THE UNKNOWN SOLDIER

Alan Robertshaw

First published in 2014 by Ohm Books, UK

ISBN 978-0-9575023-3-8

A CIP catalogue record for this book is available from the British Library.

Cover design by Bryony Hopkins

Thanks to Andrea, Jane, Margaret and Edwin for your wise counsel and to Seggy for making it all possible.

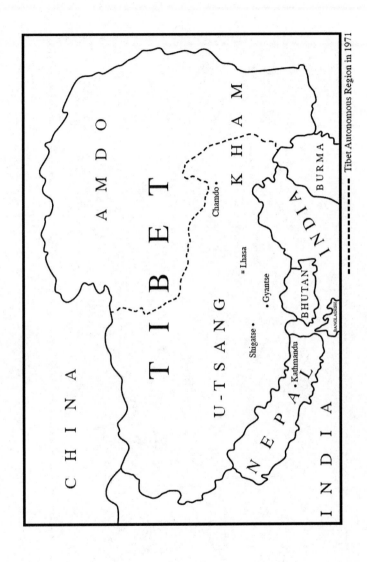

CHINA

A M D O

T I B E T

K H A M

U - T S A N G

Chamdo

*Lhasa

•Gyantse

Shigatse •

N E P A L •Kathmandu

BHUTAN

INDIA

BURMA

BANGLADESH

I N D I A

╍╍╍╍╍ Tibet Autonomous Region in 1971

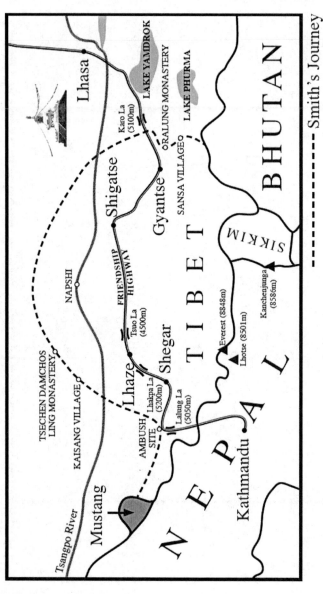

- - - - - Smith's Journey

Chapter 1

ཀ

April 1971- Friendship Highway, Tibet

Smith waited. He was good at waiting.

Usually a creature of manic action and easily bored, he could, when he needed to, wait like a cat for his prey. He needed to now.

They had arrived under cover of darkness, he and the rest, and were now well hidden in amongst the rocks scattered over the barren landscape, some half the size of a house, the perfect cover for what was planned.

Since then Smith had hardly moved except to drink a little water or eat a handful of *tsampa*. Periodically he scanned the horizon with his binoculars, the geography of the whole valley, laid out before him, becoming gradually imprinted on his mind.

To his left at the head of the pass squatted a *chorten*, that ubiquitous religious monument of Tibet, with its white painted and wind blasted square base and bulbous top stark and massive against a sky made vivid blue by the thin high altitude air. It seemed ageless, almost a part of the landscape. An all-seeing eye decorated each of its four walls, staring blindly to each point of the compass.

As the sun climbed higher in the azure sky and its rays penetrated the deep shadows amongst the rocks, the temperature began to rise, bringing occasional wafts of juniper to Smith's nostrils. He breathed more deeply, trying to capture the aroma, trying and failing to capture the memory it evoked.

Multi-coloured prayer flags fluttered on strings tied to the top of the *chorten* and staked to the ground at various distances from it, each flag about the size of a sheet of writing paper. Some were newly placed and others ripped to ragged shreds by the howling gales which routinely ravaged the pass. The wind plucked the prayers from the flags and carried them to the gods in an endless stream of devotion – a pragmatic and uniquely Tibetan method of prayer.

As it grew stronger, the wind also spun the prayer wheels set into the walls of the *chorten*, starting their brass bells rattling and ringing, like cowbells in a Swiss meadow, propelling more prayers into the ether.

Mountains towered on either side of the pass, snow permanently decorating the highest peaks in a harsh white mantle. And below, the valley stretched away endlessly to Smith's right, stark and dry as a desert, with hardly a sign of green amongst the rocks and hard-packed earth. The only other sign of human endeavour was the black snaking road uncoiling gently downwards, gradually becoming indistinguishable from the surrounding landscape as it ebbed away into the infinite distance.

Until the coming of the road not many years before, the high pass, or *la* in Tibetan, had only been navigable on foot or horseback and was closed to travellers by snow for at least five months every winter. Now trucks were able to drive this road virtually throughout the year. Running all the way from Lhasa in the east, the direction in which Smith was looking, the so-called Friendship Highway, built by the Chinese, now stretched as far as Kathmandu in the west.

It was the road and its traffic which interested Smith and the others. Apart from him, they were all Tibetans and most of them *Khampas*, warriors from the east of the country, right up against the Chinese border. Waiting did not come naturally to them, but over the last months, as Smith's value to them had become more evident, they had adapted to his ways. So they waited too.

*

It was the middle of the afternoon when Tashi spotted movement on the road far to the west.

"There," he called in Tibetan, signalling to Smith who picked up his binoculars and looked in the direction indicated.

"Seen. Three of them," responded Smith in the same language, though it was several minutes before the movement began to focus into anything discernible. The vehicles gradually grew in size to become a jeep, leading the small convoy, and two trucks close behind. Smith already knew they were People's Liberation Army vehicles, perhaps on a patrol or possibly reinforcing a garrison to the west. Not that he cared.

"Alright, get ready," shouted Pemba, the leader of the group and seasoned fighter against the Chinese, to the men within earshot. The command was quickly passed from man to man.

Smith knew that it would take about twenty minutes for the vehicles to reach the nearest point on the road to him and the Tibetans, where it was at its steepest, slowing them to a crawl. Twenty minutes for them all to think about what was about to happen and what might go wrong. Twenty minutes for any one of them to lose his nerve, panic, run. It still wasn't too late to abort the whole thing and slip away unseen. Most men wonder at some time how they would react in the face of combat. But Smith and the rest of the group already knew.

And every Tibetan waiting amongst the rocks had a reason for being there which gave them the self-discipline to meet and suppress their fear, and that reason was a monstrous hatred of the Chinese, developed over twenty years of military occupation.

They also had Smith's discipline, the instilled routine intended to fill this fearful time with purposeful activity. So they checked and re-checked equipment, cover, arcs of fire and, being devout Buddhists, nervously fingered their prayer beads.

As Smith watched through his binoculars the convoy grew closer and closer. Soon he could see the heat haze dancing off the bonnet of the jeep, and then the still distant faces of the driver and his passenger. So absorbed was he by the faces that they almost filled the lens before he lowered the binoculars. But still he could see those faces in his mind's eye. The faces of men he was about to kill. Picking up his weapon he rested it on the rock in front of him and waited.

*

At last the vehicles began to draw level with the small band hidden in the rocks, engines revving and gearboxes crunching as the drivers fought to maintain their momentum on the steep incline.

Suddenly the jeep was thrown several feet sideways by a huge explosion, instantly engulfing it in a sheet of flame. The lead truck veered wildly to avoid the inferno, but before it could get past the jeep there was another, smaller explosion and then another. Two Claymore anti-personnel mines, which the Americans had reluctantly supplied, each spraying out seven hundred ball bearings at lethally close range, ripped through the two soft skinned vehicles with devastating effect before the occupants knew what had happened.

The smell of burning fuel, paint and plastic was already filling the air. In panic men now begin to spill chaotically from the two trucks. The first contained dazed Chinese conscripts in their drab olive uniforms. With several already dead or injured by the Claymores, the survivors were now greeted with a hail of automatic gunfire.

The terrified occupants of the second truck were young Chinese civilians, all wearing their own uniform, blue Mao suits, now trying desperately to make their escape from the death trap they had so suddenly been pitched into.

Pemba and the other Tibetans briefly exchanged glances. They could not help smiling as they recognised the prey which had wandered into their trap. How many times had they seen them or their like, fanatically waving their Little Red Books in towns, villages and monasteries up and down Tibet with their enforced "re-education", beatings, often to death, and demands for the destruction of Tibetan manuscripts, art and monasteries?

The bodies of Mao's Red Guards jerked and flailed as rounds now poured into the second vehicle.

Where Smith had learned his trade, in the British Army, the Self-Loading Rifle or SLR was still standard issue, firing only a single round each time the trigger was pulled. All the *Khampas*, however, had Chinese-made AK56's, "liberated" from the PLA. This was a variant of Sergeant (Later General) Kalashnikov's Russian AK47 which was light, simple to operate and maintain, kept working under virtually any conditions and sprayed out rounds at a terrifying rate. On automatic the magazine of thirty rounds emptied in seconds.

To Smith the wooden stock and hand grip of this lethal weapon were strangely comforting, giving it a crafted, workmanlike feel as it recoiled lightly in his hands - the tool of his trade. By contrast, the plastic of the SLR now seemed to him somehow cheap, ignoble.

Right in the thick of the battle, Smith fired his rifle in short disciplined bursts as targets appeared. A soldier would fall to the ground in a crumpled heap or stagger backwards, looking in horror at the holes torn into his tunic and the blood seeping onto his chest. However many times Smith experienced battle, he never felt so alive as in that emotional no man's land, pitched between terror and exhilaration, and completely focused on the deadly task in hand. All around him was noise and chaos, but he was in control: In control of himself and the situation, the manager of violence. Later he might question what he did, even regret it, but for now there was only the moment.

"Stop!" screamed Smith above the din, suddenly aware of the profligacy of the Tibetans who continued to fire at the Red Guards even though not a man amongst them could have survived the lethal fusillade. Pemba now took up the cry and eventually the weapons fell silent.

The air was thick with the pungent smell of burning tyres, diesel and cordite. The Chinese had not been able to return a single shot, but already they seemed to be finished.

But then one of the soldiers, lain prone some way down the road, clambered to his feet and, desperately trying to take advantage of the lull, began to run downhill, picking up speed as he distanced himself from Smith and the others. They watched fascinated, but no-one reacted. For long seconds he continued his mad, desperate flight.

The cut-off group deployed by Smith three hundred metres down the road waited patiently for him to draw level with them before bringing him down with what Smith considered a suitably economical burst of fire. Falling with a bone breaking thud face first onto the hard black surface of the road, the soldier was finally still.

The whole thing had lasted less than ten minutes, but now, suddenly, it was over. The jeep continued to burn and the two trucks were heavily pock-marked, their tyres shredded and windows shattered.

Several bodies lolled from the back of the vehicles and others were sprawled on the ground around them, uniforms holed and stained. Moans and an occasional cry could be heard from the not yet dead. In the rock fall no-one moved from their cover.

After a few minutes of careful watching and waiting, Smith called out.

"Gyalo, Lobsang. Check the rear truck. The rest of you cover them." Two men moved cautiously forward. They checked the bodies at the rear of the second vehicle and seemed satisfied. One of them then dropped the tailgate, the other clutched his rifle and scanned the scene around him for danger. Two more men moved forward at a signal from Pemba and repeated the procedure with the first truck. They met no resistance so cut back the canopies of both trucks to reveal their contents, bodies and equipment littered everywhere.

"OK guys, let's get a move on," encouraged Smith as the group finally converged on the wreckage, leaving two men to look out for possible Chinese reinforcements. They began gathering up ammunition boxes and equipment from the trucks, more than enough to replace that used in the ambush.

Turning their attention to the dead, they combed through the debris of prematurely terminated lives, helping themselves to weapons, magazines, ration packs and water bottles as well as the odd souvenirs - a watch, a wallet, even a pair of glasses.

Smith stood surveying the carnage around him as the adrenalin seeped slowly from his limbs. Standing as tall as any of the *Khampas* at over six feet, his features were by now equally brown and weather-beaten, though more obviously European with hazel eyes and sharp sculpted nose and chin. His black hair had grown to shoulder length and was braided and adorned with silver bands and turquoise beads. He wore a typically voluminous dun coloured and grubby *chuba*, such an iconic item of Tibetan dress that it's very wearing was outlawed by the Chinese. With its billowing sleeves it wrapped across his slim body and extended half way down his thighs, held at the waist by a leather belt. A bandolier of ammunition was slung across Smith's shoulder Zapata-style and padded trousers tucked into heavy riding boots completed the ensemble. In most situations he could have passed as a Khampa.

"Look at this," called one of the men cheerfully to those near him. He had pulled from the pocket of one of the corpses a copy of the "Thoughts of Chairman Mao", which every Red Guard carried, and extracted something from it. The man casually tossed aside the Little Red Book. It fell to the ground and Smith noticed the wind flicking roughly through the pages. He guessed that the Tibetan gods would be uninterested in its materialistic prayers.

Smith wandered over and saw the small group leering at a photograph of a beautiful Chinese girl with short black hair smiling brightly into the camera. He turned away, suddenly saddened by the possibilities the picture brought into his mind. He probably had more in common with the men killed today, other soldiers, as they fought out a forgotten war in this most remote of places, than he had with the vast majority of humanity. But these were not thoughts to dwell on. This was what he did, what he was.

As they continued to wade through the bodies, one of the Chinese groaned and began to move. The nearest Khampa, a young man called Gyalo, pulled a knife from his belt and bent towards the wounded soldier, ready to cut his throat without a thought.

"Stop," cried Tashi. Tashi, the lama, the warrior monk, still a man of religion first and a warrior second. After the years of slaughter of his people in Tibet, he could justify killing in the heat of a war he felt compelled to fight, but not in cold blood. Smith wondered on occasions if Tashi even fired his weapon, but he never challenged his friend about this. The slender lama with his shaved head and maroon robes had other virtues more valuable to the rebels than those of fighter. He was their conscience in what they did and an ever-present link to their faith and culture. To Smith he was a friend and the reason he was in this wild and seemingly inhospitable land.

Gyalo hesitated for a second, not contemptuous of Tashi, whose wisdom and calling he respected, before looking over to Pemba. Pemba's nod was almost imperceptible. Gyalo bent over the man again and in a second his body went limp.

Tashi looked at Smith, appalled, but Smith turned away, continuing to pack ammunition into a rucksack.

Tashi would not let it go.

"We are as bad as them."

"No we're not," responded Smith in English, angry now. "You know the score. What were we going to do, treat that guy? Make him better? Take him with us? Or would just leaving him do him any favours? It might be days before another patrol comes along here. Aren't there wolves in these mountains?

"Jesus, Tashi, we can't take prisoners. We don't have food or medicine for them. They slow us down. And slowing us down means killing us." He pointed to the dead soldiers. "They don't exactly abide by the Geneva Convention. We stay alive by choosing how we fight, when we fight and knowing when to run. Now let's get sorted and get the fuck out of here." He looked directly at his friend, his tone conciliatory now. "You know I'm right. That's why you brought me here. To do what you can't."

They were interrupted by one of the *Khampas* who came running over towards them.

"Look at this," he demanded. "I got it from the jeep. Might be something interesting." The man, whose name was Lobsang, held in his hand the blackened, but intact and identifiable remains of a leather brief case.

"Let's have a look," responded Smith, impressed by Lobsang's initiative when the rest of them had assumed the jeep was too badly damaged to be worth investigating. The metal buckles were still hot to the touch and the smell of burnt leather seared his throat as Smith prised the case open and carefully slid his hand inside to extract the contents.

"What is it?" asked Pemba, joining the small group gathering around Smith. Pemba was prepared to bow to Smith's knowledge of modern military tactics, but was now ready to reassert his authority over the group. Smith greatly respected Pemba who had fought the Chinese on and off for nearly twenty years, but was still prepared to accept Smith and embrace his ideas. He in turn went out of his way not to undermine the position of the old warrior. So far this unlikely arrangement had worked well.

Smith pulled from the case a handful of smouldering files and placed them gently on the ground, fanning them out so that each one could be seen. Whilst the outer files were badly charred, most of them were virtually undamaged. Pemba picked up one and flicked through it, page after indecipherable page of Chinese characters, almost willing them to make some sense to him. But Smith knew they wouldn't.

"Tashi, can you make anything of this stuff?" called Pemba. Tashi came over and took the file from Pemba, studying it for several minutes with his scholarly gaze. The Chinese were already forcing Tibetans to learn Chinese as they encouraged more Han immigration from the Motherland and gave the best jobs to Mandarin speakers amongst the Tibetan population. But the *Khampas* were not well educated and since the invasion never stayed in one place for long. Their only contact with the Chinese was down the iron sight of a Kalashnikov. Tashi however, had spent several years in Lhasa after the invasion and had a good command of the invaders' language.

"Most of my Chinese was picked up from talking to people. I never learnt much of the written language."

"But?" responded Pemba, knowing that Tashi was, as always, being the self-effacing lama.

"But it, this one at least, it seems to be a PLA document about military deployments. Deployments of large units. Divisions, I think. It's all very technical."

"So this could be useful intelligence? Intelligence the Americans would be interested in?"

"It could be, Pemba. But I've only looked at it for a few minutes and just this one file."

"Alright. Look at them later. We can't wait here any longer. Let's get out of here." Pemba scooped up the files in his large hands and stuffed them back in the brief case.

From the debris of the raid men now began to pick up the final items they intended to take with them, slung their packs on their backs and headed away from the Friendship Highway.

About half a mile from the ambush site and well hidden, two men had been left with the horses. As the rest of the group now rejoined them they loaded up their animals and began to make their getaway.

The small, tough Tibetan horses were the perfect way to move quickly over the rugged and largely trackless terrain. High altitude and the vastness of the country meant that it was difficult for the Chinese to operate helicopters, so once away from the few roads, the guerrillas could be fairly confident of staying ahead of the PLA and disappearing into the seemingly endless Tibetan wastes. They headed west towards Mustang and safety.

Chapter 2

ཀ

Tibet

As they rode the tension in the group, built up by the attack, began to dissipate and a broad grin appeared on Smith's face at the sheer joy of the adrenalin rush from the battle and the flight from it. Mao Tse Tung was right about one thing. Power did come out of the barrel of a gun. The feeling of being truly alive had never been stronger. After all, he an Englishman, was, ridiculous as it seemed, speeding on horseback across the steppes of western Tibet with a band of warriors from another age. They could have been riding to join Ghengis Khan and the Golden Horde. Perhaps he would have fitted in just as well if they had.

Pemba looked towards Smith and as their eyes met the Tibetan smiled hugely as well.

"A job well done!" he shouted into the wind.

"It couldn't have gone better," replied Smith, still grinning. "Now it's up to you to get us away from here in one piece."

"Don't worry." Pemba assured him. "We'll be back in Mustang before the local Chinese commander even knows what has happened."

"How long will that be?"

"Two days of hard riding," bellowed Pemba.

Pemba was the leader of the group which currently amounted to sixteen men. Smith, having proved his worth, had in effect become their military adviser. This meant that he was allowed to take charge of the more technically complex operations like the vehicle ambush. Mutual respect had also lead to a firm bond of trust and friendship between the two men.

Like most *Khampas*, at over six foot tall Pemba towered over the average Tibetan. Also, unlike their Mongoloid features, his were almost European and with a characteristic beaked nose. His skin was richly tanned and a mane of black hair flew wildly behind him as they rode.

Apart from Smith and Tashi the whole group were *Khampas*, a wild and warlike tribe from the province of Kham in eastern Tibet. They contrasted sharply with the Western perception of the peaceful Tibetan, almost invariably portrayed as a monk or a pilgrim, and their proclivity for raiding caravans had not endeared them to Marco Polo or to succeeding generations of Tibetans.

Smith knew Pemba's story and that of the *Khampas* since the Chinese invasion in 1950, from long nights in Mustang when the snow and cold made fighting impossible. Then they were trapped like a medieval army in their winter quarters, waiting for the fighting season to begin.

It had been a time for Smith to prove to the Tibetans that Tashi's faith in him was justified, and that they could trust him. But it was also a time for Smith to learn what made the *Khampas* keep fighting year after year. By day they trained and scavenged for food, but by night they talked.

"At first it seemed like we could beat them," Smith remembered Pemba telling him. "After the invasion, the Tibetan Army, such as it was, never came to help us in Kham. They weren't interested in what was going on hundreds of miles from Lhasa. Never had been except when they wanted their taxes. I don't suppose we ever expected them to be. In any case they were little more than ceremonial troops with antiquated weapons.

"So we formed our own army. Chushi Gandruk, 'Four Rivers, Six Ranges' we called it, after the traditional name for our land. The land we were going to fight for. Not that our weapons were much better than the Tibetan Army's, until the Americans got involved. Hunting rifles mainly. But we were fighters and hunters. So we knew the land, our land, like we knew our own sons."

On other nights Pemba reminisced how, after an initial hearts and mind campaign, the Chinese had become more repressive and by the mid-1950's the *Khampas* were in full rebellion. In the early days they had many successes, expelling the Chinese from numerous towns in the east, notably Lithang where they had killed large numbers of Chinese troops.

But the ultimate outcome was inevitable and the Khampa

fighters were pushed ever westwards by the PLA with its vastly superior weaponry and limitless manpower. The Tibetan Army, such as it was, soon capitulated to the Chinese, leaving the *Khampas* as the only military resistance to the invasion of Tibet.

"By 1959," Pemba had continued, on yet another freezing night with the snow deep on the ground outside the tent, "we were in Lhasa. The Chinese had long since occupied the capital. Rumours were raging like fire through the city that they were about to arrest the Dalai Lama. Everyone was out in the streets when they started firing. Hundreds were killed, but we," he turned proudly to look at the other faces lit by the glow of the fire, "we helped to smuggle him out of the city, first to the Norbulinka Summer Palace and then southwards on horseback towards India. We turned west when we were sure he would be safe."

A government in exile was eventually established in Kalimphong in Northern India from where the Dalai Lama continued to wage a peaceful campaign to free his country from Chinese domination. Like every Tibetan, Pemba had undying loyalty to the Dalai Lama, but it was not in his nature to follow the spiritual leader of his country along a path of peace or into exile.

Hundreds were killed during the suppression of the uprising and *Khampas* were a prime target for being rounded up. Not all of Pemba's men escaped, but those who did continued to fight their way west.

Chapter 3

ཕ

Tibet

"I still can't get used to these stars," exclaimed Smith, laying on his back staring at the night sky. It was a late spring evening, but the sky was so clear that it was bound to freeze overnight at this altitude. They had made camp in a small side valley where their fire was unlikely to be seen from any distance, even if there was anyone within fifty miles. So far as they knew there was not.

Most of the *Khampas* dozed by the fire, chatted quietly or made tea and cooked a few yards away. Two men were deployed some distance down the valley keeping guard.

"Shall I show you how to find north using the stars?"

"Why would I want to go north? Are we moving?" Tashi showed no sign of moving.

"Fuck me, Tashi!" groaned Smith, exasperated. He took very seriously the business of being an infantry soldier and had a deep pride in his ability to live close to the land and understand its signs. It was mildly frustrating that his other-worldly friend did not share these interests.

"Don't you miss England, your family, normal things?" asked Tashi meditatively as if he had already forgotten their previous exchange. They spoke in English when the two of them where alone. None of the *Khampas* spoke the language.

"You know Tashi, I don't think I do," replied Smith, giving up on the previous conversation. "What would I do there? Get a job? Doing what? I'm not exactly the nine to five type. And anyway the weather's crap, as you know. You never stopped moaning about the rain." He paused for a moment and gazed back at the stars.

"How long is it since we left London? I've lost track of time. Not just the days, but the months. I can just about tell what season it is, but the funny thing is that seems to be about enough here. I like that"

"It's been eighteen months, I think. Perhaps a bit more," replied Tashi. Smith thought back to how they had met when Tashi was a post-graduate student at the School of Oriental and African Studies in Russell Square. The lama's English was perfect as he was the second son of a well-educated minor noble family in Lhasa who had strong links with Indian nobility. He had been sent at an early age to a boarding School in Delhi where only English was spoken.

At the age of fourteen he returned home to begin his religious education at Deprung Monastery, a massive religious community of several thousand monks situated just outside Lhasa, where he excelled at his studies. As a member of the Tibetan elite he could have expected to attain high religious office, had it not been for the uprising in Lhasa, after which the monastery was shelled by the Chinese and badly damaged. The Cultural Revolution continued the process of destruction with most of the religious icons and books being removed or destroyed as they were in hundreds of monasteries up and down Tibet.

As the life of a lama in Tibet became more intolerable, Tashi fled the chaos and eventually found himself a refugee in India along with tens of thousands of others. Having little chance of being allowed to return to his homeland, and using his family's Indian contacts, he escaped the mud and squalor of Kalimphong and continued on to England and SOAS, where he found himself persuaded to teach a Tibetan Language extra-mural class in his spare time by one of his tutors.

This unlikely project attracted an equally unlikely, but enthusiastic collection of Third Eye aficionados, explorers actual and potential, bored housewives looking for a challenge and, at the back of the room a tanned and wiry young man with short black hair and a battered copy of the 1919 edition of Sir Charles Bell's "Grammar of Colloquial Tibetan". From it Smith was already grappling with such politically incorrect phrases as "Tell him that if he tells any lies he will be flogged", "monks are lazy" and the possibly more useful "Running away when a battle is being fought is wrong".

Indeed, Smith was himself, or had been, a Third Eye aficionado, the Third Eye being the title of a book he read as an impressionable Yorkshire schoolboy. It described the life and times of a Tibetan lama, Lobsang Rampa, prior to the Chinese invasion. Like thousands of others throughout the world, Smith was fascinated by this alternative universe of magic and spirituality which seemed to have existed in the Land of Snows before 1949 and which the Chinese had now swept away forever.

Only later did Smith and the rest of the world discover that Lobsang Rampa was in reality an Irish plumber called Hoskins who did his research in the Reading Rooms of the British Museum. But strangely, it didn't matter. A seed had been sown.

The world described by Heinrich Harrier, the mountaineer stranded for seven years in Tibet after escaping from a British POW camp in India in the Second World War, was no less fascinating to Smith. And this was the real Tibet, possibly. Over the years his interest in Tibet continued as did his reading. Descriptions of Tibet under Chinese rule disturbed Smith, but so did accounts of daily life in pre-invasion Tibet, a land it seemed, at once of deep spirituality, but also of almost medieval feudal poverty and cruelty.

Chapter 4

Tibet

"Here, have some tea," interrupted one of the *Khampas*, handing each of them a metal mug from which steam rose ethereally in the firelight. Tea, Tibetan style, had taken Smith some time to adjust to, made as it was from black tea bricks and flavoured with yaks' butter which floated in ominous fatty globules on its dark surface. These days he managed to sip the noxious brew without even grimacing. In fact he found it almost refreshing.

Smith dug into his pack to produce enough *tsampa*, a kind of barley biscuit and a Tibetan staple, for himself and Tashi. This meagre diet kept most Tibetans going most of the time and served the guerrillas well when on the move.

Earlier, a dipole antenna had been erected in the camp and Smith listened almost unconsciously as he sipped his tea to the tap tapping of the radio operator checking in with the CIA. This was done at predetermined intervals or after an operation as now. Much of the time the group made it up as they went along, taking opportunistic targets as and when they could, but every so often Langley would issue directives which might or might not be followed.

"A change of plan?" called Smith. Pemba talked to the radio operator for several minutes before standing and walking over to sit with Smith and Tashi.

"As usual, you have the advantage on me, my friend," he smiled. "As you probably heard, we are requested to head north in the morning instead of back to Mustang. What do you think?"

"From what I could hear they were going to make it worth our while," replied Smith.

"Indeed," responded Pemba, unconvinced.

Chapter 5

ᄃ

October 1969 - London

Smith had been prowling the streets of London for the last six months since resigning his Commission. He missed the Army, his fellow Officers, the men, the travel. But most of all he missed being a soldier, an infantryman. The feeling that he could survive on foot in a hostile landscape with what he could carry on his back gave him great satisfaction. That he could use the ground to his advantage to close with an enemy and defeat him, or to escape from him. There was great joy in that for Smith. He didn't mind being filthy, wet and tired. He didn't mind being in the field for days or weeks at a time. Far from it – that was where he was happiest. Being Recce Platoon Commander for the Battalion gave him every opportunity to indulge his joy of soldiering. In the jungle, in the desert, even training in the Arctic. In his young life the Army had sent him everywhere and he had without question thrown himself into every conflict. Done what was required.

And then suddenly it all seemed to come to an end. The Battalion was posted back to the UK, to Aldershot, where they stagnated for nine months. Nine tedious months of military bullshit, plodding across the brown landscapes of the local training areas and finding jobs that didn't need doing. Boredom was death. Smith spent a lot of time reading and thinking.

So when he got a call to go and have a word with the OC one wintery morning he was already susceptible to an offer he didn't know he was going to get.

"Hello, Peter. Come on in. Sit down," beckoned the amiable Major Ashley Kerslake when Smith arrived at his shabby office in the Company Lines. Kerslake was in his early thirties, tall, lean, Public School, with the languid manner that so often seemed to engender.

"Let me get you some coffee." Kerslake bellowed to his clerk in the outer office and weak instant coffee soon appeared.

Smith had known Kerslake for the whole of his time with the Battalion. They had served together on numerous occasions and in some extreme situations. Kerslake was only three years older than Smith and was seen as a rising star. He made Acting Major at the age of twenty-seven and was now on his second tour in that rank.

All the more surprising to Smith then, when he announced that he was leaving the Army.

"Put my papers in already, but it could be six months before I'm out. You know what it's like"

"So what's brought this on, Ash? You're bloody army barmy. Worse than any of us."

"Bored, Peter. Bored to bloody tears. Look at this office. I hate being in an office at the best of times, but this dump is just depressing me to death.

"But to be honest I suppose I could put up with it. If it wasn't for this offer I've had. With Spartan, no less." He sounded very pleased with himself as he made this last announcement.

"Spartan?" Smith exclaimed. "How've you got involved with them?"

"You know how these things work, Peter. A guy I know who was with the Devon and Dorsets is now working for them. We met up one day and basically he recruited me. And now I'm going to recruit you."

"What? Why would I do that and why are you asking me?"

"Well, Peter, defence consultants like Spartan, as you know, are taking on more and more of the kind of work chaps like you and me are good at."

"They're bloody mercenaries, Ash."

"Such a passé term, Peter. They pay extremely well and they're offering the kind of work you like. You're a single man. No commitments. And I've been watching you. You're as bored as I am."

"And who's their MD? Bloody retired Brigadier bloody Holdsworth. That's who. Have you forgotten what it was like working for him in Malaya?"

"He remembered you as well, Peter. That's why I'm asking you."

"Eh?"

"Yes, he remembered you and when I went for a chat he asked if you were available and I said I'd ask. So I'm asking. But before you say anything think about this. He's got contracts in Africa, the Middle East, the Far East. Places we know and jobs we can do. And have a look at this."

Major Kerslake passed a slim folder across the desk to Smith which he began to read with increasing interest.

Chapter 6

ॐ

Skies over Tibet

"Fucking jump, now!" bellowed Loadmaster Wokowski in a thick Polish accent over the roar of wind and engines. Lhotse sat on the bench opposite the gaping door which led into the pitch black night, his equipment canister like an olive green torpedo squatting in front of him. A gale blew down the length of the aircraft. Lhotse's mounting fear had turned to blind panic when the green light came on over the door. He refused to budge.

The Loadmaster took a step towards Lhotse, his boots squelching in the vomit swilling gently along the floor.

"Get the fuck out that door!" Still no movement from the terrified Tibetan. Wokowski took another step and grabbed hold of Lhotse's canister which weighed about a hundred pounds and was attached to the Tibetan's harness by a coiled length of rope. As Lhotse watched with increasing horror Wokowski deftly slid the canister, lubricated by puke, across the aircraft and out of the door. In an instant Lhotse was catapulted after it into the blackness.

"Next!" screamed Wokowski.

As the rest of the half dozen parachutists followed Lhotse into the darkness the plane banked sharply and headed on a bearing south south west to the staging post in Pakistan to refuel before continuing back to base in Okinawa. The aircraft was a Hercules C 130 painted completely black with no identifying markings. It was registered to Air America, a 'legitimate' company and wholly owned subsidiary of the CIA.

"Mission accomplished. Heading home," reported the Czech pilot, finally breaking radio silence. The whole crew were Czech or Polish nationals trained in West Germany for deep penetration operations in Europe should the Cold War hot up. In the meantime they helped to keep clandestine CIA missions to Tibet and elsewhere in South East Asia non-attributable. They would fly fifteen hundred miles on three engines to conserve fuel, at an

Lhotse tumbled into the night with the awful weight below dragging him to earth. The jump had taken place at six hundred feet. This meant that he was attached to a static line which automatically yanked his parachute out of its pack as soon as he was away from the aircraft. The parachute deployed just in time to break the worst of the fall, before he hit the ground with a sickening thud and fell onto his side, shocked and dazed.

Wrestling to clear his head and take some control of the situation, Lhotse tried to get his bearings. The drop had been so quick and his panic so great that he had not been able to make anything of his surroundings on his descent. As he looked around now he could see nothing except the stars in the sky and the black silhouette of surrounding mountains.

Instinctively he began to hammer at the quick release, suddenly aware of the strength of the breeze. But before he could get free the chute billowed into life and began to drag him painfully over the rocky ground. Rolling over and over, unable to get his hands to the release, Lhotse's speed increased, His head cracked against several hard objects and only his helmet saved him from serious injury. He tried desperately to think.

Then he began to hear sounds beyond the rasping of his own body along the hard earth and the pounding in his head. At first he could not identify it, but then realised what it was. Water. Fast moving water. Now he remembered the river. The river flowing past the village where they were due to rendezvous later with the other group. The river they should have been dropped nowhere near as it was about five miles from the drop zone. Not that it was unusual for fighters to be accidentally dropped miles from the intended DZ.

Before Lhotse had time to congratulate himself for guessing correctly the parachute dragged him into the freezing and fast flowing water. Even had he been able to swim it would have been a useless skill against the raging torrent and with the weight of his soaked fatigues and equipment. Dragged below the surface his lungs screamed for air. Then his head broke through into the night, but before he could suck in precious air he was submerged again. He expected the canister to seal his fate at any second as it followed him into the water.

But instead he was swung through the water like a pendulum from the middle of the stream, and crashed jarringly onto the bank where the parachute tangled in the rocks. The canister had jammed between two rocks before it could be dragged into the water and the accursed thing had saved his life.

Lhotse lay on his back in the shallows shaken and shivering for several minutes before he began to function again. Although he had only been in the water for a matter of seconds it had seemed like an hour. The parachute was still dragging at him and he could just make out its ghostly fluttering whiteness in the pitch dark. Desperate to be rid of the thing which seemed determined to kill him, he made one final supreme effort in attacking the quick release. This time the relief was instantaneous as the monster finally stopped trying to pull him back into the river. Freed from its burden it lifted lightly from the rocks and quickly disappeared from his sight downstream. Lhotse's relief was immediately replaced by a realisation that this was an act of liberation he was going to live to regret.

But it was too late to worry. Forcing such thoughts from his mind, Lhotse opened the canister and tipped out the contents. He removed his wet and freezing clothing and stuffed it into the canister, put on his traditional Tibetan *chuba* and buried the canister in the soft sand beyond the rocks.

As he was finishing the task he heard the sound of footsteps approaching. Moving cautiously. Moving slowly. Searching. A Chinese patrol? They must have seen his torch, careful as he had tried to be. Pressing his body flat to the earth he cocked his weapon with the minimum sound and peered into the darkness. He could hear the crunch of boots on the sandy earth moving closer and closer, but still he could see nothing He was sure they were heading straight for him. Holding his breath, his heart sounded like a drum as the blood pumped in his ears, so loud he was convinced it would give him away. Then he heard whispered voices hissing to one another. They had seen him. He was finished.

As they came nearer, however, he realised that they were speaking Tibetan. But they nearly walked over him before he was sure that they were two other members of the team.

"Tendruk, it's me, Lhotse," he blurted out in relief.

"What happened to you?" Tendruk responded harshly.

"My chute dragged me into the river. I thought I was finished, but I managed to get back onto the bank."

"Where's your kit?"

"It's here. I'm just packing it. I buried my canister with the chute," he lied.

"Have you got everything?" Tendruk asked pointedly. "Do you need a hand to carry it?"

Lhotse was a tall and powerfully built Khampa who had volunteered to carry the extra weight of the bulky radio pack.

"No, I'm fine," he replied, standing and swinging the heavy pack onto his back with an easy motion.

"OK. The others are waiting for us. We'll go back and meet up with them and in the morning as soon as it's light we'll head for the village. According to the brief we'll be able to hire or buy some horses there"

Together, the three men disappeared into the darkness.

Chapter 7

ষ

Tibet

Smith woke suddenly. It was just coming light. A couple of *Khampas* were stamping around nearby to shake the cold from their limbs. The camp fire glowed with promise. Smith smiled with relief. Relief at being in a sleeping bag, fully clothed including boots, clutching his Kalashnikov, pursued across Tibet by Chinese patrols.

And not, as in his dream, back on the first night of his first exercise at Sandhurst nearly ten years before. The 'enemy' came charging through the camp without warning at about two in the morning. It was pitch dark as he struggled out of the sleeping bag, trembling hands trying to find his boots. Other cadets were on their feet and grabbing their weapons while Smith blundered around in the dark. By the time the Colour Sergeant had kicked the tent down and was shining his torch full in Smith's face he had still only found one.

"Get your fuckin' boots on Mr. Smith," screeched the Colour Sergeant in a broad Glaswegian accent. "Why's you's taken your fuckin' boots off? Where's your fuckin' rifle? You're fuckin' useless, sir. What are you? You's got thirty fuckin' seconds to get on the truck. Get fuckin' moving." Smith learned a lot that day.

Brushing off the dream along with a light coating of frost from his sleeping bag, Smith emerged into the chill of a spring morning on the high Tibetan plateau. A low mist hung in the air, but the sky above was clear blue and as the day warmed the mist would quickly burn away. He rolled up his sleeping bag and joined the others sipping tea in a rough circle around the fire. Bleary eyed men looked up and nodded acknowledgement as he filled his mug and absent-mindedly dropped a glob of rancid butter into the steaming liquid. Pemba raised an arm to silence desultory conversations.

"We made radio contact with the Americans last night and they want us to head north and meet a team dropped yesterday about two day's ride from here. A supply drop for us was made at the same time so we need to go and collect it."

"Why have they come in so close to us? What are they going to be doing that the Americans couldn't ask us to do?" asked one of the men, by the name of Rinzing.

"They are coming to collect the documents we found at the ambush site and to help us fight the Chinese" added Pemba. "These men are coming straight from Hale so maybe they need to get some experience."

"Where's Hale?" asked another man who had never heard of this strange sounding place.

"It's a training camp set up by the CIA to train our guys." Pemba's knowledge of the world beyond Tibet was as shaky as that of his men so he looked to Tashi for support.

"It's a military training camp in a place called Colorado in America and the men I've met who trained there say it's just like Tibet. High mountains, steep valleys. The perfect place for the Americans to teach our people how to fight the Chinese."

"We know how to fight the Chinese. We've been doing it for years,"

"And the Americans have been supporting us for years, with money, weapons, medical supplies, food." replied Tashi.

"But no soldiers, no artillery, no bombers. Where were they when we were driven out of Kham? When we were being slaughtered in the streets of Lhasa? When the Chinese bombed the monasteries and burned the holy relics? Raped the nuns? We're hanging on by our finger nails and they drop us a few pallets out of the back of a plane when it suits them" sneered Rinzing.

There were mumbles of agreement amongst the *Khampas*. The hopes they had all once held that the Americans were going to come to drive out the Chinese had long ago dissipated as the supply drops had become ever less frequent.

"Well," responded Pemba, reading the mood of the men, "perhaps this is a sign that the Americans are stepping up their support again. You all know communications are so bad we don't know what anybody else is doing most of the time. Maybe there have been drops all over the place. Maybe this is the start of a new push. Maybe the intelligence we found will remind them how important we are in the struggle against the Chinese."

"But honestly I don't give a damn. We fight to free Tibet of the Chinese invaders and see His Holiness return to the Potala Palace, and we're doing it with or without the Americans. So let's get moving. We're heading north." Pemba's authority was unquestioned in the group and every man rose to make ready for the day's ride.

Chapter 8

ॐ

November 1969 - Yorkshire

Smith had arrived home that morning. Not that he thought of it as home nor had done since his first posting. They sat in the pokey front room, the slanted winter sunlight attempting to penetrate its recesses.

"So it's true?" You've bloody left?" began Smith's father abruptly.

"Yes, Dad. You'll be pleased that I'm no longer a member of the oppressive Officer Class."

"Once that wud a bin true, lad. You 'ad bloody good 'A' levels. Ya cud a gone to university or summat. Bin a doctor or lawyer. Chances we never 'ad. I couldn't understand why you went to Sandhurst. I'd never heard o' the bloody place." He was quiet for a minute.

"But ya know a don't think like that now. I'm proud o' ya." Another pause.

"Perhaps you should have told me that a bit earlier," responded Smith, genuinely surprised.

"And ya know wot changed me mind? That bloody Fathers' Night or whatever you called it?" Then more ruefully, "that were probably t' most uncomfortable night o' my life."

"You bloody enjoyed it, Dad. I remember."

Smith did remember. It was the end of his first term as an Officer Cadet in New College, a term which had been a culture shock to a young man from a working class Bradford family with no experience of the Army. He had his doubts about whether he could stick it out as others fell by the wayside, but eventually his fitness, intelligence and a streak of ruthless cunning started to come through and he began to fit right in.

And then suddenly it was the last week of term, the week before Christmas. Things were a bit less hectic. A bit more civilised. Less crawling through mud and wading through the half frozen Wishstream and the lake in front of the colonnades of Old College. The last Tuesday was Fathers' Night when every Cadet could invite their father to dinner in the Cadets' Mess of New College, Royal Military Academy Sandhurst.

"I've got a confession to make about that. I nearly didn't ask you to come."

"Oh aye? Why not?"

"I don't know. I suppose I thought you'd hate it. You never showed any interest in the Army."

"'appen you were right. Anyway, I nearly didn't come when you did ask me. But then a thought a should make't effort. For you."

Again Smith was surprised at the confession made by the man who never showed his feelings. Smith's father was an overseer at Downs Coulters Mill where he had worked since he was fifteen. Since his marriage the family, eventually parents and two sons, lived in a small Victorian terraced house a ten minute walk away which he ruled as his own private fiefdom.

"A' knew a' wer' as good as any o' them, so I put me suit on, me only suit and caught t' train. But a'll tell ya what, a' wer' shitting meself by t' time a' got t' Camberley." He laughed at the memory.

"But you had a great time." And he did. Transported for an evening to another world, a world of Officers in red jackets, of Mess silver, of flickering candlelight, of conversation about lives led in exotic places, of war stories. Things he, a working man and a socialist, despised. And yet everyone was so charming, so kind, so generous. He was mesmerised. Won over.

"Yer right, lad. Ya know, I left that place wi' a completely different idea of what ya were doin' there. What ya were becomin'. So when wi came down for you're Passin' Out Parade me an ya mother were't proudest folk there. Even if ya din't win t' Sword of 'onour," he added wryly.

"Pity you didn't tell me that at the time."

"Ya know us. We're not a demonstrative lot up here. 'appen you've forgotten. You've been away that much. Anyway, am sure ya mother's told you how we felt. She's better at this stuff than me." A pause.

More angry now. "So that's why we can't understand what the

bloody 'ell your doin' now. Packin' up a good career, summat ya said ya loved, and signin' on wi a band a paid killers."

"What?"

"Spartan, that's what.That's who ya sed ya were workin' for innit. We read t' papers. Even up 'ere. I've seen what them buggers get up to."

"You don't know a bloody thing about it, Dad. I'm bloody bored with the Army. Sitting around in barracks in Aldershot all the time's not what I joined for. And it looks like Northern Ireland's the next big thing. Word is we'll be on the streets in the next year. I can imagine what your mates would have to say about that. The Black and Tans all over again. And your son in the thick of it. Grinding the faces of the oppressed Irish"

"Look lad," a more conciliatory tone now. "Look. Mebby yer right about that. Mebby I wouldn't want to see ya traipsin' t' streets o' Belfast, but I think I'd prefer that to ya killin' folk for money in Africa."

"What's the bloody difference? Killing's killing. It's not very nice, but your Labour Government's been paying me to do it. What's the difference?"

"Ya know bloody well. God, I despair." A moment's silence.

"Here, look at this." Smith's father reached over to the small table at his side where a cup of tea was going cold and picked up a battered photograph laying face down next to his cup. Staring back at Smith was the tanned, smiling face of a man about his own age wearing an army beret tugged down over his left ear.

"George," said Smith's father, before being asked. "Your uncle George."

"Yes. Killed in the war, wasn't he?"

"Which war?"

"Well, the Second World War I assume. I just remember you or somebody talking about him years ago. I've never given him any thought, I suppose. I never knew him or heard much about him and never asked."

"Well, he wa' killed afore ya were born so the never wa much point in talkin' about him. Until now."

Smith's father began to give his son a brief biography of Uncle George. Uncle George who was never going to work in the mill whatever happened and joined the Navy to escape at fifteen. Did well. Got promoted. There was even talk of him taking a Commission. Bloody unheard of in those days, but there it was. Then in 1931 the Government, trying to save money, cut sailors' pay and Uncle George found himself in the thick of the Invergordon Mutiny. It only lasted two days, but George was on his ship, The Illustrious', strike committee and got two years in military prison as a result. After that he was in and out of various jobs for being a union organiser.

"So when t' Spanish Civil War started in 1936 the wa no 'oldin' 'im back. At first he fought wi't German anti-fascists in summat called t' Thallman Column. Then when the' formed t'International Brigades he transferred to t' British Battalion."

"Why? I mean, why did he go to Spain?"

"Bloody 'ell. Don't ya know ya military history?" Smith did, but got a brief lesson anyway on how the Fascist General Franco, supported by Hitler and Mussolini, led a military rebellion from his base in Spanish North Africa against the democratically elected Republican Government in Spain. Frustrated by the refusal of their governments to intervene on the Republican side, large numbers of Brits, French and Americans and others of the Left flocked to Spain to support the Republic and so the International Brigades were formed to fight alongside the Republican Army.

"And George fought right through from t' start. He wa wounded a couple a times, but he kept bouncin' back. Cos he had some military experience he soon got some rank. But it wer alus a lost cause. By 1938 he wer a Captain. Like you. Company Commander. Better than you!" He smiled.

"Anyhow, 10th o' November 1938 he wa killed at the Battle of the Ebro." For some reason his Yorkshire dialect deserted him in naming the battle and he pronounced it in full. "That's a river in Spain. Only place abroad a've ever 'ad any interest in goin'. Don't suppose I ever will though."

Smith took the photograph from his father and held it in his hand looking into the eyes of the young man killed thirty years before. Both men were silent for several minutes.

"I wish I'd known about him before, but why are you telling me now?"

"Why d'ya wish a'd told ya afore?"

"I don't know." He paused. "It's interesting. Family history. Somebody in our family got out and did something interesting."

"Ya think that's why a told ya? Told ya now? Well it in't." He sighed. " A've realised over t' years how much you an' George were alike. Both wanted to do stuff different. Wanted a bit of adventure. Not afraid of a fight. Lookin' for a fight even. But he went t' Spain for what he believed in and your goin' to Africa or wherever for money. Now that's not right, lad.

"Since ya left 'ome a've never tried to tell you what to do. Ya moved out o' my league long since. But if ya wont listen to me, listen to George. He wa' my brother an' your uncle. Look at 'im agen. Look at that photo. A think he 'as summat to tell ya."

Chapter 9

ㅌ

Tibet

The rising sun bathed the scrubby landscape in ochre as the small party set out that morning. In the early days the *Khampas* had operated in bands of a hundred or more, but after some initial success against the Chinese their open warfare tactics had become more and more ineffective against the PLA's numerical and technical superiority. The Americans had encouraged those it had been able to train, at first in Saipan and later at Hale, to adopt guerrilla tactics and operate in small mobile groups which could travel fast, strike and disappear. These were tactics Smith new and understood. He had spent five years of his life fighting against them as the British Army desperately tried to allow Britain to withdraw in some semblance of good order from its remaining colonies. As a professional soldier he studied the opposition, literally. Now, the only book he carried apart from his battered Bell's Grammar was a Penguin edition of Che Guevara's 'Guerrilla Warfare' which was just as well thumbed. Not that it took a great tactician to see the way this war was going.

As if picking up on the point, Pemba called to Smith.

"Tell me, why do you stay with us? You know as well as I do that Rinzing is right" The two men rode side by side. They were finally beginning to feel the warmth of the sun on their shoulders.

"Look at me, Pemba. I'm one of you now. I belong here, don't I?" retorted Smith smiling, only half in irony. "Folk back home would say I've gone native, I think."

"Maybe you have, but you could easily head back for Mustang now, cut your hair and slip back into Nepal. You've done enough. Every man here respects you as a warrior. We're grateful that someone came from the West, someone with skills like yours, even if we were hoping for a few more," he smiled. "But this is not your war and anyway, it's over. You should go now whilst you can."

Smith was not one to seek or need the approval of others, but for a man like Pemba to acknowledge him as a warrior touched him deeply. This was the very term by which he defined himself.

"Perhaps you're right, Pemba. Let's finish this job and then we'll talk again." Struggling with a sudden flush of emotion, Smith spurred on his horse and pulled ahead of his companion to avoid further discussion.

They rode all day across the wide plain with the sun to their backs. It was still early in the year for nomadic herders to be seen here. In another month the whole plain would turn briefly green, and white tents would briefly punctuate the now inhospitable landscape.

Occasionally, they caught sight of wild yak in the distance. Great shaggy brown beasts with huge curling horns, they were the free-spirited cousins of the domesticated animal upon which so much of traditional Tibet's everyday life depended. Yaks provided everything from wool to butter to meat and in many places dried yak's dung was the only fuel for cooking and heating

The *Khampas* had spent their whole lives on horseback and thought nothing of the long days in the saddle, but Tashi and Smith did not find it so easy. Over the months however, they had adjusted to the pace of the group, so it was not now the ordeal it had once been. Whilst the *Khampas* took it for granted that everyone in the world could ride a horse, it was in fact pure luck that Smith could. He had never been near a horse until he joined his Regiment, which was marking time in the south of England before yet another operational deployment.

As the most junior Officer he was the Adjutant's natural choice for what the young Officers described as SLJO or Shitty Little Jobs Officer. One of the jobs included in this "appointment" was that of Officer in Charge of the Pony Club. The club was run mainly for the benefit of bored Officers' wives by an experienced Sergeant and Corporal whose full- time job it was, but with an Officer nominally in charge. Smith took full advantage of his own ample free time to learn everything he could about riding. By the time the Regiment was posted he was a more than proficient rider, although he hardly rode again until finding himself in Tibet.

Chapter 10

ག

Near Tsarang Monastery, Tibet

It was towards the end of the day that they first saw Tsarang monastery as they crested a small hill. Perched on a small rocky outcrop at the northern edge of the plain before the mountain range soared skywards, it was an unprepossessing collection of squat stone buildings with a small red tower occupying the highest point. They had planned to spend the night here.

At this distance it was difficult for Smith to make out details even with his binoculars., but as he concentrated he saw what looked like horses being led around the back of the buildings. Pemba took the binoculars and stared into the distance for some time.

"I don't see anything and in any case it could just be pilgrims, but we can't take a chance. It could be a Chinese patrol."

"If it is they might have seen us already," replied Smith. "We could skirt round the place altogether and carry on to the rendezvous. We don't need to go to the monastery."

"And if it is the Chinese? What do you think they will be doing?"

"We can't take on every Chinese patrol we meet, Pemba. Especially as there's a good chance they've seen us and we're walking right into a trap."

"We go to the monastery," shouted Pemba, loudly enough or every man to hear. This was an order.

"OK," responded Smith. "Then we need to give ourselves the best chance. I suggest we wait until the light fades more and lead the horses to somewhere where we can leave them and approach on foot under cover of darkness."

A plan was formed and they cautiously approached the monastery on foot. Lights could be seen in the windows and in the silence of the plain occasional shouts and bawdy male laughter rang out across the cold empty steppe. Not the natural sounds of a

Tibetan nunnery. As there was no courtyard in the monastery the horses had been left tethered outside. Now his eyes were adjusted to the dark Smith could make out their silhouettes with his binoculars. He guessed that there were about a dozen. It was now a calculated risk and the odds seemed good. Two men were sent forward to dispatch the guard who had been left with the horses, the red glow from his cigarette giving away his nonchalant presence. They returned in a few minutes, the blood black and thick like oil on their knives in the star bright night.

Splitting into three groups they made the final approach to the monastery from different directions. On reaching the first building Smith climbed onto Gyalo's shoulders and clambered up onto a window ledge.

Smith helped Gyalo and another Khampa up onto the ledge and all three dropped silently into a corridor. He stood in the dim light, back pressed against the rough whitewashed wall, a knife raised in his right hand. Through a door to his left he could hear satisfied groaning and an occasional whimper. He had been listening to these sounds for what seemed like forever and his skin crawled. With a supreme effort he forced himself to wait another minute, listening, to be sure that his eyes were accustomed to the light. His hand involuntarily gripped the knife more tightly and he took regular deep breathes to keep himself calm as he became more certain of what he was about to encounter. A trickle of sweat ran down his sleeve. Part of him cried out to let Gyalo take the lead and deal with this. How many more horrors did he have to see?

But he knew that he had to keep facing his demons and stay focused. Clear the mind. Deep breathe. Go.

With his foot he gently pushed the door. It hardly made a sound as it swung open on simple rope hinges. In an instant Smith was in the room and staring at a man's pale buttocks pumping rhythmically in the flickering light of a pair of butter lamps. A young girl, wide eyed with fear, stared back at him from beneath the young soldier who was still too pre-occupied to be aware of the intruder.

In one swift movement, Smith crouched and hooked his left arm around the man's neck, lifting him off the girl. At the same time the knife plunged into his back. As Smith twisted the blade there was a sickening sound of escaping air as the soldier's right lung punctured and collapsed. Frantically, the man sucked in oxygen and his arms and legs flailed wildly. But it was to no avail. Smith drained

41

himself of compassion as the man's head was forced further and further back until there was an audible crack. The body went limp in Smith's arms.

He withdrew the knife and quickly wiped off most of the blood on the dead man's jacket before lifting the body completely off the girl. Only then did he see the four pockets on the tunic indicating that this hero of the revolution was a PLA Officer.

The young nun pulled her habit down over her exposed thighs and shuffled backwards on her haunches into the dark recess of her tiny cell. She pulled her knees up as tight towards her as she could, and clutching them in her arms began to rock gently from side to side, whimpering. As Smith tried to approach her she cowered in fear.

"Stay here and keep quiet," hissed Smith before disappearing down the corridor.

The two *Khampas* who had entered this side of the building with him were now ahead of him and carefully opening the doors of other cells down the corridor. They were empty. The only sound was that of male laughter and shouting somewhere beyond the corridor. Then a distant burst of gunfire and the laughter was instantly extinguished. Smith drew his 9mm pistol and the three men sprinted the few steps to the end of the corridor where they faced a closed door.

Smith nodded to the lead Khampa who kicked in the door and allowed Smith to step swiftly past him and into the room. The adrenalin rush heightening his senses, he instantly assessed the situation and fired single shots at three soldiers before they could rise from the floor. Two other men struggled to their feet, but the *Khampas* were quickly on them, smashing them to the ground with the butts of their AK's.

Smith had been involved in house clearances before, but though they had trained for this in Mustang, the *Khampas* had never put his principles into practice. So Smith was relieved that they had not sprayed the room with automatic fire as he had half expected.

The room was of a substantial size with a high ceiling supported by red painted rough wooden pillars. An altar-like structure ran the whole length of the rear wall covered with rows of brass butter lamps which caused the weird murals of red and gold dragons to dance eerily in the spluttering light. Two nuns were hanging naked by their hands from ropes tied to beams in the ceiling and three others huddled together below the altar, obviously awaiting the attentions of the soldiers.

The only other door was at the far side of the room. Smith signalled to one of the *Khampas* who bounded over to the door and stood to the side of it with his AK at the ready. Smith reckoned from the number of horses they had seen outside that they had accounted for nearly half of the Chinese patrol already and so barring a disaster the others should have already been dealt with by the larger Tibetan force. But he could take no chances. At another nod from Smith the first Khampa carefully opened the door and slipped out of the room. Smith and the other Khampa quickly followed, backs pressed to the wall of the new corridor they found themselves in. It was badly lit, but their eyes soon re-adjusted as they tentatively advanced. Suddenly, a figure appeared, silhouetted in the light beyond and Smith dropped to one knee ready to fire. Just in time he recognised the outline as that of a Khampa and stepped forward to be greeted by Rinzing.

"What's happening?" he demanded in a loud whisper.

"We've cleared right through the building apart from this wing as far as we can tell," replied Rinzing.

"How many of them?"

"Eight. Pemba is in the main hall and some of the men are still making a final sweep to be sure."

"OK. How many nuns?"

"I've seen five dead and a couple injured and about another ten who seem alright"

"Go back and tell Pemba we're OK and were going back to help the nuns we've seen down here. We'll bring them all to the main hall in a few minutes."

Smith and the *Khampas* retraced their steps to find the three nuns still in a terrified huddle. They seemed to be physically unharmed and Smith tried to placate them briefly, before they all turned their attentions to carefully cutting down the other two women. The men could now clearly see, to their horror if not surprise, the livid marks of cigarette burns on their backs and thighs. One of the men quickly left to find Tashi, whose medical knowledge was obviously needed. Smith left the other Khampa to look after the nuns as best he could whilst he quickly returned to the cell of the young nun at the end of the corridor.

She still sat in the corner of the room with her legs drawn up tightly in a foetal huddle, staring with terror at the body sprawled across the cell, now in a pool of congealing blood. Smith approached her slowly and she immediately tried to draw away from him.

"It's alright," he tried to assure her. "He's dead. He can't hurt you any more. Come on. Stand up and we'll go and see the other sisters. They're OK," he lied. "And we have a doctor with us."

She shrieked and shook as he reached out and took hold of her, but he persisted, putting his arms round her, lifting her up onto her feet and holding her tightly to him so she could not resist. He was suddenly aware of how slight she was and looking into her face she seemed little more than a child. He was also acutely aware that he had no idea how best to handle this, but years of training and experience of violent and unexpected situations had taught him to take control, do something and worry about whether it was the right thing later.

Firmly, but as gently as he could he led and dragged her down the corridor. She ceased resisting, but continued to sob quietly. In the other room someone had produced tea which the uninjured nuns sat sipping. Tashi was stooped over one of the injured women, both of whom were now laid on the floor covered by blankets.

"This girl's been raped by one of the Officers." Smith announced baldly to Tashi in English as they entered the room. "Can you have a look at her?" Tashi looked up at the young face. Smith wondered how many times had he seen that face before, the face of countless women violated by the Chinese since the invasion began? He knew that rape was not just a random act of undisciplined troops, but a weapon to be used to demoralise the enemy. Tens of thousands of nuns were driven from their monasteries and untold numbers of them had been raped or forced to marry men from the endless tide of immigrants being encouraged to colonise Tibet from China proper. All part of a deliberate policy to destroy Tibetan culture and dilute Tibetan ethnicity.

"What is your name?" Tashi asked the girl as he approached her, but she refused to answer. Tashi led her gently into the light of the room and indicated for her to sit on the floor, which she did, immediately adopting her foetal position again.

"What is her name?" Tashi addressed one of the uninjured nuns.

44

"She is called Chungla and I am Tseten," replied the nun, who Smith could now see was not much older than Chungla.

"Alright, Tseten, will you help me?"

"Of course, Rinpoche She is the *Tulku*." Tashi and Smith looked at each other, shocked by the girl's addressing Tashi in the form used for only the most senior and revered lamas.

"Why the fuck is she calling you Rinpoche, Tashi and what's this about the *Tulku*?" hissed Smith, reverting to English.

"I...I don't know," stuttered Tashi before regaining his composure. "The girl is shocked, probably delirious. Doesn't know what she's saying. She's had a terrible ordeal. They all have. Now, do you want me to help this girl or not?"

"You're a shit liar, Tashi. We'll talk about this later" Tashi looked even more uncomfortable as he turned his attentions back to Chungla.

"Chungla has been attacked by one of the Chinese soldiers and I need to examine her, so I want you to assist me, Tseten. Are you a friend of hers? Can you do that?"

"Of course, Rinpoche" responded the girl again to Tashi's horror.

"Why are you calling me that?" he responded sharply, to silence her before Smith could get involved again. "No, do not reply. Just come over here and please do as I tell you." Tseten looked confused and embarrassed at Tashi's rebuke, but began to comfort her friend who seemed to relax a little. She then whispered something to her friend which the others could not hear. Chungla looked at Tashi. As he approached she was immediately more compliant and he began his examination.

Smith left them and headed to the main hall, a larger and obviously more important version of the room he had just left. Thick, rich rugs adorned the floor and the room was furnished with various red painted wooden chests and seats inlaid with gold. A huge Buddha sat on the altar. Hanging from the ceiling were colourful silk panels and white katas, silk scarves traditionally presented to the monastery by important visitors.

Also hanging from the ceiling beams by their arms were two terrified men, being beaten by a couple of *Khampas* to the encouragement of a small audience of other *Khampas* and nuns.

"Pemba," Smith shouted, "what the hell is going on? Cut them down, now!"

"This is not your business, my friend. You have no authority here. If you have no stomach for this, leave us. We know what to do with this scum. In any case they may have information." Smith looked directly at the two terrified faces, only now realising that one of them was Tibetan.

"Yes, my friend, a traitor working with the Chinese. And the other is a Red Guard. You know why they were here? Thamzing. How many times have we seen this?"

Smith knew that Thamzing was the method of re-education introduced into Tibet by Chinese Communist cadres. At first it involved the study of Marxist-Leninist doctrine and the introduction of collectivisation. But in time it required Tibetans to denounce themselves and their neighbours. During the Cultural Revolution, Red Guards regularly beat and tortured 'reactionaries', 'counter-revolutionaries' and the 'running dogs of capitalism', often to death. Monasteries and their inhabitants and contents were a prime target for Thamzing.

"Every man here has lost family and friends to these bastards. I watched my own brother die at their hands back in our village in Kham."

"This is just revenge, Pemba. What about your Buddhist ideals?"

"That's just what they are, my friend. Ideals. Ideals that, after ten years of killing and dying, have become meaningless in this place. Even Tashi is a warrior first now and a lama second."

"OK, Pemba, I'd like to argue this one out with you, but I guess I'm not going to win," replied Smith, and before anyone in the room realised what was happening, he raised his pistol and shot the two unfortunates dead.

"Is that all of them accounted for?" he asked. "We need to think about getting out of here."

Chapter 11

US Embassy, New Delhi

When it opened in 1959 the celebrated architect Frank Lloyd Wright described the US Embassy in New Delhi as one of the finest buildings of the last hundred years. Pat Reagan was not going to disagree with that. As CIA Station Chief he had a spacious, tastefully furnished, air conditioned office on the first floor of the embassy, looking onto a steady stream of traffic heading for the city centre along Panchsheel Marg. Just visible above the buildings on the opposite side of the road were the trees of Jayanti Park where Reagan often took a solitary lunch when the weather was not too unbearably hot. Today was what passed for winter in New Delhi and he could be in the park in five minutes, but other business pressed.

Reagan was a plain speaking Irishman from Boston. With his close cropped dark hair, a powerful chest straining at the buttons of his short sleeved shirt and a confident, almost brash manner, the forty-one year old could easily be mistaken for the US Marines Colonel which he might have become. Like many in the Agency he had been poached as a young officer from the Marine Corps which was a natural recruiting ground for a certain type of person. Reagan's Columbia degree in Oriental Languages and military experience made him that type of person.

Having spent two eventful and dangerous years in Saigon including during the Tet Offensive of 1968, he was now enjoying the promotion which the job in New Delhi gave him, but missing the action of Vietnam.

"Come on in, Martin," beckoned Reagan to a tall, blond, tanned, athletic man in his mid-thirties who tentatively opened the door to Reagan's office.

"How's things down at Haus Kaus?"

"Er, fine," replied the newcomer as he looked across at the smartly dressed stranger sprawled on an armchair opposite his boss.

Martin Larsen could have been Scandinavian from his appearance, but actually hailed from Santa Monica and had read International Relations at UCLA before joining the Agency. For the last five years he had been on the Tibet Program, first as a Senior Instructor in tactics and tradecraft at Hale and for the last eighteen months as head of the Special Service Center here in New Delhi. The SSC was the hub for all the CIA's Tibet-related activity and was based in a top secret safe house in the Haus Kaus district of the city near the University.

"This is Stephen Chivers. He's my opposite number in Six over at the British High Commission. Him and me go back a long way. Isn't that right, Stevie?" Chivers winced noticeably at being referred to as Stevie, but quickly recovered and leapt to his feet smiling broadly to begin enthusiastically pumping Larsen's arm.

"Hello. Nice to meet you."

Larsen was a little taken aback by such an effusive Brit, as these guys were, in his limited experience, usually pretty buttoned up. Not the plummy accent he expected either, but something he guessed as being more northern.

"Steve was their man in Saigon back in '63 when I did my first tour there, before the shit hit the fan. Great times, eh Stevie? And a great town." Chivers smiled in agreement.

"OK," continued Reagan, becoming more serious now, "let's get down to business." He indicated to the armchairs set around a glass coffee table and they all sat down. A pot of coffee and three cups and saucers were set out on the table, but, unusually, there were no files in evidence as the meeting began.

"Stephen, do you want to kick off on this?"

"Well, Martin. Do you mind if I call you Martin?" Not waiting for an answer, Chivers continued. "Well, to get right down to it, it's been drawn to our attention that one of Her Majesty's subjects is fighting with the Tibetan rebels, with your boys in fact, against the PLA. Also, from what we hear he is, in his own small way, and depending on your point of view, being quite effective."

"And what is your point of view, Mr. Chivers, if you don't mind me calling you that?" interjected Larsen sarcastically. He hadn't been in the room two minutes and he was already on the defensive.

"Martin," Reagan admonished, "what the hell is this all about?"

"How do you know about this guy?" responded Larsen to

Chivers.

"Never mind how we know," interjected Reagan. "We know, and now that we do, something is going to have to be done about it. But first, give us the back story on this. How long have you known about this and why haven't you actioned it yourself? Jesus, you're an experienced Officer, Martin. Can't you see the implications of this?"

At first Larsen was silent. Reagan leaned towards him, staring intently, aggressively.

"Alright," began Larsen, outmanoeuvred. "About six months ago one of our Tibetans, a Hale graduate who we called Ed (we gave them all western names at Hale) wandered across the Indian border with a group of refugees. He'd been infiltrated into Tibet overland with a small team about three years ago and we lost contact with them nearly straight away. It turned out they were ambushed by the PLA days after they got back into the country. Probably betrayed by the locals in what was supposed to be a safe village. Not that unusual, sadly.

"Anyhow, the whole team was killed with the exception of Ed, who managed to run for it. He headed west towards Mustang and eventually linked up with another outfit.

"To cut a long story short it seems this European guy and some monk joined the team at some stage, after which, according to Ed, they moved up a gear, or several gears more likely. This team weren't amateurs, they'd been fighting the Chinese for years already, but this guy seemed not only to know what he was doing, but to put the umph back into them.

"So then they get involved in some fire fight. One of many if Ed is to be believed. And Ed gets separated from the group. They don't have radios or any of that shit up there, so Ed's on his own again. He heads south and eventually turns up in Kalimpong and from there he contacts us."

"So how reliable is this Ed?" enquired Reagan.

"He was fully debriefed by one of my guys in Kalimpong. He was convinced that Ed was telling us the truth. But the fact that he contacted us when he got to India and that this story has no obvious other motivation convinces me that it is true."

"So why did you do nothing about it?" asked Chivers, obviously irritated.

"Because, Pat," began Larsen, addressing his superior. "Because my job is supposed to be to make the Tibetan resistance as effective as I can. This guy seemed to be making that job a bit easier and it wasn't even costing us a dime."

"Wo there! Just back up a little, fella. You know better than me, or you should do, that this situation is a whole lot more fluid now. The Chinks aint the problem to Uncle Sam they used to be. In fact if Kissinger gets his way the President's gonna be their best buddy before we know where we are. Those Chinese divisions tied down in Tibet are divisions our government wants to see eyeball to eyeball with the Russkies along the Sino-Soviet border. The Russians are the State Department's public enemy number one and we want them watching their back." Reagan paused.

"So your guys are no longer part of the solution, they're part of the problem." Another pause. "You know what I think, Martin? I think you're too close to this. You've been working with these people a long time and you've got to like them too much. Hale is closed down and this operation is running down. Before long all your Tibetan boys are going to be looking for jobs and if you don't want to join them get with the program. You understand me?"

No reply. Reagan continued, calmer now.

"As a matter of interest, Martin, do we know who this guy is? Is he a Brit or what? Could he be some kind of mercenary?"

"All we know is basically what I told you. It seems he met the monk in London and Ed was convinced he was a Brit. It seems a reasonable conclusion that he was a soldier at some time and the Brits get as much field experience as anybody these days. He was probably an Officer in my opinion. Ed guesses he was about thirty years old. Apparently, he calls himself Smith.

"I doubt he's a mercenary as nobody up there has any money to pay him. God knows what his motivation is, but I don't think he's linked to anyone outside. Do you want me to find out any more?"

"No Martin. What I want you to do is get rid of him before the PLA catch him. Can you imagine how much political shit is going to fly if they caught a Brit charging round China killing their people? Or even worse, if you've got all this wrong and he's American. A US 'military advisor' in the field with some ragbag rebel army on Chinese sovereign territory. Jesus! They'd have a fucking propaganda field day."

"Hold on Pat. The whole point is that Tibet is not part of China. The Tibetans have a good legal case and that's why Uncle Sam was prepared to support them in the UN. We were, we are doing something good here. Perhaps you never heard this, but the International Commission of Jurists concluded back in 1959 that what the Chinese were doing in Tibet constituted genocide under the UN Genocide Convention. And things are probably a whole lot worse now. I'm proud to say that we've been doing something, even if not enough, for these people." Larsen turned to Chivers, more angry now.

"If Britain had supported the UN Motions on Tibet perhaps they would have got international backing. But you couldn't support it because all the colonies you were still trying to hang on to would have been clamouring for independence, which of course they all got anyway as it turned out"

Before Chivers could respond Reagan charged in.

"What the fuck are you talking about, Martin? This shit is all history. Don't quote conventions and UN motions to me. In the here and now we have a problem and I want you to deal with it"

Larsen was about to launch into another diatribe, but realising that it was futile, bowed to the reality of the situation.

"OK, what do you want me to do?"

"Jeez, Martin! OK. In words of one syllable. Kill the son of a bitch. Do it soon and don't leave a body lying around for anyone to find."

Back at the safe house Larsen sat in his office reflecting on the meeting and what a complete naive shit head he had shown himself to be in front of his boss and the supercilious Limey. The trouble was they were right. He was not the only one to have got too involved with the Tibet Program, the Tibetans they trained and the cause they were fighting for. He knew several of his colleagues felt the same way.

But every mission came to an end and you moved on. Sometimes you were on the right side and felt good about what you did and sometimes you let your allies down, let them die, and worse, in the best interests of Uncle Sam. That was the name of the game. It was what you got paid for.

Larsen was sure they had been on the right side this time and he had tried to keep the Program going even when he knew the funds were being cut and every fighter was being prepared for an eventual end to American support. They hadn't made a parachute drop of fighters or supplies since God knows when. All the guys trained at Hale who were still in the field were now under strict orders to collect intelligence only and not engage the PLA. Reagan was right. It was over.

Larsen knew that the only people hitting the Chinese now were the few independent groups still out there and that's why he had ignored Smith or whatever his name really was. He had known the potential dangers of doing this, but he could not pull the plug on this guy. How many times had he laid awake at night since he had heard of Smith's existence and imagined what was in the man's mind and how he lived? Larsen was an adrenalin junkie and a romantic and that's why he joined the Agency. His job had him doing things that most people only dreamt of and sometimes, like with the Tibet Program, it was even worthwhile, but still he spent ninety percent of his time behind a desk and always at the beck and call of somebody or some policy higher up the food chain.

Smith, in Larsen's imagination, did exactly what he wanted. He had chosen his cause for whatever reason and he fought for it, literally. He rode a horse, for God's sake, and slept under the stars. His life must be on the line every single day. He didn't even get paid.

What was he up to, what was he thinking right now, Larsen wondered? He seemed to prowl the vast Tibetan Plains like, like what? Like a snow leopard. That was it. This man was a predator. But he was also on the endangered list. And how ironic that Larsen was the man who had to make him extinct.

Larsen's reverie was interrupted by a knock at the door.

"Come in."

A Tibetan, obviously a Khampa from his height and features, but dressed in casual western clothes, entered Larsen'soffice.

"You sent for me, boss?"

"Yes, Lhotse. Come in. Close the door." Lhotse was one of eight Tibetans currently doing desk jobs at the SSC. Several of them had attended courses in International Relations, Politics and US History at Cornell. Between them they were a veritable Tibetan think tank as well as a military operations base.

"I'll get right down to it. How would you like to go on an operation, Lhotse?"

"With Unit 22?" enquired Lhotse doubtfully. Unit 22 was set up by General Uban as an Indian Army Special Forces unit. As fighters were stood down in Tibet they were redirected by the CIA into Unit 22 via the SSC so that their expensive training and talents were not wasted.

"No." Larsen re-assured Lhotse. "How would you like to go home? We're putting a team together asap and I've got a very special job for you."

Chapter 12

ཐ

Tsarang Monastery, Tibet

With help from a couple of the *Khampas* the nuns managed to prepare a simple meal. Apart from those deployed as lookouts and Tashi who was still attending the injured nuns, everyone congregated in the main hall of Tsarang Monastery and the men at least, ate enthusiastically.

"So, what now?" Smith asked Pemba as he scooped the last of his food from his wooden bowl.

"We head for the RV as planned."

"And the nuns? If we leave them here they're dead meat and if we take them they're going to slow us down. The PLA are going to miss these guys sooner or later and they're going to come looking for them."

"This I realise, Peter," replied Pemba, slightly exasperated, "but do you have a better idea? As you say our choices are limited. They come with us. They are our people."

"OK," agreed Smith. "So let's get out of here as soon as it's light. And then we need to get rid of them as soon as possible. Presumably most of them come from villages fairly close by. Can we dump them off at a small town or village a reasonable distance from here where they can disappear back to their families?"

"We're only about a day or so from Kaisang were the RV is. It's a small town and once we have conducted our business they can be left there. It is a risk, but no more than anything else we can do now. If the Chinese really want to find these women you and I know that, whatever we do, they will. Let's hope they are more interested in finding us and we can draw them away from here."

"Yes," agreed Smith again, trying to close his mind to the possibilities.

Filling another bowl with food, Smith rose and walked down the corridor to where Tashi was still at work.

"Some food for you, Rinpoche," he announced in English, smiling at his friend.

"So tell me what secrets you've been keeping from me."

"Later, perhaps," replied Tashi doubtfully. "For now there are more important things."

"OK. How are the patients?"

"Better than I first thought. Very shocked, but physically, yes, pretty good considering."

"Good, because we travel as soon as it's light."

"All of us?"

"That's Pemba's plan, and he's right. We can't afford to hang around. So eat up. I'll go and get some food for the ladies if you think they're up to it."

It was still bitterly cold as they began to load the horses. There was just enough light from the early morning sun to fasten buckles and straps with rapidly numbing fingers. At least, with the PLA horses, everyone had transport. Two small rickety carts had also been retrieved from the depths of the monastery and hitched up to two of the spare horses. Pannier baskets had been strapped to the other surplus animals.

The *Khampas* had slept little once it was realised that there was enough transport not only for the refugees, but also for the Chinese soldiers, or at least their bodies, and their equipment. So far as it was possible, every sign of the previous night's encounter had then been erased from the Monastery, the bodies piled into the carts and their equipment spread around the party.

The Chinese may arrive tomorrow or in a month's time depending on when the patrol had last reported its position. Hopefully, a superficial inspection of the Monastery would give the impression that it had been abandoned, a far from foolproof plan, but one that improved their chances of escape.

Soon they were under way. Two men were immediately sent ahead to recce and check the route, but for the rest the going was painfully slow. The nuns could all ride, but not well and not quickly with the injuries some had sustained. The carts also looked as if they would fall apart at any minute as they rumbled over the rocky ground.

Smith could feel a knot tightening in his stomach as he willed the party on and silently prayed that they would be able to lighten their load before the PLA overtook them.

Many of the great rivers of Asia rise in the fastness of the Tibetan Plateau. As the party made their tortuous progress northward the countryside began to close in around them until they arrived at the banks of a tributary of one of them, the Tsangpo which becomes the mighty Brahmaputra and eventually floods into the Bay of Bengal two thousand kilometres away.

A more well defined track appeared now, leading them along the river bank as the torrent raged milky white with ice melt beside them. The solution to the problem of disposing of the bodies was now at hand. Weighted down with rocks and surplus equipment the first cadaver was experimentally tossed into the stream. Greedily grabbed by the foaming waters it quickly disappeared. Whether to the bottom or downstream they could not tell, but it was the easiest solution to a substantial problem and Pemba decided that they must take the risk. One by one the corpses were dispatched without ceremony into the hungry river. With luck it would keep the *Khampas'* secret long enough for them to make their getaway after the rendezvous.

The carts were broken up and what wood could be carried for firewood was loaded onto the horses. The rest was scattered and hidden some way from the track.

Even with the whole party now on horseback progress was agonisingly slow and it was clear that what had originally been planned as a day's journey was going to take probably twice that.

Constantly on the lookout for danger, Smith was finally starting to relax when, late in the afternoon of the first day, he heard frantic shouting and waving from the *Khampas* who were riding ahead of the main group. Almost before he saw the aeroplane, Smith heard the whine of its twin engines as it raced towards them down the valley. Instinctively, everyone ducked as it soared a couple of hundred feet overhead. It was gone before they could even think of taking cover, but Smith knew that it would be back.

"Tell them to keep in line," yelled Smith to Pemba, guessng that a panicked rush for cover would convince the Chinese that they had something to hide. Pemba responded and the party continued to trudge forward in a ragged line.

A few minutes later the plane did re-appear, now heading towards the party down the valley from their rear. It had been long enough for the crew to radio back to base for instructions. Or perhaps they already had instructions to strafe anything suspicious and were returning for a better target. Everyone strained to look over their shoulders at the approaching aircraft. Smith felt naked, already imagining the rounds ripping into his flesh.

As the plane bore down on them for a second time, they expected at any second to hear the staccato sound of machine gun fire. Spontaneously Smith began to wave in a friendly fashion to the approaching aircraft as it came lower and lower.

"Wave!" he shouted.

"Wave!" bellowed Pemba, taking up the cry and raising an arm to greet the approaching aircraft. "Wave!"

Other members of the party instantly followed suit so that, by the time the plane was overhead, nearly everyone was flapping both arms in the air frantically and smiling inanely. To their amazement and relief the guns remained silent as the pilot hurtled low over their heads once more, tipped a wing, straightened up and flew on up the valley.

"Jesus!" said Smith loudly in English to no-one in particular.

No more planes were seen that day and Pemba eventually decided that they would rest for a couple of hours before any search party could close in on them and then continue travelling through the night for as long as the weaker members of the party could keep going. The nights were cold and clear with a bright half-moon, meaning that sleeping in the open was not a good option for the women but travelling still was.

As they progressed in the darkness most of the party led their horses and only the injured nuns continued to ride, each led by a Khampa. The trail was now well defined by the light of the moon and continued to follow the riverbank for several miles. Pemba walked at the head of the main party. At around midnight he saw the two *Khampas* who had been sent ahead, sat by the trail, holding the reigns of their horses.

"The bridge is just ahead," announced one of them, Gyalo, who knew the area well.

"What's it like?" asked Pemba.

"As I warned you. It's bad enough taking animals across in daylight, but at night..." His answer tailed away into the night.

"Alright," called Pemba to the rest of the party which had now come to a halt behind him.

"We're going to have a rest here for a few minutes."

"Let's have a look," he continued, turning to the two men. They left their horses and walked towards the bridge, Smith following behind them. The trail rose quickly now and it was soon clear that the bridge spanned a narrow point where the river was squeezed between bands of rock. As the little group approached the bridge itself the roar of the river, suddenly compressed into the channel, had them shouting to communicate.

"Not good," bellowed Pemba above the roar. "Not good at all." They were now standing on a natural rock platform about twenty feet directly above the river. On either side of them a stout wooden strut rose about ten feet into the air and from the top of each a thick rope stretched behind to some unseen anchor point. To their front the ropes dipped away out over the thundering torrent, disappearing into the darkness. More ropes stretched from the base of the struts and these were linked by planks to form a narrow walkway. A cats' cradle of thinner ropes interlinked the main ones forming a sort of flimsy fence and hand rail on either side of the bridge. As they watched, the whole structure swayed vaguely before them.

"Perhaps we should wait until daylight." Shouted Pemba.

"But that's hours away," responded Smith. "We need to keep moving, Pemba. It's shit, but I still say we go."

"OK," agreed Pemba without further discussion and they returned to join the main party.

Apart from the danger of crossing the bridge, Smith and the others were all too aware of the ever present possibility of an attack by the Chinese. They would be particularly vulnerable crossing the bridge, so four *Khampas* were sent across first on foot to secure the ground on the other side. Smith watched anxiously as they were swallowed up by the night. With no tactical radios they could never be sure what was happening to anyone out of sight of the group and they might not even hear the sound of an ambush on the other side above the noise of the river.

Another four *Khampas* were deployed to secure their rear and two men were left to look after the horses of the forward and rear parties.

Gyalo was given the task of making the first crossing with a horse. He led his mount to the edge. A fine dusting of frost, sparkling in the moonlight, now covered the narrow wooden walkway as it sloped away from him. The white foaming waters of the angry river swirled and leapt below. Gyalo had to bellow to his horse for it to hear his commands as he pulled the reluctant beast forward. Its head dragged wildly at the reigns and its hooves clattered on the wooden walkway as it was eventually coaxed onto the bridge. At first the horse's legs thrashed and it struggled to retain its footing as the narrow bridge sloped down into darkness, but as Gyalo led it further forward it settled to the precarious surface and soon man and horse had reached the lowest point to which the bridge sagged. They then began to climb out of sight towards the far bank and safety.

The next Khampa and the next followed as closely as they dared so that each horse behind saw as little as possible of what was to come. This plan worked well with the experienced horsemen and they even managed to get the two most seriously injured nuns across without incident, lashed to their horses to prevent them falling.

Smith and Tashi crossed next followed closely by the young nun, Chungla. As she and her horse began to climb up from the lowest point of the bridge, the horse suddenly reared without warning. Chungla clung bravely to its reigns, now dragged high above her head and almost lifting her off the bridge as the beast reared in terror. Smith and Tashi immediately saw what was happening, but the bridge was too narrow for them or the men behind to pass their mounts. They raced to the end of the bridge, let go of their horses and turned to dash back down the bridge.

In the meantime, the panicked horse crashed down on Chungla, knocking her to the floor of the narrow bridge. Having nowhere else to go, the animal now charged wildly forward, about to trample the injured nun. She saw the danger and instinctively rolled sideways, over the side of the bridge. Her chest caught on one of the vertical ropes and she managed to hook her arms around it as her legs waved wildly in the air feet above the icy torrent. She screamed in terror as she clung precariously to the cold wet ropes.

Smith and Tashi were now sliding down the bridge towards the girl, with the panicked horse heading straight for them, about to trample them both. At the last second Smith grabbed the rope handrail and swung over the side as the horse dashed past him. Tashi was a few metres behind and managed to turn and scramble back up to the far side of the bridge, pursued by the terrified horse.

The rope was as hard and cold as iron cable in Smith's hands, and for an instant panic welled up inside him as he doubted whether he could pull himself back onto the bridge. A glimpse of Chungla's thrashing body only feet away cleared his mind and with a huge effort he swung his legs up onto the wooden floor of the bridge and slithered back to safety. He then lunged forward and managed to grab the nun's shoulders.

As he struggled to pull her back from the edge the whole bridge suddenly shook violently and she slipped from his hands. Farther along the bridge the terrified horse had reared again before catching up with Tashi. Its hind legs sliding on the icy incline, the animal crashed sideways into the ancient side ropes of the bridge. Unable to resist the sudden force, they snapped like string and the beast plunged headlong into the icy stream. For an instant Smith saw its terrified eyes caught by the moonlight, above the hissing foam, before it disappeared forever from view.

Chungla was quickly losing her hold on the ropes and now hung fully extended below the bridge, her feet dipping in and out of the white chaos below her. Smith scrambled back to the girl and straddled one of the upright ropes so that he could not be dragged into the river with her, before leaning forward and grabbing her cold slender arm with one hand. She looked up at him with obvious relief on her face, seemingly more confident than he was that he would rescue her once again. Her look turned to one of horror as her arm began to slip through Smith's grasp, the cold and the dampness of her skin making it virtually impossible for him to hold her any longer. Her small hand was now gripped in his.

"It's alright, I've got you," he shouted, knowing that he was going to let her go at any second. "Hang on." Again he could see that look of absolute trust in her face even as he was about to let her die in the icy river. He had to hold on to her.

And then suddenly other hands were reaching down for the girl as two *Khampas* arrived and between them quickly grabbed her and hauled her back to safety. Clinging precariously to the side of the bridge undamaged by the lost horse, they then inched their way to the far side of the river and safety. As they stood once again on solid ground, Chungla, to Smith's surprise, threw her arms round him and began to sob with evident relief. He reluctantly held her frail body in his arms, avoiding the eyes of the other Tibetans.

The bridge now lurched seriously to one side where the horse had fallen. Pemba was soon across the damaged bridge and organising the men who were already safe. Ropes were lashed over the gap on the damaged side to provide some protection, psychological if nothing else, and soon the process of crossing began again with *Khampas* cautiously leading the remaining nuns and horses to safety.

Finally, the whole party was safely across. Chungla was apparently no worse for wear, but it was decided to rest for a while. A simple meal was produced and once consumed they again set out into the darkness with two *Khampas* riding ahead and two trailing in the rear.

"Time for a talk," announced Smith as he drew his horse alongside Tashi.

"Yes?" enquired Tashi as if he did not know where this was leading.

"Yes indeed, Rimpoche."

"Alright, what's the problem?"

"I don't know. I suppose it is just a bit of a surprise to find that my old friend Tashi's an incarnate lama, Tashi Norbu Rimpoche."

"It is no longer wise to advertise these things, Peter, as I think you know."

"Yes, but this is me, Tashi."

"It is simple enough. My medical and religious studies at the Deprung Monastery were complete. I was about to become Abbot of a monastery outside Lhasa. My training and family connections made this a natural step. And then Deprung was bombed and I was forced to flee. The rest you know.

"In India and London my status at home seemed less and less relevant to what was happening around me. No-one who is not a Tibetan would refer to me in this way. I got out of the habit of being Tashi Norbu Rimpoche, if you'll excuse the pun." They both smiled.

"And as I said, in our situation here, it is better to be as anonymous as possible if we are captured. Senior lamas get special attention from the Chinese."

"So what about the girls? How did they know you? Have you been to Tsarang Monastery before?"

"No. They said they knew that I, er, that we would come. They've been waiting for us for a long time."

"How did they know we were coming? Did the Chinese know? Was that a trap back there? How long have they been waiting?" Smith the soldier needed to know if they were in even more danger than he already thought.

"Peter! Calm down. They have been waiting for years."

"Years? What the hell do you mean?"

"Chungla is a *Tulku*. You heard them say that. You know what that word means, don't you?"

"Yes. She's been recognised as an incarnation. I thought only guys could be *Tulkus*"

"That is not correct, Peter. Most *Tulkus* are men, but not exclusively. Women also seek to escape from the endless cycle of life and death by finding enlightenment and many have succeeded. In a previous life Chungla was one of those. At that time she chose to return to this world to assist others in achieving enlightenment. She did this by becoming Abbess of Rongbuk La Monastery near Shigatse."

"So how did a teenager, how old is she, fourteen, fifteen, how did she get herself voted in as Abbess?"

"I'm sure you know this, Peter. In the same way that the Dalai Lama was found when the Thirteenth died. When the old Abbess died a small delegation was sent to Lhamo Latso, the Oracle Lake. They saw a vision which directed them to a small village. Here they showed items to several possible candidates, young girls aged about four years old. Chungla was the only one to correctly identify the items which actually belonged to the old Abbess on every occasion. She also had a birth mark on her arm in the same place as her predecessor."

Tashi continued to describe how the young girl was taken from her family of poor farmers and ensconced in relative luxury at Rongbuk La. Here she began her studies in Buddhism to prepare herself for a life as a nun and Abbess.

"And what about the families? What do they make of all this, Tashi?"

"They are very happy, Peter. Their son or daughter has been granted a high honour and what you would think of in the West as a career and status. They can visit their child often and benefit materially from the largess of the monastery."

"I'm doing my best with this, Tashi. I like the idea of incarnation. So the Buddha tells me that if I want to come back to a better situation in the next life I've got to be good in this one. And if I keep at it I'll eventually attain Nirvana. It's a pretty clever way of persuading people to live good lives, social control even, and impossible to disprove."

"I thought you were interested in Buddhism, trying to follow the path."

"I am, but for some reason belief isn't my strong point. Anyhow, what happened to the girl?"

"Her monastery, Rongbuk La, where she was destined to be Abbess, is near Shigatse, Tibet's second city after Lhasa and power base of the Panchen Lama. As you know, he is the most important Lama in Tibet after the Dalai Lama. So when the Dalai Lama fled to India in 1959 the Chinese wished to use the Panchen Lama to win over ordinary Tibetans. At first he did as the Chinese wanted, but then he became difficult. In 1964 they finally lost patience with him. He was arrested and he's still locked up in Qincheng Prison near Beijing.

"After the Panchen Lama's arrest the Red Guards came and destroyed the Samdrubtse Dzong in Shigatse. It was over six hundred years old and almost as important to our culture as the Potala Palace in Lhasa. Then they started on the monasteries. Rongbuk La was flattened and many of the nuns were forced to marry or become prostitutes. But the nuns had seen this coming and they had already smuggled Chungla to safety."

"How old was she when all this was happening?"

"She was ten years old. Since then she has been waiting for us. As I told you, she knew we would come to help her. She has special gifts. You will see. You are a cynical man, Peter, but you will see that a *Tulku* does have knowledge and powers acquired over many lifetimes."

"No I won't, Tashi, because we're getting rid of her and the rest of them in Kaisang tomorrow."

"I don't think we can do that Peter, because we have to take her away from here, to safety. To the West."

Chapter 13

ར

PLA Headquarters, Shigatse, Tibet

The Headquarters of the PLA Military Sub-Command covering the South-West of Tibet, the area where Smith and the *Khampas* currently operated, was based in Shigatse and Colonel Zhu De was Second-in-Command of the garrison. Zhu hated Tibet and he hated Tibetans. He hated Tibet because it was the coldest and bleakest place he had ever served. It made him crave the heat of his native Hunan Province, even though he had hardly been back there in the last twenty years, going without question wherever the PLA, all the family he now had, sent him. But the more time he spent in the grey concrete world which was the Headquarters, the more he dreamed of the sub-tropical land of his childhood.

He hated the Tibetans for their ingratitude. Now on his third tour in this benighted place, he had seen from the early days of the liberation of Tibet the feudal poverty and ignorance of the ordinary people, the swaggering arrogance of the Lhasa aristocracy who owned much of the land, and the superstitious mumbo jumbo encouraged by the endless monasteries which seemed to own the rest of the country.

Mao had been right to exercise China's legitimate claim to sovereignty over Tibet at the earliest opportunity after the Communist Party gained control of China. Tibet was part of China and always had been. To Zhu there was no doubt about that. And the plight of the people of Tibet under the yoke of a feudal theocracy could not be ignored.

Zhu had joined the Party on the Long March as a young man in 1935, fighting first the Nationalists, then the Japanese and then the Nationalists again until victory finally came for the Chinese Communist Party in 1949. He was there with Mao in Tianenmen Square that same year when The Chairman declared that "China has stood up" after two hundred years of civil war and foreign domination. Tibet, Zhu believed, had the right to stand up as well.

So why after twenty years of Communism, the creation of the

Tibetan Autonomous Region within the motherland, the land reform, and the sweeping away of the blood sucking monasticism, were these people still trying to kill his men and bring back the imperialist supported Dalai Lama?

Zhu brushed such thoughts from his mind as a knock on his office door brought him back to present concerns

"Enter." The door opened and Captain Deng strode confidently into Zhu's drab office. Deng was the Garrison Intelligence Officer. At the age of twenty-eight he was more than thirty years younger than Colonel Zhu and looked even younger. He stood smartly to attention in front of his superior Officer as the latter studiously ignored him, instead concentrating on lighting a cheap and foul smelling cigarette produced from a packet on his less than tidy desk. Finally Zhu looked up, taking in at a glance the smart dress uniform, the slicked back hair and imposing height of the younger man, looking as if he had just returned from a military parade. By contrast Zhu himself was short and stocky with grey close cropped hair and his battle fatigues and combat boots suggesting he might need to leave on a operation at any minute. He wished.

Deng was a graduate of Beijing University and spoke Tibetan well. His language skills had proved useful to him as an interrogator at the notorious Drapchi Prison in Lhasa, enforced home of many of Tibet's political prisoners, as had his zealous pursuit of information from the hapless inmates.

"Show me on the map, Deng," began the Colonel brusquely as he strode over to a detailed map of South West Tibet displayed on the opposite wall of his windowless office.

"Show me where you found the parachute."

"Here, Colonel." Deng pointed to a spot on a thin blue line on the map, the course of the upper reaches of the Tsangpo River.

"So that's about a hundred kilometres from here. Anything of interest around there?"

"Nothing, Colonel, or at least nothing obvious. As you can see, it's a pretty isolated area, a few small villages and monasteries dotted around.

"Much like the rest of the country," he added. "The nearest village is called Kaisang." Deng paused.

"Kaisang," repeated Zhu after a minute, obviously recognising some significance in the name.

"Isn't that one of the places we've been getting reports about? That the locals are supporting this trouble-making nun, Thrinley Choedron. Are we assuming this parachute drop is something to do with the uprising in Nyemo? Bring me up to date on the whole sorry saga, will you Deng?"

"Well, Colonel, as you'll recall, this whole thing started in Barkhor, well away from our Tactical Area of Responsibility. Choedron and her supporters killed about fourteen members of our Propaganda Team in the town last month. Apparently a pretty bloody affair. Reports say they chopped off their arms and legs."

"And remind me what we did about this Captain." Deng was silent for a moment and before he had time to gather his thoughts Zhu answered his own question.

"Nothing! We did nothing. And why? Well, I'll tell you why. Because everyone back in Lhasa assumed this was part of the bloody chaos your cronies the Red Guards have been allowed to unleash across the whole fucking country. Flattening monasteries, murdering nuns, monks and peasants alike. I don't give a shit about these people, but I do care about us making a success out of our mission here. And the antics of the Red Guards haven't helped. Choedren and her followers are the chickens coming home to roost on this, Deng. It's our men they're hacking up." The Colonel took a breath before continuing his diatribe.

"I was with Mao on the Long March, Deng. Before you were born. He led us literally out of the wilderness and into power. But," a pause "but now he's more obsessed with hanging onto power and politicking in Beijing. And idiots like you can't see that, Captain Deng. You thought unleashing the Red Guard was all about purifying the Party and the country. In the same way you purify them in Drapchi, I suppose? How bloody naive of you, Deng!

"Then, like all the rest of them, you thought this blood thirsty nun and her pals were part of all that. You and our masters in Lhasa, and even in Beijing, can't tell the difference between the Red Guards and Thrinley Choedren. Well, I'll tell you the difference. Whilst the Red Guards are going round beating and killing anyone they decide is a counter-revolutionary, this nun and her supporters are only interested in getting rid of us, the occupiers as they see us.

"The PLA's split down the middle with all this politicking and

67

because the faction you seem to support in the Army have allowed, even encouraged so much death and destruction they can't see that this is something different. That's why, instead of them being crushed at the start, they're running out of control in a hundred towns and villages from here to Lhasa and now, it seems way to the west as well.

And worse still, the CIA seems to have somehow got in on the act."

Deng looked flustered and dismayed at this attack on his allegiances and competency and seemed about to launch into a defence of himself and the faction he supported, but Zhu cut him off with a raised hand.

"So Intelligence Officer," he began, calmer now, drawing his junior back to the immediate business in hand. "What intelligence have you gleaned from your interrogations that's going to let us get back on top of this situation?"

"Well, sir," began Deng. "I interrogated the man who handed in the parachute, a peasant from a hamlet about ten kilometres downstream of Kaisang. He found it tangled in bushes on the river bank. But it's anyone's guess how far it might have been washed downstream.

"I dispatched a patrol to the area, but they found nothing else of interest nearby. So they split into two, one following the river towards Kaisang where they should be any time now. The other headed off to check other villages and monasteries in the area away from the river. They're now overdue in reporting in."

"That's excellent news," sneered Zhu sarcastically.

"As you know, Colonel, communications are far from reliable in the mountains, so I was not concerned at first. But this afternoon we sent out a reconnaissance plane."

"And?"

Deng reached into his leather briefcase and extracted a slim file which he lay on the Colonel's desk and flipped it open.

"Here are the photographs, or at least the ones of any interest." Deng turned each picture over in turn, allowing Colonel Zhu a few seconds to study each one.

"Who are they?"

"I have no idea," stated Deng frankly. "They are clearly armed, but then so are most of these people if they are travelling with a caravan. And here you can see they are waving at the plane so they seem innocent enough." He paused for effect. "But look at this." Deng reached into his briefcase again and pulled out another item, a magnifying glass in four short steel legs which he stood on top of one of the pictures. Zhu squinted into the glass and the image sprang at him in glorious 3D.

"An AK56," exclaimed the Colonel. "I wonder where they got that, Deng? We need to find out."

Chapter 14

Tibet

The party left the track leading to Kaisang to make a detour into the nearby hills. The sun was now bright and high in the piercing blue sky. After about an hour, one of the *Khampas* called out and pointed to a spot high up in the hills on the other side of the valley.

There it was again. Quite clearly, the regular flashing of a mirror reflecting the sunlight in their direction. A simple but effective way to communicate in the mountains.

"That's them. That's their signal," called out Pemba. He leaned back over his saddle to wrestle an object, a small flat square of polished metal, from his pack and hold it at arm's length in the direction of the sun, tilting it slightly to and fro. The reply came immediately from the opposite hillside.

Soon a small band of men in traditional *chubas* could be seen emerging from their hiding place and leading horses encumbered with packs down the rock-strewn slope. Within minutes the newcomers were being welcomed with smiles and embraces as they joined the main band.

"Welcome friends!" announced Pemba.

"Welcome to you," replied Tendruk, the leader, in mock anger. "We've been freezing to death for two days in these hills waiting for you."

They found a suitable place for a camp nearby so that news could be exchanged. Guards were posted and cooking fires discreetly lit. Soon water was boiling for tea and hot food was passed around amongst fighters and nuns. The nuns were of hardy stock and even those with the worst injuries had coped well with the arduous journey and were showing signs of recovery, at least of physical recovery, though no-one could tell what mental scars they might have. This was part of the scarring of a whole people.

Smith sat eating alone as a small group formed around one of the fires, consisting of Pemba and a couple of his closest lieutenants and the newcomers led by Tendruk. It suited him to maintain his anonymity for the moment and Pemba would eventually tell him anything he needed to know. Nor did Tashi involve himself in the discussions and after a few minutes he picked up his food and joined Smith.

"Well, Tashi, what do you think? He spoke in English and Tashi responded likewise.

"About what?"

"About what we do next."

"I already told you. It is now my duty to help the *Tulku*. Her monastery, her position here in Tibet, has been destroyed and it is now her task to take her knowledge, her potential, to where it can best be of use. And that is in the West. She must go to where she will be heard. Where there are willing ears. America, California perhaps, or even England. As you know we now have monasteries established in such places and she will keep our culture, our religion, alive there."

"What is so special about her?"

"She is a *Tulku*."

"I know. You keep telling me that."

"That is enough, Peter. She has lived many lives and accumulated much wisdom. It is her and our destiny to be born in these times. What the Chinese call being alive in the bitter sea. Our culture is under great threat and must not be allowed to die. It must be taken to a place of safety where it can be nurtured until the time is right for it to return to bloom here in Tibet.

"But the irony is that as the Chinese try to destroy us and our ideas, so they are now blossoming in your world, in the godless West which is desperate for a spirituality like ours."

"So how are you going to get her out of here and to the West?"

"With your help, Peter."

"Hold on. How do I come into this? I'm a soldier, not a bodyguard. I came here to fight. For a free Tibet. A lost but noble cause, someone described it as. Now who was that?" He paused. "Oh, I remember, it was you, Tashi. If you remember it was you who persuaded me to come, though with a line like that I can't now think for the life of me why in God's name I agreed."

"You came to help us. Perhaps you are the only person from the outside world who came, Peter. Almost certainly you are. The CIA sent money and equipment and trained out fighters, but you came and risked your life with us. You still do. That makes you unique. Unique in your desire to help Tibet and its people.

"But you can see as well as I can that the fighting is almost over. I am not a warrior, but I have done what I had to do. Now I can help the Land of Snows in another way and so can you.

"We are not running away. It will not be easy and there may well be more blood on our hands, but we must get Chungla to the West. Doing this will now be the greatest contribution you can make to Tibet.

"Oh, and by the way, Peter, she believes that one of the newcomers might mean you harm. We need to part company with them as soon as possible."

Before Smith could respond to Tashi's warning Pemba called to Tashi who rose and walked towards the small group. Soon instructions were passed to everyone in the party that they were proceeding towards Kaisang.

Chapter 15

ৎ

Kaisang, Tibet

Whilst the rest of the party remained hidden from view Pemba, Tashi and Smith scrambled onto the summit of a hill with a good view down onto the village of Kaisang. The square flat roofed adobe houses could be seen dotted haphazardly amongst greening fields where a few horses and yaks grazed. Away to their left were the buildings of Kaisang monastery, or what remained of them. As the three men trained their binoculars on the centre of the village three crow-pecked heads impaled on wooden spikes came into sharp and grisly focus.

"What the fuck?" exclaimed Smith as the three men lowered their binoculars and looked at one another.

"The Chinese?"

"I don't know," replied Tashi. Then, thinking for a few seconds he continued.

"I'm sure I can see other people moving around and there are definitely animals in the fields. No sign of damage to buildings, apart from the monastery, but that looks as if it was done a while ago."

"Well we need to find out what's going on before we wander in there," interjected Pemba. "We need to send someone down to take a look."

One of the nuns whose family lived in Kaisang was dispatched to the village in the hope that she would attract no suspicion if the Chinese were around. The young woman led her horse as casually as she could towards Kaisang, eagerly watched from the group's vantage point.

She finally returned a couple of hours later and described to

Pemba and the others what had happened.

"No Chinese soldiers or Red Guards have been to the village for weeks. There were five Chinese cadres there and they have all been killed."

"Killed by who?"

"By the villagers. My mother says they have been pushed around for long enough. She told me that last week people came from other villages and told them what had happened there. That people were rising against the Chinese and the Chinese soldiers were doing nothing about it. So they did the same. They killed the Headman and everyone who has supported the Commune. Those heads on spikes are him and his wife and daughter."

Pemba and Tashi looked at one another.

"Perhaps our time has finally come," pronounced Pemba.

"Perhaps," responded Tashi, sounding less than convinced. "What do you think, Peter?"

"It does not matter what he thinks," responded Pemba before Smith could express an opinion. "Peter, you know about fighting, but you do not know our people. About this country. Even the CIA have started to support us again. They know what is happening."

"I wish you were right, Pemba, but you've talked to Tendruk. You know what they said about their mission and their instructions for us. To observe and report back. Not to engage."

"Because they think we are too few and too weak. That the people, the peasants and the monks will do the job. But we can't stand by and watch. We are warriors. We fight. And in any case, we do not take instructions from the Americans. We have not been to Hale. We are our own men"

Smith looked up to heaven.

Chapter 16

ঽ

October 1969 - London

Following the weekend with his parents in Yorkshire, Smith returned to London. His thoughts frequently returned to the conversation he had with his father and to his dead uncle. The seed of doubt had been sown, as his father had intended. Getting out of Spartan was not a problem. They had promised him a contract and he had said that he was available, but that was as far as it went. If he turned it down they would find someone else. He would be forgotten about. But is that what he wanted? He didn't know. And if he didn't go what would he do? This was the reason he had left his beloved Army.

On a whim he had signed up for a class in Tibetan at SOAS and this was about the only constructive thing he was currently doing. He had studied French and German at A Level and Russian at Sandhurst. The latter had shown him that he had something of an aptitude for more exotic languages and the Tibetan was now progressing surprisingly well. But then he did have little else to do with his time.

He quickly became friendly with the class tutor, a Tibetan called Tashi. Soon the more enthusiastic members of the class were meeting every Wednesday evening in the predictably named Shangri La Tibetan Restaurant not far from Russell Square, ordering meals in halting Tibetan and quizzing Tashi about life back home.

One Wednesday evening Smith, Tashi and two other students, a middle-aged woman called Mary and an attractive (to Smith at least) woman in her mid-twenties called Abbi climbed the steps to the first floor dining room of the Shangri La, dimly lit and tiny, with seating for only about thirty people. As usual, the owner, always referred to as Mr. Thondup, came rushing and beaming to greet the new arrivals as soon as he saw that Tashi was with them. The place was already busy, but they were shown to a reserved table by the window.

"The menu in English or Tibetan?" ventured Mr. Thondup.

"Tibetan, naturally!" encouraged Mary, although she and the rest of the party knew that she could still hardly make out a word of the strange hieroglyphs which would come sliding across the requested menu.

"And one in English," mouthed Tashi in Tibetan whilst Mary was engaging Smith in conversation.

"Every time I come here I wonder how they possibly manage to pay the rent on this place, never mind make a profit."

"I know what you mean," replied Smith. The same thought had crossed his mind.

The menus arrived and the three students grappled with the strange text to see if they could turn it into something worth eating. They had tried this exercise on previous occasions and so could memorise a few of the items, but when Smith started to study the piece of card in front of him it was as if a blurred image had suddenly come into focus. Something had clicked and he could actually read the thing, or at least most of it.

"I'll have the spring rolls to start and the Monk's Casserole, I think," he announced proudly.

"That's what you had last time, Peter" announced Abbi, smiling.

"I can bloody read it," responded Smith defensive and deflated.

"I know you can. I'm only joking. I have no idea what you had last time. You're streets ahead of the rest of us.

"Well," replied Smith sheepishly, "I have more time than the rest of you. And I had been practicing before I started the class."

"How come you have time on your hands?" probed Mary.

"I'm out of work."

"Oh."

"Well, strictly speaking, I'm waiting for a new contract to start, but I'm having second thoughts about it."

"A contract doing what?" chimed in Abbi. Both women found Smith interesting. He was tall and athletic, not unattractive and obviously intelligent, but he was never very forthcoming, which only added to the possible mystery.

"International development stuff," began Smith vaguely. "Ah,

Tashi, I think I've made a breakthrough with this menu," he announced, avoiding further discussion, as Tashi returned to his seat from his chat with Mr. Thondup. "We were just wondering how they make any money in this place."

"Well, let's order some food first." He signalled towards the kitchen door and Mrs. Thondup came scuttling across with a pad. Smith ploughed ahead confidently in his ungrammatical, but by now quite intelligible Tibetan, confirmed by Mrs. Thondup's silent scribbling.

"And you?" asked Mrs. Thondup to Abbi.

"God, I'm sorry," interjected Smith sheepishly. "I'm so bloody keen to show how clever I am."

"Don't worry," replied Abbi indulgently as she proceeded to make an equally accomplished job of her order.

Mary did not fare so well and was soon blushing and stammering as Mrs. Thondup patiently tried to make sense of what she wanted. In the kindly guise of assisting Mary, Tashi ordered for her.

"I know the words, but as soon as I have to use them my mind goes blank", she apologised.

"Don't worry. You're doing really well. It is not an easy language and takes much practice. These two have been working hard." Smith and Abbi smiled conspiratorially at one another and Smith was amazed to realise that he had not registered before just how attractive she was. Her hair was dark, as dark has his own, straight and cut in a short bob which accentuated the roundness of her face and what he took to be an Irish complexion and brown eyes. Lipstick was the only make-up he could discern, subtly applied to great effect.

"OK Tashi, so how does this place survive? It's great, but it hardly looks a money spinner to me."

"It is interesting that you should ask this Abbi, because it is pertinent to something I was going to mention to you all." The others waited, intrigued.

"You are in fact correct that Mr. Thondup, excellent host and chef that he is, struggles to make a profit, West London rents being what they are. So the restaurant is supported by Samye Ling."

"Who?"

"Not who, but what, Abbi." Tashi paused as Mr. and Mrs. Thondup arrived with the starters.

"*Tu-jay-cha*, Thank you," they all, even Mary, managed in convincing Tibetan.

"So. To continue. As I am sure you all know, large numbers of my people have left the Land of the Snows since the Chinese invasion, and whilst many have gone no further than the Indian border, a Tibetan Diaspora is now establishing itself in the West, in the USA, Canada and elsewhere, but also very much here in Britain.

"These people are not all poor refugees. Some are wealthy individuals who have brought resources from Tibet or already had wealth in India or the West. Others are lamas who have been able to escape with at least some of the wealth of their monasteries and also with artefacts and the wisdom of our religion.

"And recently they established a Tibetan Monastery in Scotland at a place called Eskdalemuir. The monks help Mr. Thondup so that we, independent Tibet, the Dalai Lama, have a presence here, even if for now only a small one, in this great city."

"I didn't know there were any Tibetan Buddhist monasteries in the West."

"Well, we are not keeping it a secret, Mary. Quite the reverse. Our culture is under threat at home, but it must survive and in the short term that may only be possible here. And that is what I wanted to ask you. If you would like to visit Samye Ling with me? To see some of our culture first hand. And to practice your language skills as well"

Chapter 17

ধ

A1, North London

Mary couldn't make it, but, on an early spring Saturday morning a couple of weeks later, Smith and Tashi left London heading North on the A1 squashed into Abbi's racing green Mini Cooper.

"This is a nice car. Have you had it long?" enquired Tashi as they roared up the outside lane with Abbi obviously enjoying the freedom of the open road.

"I bought it new a year ago and I love it."

"It is a very nice car," endorsed Tashi, who could not drive and knew nothing about cars and their relative merits.

"Did you say you didn't have a car at the moment, Peter?" continued Tashi, warming to his theme.

"That's right," replied Smith noncommitally. Since leaving the Army and moving to London, Smith had realised something that had never occurred to him before, but then it had never really mattered before. The Army was his home. When in the UK he had a decent furnished room in a Mess and good food and plenty of it appeared regularly. He never cooked or washed up or made a bed. In the field he had what he could carry on his back and that was it.

The sad truth was that he owned virtually nothing. Only it had never been sad until now. But when he had moved from the Mess in Aldershot everything he possessed fit into a single MFO box.

"Bloody hell!" exclaimed Gus when Smith had arrived at his mews cottage in Kensington. "Is that it?" And it was.

Gus was a Captain in the Scots Guards and about to be posted to Hong Kong. Not looking forward to two years of chasing "eye-eyes's" (illegal immigrants) trying to escape from the People's Republic to a better life in Britain's free market paradise in the east. But happy to let his old friend Peter have his West London pied-a-terre for the duration rent-free.

"So how do you get around?" continued Tashi, glancing over his shoulder at Smith sprawled out on the tiny rear seats.

"On the bike," he responded brightly.

"You cycle? In London? That's very dangerous, isn't it?"

"Motorbike," corrected Smith.

"Still bloody dangerous though. I didn't know you had a bike. What type?" enquired Abbi.

"Triumph Bonneville." As his recent stock taking had shown, this was his only significant possession, the only thing he owned worth more than fifty pounds. Already half way to being a Buddhist he thought, smiling to himself.

"God." Abbi continued with her train of thought. "I've never been on a motor bike." It quickly became apparent that Abbi was the kind of woman who should have been on a motorbike and that now she realised this it was an omission which needed to be corrected soon.

"Haven't you? That's surprising." Then silence.

Tashi looked over his shoulder to see Smith smiling knowingly at him.

"Stop this, Peter," he admonished. "He is being very cruel to you, Abbi."

"Yea, of course I'll take you out on the bike. If you want to risk it. We'll sort out a helmet and get something organised when we get back to London, if you like."

"I'll hold you to that."

The conversation resumed over three cups of what passed for coffee at a service station on the A1.

"I never asked you what you did for a job, Abbi," began Tashi, smiling serenely over his cup.

"At the moment I work for UNICEF. As an operations manager."

"What's that?"

"Well, sadly it means being stuck in an office making sure our people on the ground are doing what they're supposed to be doing and have the resources we're trying to get to them in the middle of some disaster area on the other side of the world. I was a field worker with Christian Aid and then Save the Children, but climbing the greasy pole led me back to a desk."

"Your work sounds very interesting, Abbi," added Tashi. "How did you get into this kind of work?"

"I did a degree in Peace Studies at Bradford. From that international development seemed an obvious career."

"Just the opposite to me," mused Smith. "War Studies is more the order of the day there."

"Oh yes. I remember you saying in the restaurant you were waiting for a contract. To work abroad. Not in development work, I assume?" enquired Tashi.

"No. Not exactly," replied Smith vaguely. Then more brightly, "but I'm having second thoughts about that."

"I told you before, you should think about working for an NGO, Peter. I've known a few ex-army guys over the years, advising on mine clearance, logistics, that sort of stuff."

"Yeah, well. I'm not sure how much use my skills would be to UNICEF, or anyone else, Abbi."

"You might be surprised, Peter," chipped in Tashi. Smith screwed up his face as he forced down the dregs of his coffee and they returned to the car.

Chapter 18

ק

Kaisang, Tibet

Still huddled below the crest of the small hill from which they had been observing Kaisang, Smith and the others watched in horror as white phosphorus shells began to land on the roof and surroundings of the monastery. In no time at all, dense white smoke was swirling around the buildings and soon the timbers, bone dry in this rainless land, began to ignite. Acrid smoke poured down on the box-like buildings, drifting across the whole settlement. Fires could now be seen, in buildings and hay ricks. The grisly spiked heads disappeared and re-appeared intermittently as the smoke spread. Members of the still living population could occasionally be spotted darting between buildings in obvious panic.

Suddenly, the group on the hill were aware of a distant roaring which quickly came closer and distilled into the deep growl of diesel engines. As they looked to their right a line of six PLA Type 63 Armoured Personnel Carriers swung into view. Their tracks tore at the distressed earth, throwing up swirls of dust as they stormed towards the village. Expecting no resistance, the commanders and gunners of the squat vehicles had left their top hatches open to give them a clearer view as they advanced.

"Where the fuck did they come from?" exclaimed Smith as they continued to watch, mesmerised by the scene unfolding below them.

A few hundred metres short of the first buildings, the APCs slurred to a halt in a rough extended line, each about thirty metres from its neighbour. The commander of one of the vehicles towards the centre of the line looked to be speaking briefly into his radio. Almost as one, the metal doors at the rear of each vehicle swung open, disgorging a cargo of about a dozen men in drab olive uniforms, webbing pouches at their waists and wearing steel helmets, each man clutching his AK56.

They moved swiftly round the vehicles to form an extended line ahead of them and continued to move towards the village at a determined walking pace. The vehicle gunners could be seen pulling back the cocking handles of the mounted 7.62 machine guns, ready to provide covering fire in the unlikely event that it was needed, or to mow down villagers on request.

The Chinese soldiers were now disappearing in and out of the smoke and wispy fingers of white reached as far as the line of APC's.

"They will destroy the village!" screamed Pemba almost in tears, suddenly scrambling to his feet. Smith grabbed him and dragged him back down behind the skyline.

"Get off me!" raged the powerful Tibetan, but Smith clung to his friend.

"What are you going to do?"

"Fight!"

"How?"

"We have our horses. We can attack."

"Are you insane?" Both men were now breathing heavily as they continued to wrestle in the dust. "Listen. We cannot win against them. In the open we have no chance. We need to get out of here before they see us."

"No," was Pemba's emphatic response, as with a supreme effort he finally broke free of Smith and pushed himself exhaustedly onto his hands and knees. "You do not need to join us. You have done enough." His tone was suddenly contemptuous. For a second Smith felt the fight drain from him under this assault, more violent than any physical attack.

"Listen to me, Pemba," he forced himself to respond. "There are too many of them. We can't save the village and all we will do is get ourselves and the nuns killed if we try."

"We cannot leave them to die. We must fight. They are our people."

Smith realised that this was an argument he was not going to win and that his fate was inexorably tied up with that of the other fighters. He was in no position to go it alone. Pulling his pistol from inside his *chuba*, he pointed it menacingly at Pemba. After the incident at Tsarang Monastery there was little doubt that Smith meant business.

"OK Pemba", gasped Smith. "I'll tell you what we'll do. There's not going to be any cavalry charge. Get the men up here, and bring the RPG's and one of the Dragunovs. Tell them to keep out of sight of the village. Tell Tendruk to leave some of his men to guard the horses and take the rest of his men and the nuns and head up the valley away from the village. This way at least some of us might survive.

"Think about it, Pemba," he exhorted, both men silent except for their panting for breath after their exertions.

Smith thought that Pemba would at least argue, but, after a couple of minutes the Khampa leader, calmer now, simply turned and bounded down the reverse slope of the hill towards the waiting group of fighters and nuns.

"Tashi, go with him. Make sure he does what I said."

"How will I do that?"

"You'll find a way. He'll listen to you." The lama followed Pemba without another word.

Smith watched anxiously as Pemba gesticulated wildly at the group, Tashi now at his side. He half expected men to start mounting their horses ready for a frontal assault on the Chinese, but to his relief the majority of the fighters were soon making their way on foot up the hill behind their leader.

"Here," was all Pemba said as he thrust a long object wrapped in canvas into Smith's arms.

"Let's see what's happening. Tell everyone else to stay here til we call them up." Smith crawled as Pemba quickly briefed the others and followed him. Smith now peered cautiously over the brow of the hill. The APCs had not moved, but the line of advancing soldiers was already in amongst the buildings of the village.

"Get the RPG's up here and the rest of the men," ordered Smith as he continued to view the drama through his binoculars. Rocket propelled grenades with High Explosive Anti Tank (HEAT) rounds were soon ready to fire. Smith knew from experience that irregular troops like the *Khampas* had a poor record of hitting the target with any weapons, never mind Soviet built RPG7s which they rarely, if ever, got a chance to practice with. He had once almost been the victim of a similar weapon, but his assailant made the mistake of trying to fire it at his vehicle from the open window of a car. The back blast had incinerated the firer and the other occupants of the car and Smith lived to tell the tale.

Whoosh!! The first round went scudding off in the general direction of the APCs, but exploded harmlessly in the ground nearby. But before the Chinese realised that they were under attack the second weapon fired and against the odds hit the nearest APC in the flank. It exploded in a ball of flame as the crew dived for safety, one with his fatigues already on fire.

Smith lowered his binoculars and quickly unrolled the canvas bundle to reveal the Dragunov, another Soviet weapon used by the PLA and liberated from them in a past raid. It was a simple, but reliable and effective sniper rifle. He wrapped the sling tightly round his forearm for extra stability and peered down the telescopic sight. Smith had never been the best shot in the Battalion, but he had been good enough to take a team to the National Rifle Championships at Bisley once, where they came next to last. Now was the time to suppress such memories.

He swung the sight round to the vehicle from which he thought the original order to disembark had been given. Take out the Officers first. A time honoured principle of soldiering, and especially so in the War of the Flea where, once the decision has been made to hit the enemy, scarce resources need to be used to maximum effect.

So Smith held the rifle, stock firmly in the palm of his left hand, pushing the butt solidly into his right shoulder, trying to steady his breathing so that with each breath the cross-hairs returned to the target. He aimed off slightly to allow for the wind blowing from his left to right, and fired. The man must have heard the shot and ducked into the turret. No. Smith could still see him. Slumped below the lip of the turret. A hit! As if to confirm his diagnosis, a figure appeared in the hatchway trying to pull the wounded man into the vehicle. Smith fired again. The soldier looked round, shocked, but before he could react Smith fired a third time, sending the man sprawling over the roof of the APC.

Smith swung the rifle round in the hope of picking out another target, but by now everyone was getting the message and turret lids were crashing shut on every vehicle. Even this was in the rebels' favour as it meant that drivers and commanders in the APCs, now battened down, would have a much more restricted view of the *Khampas* and where they were firing from.

In the meantime, the other *Khampas* had needed no instructions to begin firing at the enemy. The Chinese foot soldiers took cover where they could amongst the buildings and behind the low stone walls of Kaisang as automatic rounds began to fall amongst them. The Tibetans could see from their hilltop vantage that the Chinese had soon taken several casualties.

"Hit the APCs!", cried Pemba and more RPG rounds were launched at the exposed vehicles. Battened down, they were finding it difficult to identify where they were being attacked from, but it would not be long before they knew and began to return fire. Before they could, a second APC took a direct hit and a third had a track ripped off.

Then the mortar rounds began to land on the hillside, well short of the Tibetans at first, but creeping inexorably upwards towards the *Khampas'* positions. This was now accompanied by heavy machine-gun fire from the undamaged vehicles and automatic fire from the infantry in the village. The Tibetans kept returning fire as best they could, but they had little cover, having had no time to dig shell scrapes.

"Pemba!" shouted Smith. "We're going to be taking casualties if we don't get out of here soon. We need to do something."

"What do you suggest?"

"Get most of the men away now, whilst some of us stay behind to hold the Chinese up." Pemba agreed and began to shout orders to his men, several of whom began to crawl back from the edge of the hill and then to scramble down the reverse slope once they were out of sight of the enemy.

"And you, Pemba!" bellowed Smith.

"I am not leaving!"

"If you don't get away the others won't. You need to lead them Pemba, if we're to have any chance of getting away in good order."

"What about the village?" Smith wanted to answer that he had told Pemba the whole thing was a waste of effort and potentially more lives, but for the satisfaction it might have given him it would only do more to dissuade Pemba from leaving.

"We've given the Chinese something to think about, given them enough casualties to take their mind off the village. They're going to come after us now. So we've bought them some time. It's the best we could do." Smith knew time was something the Chinese had plenty of and that if they did not destroy the village now they would be back when they were ready. This was not something they were going to forget about. But there was an outside chance that at least some of the villagers would have time to make a run from it, desert their homes and leave, assuming they had anywhere to go.

"Go, now Pemba. Please. I'll stay and gradually send back the rest of the men to follow you. You know where to head for." Mortar shells continued to explode around them as the two men shouted at one another over the deafening noise. Finally, Pemba, defeated, clambered to his feet and began to head down the hill, looking back once before picking up speed as Smith watched him go with relief.

Getting back to business, Smith began firing the sniper rifle at any targets he could see on the edge of the village as the few remaining *Khampas* kept up their fire. The ground between the hill and the village offered no cover for the infantry who were not going to launch a frontal attack whilst a sniper was picking them off. However, the APC's were less vulnerable and the undamaged ones had by now swung round in the direction of the hill, driving slowly and determinedly towards it as their machine guns continued to chatter and spit rounds at the Tibetans. Smith could see that the scarp slope would be too steep for them to drive right up, but that they were going to be able to get dangerously close.

Smith dismissed more of the *Khampas* as the vehicles approached so that now only he and two others remained. He rolled onto his back as the others continued firing so that he could reload the Dragunov for what he hoped would be one last time before he made his escape. Rolling back onto his stomach and peering down the sight again he immediately saw a target amongst the soldiers on the edge of the village and fired. The man fell, clutching his leg. Another soldier dashed out to help him. Smith watched fascinated, for what must have only been a couple of seconds as the man struggled to drag his comrade into cover. Then he fired. The rescuer flew backwards as if hit by a train as the full force of the high velocity round hit him in the chest. He lay spread-eagle on his back. Still.

Smith continued to watch the injured man, whom he could now distinguish clearly through the sight. He fumbled in his webbing and produced a field dressing, which he clamped onto his wound. Smith waited another minute to see if anyone else would attempt a rescue, but no-one did. He fired again. The wounded man's scream could be clearly heard from the top of the hill as he pawed vainly at his other leg. None of the soldiers in the village were going to be coming out of cover for a while now and they were going to be forced to listen impotently to the whimpering of their comrade for some time.

By now the APCs were half way up the hill, within two hundred metres of the Tibetan's line. Time had conflated to only a few minutes for Smith. But in the real world, the world of offices and shops and cafés and husbands going home after work and children walking to school, a couple of hours had passed since the Tibetans had launched their attack. Finally accepting this strange anomaly in the space time continuum, he decided that they had done enough. Enough to allow the rest of the party to make an escape to where the Chinese would not be able to easily follow. Enough to give the villagers of Kaisang a slim chance of escape. And most importantly, enough for Pemba to convince himself that they had done something, had not entirely abandoned their own people in the face of a Chinese assault.

"Get off that last round!" shouted Smith and with a whoosh a rocket launched and exploded right into the driver's viewing aperture, engulfing the lead vehicle in flames.

"Now go!" called Smith and the two men, who did not need too much encouragement, dashed away from the battle, almost bent double and sprinting as fast as they could downhill.

Smith continued firing the Dragunov intermittently, at the APCs, which at this range might just be penetrated by his rounds. Firing at anything that moved, or at nothing in particular. Just keep them pinned down and uncertain, especially in the APCs which were now so close to his position and whose troops were no doubt desperate to get at whoever was on that hilltop. They kept up a steady rain of machinegun fire as Smith did his best to keep them guessing as to where he was or how many men were with him. At last he decided he had bought himself as much time as he could and throwing the rifle over his shoulder made a run for it, expecting at any second to be caught in a deluge of gunfire. Zig-zagging this way and that he rapidly picked up speed, his heavy boots kicking up a cloud of dust in his wake.

Chapter 19

October 1969 - Eskdalemuir, Scotland

Beyond the Borders town of Lockerbie the road narrowed considerably as it meandered through the Lowland countryside. Abbi seemed to still be enjoying putting the car through its paces and testing the limits of its handling ability as Smith was pitched from side to side on the back seat. He said nothing about Abbi's driving as he watched the world outside fly by. After a few miles they turned left by the chapel in the tiny hamlet of Eskdalemuir, and soon they were parking the Mini in the spartan precincts of the putative monastery at Samye Ling.

The community was based around an old two-storey hunting lodge built of red border stone called Johnstone House, located right by the River Esk. What made this a particularly propitious site for the Tibetans was the fact that a tributary river joined the Esk at a right angle to it and the tributary pointed directly behind the main house. Here they intended to build the Tibetan Temple and it was planned that a traditional quadrangular Tibetan monastery would grow from that first vital building.

Already, gardens were being cultivated and outbuildings converted to workshops. Prayer flags adorned some of the buildings and prayer wheels clattered in the icy wind. Around the house stunted oaks draped with bearded lichen were testimony to the damp climate of the valley the Tibetans had chosen as their new home, almost as isolated a location as they could have found in Britain. Above the monastery sheep grazed on the meagre pasture which turned to acre after endless acre of unsympathetic conifer plantation higher up the valley.

"Welcome!" greeted Dave in a thick Glaswegian accent as the trio entered Johnstone House. Dave was a novice at the monastery, one of the first non-Tibetans to commence training for holy orders as a Tibetan lama. He had a shaved head and a thin almost drawn face, adorned by a pair of wire-framed National Health Service glasses. At this early stage of his training and the monastery's development he was also general factotum.

"It is good to be back, Dave," replied Tashi. As soon as he walked through the door and saw the symbols of his faith and lamas dressed in maroon robes he seemed to Smith to be transported back to a life he guessed he had lost forever in his homeland.

"You're staying for three days, I think."

"That's right."

"I'll show you your rooms." Dave stood and as he did so his maroon robe slipped from his right shoulder to reveal to Smith and the others a series of distinctly un-Tibetan tattoos snaking down his arm. Unaware or oblivious of their stares, Dave led the small party up the curving wooden staircase to the landing and along a corridor to two simply furnished rooms on the first floor. Smith and Tashi would share one room and Abbi would occupy the other.

As they already knew, the rules of the monastery for visitors were:

1. To protect life and refrain from killing.

2. To respect other's property and refrain from stealing.

3. To speak the truth and refrain from lying.

4. To embrace health and refrain from intoxicants.

5. To respect others and refrain from harmful sexual activity.

The relationship between Smith and Abbi had developed rapidly in the last few months. They had no reason to think that their sexual activity was harmful, but they decided to refrain for the duration of their visits to Samye Ling. Just in case, they joked.

Smith had already begun to reflect more on his life in the light of these seemingly simple tenets. He had always seen his chosen profession of soldier as essentially noble and with one obvious exception he could look back on his time as a warrior with an honest belief that he had lived by these principles. Now, following Tashi's lead, he had even stopped eating meat. The philosophy of Buddhism was slowly beginning to permeate his way of living and thinking.

"Tashi's asked me if I'm interested in going to India with him."

Smith and Abbi were the only occupants of the aptly named butter lamp room. The pale orange light of a thousand flickering butter lamps washed over their faces as they knelt side by side.

"What? When? Are you going to go?" Smith smiled, inwardly pleased that she had shown such obvious concern and regret that he might be leaving.

"He's going to Daramsala at the end of term. He thought I might be interested in doing some travelling. Seeing the Tibetan community in exile. Absorbing myself in the language. We might even get an audience with the Dalai Lama," he added, smiling. "Not that autograph collecting's really my thing."

"You're going to go, aren't you?" Smith could not tell whether her tone was amazement or reproach, but he ploughed on regardless.

"Well, what else have I got to do? And, you know what? I've realised that, although I've been to endless exotic places, they've always been work. The Army. Most leaves I went home to my parents or stayed with friends in London. I've virtually never been abroad on holiday."

"Some weird holiday!" responded Abbi, now sounding decidedly jaundiced about the whole project.

"Hey, it'll only be for a few weeks. And when I get back perhaps I'll apply for a proper job, whatever that is.

"In any case, if a good development job came up in some benighted hole on the other side of the world, wouldn't you be off like a shot if it suited you?"

"That's not fair. It's not the same thing at all."

"Of course not," agreed Smith wearily.

"How come I don't qualify for an invite to India, Tashi?" The trio shared a table for lunch in the simply furnished monastery refectory. Tashi appeared bemused.

"Peter tells me you're taking him off to Daramsala."

"Did he? Oh." Tashi looked at Smith and Smith looked at Tashi, but said nothing.

"Well, yes, but it was only a thought."

"You're up to something Tashi. I don't know what, but you've got plans for Peter, haven't you?" Smith looked quizzically at Tashi.

"Not at all Abbi. I simply asked Peter because I thought it would be an interesting experience for him. And he has the time. You have a job. Would you come if I asked you?"

"I might."

"Then come, by all means." Tashi called her bluff. They both looked at her.

"Hey, that's a great idea," enthused Smith, looking Abbi in the eyes.

"OK, you bastards, you're right!" she responded petulantly. "But it's not fair. Everybody's on the Hippy Trail now. Even one of the typists at work. She just handed in her notice about two months ago. Next thing we heard she was on this thing called the Magic Bus. Turns out there's a bus, a double decker bus for God's sake, that you can catch in London and, ding ding, off you go to Nepal.

"You'll probably both end up in Katmandu and I'll be slaving away behind my desk to pay for my stupid car and my stupid flat."

"But, Abbi, you love that car. We love that car. How would we get up here otherwise?"

"Double bastard," was all Abbi could manage. They had made their decision, whatever they were up to, and she had made hers.

Chapter 20

অ

London

"When are you leaving?"

"What?" shouted Smith into the wind.

"You can hear me alright," Abbi shouted back into his right ear. "You don't want to talk about it, that's all."

The Bonneville engine made a satisfying roar in Smith's ears, unlike Abbi's questions, as his foot nudged the gear shifter and the bike slid into fourth. Doing sixty now, and they were only half way up Kensington High Street. Then down through the box as they approached Holland Park. The lights were red, but there was no traffic and Smith ignored them as he and Abbi leaned vertiginously to their right turning into Earls Court Road. They quickly picked up speed again as Smith worked his way rapidly back through the gears, only to break sharply as they swung left into Lexington Mews. Smith jammed on the brakes outside number seventeen and Abbi involuntarily cannoned into his back, their helmets knocking together audibly.

"Jesus, Peter. You're bloody insane," smiled Abbi exhaustedly as they clambered off the bike and pulled off their helmets.

"And you've become a regular Hell's Angel", responded Smith, looking at her standing on the pavement in a pair of well fitting faded denim Levi's and his leather jacket zipped up to her chin, two sizes too big for her.

They had spent the evening in various bars in the West End although Smith had hardly drunk anything except orange juice. It seemed to her that it wasn't alcohol he needed to have a good time. In some disco they had cavorted around the dance floor as the Doors "Light My Fire" blasted their eardrums. Abbi was bemused to discover that they were his favourite band, closely followed by Pink Floyd. He seemed invigorated.

Only minutes before he had left Abbi in the bar whilst he went to the toilet. As soon as he was gone some bloke in crimson velvet flares and a blue soldiers dress jacket with high collar and brass buttons, all undone, now all the rage on the King's Road, came over and started chatting Abbi up. He wasn't bad looking, tall, with long blonde hair which he kept sweeping back with his hand. She was flattered, though not interested, but before she could tell him this Smith returned.

"Who's this? Are you going to introduce us?" asked Smith pleasantly as the young man continued to talk to Abbi, ignoring him.

"This is, er, I don't know your name."

"Simon," said the young man, turning to Smith. "Who the fuck are you?" He sounded angry now and a little drunk.

"Peter. Do you know Abbi?"

"I'd know her better if you'd fuck off." Abbi looked anxiously at Smith. Smith took a step backwards.

"Nice jacket. I used to have one a bit like it. A soldier's jacket," continued Smith in a friendly conciliatory tone.

"Have you ever killed anyone?" Smith's tone was now icy and the smile had disappeared from his face. Abbi noticed that his feet were now slightly apart, one forward of the other, and his hands were clenched into fists, but he looked strangely relaxed.

"I didn't think so," he added when the man didn't reply. He seemed to have finally sensed through the alcohol what Abbi had already recognised, the aura of menace and impending violence which Smith was able to emanate. Suddenly his demeanour completely changed.

"I, I only wanted a chat," began the man, haltingly. "See you." He turned to Abbi briefly, trying to force a smile, before pushing his way into the crowd. Abbi looked at Smith.

"What? I didn't do a thing. What did I say?" He smiled. She smiled. She guessed the adrenalin saw him through the rest of the night.

Abbi had not been so restrained. She was still drunk at five o'clock on the following morning and the remains of the dope she had bought from some guy in the Kings Road was still in her bag. It was a beautiful late spring morning so they had decided to come back via the 'scenic route', as Smith described it, along the Embankment.

"Didn't Lawrence have a bike?" asked Abbi as they stood momentarily admiring Smith's machine in the early London light.

"Lawrence who?"

"Don't be obtuse. TE Lawrence. Lawrence of Arabia."

"What made you ask that?"

"I don't know. Just popped into my head. Probably an LSD flashback."

"A what?"

"Only kidding," she giggled. Smith wondered if she was.

He opened the door of Gus' mews cottage and they entered the tiny, but expensively furnished sitting room. Abbi flopped down on the battered leather settee which she guessed had been in Gus' family for generations. Smith disappeared into the kitchen to the accompaniment of running water and clattering pots. But soon the only sound was the gentle bubbling of the coffee percolator, the smell of fresh ground coffee wafting into the room.

"He had a Brough Superior," called Smith from the galley kitchen.

"Finally!" exclaimed Abbi.

"Well actually he had a load of them one after the other. 980cc with a written guarantee from Brough that every bike had done a ton over a measured quarter mile. That was fast in the Thirties. My bike only does a hundred and ten flat out."

"Along the Embankment," Abbi joked.

"They're worth thousands now. Tens of thousands. The ones he owned. He was killed on one of them."

"Yes, I remember now. I saw the film." Abbi was suddenly serious. "You won't get killed, will you?" Smith came back into the living room with two cups of dark, steaming coffee.

"On the bike? No. You've seen how careful I am."

"Don't joke. I mean in India or wherever you're going."

"What do you mean "or wherever?" That's where we're going. India. Next week. Wednesday, as it happens. Tashi only told me yesterday. But we'll be back in about eight weeks."

"Will you?"

Chapter 21

PLA Headquarters, Shigatse, Tibet

"What's happening, Corporal?" Colonel Zhu had been called to the Operations Room, having been told that the force dispatched to the village of Kaisang had run into some kind of problem. He had assumed that it would be a fairly straightforward mission to teach a bunch of recalcitrant villagers a lesson or two. With Major Leung in charge the Colonel had been particularly confident of a positive outcome. What could go wrong? Well, anything in this ungrateful place.

"Alpha Company are reporting a contact, Sir."

"A contact? With who?"

"Tibetan bandits, splitists, Sir. So it seems."

"Casualties? Are there casualties?"

"Er, yes, but we don't know how many," the Watchkeeper stammered, intimidated now by the rising anger of his superior Officer.

"Give me the radio, Corporal." Colonel Zhu snatched it from his hand.

"Hello, get me Major Leung, this is Colonel Zhu, over." He abandoned any pretence of radio security. He needed the facts and quickly. One thing he could be sure of was that any Tibetan partisans there may be around would not have the technology to monitor his radio net.

"Sunray down, over." Zhu was momentarily stunned by this news. Major Leung was dead or badly injured.

"What? Who am I speaking to, over?"

"Lieutenant Bin, Sir. Number One Platoon commander. I have taken command of the company, over"

"Where is Captain Deng, over?" Deng had been keen to go on this mission and Colonel Zhu had reluctantly agreed, considering that perhaps Kaisang deserved Captain Deng after all. He did not expect Deng to have taken over command of the company if there was any fighting to be done, but as that now seemed to be over, he assumed Deng would be asserting his authority.

"Captain Deng is being treated by the medics, Sir. He has a very serious chest wound. I am the senior Officer here. What are your instructions, over?"

"Give me a full sitrep in five minutes, Lieutenant. Out." Deng was wounded! Seriously wounded. Well, perhaps this operation was not a complete disaster after all.

Lieutenant Bin quickly gathered the information needed for his situation report. As military protocol required, he then reported back to Colonel Zhu the various statistics he had gleaned on the state of the company, the enemy force, casualties, supplies, the condition of his vehicles and so on, which summarised for the Colonel what had happened at Kaisang in the last hour. Zhu considered the information for a few minutes, shocked that such events were still happening in the Tibetan Autonomous Region after all the years he and the PLA had spent trying to pacify it.

"Hello, Lieutenant Bin. Are you there, over?"

"Bin here, Sir, over."

"You have rounded up all the villagers? That is good. Try and identify the ringleaders and bring them back here for further interrogation. We will get some answers from these people. Treat any of their casualties and bring in any too serious to deal with locally."

"Yes, Sir, over."

"I want you to take a small force on foot and check the direction the bandits came from. See if there are any signs of others still alive and if so track them down. Report in every six hours.

"Give command of the rest of the company to Lieutenant Chang and tell him to return to base, apart from a small reserve with your vehicles to await you in the village, over."

"Understood, Colonel, over."

"Out." Zhu put down the radio and moved over to look at the large scale map of the area on the Ops Room wall. Even now, vast swathes of the country were still unmapped or covered by maps of dubious accuracy. The Colonel wondered how much he could rely on this map. He had never been to Kaisang, which until now had had little significance. It looked from the map as though a narrow valley led away from the village to the north west and Zhu could see how it might have given the bandits cover from his company, even on horseback, until they were within firing range of his men. The valley also seemed to offer a good escape route for any who survived. Lieutenant Bin did not think he could get his vehicles up there and the map seemed to confirm this.

Perhaps there had been no survivors, but it seemed unlikely to Zhu that men on horseback would have been accurate or lucky enough to have identified and shot his two most senior Officers. Somebody had given them covering fire. And that somebody had got away.

He picked up the telephone on the Ops Room desk.

"Colonel Zhu here. Get me the airfield."

Chapter 22

ಠ

Kaisang, Tibet

Smith came slithering over the loose scree towards Lhotse. He smiled back at the Tibetan who began to swing his M16 from his shoulder. Unlike the *Khampas*, the Tibetans inserted by the CIA were equipped with American weapons. As Smith came closer he called out to him in English.

"Why you, Lhotse?" The look on Lhotse's face changed. He hesitated for a split second by which time Smith was already upon him, knife in hand. Smith palmed away the rifle with his left hand and used his momentum to topple Lhotse backwards down the slope. He fell heavily, winded, and with Smith on top of him, the knife now at Lhotse's throat.

Lhotse knew he was finished. What he had seen and heard in the last couple of days only reinforced what he had been told by Larsen before his deployment. Instinctively, he played for his life, anyway.

"Stop, Peter, please!"

Smith's mind was racing. When he had called to Lhotse it had been a genuinely innocuous question about why they had chosen to leave him behind to wait, but the change in Lhotse's eyes had immediately brought to mind Chungla's warning about danger from the newcomers and he knew the threat was Lhotse. He also knew that any weakness of his resolve in such a situation could easily give the upper hand and therefore Smith's own life, to Lhotse. The man was a warrior and had been trained in God knows what by the CIA. He should finish it now.

But he did not. He pressed the blade firmly against Lhotse's jugular.

"Move and I'll cut your fucking head right off," snarled Smith. The heat of Smith's breath burned on Lhotse's face.

"Now, tell me why I shouldn't do just that. You were going to kill me." As Smith articulated the thought, his body tensed, and it seemed the coup de grace would come, but again it did not. Smith wanted, needed, answers.

"My boss gave me a chance to come back, back to the Land of the Snows, and I took it. In return he wanted me to kill you. He told me you were a danger to the future of our operations, our cause. I had no reason not to believe him. So I agreed." Smith's hand tensed and he pushed the blade into Lhotse's skin.

"But," he quickly added, "I received another signal yesterday evening. As you know, I am the radio operator for the group. He told me there was a change of plan. I was not to kill you."

"Why should I believe this shit, Lhotse? You're just wriggling to save your own life."

"He told me to tell you a name. If I was going to kill you, I would not have a name to give you. We would never speak of this matter."

"What is the name?"

"Abbi, A-B-B-I, Abbi. Does that mean something to you?

Chapter 23

New Delhi

Larsen had never before ventured so far into the old walled city of Delhi and certainly never so far into the alleyways of Chandni Chowk. As he proceeded, elegant Haveli, pre-colonial mansions with high ceilings and hidden courtyards, gave way to narrow lanes of workers tenements lined with tiny shops, workshops and eating houses as Larsen struggled to follow the directions jotted on a scrap of paper in his hand. The lanes were alive with noise and bustle, but he felt no sense of danger from the endless stream of Indian traders, shoppers and workers flowing around him although he was virtually the only white face, towering over the native populous.

Turning right into yet another narrow lane of sound and colour he soon spotted the incongruous sight of an Englishman in a crumpled linen suit sipping tea at a tiny table below a sign declaring the establishment to be 'The Moonlight Teahouse'. Chivers immediately spotted Larsen and rose to acknowledge him, at the same time doffing his sweat-stained Panama hat, every inch the Graham Greene caricature. The contrast in appearance to the Stephen Chivers Larsen had last met in his boss's office a few days earlier was so pronounced that Larsen almost commented as the two men smiled at one another and shook hands. At the last minute Larsen had second thoughts and simply followed Chivers' directions to join him at the tiny table.

"Glad you could make it Martin," Chivers announced. "Let me order you something." Chivers hesitated. "Unless you're up on the food in these parts."

"No, I've never found myself in this part of town before. You show me the ropes." Larsen could not tell whether Chivers was pleased or embarrassed at his presumption of Larsen's ignorance. He waved an arm in the direction of the interior of the teahouse and a waiter, a small man in dirty white shirt and trousers and sporting a huge black moustache appeared almost immediately. Words were exchanged by Chivers and the waiter in what Larsen guessed to be Urdu and the waiter disappeared back inside, apparently knowing their requirements.

"I'm suitably impressed," commented Larsen, perhaps a little too tartly.

"Don't be," responded Chivers, smiling. "I grew up here. My father worked in the Embassy and I went to school here for six years. The Embassy School admittedly, but at that age you pick up languages easily and I had an aptitude."

"So it runs in the blood?"

"What?"

Larsen looked to either side before saying "This kind of work."

"O God, I see. No. Not exactly. My father was the messenger from the Post Room. But I have to say the attractions of the diplomatic life were obvious to me even then and the rest, as they say, is history. Ah, here's lunch."

The waiter had re-appeared and proceeded to set our various items before the two men. Fresh tea was poured and the man retreated to the sound of what Larsen assumed to be thanks from Chivers.

"Parathas," announced Chivers. "Basically flatbreads fried in ghee, provided for honoured guests," he added with another smile. "Those are stuffed with vegetables and those," he waved a hand across the table, "are plain. For dipping in yogurt or pickle. Pretty obvious, I suppose." He proceeded to roll one of the parathas into a small tube and, in spite of his previous directions, dipped it in his tea.

"Tuck in."

They ate in silence for a few moments.

"The tea here is excellent, as well. I have a secret passion for real Indian tea. That's why I come here."

"And why do I come here?" enquired Larsen.

"Well, I thought we got off on the wrong foot back there." Chivers waved vaguely over his shoulder to indicate, Larsen assumed, Pat Reagan's office in the US Embassy, even though it was geographically in exactly the opposite direction.

"Did we? The message from you and Pat seemed pretty clear and unambiguous."

"Look Martin, I've known Pat Reagan for a long time and he's a great bloke to have on your side when the chips are down. But, like a lot of you chaps, he sees things in very black and white terms. At our last meeting I felt you were not quite like that. That things are a bit more nuanced for you, if you know what I mean.

"So when you called me after the meeting to ask just what we knew about this chap careering around Tibet, I had to admit to myself as well as you, that we knew damn all. And in a way that doesn't matter, because he's still a problem that needs dealing with. But you made me think." Chivers paused to munch on a now somewhat soggy paratha, before continuing.

"I decided you were right. He shouldn't be the unknown soldier, so to speak. We should find out something about him."

"But," interjected Larsen, "wont that make it more difficult to 'deal with him' as you describe it?"

"To be honest, no. I was hoping that you were going to tell me the job's already done. Are you going to tell me that?"

"No. The wheels are in motion, but as you'll appreciate, this is a very arm's length operation. Comms are very poor and we have to let the thing take its course."

"Well, Martin, I hope that what I have to tell you isn't going to change your mind. You're not going to go wobbly on us, are you? I just did this as an academic exercise, to see how much it might be possible to find out about someone from nothing, but if it's going to personalise this too much for you then we can put a lid on it now." Chivers looked at Larsen intently.

Larsen struggled to control his anger. It surprised him to realise that he was not angry because Chivers was questioning his professionalism, but because the limey bastard had hit on the truth. He did care about what happened to Tibet and the Tibetans. Like many who had worked with the Tibetans at Camp Hale he had formed a genuine attachment to them and their land. As those on the Tibetan Program had learned more about the country, its traditions, its religion, its language, many of them had developed an affection for its people and the rightness of their cause. It was an affection which stayed with these unsentimental CIA agents long after the Tibet Program was rolled up, in a way which never happened to them in Vietnam or Cuba or in the numerous other clandestine wars fought to maintain Uncle Sam's overseas interests.

"Of course not. Don't jerk me around Chivers. Just tell me what you found out." Did he protest too much? It seemed not, as Chivers launched into the story he had managed to piece together. Larsen guessed that he was too pleased with what he had found to keep it to himself now. The char wallah arrived with more tea and as he left Chivers began his story.

"I don't know for certain that this is our man of course, but it seems pretty likely. What do you know about him Martin?"

"Not a great deal. You know what?"

"Indulge me Martin."

"OK. We believe that he's British. Probably an ex-soldier and that he's been in Tibet for a year or more."

"And?"

"And what?"

"Any likely conclusions to add to these very basic alleged facts?" Chivers prompted.

"Well, he's operating in Tibet and has been for some time so he probably speaks the language well. And for the Tibetans to accept him he must have something they want. Military skills, probably, which suggest an Officer or Senior NCO rather than just a foot soldier. That's probably reinforced by his language skills"

"Yes, good. So assuming these simple facts, I checked out where you can learn Tibetan in Britain, and it's hardly surprising, but lucky for us that there are very few places. An undergraduate course at SOAS, one in Oxford and a couple of adult education classes in London. It wasn't difficult to get a list of all the men who had attended these courses in the last five years and narrow that down to the ones in the likely age bracket. Seventeen suspects in all. Then, the very next thing I tried came up trumps. Look if any of them appear on the Army List."

"What's the Army List?"

"What it says. A list of all the Officers currently serving in the British Army and published every year. And on the List until two years ago was a name, the same name as a chap who also started Tibetan evening classes at SOAS not long after. A bit of simple cross-referencing proved it was the same man. Our man. Got to be."

Larsen was impressed. "Did you find out anything else?" Chivers produced a slim folder and handed it to Larsen. "My treat," he said. "You were right. It's quite an interesting little story. I've only included the basic facts and a couple of known associates, so to speak. Just for your interest. We could have pulled his whole military record, school, family, the lot. But what's the point? In fact the less anyone else knows about this the better. That's the only copy, so I know you'll know what to do with it when you've read it.

"Now eat up and then I'll lead you out of this maze."

Chapter 24

Kaisang, Tibet

Smith's mind was in turmoil. How did they know about Abbi? What did they know? Who the hell were these people and why were they so interested in him? But another voice screamed out in his head, Get away from here. The Chinese could be here any minute. He needed to move and catch up with the others. Get them all to safety.

So what to do about Lhotse? Killing him now was probably the safest option for his survival, but he needed answers and Lhotse had them.

"OK, on your feet." He dragged Lhotse up and pushed him towards his horse. "We're getting out of here, but any tricks and you're dead." Smith picked up Lohtse's M16 and slung it over his shoulder. He quickly packed the sniper rifle and swung onto his saddle. Lhotse, regaining his composure, quickly clambered onto his own horse and rode in the direction Smith indicated up the valley.

With Lhotse leading, they rode at a wild pace, Smith frequently looking over his shoulder for signs of pursuit, but seeing none. They made good progress over the firm dusty ground of the valley bottom, but after about an hour the valley began to narrow noticeably and the ground underfoot became much rockier and more difficult for the horses. The pair had to slow to a walking pace so the animals did not stumble.

"Time to talk, Lhotse," prompted Smith angrily. "I need to know what this is all about. Who is so interested in me and why?"

"My boss, Martin Larsen. He works for the CIA. He trained me at Hale. I've known him for years as a friend as well as my boss. So I trusted him. Still trust him. He briefed me for this mission. Like I said, he told me you were a threat to our operations here, probably a traitor giving information to the Han.

"I believed him. Why wouldn't I? He's my friend, but he also has all the information available to the CIA on Tibet at his fingertips. He knows better than any other American what is going on with our resistance here and he genuinely believes in our cause."

"So he told you to kill me?"

"Yes."

"And then he suddenly changes his mind?"

"Yes."

"Why? What changed, Lhotse? What changed in the few days since you've been here?" Smith suddenly produced a pistol from inside his *chuba*, cocked it and pointed it threateningly at Lhotse.

"Think, Lhotse. Time's running out for you, my friend."

"I think that he changed, Smith. Changed from the man taking orders to the man he truly is. An honourable man who decided that his orders were wrong and that you did not deserve to die." Was this true? Did any of it make any sense?

"Alright, how did this Larsen know who I am and that I am here?"

"Some refugee who had ridden with Pemba got back to New Delhi and was debriefed by the CIA and he told them about you. Perhaps he knew you. I don't know. They did a bit of research with the British and they seemed to find out about you for us. They are afraid that if you are caught or killed by the Han that you will cause great embarrassment to their governments. The simplest solution was to get rid of you. I was to kill you and hide your body."

Smith suddenly felt very exposed. Not only were the Chinese trying to kill him, but the Americans and his own Government, the Government for which he had put his life on the line more times and in more places than he could remember, wanted to murder him and hide his body. How could he, one man alone, stand up to this? With the pistol still clenched in his hand, he almost over-reacted and in anger and frustration shot Lhotse on the spot, but managed to control himself sufficiently to get his mind working again.

After all, hadn't he put himself in this position? He knew when he came to Tibet that this was no game, or that if it was, it was a very dangerous one. And now it had become even more dangerous than he could have imagined.

"What do you know about Abbi? How is she involved in this?"

"I don't know. Larsen just told me that if things went badly between us I was to mention that name, as the fact that I knew it might slow you down. And it did. I don't know anything else about this person."

Was this true? Smith was inclined to think that it made sense. But it didn't matter. What mattered was that they knew about Abbi. Had access to her. Knew that this would make him feel vulnerable. What might they do to her?

"So what do they want now? What does your Mister Larsen want?"

"They want you dead," answered Lhotse flatly. "Only Larsen has changed his mind. I don't think the men who give him his orders know that. I think that he is pretending that I have killed you in the hope that you will, as is very likely, soon be finished off by the Han, or that you will run for it. You can do that, you know. You can still get away from here in one piece. You are three days hard ride from Mustang."

"I think you've said enough, Lhotse," replied Smith quietly. "Follow me."

Leading the way, as well as checking behind, Smith was now looking more intently up the steep sides of the valley. Soon he indicated that they should veer off at an angle to the valley bottom leading them gently up the right hand side of the valley. In a few minutes they had gained several hundred feet. Smith called a halt and drew out his binoculars. Lhotse followed suit.

They now had a commanding view of the valley below and as they turned their horses they could see far down the valley in the direction of Kaisang. Still no sign of pursuit, but both men knew that the Chinese would come. They would also scramble a plane, but hopefully, with darkness only an hour or so away, that would not be before tomorrow.

"What are we going to do?" asked Lhotse.

"What you're going to do, Lhotse, is to slow them down to give the rest of us a chance." Smith pulled the Dragunov from its place on his saddle and handed it to Lhotse. He started to slot rounds into a couple of magazines.

"Did they teach you to shoot at Hale?" Lhotse nodded. He had indeed spent a lot of time on the firing ranges of the training camp back in Colorado and been good at it.

"OK. We're going to find a good firing position for you. Wait until its dark and if they haven't shown up follow us." They scrabbled around in the rocks for several minutes checking out possible positions for their amount of cover and lines of fire until they found one Smith was happy with.

"OK, this'll do." Lhotse wriggled into position facing down the valley. "You know the name of the game. Aim to wound a couple of them. Keep them pinned down until its dark and then get the hell out of here." Smith handed the magazines to Lhotse. "These will be enough to do the job. I'll tether your horse over here." He led the two horses further up the valley. "Good luck!" he called as an afterthought.

Both men knew that Lhotse was going to need a hell of a lot of luck. If the Chinese came and he engaged them his chances of getting away were slim. Even if he did, could he catch up with the others, not knowing for certain which direction they had gone? It was also unsaid between them that there was nothing to stop Lhotse giving Smith a few minutes start and then leaving his post and following at a safe distance. A double bind. Would Smith wait up the trail to see if he was followed? In this case Lhotse knew he was a dead man. But Smith was also giving him the chance to prove himself. Lhotse settled down for a long wait.

As he lay in his lair periodically scanning the terrain to his front, Lhotse's right hand instinctively felt for the hard outline on his left forearm. A cyanide ampoule taped there before the parachute drop. Back at the airfield it had seemed like a bit of CIA dramatics, but now, alone on a remote mountainside with a troop of Chinese infantry about to overwhelm him it provided a macabre comfort. He had never before allowed himself to wonder what he would do in this kind of situation. Until today his youth had made him invincible. The reality of being captured by the Chinese and recognised as an infiltrator was suddenly all too real. Now he could think of nothing else.

And worse still was the knowledge that he was probably the instigator of his own demise. He had told no-one about the loss of his parachute into the river, but it now all seemed much more than coincidence that the PLA should arrive in Kaisang so soon after the parachute drop. Of course there were other explanations. The Chinese had patrols in the area which could have seen signs of the team after the drop. Or possibly they had been betrayed by a villager. Not all Tibetans hated the Chinese, especially if there was cash to be earned. Many of the local Tibetans had no more love for the Khampa rebels than for the PLA. Both were seen by some as foreign invaders who brought trouble they did not need. But try as he might, Lhotse could not convince himself that his current plight was the fault of anyone but himself.

How different things had turned out from the optimistic beginnings when a younger Lhotse found himself in the Colorado Mountains several years earlier. Speaking no English, but identified for his leadership potential whilst in the Tibetan exile community in Northern India, he was smuggled half way across the world to the strange yet familiar Colorado Mountains in which Camp Hale was based. The soaring peaks and the deep winter snow soon had him almost convinced he was back home in the Land of the Snows. It was the perfect place to train Tibetans to fight in their own country.

The CIA instructors, struggling to master Tibetan pronunciations, soon gave up and gave all their students western names. Soon after he arrived, Lhotse became Larry. Larry proved to be an exemplary student. With little formal education, but with a sound informal education in hunting and, briefly, of fighting the Chinese in his native Kham, Lhotse was highly motivated and suited to the trade of guerrilla fighter.

The Americans had discovered early on that their Tibetan recruits had tremendous lower body strength and could walk uphill all day. They also had no fear of heights. These were ideal characteristics for potential mountain fighters. However, their upper body strength tended to be poor and much time was spent in Hale's small gym addressing this so the recruits could control a parachute and carry the equipment they would need once dropped back into Tibet. Larry loved it. He loved it all. The training, the mountains, the tight-knit community of comrades ready to fight and die for each other and for their homeland and the Dalai Lama.

During the eighteen months Lhotse spent at Hale, Martin Larsen was one of the senior military instructors, teaching tactics to Lhotse's intake. Many of the CIA officers who worked at Hale or elsewhere on the Tibetan Program were greatly impressed with their students' dedication and cheerful optimism and formed strong bonds with them. Lhotse and Larsen became firm friends and the more the two men talked the better Lhotse's English and knowledge of the world outside Tibet became.

Weapon training, demolition, advanced radio classes and tactics were all on the curriculum and the lessons were reinforced by constant clandestine exercises in the snow filled valleys surrounding the camp. The team was ready. But as the time for Lhotse and his fellow students to "graduate" approached the changing political situation was becoming more obvious to Larsen and the other CIA staff at Hale. Drops into Tibet had just about ceased and the likelihood of Lhotse using his new found skills became remote. As a sweetener a select few of those who had made the most progress were offered places at prestigious US universities. Lhotse was one of the lucky few.

But now the urbane young Columbia graduate, who had never fired a shot in anger, was suddenly aware that whilst his reverie had taken him to happier times a PLA soldier had unwittingly wandered into his field of vision. With shaking hands Lhotse grabbed his binoculars and scanned the view to his front. Only the one man was visible now, fully formed in Lhotse's lenses as he cautiously skirted a small rise. Point man.

"Take him now!" insisted a small voice in Lhotse's head, "before the others appear. They won't see the flash from your fire. They won't know where you are. Do it now!"

Letting the binoculars fall, he raised his weapon and stared down the telescopic sight. At first it seemed to swing around wildly, but as he wrestled with it the thing settled to the rhythm of his breathing. The target was in the cross hairs.

He pulled the trigger. The rifled kicked upwards, but the sight settled back to where the target had been. A good sign, but no sign of the target. Had he missed? Then he heard it. At five hundred metres the screams of a wounded man could not be mistaken. Staying focussed, Lhotse swung the rifle to left and right to engage another target. And there it was. Another Chinese soldier darting forward to help his wounded comrade. More confident now, Lhotse let the man run into his sights and fired off a second round, aiming for his midriff. The man went down.

By now others were appearing over the rise, but they did not need the shouts of their Officer to make them hit the ground as the second shot rang out. Lhotse didn't know where he had hit the second man, but he was sure that he had.

Clutching the Dragunov, he shuffled backwards from his hiding place and then crawled until he was sure he could not be seen when he rose to his feet and, bent double to reduce his profile, ran as fast as he could towards his horse. He had done all that Smith had asked or could have expected of him. Hopefully, the Chinese had two injured men to casevac and it would be some time before they were even confident enough to get close to them. Then at least four men would be needed to carry each man, tying down possible nearly half of the pursuing force. As Lhotse swung onto his horse the light was already fading and he thought he felt rain in the air.

Chapter 25

ཁ

Tsechen Damchos Ling Monastery, Tibet

"With a magazine of twenty rounds, load!" Smith bellowed out the command in true skill at arms training fashion. A small brown hand reached out, sweeping gently back and forth across the dusty flagstones. Quickly detecting the curved metal shape of the magazine, the hand grabbed it firmly and whisked it through the air to clamp it straight into the waiting cavity of the AK56. Chungla smiled as the magazine went home with a satisfying clunk. Smith was relieved that she had never seen a war film and so did not need to resist the urge in most soldiers to then bash the magazine from beneath in a macho fashion, which leads to rounds jamming in the chamber.

"Make safe!" The girl pressed the release and removed the magazine, cocked the weapon to make sure that any rounds in the chamber were ejected, re-engaged the magazine and flicked on the safety catch. The weapon could not now be fired by accident.

The young nun sat cross-legged on the flagged floor of the monastery courtyard, her slim girlish form an incongruous sight in her maroon nun's robes, her delicate hands clutching the automatic rifle across her body. Smith sat opposite her in pair of battered Levi jeans and a grubby tee-shirt, his long dark braided hair flicked behind his ears. He sensed that the girl was smiling, but the white cotton scarf tied around her head to blindfold her made it difficult for him to be sure.

"How did I do, Master?" she enquired with an ironic emphasis on the word "master".

"OK," he responded. "You did OK."

"I'll show you OK," she replied in mock anger. "Look at your watch." As his eyes turned automatically to the battered timepiece on his wrist the girl held up the rifle and deftly removed the magazine again, cocked the weapon once more to make sure it was clear and allowed the working parts to slide forward. With impressive speed and dexterity, she removed the top cover and put it on the ground by the magazine. Next came the bolt and the bolt carrier, then the gas piston and then the recoil spring assembly. She named each part in mangled English as she released it from the weapon. Smith didn't know the Tibetan terms and she had proved a good mimic of his English as he had showed her each part. As he watched her the words of a poem he had memorised years before began to play through in his mind.

In mere seconds every item was laid neatly parallel to the next and then finally the skeleton of the rifle was laid across her crossed legs.

"Stop!" she called. Smith hadn't been able to focus on his watch to time Chungla's effort, she had started so quickly, but he didn't need to in order to know that plenty of his soldiers back home would have been envious of her performance.

"That's good," he acknowledged begrudgingly. "Now put it back together. Go!" She snatched up the AK and, holding it upright with the butt resting on the ground, began to methodically slam the parts back into place. As rapidly as she had disassembled it, the deadly jigsaw puzzle was again complete, sling clipped in place and the weapon cradled in the young girl's arms.

"Alright, I have to admit it. That was impressive. But you had a good teacher," he laughed. Chungla pulled the scarf from her face, dark eyes lit up by a wide grin of pride and pleasure.

Smith suddenly realised that this was the first time he had seen her smile since their terrible encounter back in Tsarang Monastery. Weapons training as therapy. My God, he thought.

They had arrived at Tsechen Damchos Ling Monastery two nights earlier, after a virtually continuous forced march through the mountains, their route constantly twisting and turning in an attempt to shake off the enemy. The nuns knew the area well and believed that Tsechen Damchos Ling would be sufficiently isolated and welcoming to give them time to recuperate.

Smith caught up with the group just after daylight on the morning following his leaving Lhotse to defend their rear. He had kept going through the night until he could no longer be sure of the route the rest had taken, at which point he rested briefly until dawn. As soon as it was light he set off wondering now if he would catch them or whether he had lost their trail. Thoughts of how long he, an Englishman, stranded alone on the inhospitable Tibetan plateau in the middle of a war could survive began to eat into his consciousness. Forcing the panic to the back of his mind he pressed on for another hour, when he saw a huddle of people and horses ahead. Checking with his binoculars that it was Tashi and the others, he spurred his horse on.

"What are you doing sitting around in the open, Tashi?" He tried to sound angry and professional, but Tashi detected the relief in his voice.

"The trail splits here and you could have missed the way we went. We could not afford to loose you, Peter," he flattered Smith, although it was true. They still needed his skills and resourcefulness.

"OK," Smith was easily mollified. Then with a sense of urgency, "but let's get moving now".

Like their medieval European counterparts, Tibetan monasteries and their inhabitants, in Smith's view, ranged from the greedy, venal and worldly wise to the aesthetic and spiritual. As a general rule, the smaller and farther from Lhasa a monastery was, the more likely it was to tend to the latter characteristics. Despite the obvious danger to the establishment and its inhabitants, Tsechen Damchos Ling, in the form of its aging Abbot, welcomed the fugitives with open arms.

The buildings of the monastery, from a distance, resembled a series of stone boxes stacked one behind the other in a linear profile as they gradually scaled a forty-five degree slope half way up a remote Tibetan mountain side. Guests to the monastery, including the current newcomers, were accommodated in rooms on the lower levels. The courtyard in which Smith and Chungla had been training was located between two of the larger buildings about half way up the monastery complex.

"Peter! Peter! What the hell are you doing?" Interrupting Smith's thoughts, Tashi came splashing across the open courtyard towards where Smith and Chungla were sheltering from the rain. Water ran down the stone-slabbed roof above them and fell in a curtain to their front. It rarely rained in this part of Tibet, but for the last four days low damp clouds had sat over the mountains, with regular showers providing welcome respite from the long dry days of spring. It was not just the crops which were benefitting. The weather had provided the perfect cover for the fugitives to make good their escape from the village of Kaisang and their Chinese pursuers.

Tashi burst through the curtain of water into the dry, shaking himself and scowling at the two figures in front of him as he did so.

"What's going on here, Peter?" he repeated in English.

"Naming of Parts, Tashi. To quote Henry Reed," he began, in his best Tommy Atkins voice, to recite the poem which had sprung into his mind earlier, and which suddenly seemed appropriate and important.

"To-day we have naming of parts. Yesterday,

We had daily cleaning. And to-morrow morning,

We shall have what to do after firing. But to-day,

To-day we have naming of parts. Japonica

Glistens like coral in all of the neighbouring gardens,

And to-day we have naming of parts."

Looking somewhat bemused, Tashi tried again, still speaking in English. "What is she doing with a rifle, Peter? She's an incarnate, a *Tulku*. And she's a child! A child. Look at her." They both looked at the child/woman crossed legged in her maroon robes, holding a loaded AK56 defiantly across her slim body.

"And this you can see is the bolt. The purpose of this,

Is to open the breech, as you see. We can slide it,

rapidly backwards and forwards: we call this,

easing the spring. And rapidly backwards and forwards,

The early bees are assaulting and fumbling the flowers:

They call it easing the Spring," continued Smith unabashed.

"Written by a man called Henry Reed, one of the few war poets of the Second World War. Part of my culture, Tashi. A culture I'm starting to forget trapped in these mountains."

Smith's seeming frivolity just antagonised Tashi further.

"Poems about war. AK56's. That's your culture and that's the problem, Peter." Turning to the girl, he continued, speaking now in Tibetan.

"Chungla, what are you doing? You are a *Tulku*. This is not our way. Not the Lord Buddha's way. This is against all the training you have received, the life you have lived since you entered Rongbuk La."

"Rimpoche," replied the girl after a moment's silence. She rose gracefully to her feet and hooked the sling of the rifle over her head so that the weapon sat diagonally across her slim back, muzzle pointing to the ground, as she had been taught by Smith, to keep rain out of the barrel.

"With great respect, Rimpoche, since I took holy orders Rongbuk La has been destroyed by the Chinese. Rongbuk La, the monastery I was destined to be Abbess of. I was nearly killed. I had to hide for weeks in the mountains, virtually starved and frozen to death. I was still a child, Rimpoche. Since then I have lived in constant fear. Fear that the Chinese will come. That someone will identify me to them.

"They didn't recognise me when they came to Tsarang, but they raped me anyway. I have never been with a man, Rimpoche, never even known men apart from my brothers and father, but this is what they did to me and this is what they have done to our land. And what good has our praying done? Tell me that, Rimpoche. Tell me!" Although she spoke with composure and with respect for Tashi, tears were now running freely down her smooth brown skin as she looked forlornly at the two men before her.

"But he doesn't have the answers, Chungla." He looked at Smith.

"I once thought that he and his kind did, that soldiers and the CIA could help us, but believe me they don't." Tashi stepped towards her to take hold of her, but Chungla backed away from him.

"Look what you've done to her, Peter," snarled Tashi, turning to Smith and switching to English again. "Since we found her she's become infatuated with you and you've taken advantage of that to corrupt her. Look at her!"

Smith was shocked and hurt by the anger of his friend now being projected at him.

"I didn't rape her, Tashi. I didn't burn down her monastery," he retorted also in English so the girl could not understand. He resisted the urge to add that he had risked his life to save her and this was the thanks he got for it. That he had not sought out the girl whilst they had been on the trail. Thought that he had nothing to say to a young teenage Tibetan girl with a, to him, almost incomprehensible upbringing.

"She sought me out since we've been here, Tashi," he continued defensively. "While you've been chatting to the Abbot and catching up on lost praying time, this young traumatised girl has been left to her own devices. It's given her time to think. Probably too much time and too much thinking. She asked me about the AK, to show her how to use it and I refused. But she persisted till I gave in. I was bored and she was keen." Tashi was silent and Smith continued, gaining confidence in his cause.

"But I thought about this as well. So let me tell you a little story, Tashi." He smiled.

"What story? What are you talking about, Peter?"

"About Che, Che Guevara."

"Ah! Your hero. Another part of your culture. Another warrior. What does he have to do with this? With Chungla?"

"He's not my hero, Tashi," blurted out Smith, suddenly feeling like a schoolboy in some playground argument, denying heroes, but never mind. There was a point to be made.

"Castro originally took Che on as a doctor. Apparently, one day they were ambushed in the Sierra Madre Mountains by the Cuban Army and had to make a quick exit. They needed to grab what they could and get out of there. The way Che tells it, there was a pile of kit including his medical supplies and a box of ammunition. He could only carry one thing. Without thinking he took the ammunition. The doctor took the ammunition and the rest, as they say, is history."

"The rest is bullshit, Peter, and so is that story I bet."

"Maybe, Tashi, but you're missing the point."

"No I'm not, Peter." He looked at the tiny implacable figure of Chungla in front of him, and turned and ran back out into the rain.

Chapter 26

�

PLA Headquarters, ShigatseTibet

Unfortunately for Lhotse, the bullet hit his skull, rendering him unconscious, but not killing him. Concerned that there may be other snipers in the hills the soldiers approached his fallen frame slowly, giving him plenty of time to die, but Lhotse clung stubbornly to life. When the Chinese realised that he was still alive they casevaced him back down the valley in the growing darkness alongside the soldiers he had shot. One died before they reached the vehicles. The other screamed from the agony of his abdominal wound with every jolt of the stretcher over the rough ground. It was over thirty minutes before a medic got enough morphine into him to quieten him, but Lhotse was unaware of any of this

The two casualties barely survived the journey in the armoured vehicles back to the military hospital in Shigatse. But on orders from the top and amidst much resentment, with the best treatment locally available, Lhotse recovered consciousness after three days. He was delirious and confused for several more days and slept most of the time, being hand fed by a kindly orderly at regular intervals. As his strength increased, memories of recent events, the parachute drop, the attack on Kaisang and the fight with Smith, began to return.

As his mind cleared and the room he was in began to come into focus for the first time, he reached instinctively for his left forearm. He could not remember quite why, but an instinctive panic flushed over him when his fingers traced only the smooth skin of his arm.

"Is this what you are looking for?" enquired a voice in Tibetan. Lhotse struggled up the bed to raise himself enough to see the owner of the disembodied voice.

"Once you have told me what I want to know, perhaps I will give it back to you. Perhaps." Captain Deng had not been as badly injured as at first thought and had made a rapid, if not yet complete recovery. He was now keen to get back to work. In his hand he held Lhotse's cyanide capsule.

"Enter", shouted Colonel Zhu, in response to the gentle knock on the inner door of his office. His orderly, Corporal Li, put his head around the door. The Colonel's office was a Spartan affair with a large desk in the centre, tidy of all clutter as always. The solitary window had a dreary view onto the large concrete parade ground beyond and soldiers could be vaguely heard stamping around outside. There were no family photographs on the wall or on Zhu's desk, the only picture adorning the office being a monochrome photograph of a proud looking Zhu in Tiananman Square with Mao beaming at his side.

Cabinets with files and reference books neatly lined the walls. The only concession to colour in this drab grey room was the strip of medals adorning Zhu's olive green dress uniform which hung from a hanger on the door of a steel locker standing in one corner.

"Captain Deng is here to see you, sir."

"Show him in, Li," responded the Colonel with mixed feelings. He was eager to hear what intelligence Deng had acquired, but did not wish to resume his jousting with the man. Nor did he wish to know how the information had been obtained. A heated discussion with his superior officer, the Garrison Commander, had seen Zhu overruled on the issue of how the interrogation of the Tibetan terrorist should be conducted. The Commander wanted results yesterday and was happy to give the psychopathic Deng free rein to get them.

If Deng got the information, his star would seem to be once again in the ascendancy. Zhu doubted whether information extracted by Deng's methods could be relied on. He was no sentimentalist, but he had fought the Japanese, the Nationalists and now the Tibetans and he knew from bitter experience that men in extremis tell you what they think you want to hear. But only time would tell whether he was right this time.

Deng entered Zhu's office with a self-satisfied smile on his face and a slim file in his hand.

"Thank you for seeing me, Colonel," he began. "Here is the information I believe you were waiting for." He placed the file on Zhu's desk.

"And our prisoner, Deng. How is he progressing?"

"I can't say that he is well, Colonel, but he will survive to stand trial, if that is what you want."

"It is, Deng," responded the Colonel without emotion. "I hope that you obtained all the information he had to give us." Zhu made this statement sound more of a threat than a comment.

"I'm quite sure of that, Colonel Zhu. He was most helpful."

"Well, let's see." Zhu picked up the file and began to read. Deng began to retreat.

"Stay where you are, Captain Deng. I may have some questions for you." He did not invite Deng to sit as he proceeded to scour the pages of the report, underlining here, scribbling a note there.

It was nearly twenty minutes before Zhu slid his round wire rimmed Party approved glasses to the end of his nose and glowered over them at Deng. The Intelligence Officer was struggling to conceal the effects of standing in front of Zhu for such a period of time.

"Are you alright, Deng," enquired the Colonel. "You look decidedly unwell. Shall I call the MO?" He sounded genuinely concerned.

"No need for that, Colonel. I'm fine. Just not completely recovered. Would you mind if I sat down?"Zhu guessed that he was near to collapse.

"Do you believe that he knew nothing about the briefcase? That it was destroyed in the vehicle?" enquired the Colonel, ignoring Deng's request

"I was very insistent on this matter, Colonel, and the Tibetan denied that he knew anything about it."

"So he and his team were parachuted in to reinforce and resupply the terrorists and for no other reason?" insisted Zhu.

"Yes, Colonel"

Zhu was quiet for a few seconds, and then continued.

"Tell me what you think we should do now we have this information, Captain," continued the older man in a pleasant tone,

"I, I...." Deng paused and Zhu was sure he was going to collapse any second.

"I, I think that...." He lurched forward hands outstretched to break his fall, but still catching his head on the side of Zhu's desk as he fell. Zhu stood and came around the desk, taking hold of the half-conscious figure. He lowered the injured man to the floor. The Colonel put his mouth close to Deng's face.

"How do you feel, Deng?" He hissed, pressing his hand where he new Deng's wound to be and clamping his other hand over Deng's mouth. Deng's face was white, sweat poured down his forehead and his eyes stared at Zhu in terror.

"I just want you to experience a little bit of what you did to that Tibetan, Deng. It's stupid, I know, but I want you to think about, to feel what you did to him. What you do.

"He was a soldier, Deng. On the wrong side, but still a soldier. He deserved better than you. And if your intelligence is wrong men are going to die needlessly. And you will regret that."

As suddenly as he had seized him, the Colonel released Deng. "We'll talk again when you're feeling better," He smiled.

"Li!" he bellowed. "Li, get a couple of medics and the MO in here immediately. Captain Deng looks distinctly unwell," and turning to look down at Deng, "I think he returned to his duties before he was ready."

As soon as Deng had been stretchered down the corridor, Zhu picked up the telephone.

"Tang! Meet me in the Ops Room in ten minutes." He slammed the telephone back in its cradle, scooped up Deng's file and headed out of his office.

"Follow me, Li." The orderly scuttled behind his boss, pen and pad in hand.

"Get on to the OC Recce Flight and tell him to be in the Ops Room in thirty minutes with a weather forecast. Then go to my quarters and pack my kit. And then pack your own, Li. We're going to get our boots dirty." The Colonel knew only too well his corporal's feelings about going into the field, but he had little time for 'shiny-arsed soldiers', not a little afraid that he was becoming one himself So Li was going to get some combat experience whether he liked it or not.

Major Tang's Bravo Company was now the standby Company, currently on six hours notice to move. This meant that no man in the Company could leave the garrison, personal equipment was packed and all the Company's kit was loaded onto their vehicles.

"There you are Tang," Zhu greeted his Company Commander warmly. Tang was relieved that he had beaten the Old Man to the Ops Room and even more so to see that he seemed to be in a good mood. Word was already spreading regarding Deng's "relapse" and Tang had not known what to expect. Like Zhu he was a career Infantry Officer and had seen action in his youth as an "advisor" in North Korea during the Korean War. He had been posted to the Tibetan Autonomous Region on three occasions now, interspersed with tours elsewhere in the Motherland, and so knew the TAR and its people well, or as well as any PLA Officer could.

"We're going to have a bit of an outing, Major." He tossed Deng's report towards Tang.

"We, Sir?" Tang was puzzled. One of the good things about operating in the TAR was that, as a Company Commander, he was usually virtually autonomous once he got his Company out of the Garrison.

"Yes, Tang, we. These bandits have caused us enough trouble. I'm going to take personal charge in the field of the operation to round them up. We'll probably need to mobilise Charlie Company as well, so I will take overall charge." Colonel Zhu could not hide from Tang his own excitement at the prospect of getting down to some good old-fashioned soldiering instead of festering in his office whilst terrorists and Red Guards ran amuck on his patch. Tang realised that he was going to sort this one out himself.

"You need to take that report away and read it." Zhu nodded in the direction of the file in Major Tang's hand.

"Read the report, get your men ready for an immediate move and be back here in one hour for a full briefing." Tang hesitated momentarily in case there was anything else. There wasn't.

"Yes, Colonel", he snapped finally, saluting and turning on his heels he stamped out of the room. He opened the Ops Room door to be greeted by Captain Lo, OC of the Garrison Recce Flight.

Tang and Lo passed one another and both men looked into the eyes of the other, Lo trying to detect in Tang's an inkling of what was afoot, but without success.

Lo saluted as he approached Colonel Zhu.

"Over here, Lo," beckoned the Colonel. He was pouring over the large scale map of the Garrison's Tactical Area of Operations laid out on the Ops Room table. The large room was dimly lit around them, illuminated only by an occasional reading light and the glow of radio equipment, except for the map table itself which was bathed in an intense light like a pool table in a cheap bar.

"Firstly, Lo, I need a weather report." Lo, still standing, opened the folder he was holding, although he didn't need to refer to it as he already knew its contents.

"Well, Sir, this unusual low pressure which we have been experiencing over the last few days now looks set to clear away to the south towards Northern India as high pressure pushes in from the north."

"Which means?" enquired the Colonel, impatient to move on.

"Which means, Sir, that the weather is rapidly improving. The rain and low cloud has now just about gone and by tomorrow we will have clear skies and excellent visibility."

"So you'll be able to get those planes of yours in the air." A statement, not a question.

"Yes, Sir," Lo agreed. "What are we looking for?"

"Bandits, Lo. Bandits." Zhu smiled, thrilling again at the prospect of the chase.

"Probably the same group you mistakenly took to be innocent traders on your last outing, Lo," the Colonel admonished mildly.

"Or what's left of them. They've got a couple of days start on us from Kaisang village. We know they headed west in the first place. But our foot patrols soon lost track of them and they could then have gone in any direction. However, Lo, it is more than possible that they have some valuable intelligence belonging to us which they may have managed to retrieve from the highway ambush. If so, we need to get it back and they need to get it out of the country. The Yankee Imperialists are going to be very interested in it if they get their hands on it."

Zhu showed Lo on the map where Smith and the others had carried out the ambush, where Lhotse's parachute had been found, the location of Kaisang village and the route the fugitives had taken from the village after the battle there.

"So it seems pretty clear where they are going, Lo. Do you

agree?" Captain Lo did agree.

"Mustang."

"Indeed, Captain," confirmed Zhu. "And to get there they have to cross the Tsangpo. At this time of year the river is a raging torrent of freezing melt water so they are going to have to cross at one of the bridges, and we will be waiting for them. There are only four bridges that they can cross at according to our maps." The colonel pointed them out on the map.

"Here at Napshi, at Matho, then at Chala, and finally at Kyakyaru. So, Captain, we're going to deploy at each of these bridges and wait. But in the meantime we need you to recce the river between here and Kyakyaru to confirm that there are no other crossing places. And we also need you to sweep every valley north of the Tsangpo in the hope that we will find them before they even get to the river." The Colonel paused.

"It's a great shame, Lo, that we can't get you some helicopters up here. I've got to admit that the Americans have shown us the way in Vietnam. Helicopter gunships, troop carriers, resupply, casevac. They do it all by helicopter. Across that jungle in minutes."

"I'll be as happy as you, Colonel, when someone can get us some that will fly reliably at these altitudes. But in the meantime..."

"I know, Lo, I know. So we have to make the most of what we have. I want your planes in the air at first light tomorrow and they'll be up there until we find this splitist band and deal with them. We have to deal with these terrorists and recover what they stole from us."

Chapter 27

Tsechen Damchos Ling Monastery, Tibet

Leaving Chungla with the AK56, from which she now refused to be parted, Smith went into the monastery and groped his way down two flights of dark stone stairs to his tiny cell. A handful of butter lamps flickered a dim light across the room. The only contents were a hard bed on which his sleeping bag was spread and his saddle bags with a few items of his meagre kit spilling from them. He crashed down onto the bed, his mind in a rage after the exchange with Tashi. Smith could understand, just about, why Tashi would be angry that Chungla might be turning her back on her religion. But hadn't Tashi done exactly the same thing as her, turned from the path of peace which his religion demanded? Had he got it wrong, misunderstood Tashi? Memory and truth were ephemeral things so he had to focus on what had happened.

His thoughts drifted back, back to England where he had met Tashi, or to be accurate Scotland and the monastery at Sami Ling. How strange that monasteries should be having such a profound effect on the life of a thoroughly Twentieth Century soldier. Had he become a modern crusader? Had his crusade become as morally corrupt as that of Simon de Montford or Richard the Lionheart?

"I'm going back to Daramsala soon, Peter," Tashi had begun. Why don't you join me? Just for a couple of weeks. Your language would improve enormously in a Tibetan speaking environment, and whilst it is not exactly Tibet, it would help to put the language into its culture."

"I'm not sure I am that bothered about improving my skills, Tashi. I'm enjoying this," he waved one hand generally around the room to indicate the monastery, "but when am I ever going to use Tibetan except here or with you? This was all just a whim to help fill in the time I had on my hands."

"Oh." Tashi did not hide his disappointment. "I thought you were interested in Tibet. Had been for years you said. Since you were a schoolboy."

"I was. I am," agreed Smith.

"Well then," continued Tashi, more enthusiastic again, "With me as your local guide, you'll get a real insight into my country. A cultural holiday of a lifetime," he smiled.

Smith capitulated.

So it was agreed. The news was broken to Abbi and flights were soon booked. The pair flew to Delhi on a sunny day in June. From Delhi, they continued by train to Simla. The European back packing hippy and the Buddhist monk heading for the Himalayas created little interest in late 1960s India. At Simla they picked up the narrow gauge railway to Kangra and completed their journey in a less than roadworthy taxi to their final destination, hard up against the old Northwest Frontier.

"Here we are, McCleod Ganj," announced Tashi as they entered the small Himalayan town where the Tibetan Government in Exile had been based since just after the Lhasa Uprising of 1959 and the subsequent flight of the Dalai Lama to India and safety. The town was located a mile or so beyond Dharamsala itself and was in effect a northern suburb of it.

"You should feel at home here, Peter. This was a British Hill Station. Your forebears came in the summer to get away from the heat of the Punjab. One of your famous Gurkha Regiments was based here."

"My forebears, as you call them, Tashi, were all slaving away in the mill in Yorkshire, not swanning around India. But this bloody rain is making me feel right at home." It was June, the start of the monsoon season, and the rain hammered incessantly on the windscreen of the taxi, the aging wiper blades barely coping with the deluge.

"Do you know somewhere we can stay tonight?" Tashi addressed the driver.

"Of course," replied the driver enthusiastically. "My cousin has a place. Well, he's not exactly my cousin, but..."

"And where is this place?" interrupted Tashi, before they heard any more of the driver's complex family network. From the journey so far he seemed to be related to every Indian resident of the town from the mayor down.

"The Kunga Guest House, on the Bhagsunath Road," the driver responded cheerfully, unabashed by Tashi,s interruption. "A very good place to stay. Very clean. Very nice."

And it was. Very clean and very nice.

"But what are we doing here, Tashi?" a bemused Smith was finally able to ask as he threw his back pack down on the bed in the simply furnished room the owner of the Kunga Guest House had led them to.

"I thought you knew everybody here. I was expecting the red carpet treatment arriving with my influential pal Tashi. Not spending the night in a B&B."

"Shush, Peter, they will hear you. There is nothing wrong with this place."

"Believe me, Tashi, I've slept in worse places, but I won't bore you with that. I just thought, being with you, I was going to be a guest of the Government, even if it is a government in exile."

Thinking about it later, Smith was never sure just when he had realised that this was all part of Tashi's master plan. His plan to get Smith to go with him, at least to Mustang and probably into Tibet itself. So Tashi did not want Smith to seem like anything other than one of the thousands of Western visitors to Dharamsala and McCleod Ganj, come to catch a glimpse of the Dalai Lama and perhaps visit the holy sites around the place.

Chances were that no-one cared what Smith and Tashi did or that Smith would go no further than McCleod Ganj, but Tashi had not wanted to take the risk, Smith realised. The Tibetan exile community in the town now ran into several thousand, many living in poverty with few jobs available to them. Some were bound to be in the pay of the Chinese. Smith being hosted in any official way by the Tibetan community was not part of Tashi's plan, so that there could be no repercussions later.

McCleod Ganj huddles on a hillside about seven thousand feet above sea level, surrounded by dense forest. Towering just to the north are the higher peaks of the Dhauladhar Range with the highest peak, Hanuman Ka Tibba, reaching eighteen and a half thousand feet and dominating the town. For the next couple of days the mountains were invisible in the mist as the rain continued.

Smith explored the town in short dashes between tea shops, restaurants and bookshops. Not that there was much to explore and he was soon spending most of his time reading trashy novels on his bed, sipping tea and chatting with Tashi or the owner of the guest house. There was, after ten years of refugees trickling into the town, a distinctly Tibetan atmosphere to the place, with prayer flags and wheels in abundance and food vendors and monks on the streets. Smith was acclimatising not just to the altitude, but to Tibet.

When out alone, Smith also practiced his Tibetan on any exiles he ran into who were willing to chat, which, being an affable people, they usually were, and especially so on meeting a Westerner who spoke their language. This in spite of Tashi trying to find plausible reasons to discourage him as such behaviour was bound to attract talk. Not many westerners spoke Tibetan.

Tashi periodically disappeared on mysterious missions on which Smith was not invited, but as the weather improved they also ventured further afield together. One walk took them to the Church of St John in the Wilderness surrounded by pine forest in the direction of Forsyth Ganj. The squat slate building, surrounded by a very British graveyard and dating back to the middle of the Nineteenth century, reminded Smith of a Lakeland church. The chill air of the mountains made him think briefly of past walks in the Cumbrian fells. But he was soon engrossed by the gravestones with their potted histories of soldiers and government officers, their wives and children, who had died thousands of miles from home, now buried in what felt very like a little piece of England in the Himalayas.

"Here, Peter," called Tashi, trying to enter into the spirit of it, but privately seeing little interest in the graves of foreigners a hundred years dead. "One of your forebears." That word again.

"Lieutenant Crispin Nicholson, 66th Batallion the Gurkha Light Infantry." Smith wandered over to look and read out the rest of the inscription.

"Died 16 November 1863, in the twenty third year of his life, from injuries sustained after falling from his horse in a polo match. Erected in his memory by his fellow Officers."

Smith could not help wondering what this young man would have been like in life. A brother Officer and an infanteer, separated by a century, a century in which it became just about possible for mill workers sons to go to Sandhurst. How shocked would Lt Nicholson have been by that? Smith turned away and the ex-soldier and the monk headed back towards the town, each deep in their own thoughts.

Finally, after several days in McCleod Ganj, Smith was allowed by Tashi to graduate to visits to the Tibetan sites in the town. Tashi took him to Namgyal Monastery located on the edge of town. The monastery had transferred itself from the homeland after 1959 and now housed about a hundred monks. Smith managed to restrain the urge to show off his ever improving Tibetan as he and Tashi now talked together in that language exclusively when they were alone. Smith still couldn't see the problem with using the language in public and Tashi's feeble explanations were unconvincing. However, he went along with his friend's request.

In the sunny courtyard young monks in maroon robes took part in traditional debates, accompanied by much waving and clapping of hands, as they discussed pressing religious matters. Bemused tourists stopped to watch the spectacle before heading for the temples and restaurant.

"What's going on?" asked Smith.

"This is now the Dalai Lama's monastery and he established it to represent all the main schools of Tibetan Buddhism. But traditionally, all of them used the same teaching methods for their lamas and a main part of this was debate. I spent hours every week debating with my Masters over many years. My examinations were in the form of a debate with the senior tutors of my monastery. It is entertainment for the tourists, but it is also our way of training the mind. Our beliefs are passionately held and hotly debated."

"So what were these schools you mentioned, Tashi?"

"It is very complicated for an outsider to understand the doctrinal differences and I will not try to explain them, but the four main schools of our religion are called the Nyingmapa, Kagyupa, Sakyuapa and the Gelugpa. They are different sects if you like. In the same way as your Roman Catholics and Protestants are all supposed to be Christians, but could have wars with each other, our sects have rivalries which have turned nasty in the past."

"How nasty? Smith was genuinely surprised.

"Very nasty, Peter. And that is the point. The Gelugpa lamas wear yellow ceremonial head dress and the other sects wear red and this rivalry between the Red Hats and the Yellow Hats, as they have become known, went on for several centuries before the Chinese invasion.

"But when he arrived here, the Fourteenth Dalai Lama, Tenzin Gyatso, realised that such internal bickering, if had not been before, was now irrelevant and a distraction. Our country was occupied by a foreign power and we were arguing about metaphysical niceties. So this monastery is what you might call ecumenical. It subscribes to no particular school and has members of each of them."

"But presumably the Dalai Lama is a member of one of these schools."

"Yes, since the Seventeenth Century of the Western calendar successive Dalai Lamas have been members of the Gelugpa or Yellow Hats, so they have at least in theory been in the ascendancy. The Panchen Lama is also a Yellow Hat."

"And the Panchen Lama is the second in command?"

"You're military terms do not exactly describe it, Peter, but you are nearly right. Traditionally, the Panchen Lama had his seat at Tashilhumpo Monastery in our second largest city, Shigatse. Much of the monastery was destroyed by the Red Guards, but fortunately these were mainly accommodation and administration buildings. The PLA stopped the Red Guards destroying the main religious buildings as they had captured the young Tenth Panchen Lama and used him as a puppet after the Dalai Lama fled Lhasa. The Chinese also completely destroyed Shigatse Dzong in 1961. It was a very important building to us Tibetans, asmaller version of the Potala Palace in Lhasa, home of the Dalai Lama until his exile, but it was torn down stone by stone", concluded Tashi bitterly.

"So he supported the Chinese, the Panchen Lama?"

"Yes, for a while. Without the Dalai Lama, he was the senior Tibetan religious and political leader. But he probably had no choice. He was young, inexperienced and a virtual prisoner.

"But then in 1962 he presented a petition to Zhou Enlai, the Chinese Prime Minister, listing many complaints of brutality carried out by the Chinese since the invasion. At first they seemed to be listening and Zhou Enlai was sympathetic, but then Mao turned against the Panchen Lama and he was arrested in 1964. So far as we know he is still in Quincheng Prison where so many of our people who have spoken out against the Chinese have ended up. It is a brutal place where Tibetans are routinely tortured and executed"

Smith did not know how to respond and the friends fell silent.

They crossed a stone paved courtyard leading to the adjacent Dalai Lama's temple, known as Tsuglag Khang. Preferring to make the most of the fine weather, they did not enter the complex with its traditional Tibetan statues, religious icons and butter lamp lit chapels, instead choosing to wander along the periphery of the low white painted buildings. Large decorated brass prayer wheels were set into the walls and Smith absent-mindedly spun one occasionally as they passed by, setting it off clattering and rattling behind them. Tashi seemed to be lost in thought for several moments and Smith waited for him to speak again. At last he continued.

"There is so much you do not know about our country and the suffering of its people, Peter," he insisted intently, looking directly into his friend's eyes. "But you know more than most people and you have proved by your reading and by your study of our language that you have a great interest in our plight. Is that true, Peter?"

"Yes it is, Tashi." Tashi hesitated momentarily as if thinking of the right words with which to proceed.

"So would you like to help us?"

"Yes, of course, Tashi. But what can I do. I don't have any skills that you could use. I'm not an aid worker like Abbi." He paused.

"Have you asked her? She could probably do something useful for your people with her contacts and experience. Are there Western aid workers here now?" Tashi ignored his question, apparently intent on his own line of reasoning

"You do have skills, Peter. Skills which could be of great use to us. Not here and not to the exile community. But to the people I know and who I am going to join when we leave here. I am hoping that you will come with me."

"You've lost me Tashi."

As they walked past the end of the building there was suddenly a distinct fragrance of juniper smoke in the late afternoon air. The aroma reinforced to Smith the exotic nature of the location he now found himself in, a Tibetan monastery high in the Himalayas, and he would in the future always associate it with what he was now about to do.

"The skills we are interested in are your military skills," Tashi finally blurted out, seemingly seeing no better way of approaching the subject.

"My military skills? You're a Buddhist monk, Tashi. I don't know what you're thinking of doing with any military skills I might have, but last time I looked you people were pacifists. And who is this "we"?"

"You did not look in the 'Land of the Snows'. It is true that we are pacifists, or were, but for many of us, layman and lama alike, we can no longer accept meekly the suffering imposed upon us. As long ago as 1959 the International Commission of Jurists told the United Nations that the Chinese were guilty of committing genocide in Tibet. This is a matter of public record, Peter, for those interested to read such things. This could not go unanswered.

"So we had to act. We have been resisting from the beginning and still continue to do so twenty years after the illegal invasion of our lands."

"Have you fought, Tashi?"

"No. My role has been to raise funds, to buy equipment, to increase awareness and gain support for our cause in the West. But now no-one is listening. As I said, it is ten years since the world was told that the Chinese were trying to destroy our people and culture. Where are the television documentaries and news items exposing this on your BBC?

"But others fight and die whilst I continue my studies in London and live a comfortable life. I can do this no longer." Smith took hold of Tashi by the shoulders.

"Listen to me, Tashi. I don't know much about your war, but I know enough to tell you that without a shadow of a doubt you are contributing far more to your cause by continuing what you have been doing than you will by taking up a gun. You're not a soldier. You're not trained. But even if you were, you'd just be a tiny cog. What difference are you going to make, compared to the difference you are making now?"

Tashi shrugged Smith's hands from his shoulders and continued to walk. Smith quickly joined him.

"I know all these arguments. I have heard them in London and now I am hearing them from my friends and others here. But none of this alters how I feel. I know what I must do." He paused.

"There is a Khampa leader called Pemba. A great fighter. He has been fighting the Chinese from the start. We met in Lhasa during the Uprising of 1959. He now has a *Magar* in Mustang and he and his band attack the Chinese from there. I am going to join him. It is decided"

"Woah there! *Magar*s? *Khampas*? What are they?"

"*Khampas* are a warrior people from the east of our country. Their lands were almost the first to be invaded by the Chinese in 1949 and they have been fighting ever since. Those who did not submit were killed or retreated. Pemba and his men have been driven back to the western edges of our lands and now take refuge across the border in Mustang. Mustang is in Nepal, but it is culturally part of the Land of the Snows. The *Khampas'* military camps are called *Magar*s and there are several in Mustang, including Pemba's. I am leaving in a few days to join him and I am asking you to come with me." Suddenly Tashi's mood seemed to lighten as if expressing his intentions aloud had in some way manifest them as his destiny and he no longer needed to struggle with himself or anyone else to justify what he was about to do.

"Ah, here is the restaurant. Shall we have some tea?" asked Tashi brightly.

A bemused Smith was led into the simply furnished refectory-like room. They sat at a table and ordered Indian tea and some sweet cakes. Small groups of tourists chatted and ate at nearby tables as Smith tried to absorb the most preposterous proposal he had ever received. Even more preposterous than that from the lady-boy who had propositioned him in a bar in Penang on a brief period of leave from the jungle.

"Look, Tashi. Even if I wanted to join you, as I said, one more soldier can contribute very little and that applies as much to me as it does to you."

"I am not thinking of you as a soldier, Peter, but as a military advisor. We get money from the Americans. We get equipment from them and even training for some of our men in a special training camp. But we do not have military advisors on the ground. No-one comes to help us. You could be a military advisor. In Mustang. Our men need training in modern weapons and tactics. Your government, the Americans, the Russians, they all send military advisors to help governments they wish to prop up. Why should we not have such advisors? We can pay you.

"You are a professional soldier, an Officer who has fought in many places. Didn't you tell me once that you were going to join a private security company when you left the Army? What is so different in that to working for us? We might not have as much money as them, but we have a just cause."

Smith tried to take it all in, Tashi's offer, what was going on in Tibet, but needed to be sure he had this right.

"The Americans fund you? The American Government?"

"Yes, Peter. The CIA have done so for many years."

"The CIA? Bloody hell! I didn't know anything about that." Smith was genuinely surprised.

"Why would you? We do not advertise it. The Americans do not advertise it. But it is so. We are an irritant to the Chinese and the Americans like to encourage this. We are a side show of the Cold War. They give us money and weapons and take some of our people to a place called Camp Hale in Colorado for training. This was all set up by the Dalai Lama's brother Thubten Norbu who has had close contacts with the Americans for many years, since the Uprising."

"So the Dalai Lama supports this?"

"He cannot support it and keep his position of non-violent resistance which has given him prestige in the world."

"But he knows about it?" Tashi was silent.

Smith thought about all this for a few moments. Tashi sipped his tea and looked out onto the sunlit garden beyond the window.

"So Peter," he continued at last, "will you come?" The opportunity to persuade Smith, had there ever been one was slipping away. Why would he come? It was indeed a ludicrous proposition.

Smith was silent, his mind running through what Tashi had told him about the Americans and about the plight of the people of Tibet. And, yes, Tashi was right. He had been prepared, eager even, to go and work for Spartan, doing whatever they wanted him to do if the money was right. He also remembered his father's story of Uncle George who had died fighting for what he believed on the Ebro River in Spain. His father wanted him to do something decent, something worthwhile, but at the time Smith had no idea what that might be.

Perhaps in a strange way Tashi's offer was what Smith was

looking for and he had known this in his subconscious when he had agreed to come to India with him. As long as he could remember he had craved adventure and been terrified of being ordinary, living an ordinary life. Perhaps Tashi was offering Peter Pan the opportunity to put off growing up for a while longer.

"Yes," replied Smith simply. "Yes, Tashi, I will come with you."

Chapter 28

ཕ

Tsechen Damchos Ling Monastery, Tibet

Smith climbed the rickety wooden ladder to the roof of the building used by the monastery to accommodate guests. The rain had stopped some time ago and a mist of steam rose from the flat roof as the heat of the sun began to penetrate the thin mountain air. The clearing clouds revealed a magnificent vista of steep valleys and snow capped mountains way to the north. The other men of the party were already sat, huddled in their *chubas*, rifles on the floor by their sides, forming a small circle. Heads turned towards Smith as he climbed over the parapet.

"Welcome," said Pemba to Smith as he took his place. "Now we are all present. Let's begin." He paused a moment and no-one interrupted the silence.

"The rain is passed and so the Chinese will be on our trail. No doubt they are already out looking for us. We need to get moving immediately. We must endanger the monastery no longer." He paused again before continuing.

"We have news Lhotse was taken alive by the Chinese. We must assume that they know everything he knows." There was a shocked silence amongst the group, broken by Smith.

"How do you know this?"

"We have our sources."

"Who? Where?"

"Inside the Chinese headquarters. That is all anyone needs to know. This man is trusted and has risked his life to give us this information. So, we must use it. We need to get to safety in Mustang as soon as possible and this is the route I propose." Pemba leaned forward and began to smooth a crumpled and aging map on the floor in the middle of the group.

"Is he alive?" It was a woman's voice. The men looked over to the parapet where the slight figure of Chungla now stood, still in her nuns robes, her rifle still slung over her thin shoulders.

"Yes, just about," responded Pemba.

"And what will happen to him?"

"It is beyond our control," replied Pemba trying to avoid the issue and return to his map.

"Please! Tell me what will happen to this man."

"Well, as they have not killed him they'll probably take him back to Lhasa for some mock trial and then they'll execute him or send him to Quincheng and work him to death. But we can do nothing about it. We must put it from our minds and concentrate on the safety of the party here and the intelligence we have for the Americans. It could be vitally important."

A sombre silence fell over the group at this articulation of the reality of Lhotse's fate. In the silence a bell could be heard ringing in the depths of the monastery. Prayer flags fluttered listlessly around the party in the light breeze as they avoided each others gaze.

"We cannot allow this to happen," stated Chungla baldly. "We must rescue him." The circle of men now looked at one another, not sure whether to laugh at such a naive suggestion from the *Tulku*. The wisdom accumulated in her past lives had obviously not yet manifest itself in the mind of the young girl.

Pemba spoke for them. "We are all sorry at what has happened to our comrade, incarnate one. We respect your concern for him. But we who have been fighting for many years understand the reality better than you. Lhotse is in a cell in the headquarters of the Chinese surrounded by who knows how many Chinese soldiers. We don't know how badly injured he is. It is impossible to help him." He turned back to the group and the map in front of him.

"This man is your comrade," the girl persisted. "He went to America to learn how to fight for us. He risked his life by coming back here to help us all, and you are just going to shrug your shoulders. What kind of men are you?" Some of the group shuffled in apparent embarrassment at Chungla's indictment, but no-one responded

Chungla stepped down from the parapet to join the group, the muzzle of her rifle scraping on the adobe wall as she did so. Standing next to Smith and looking down at him, she spoke again, more confidently now.

"And you, military advisor, what do you advise? Does your army in the West leave its comrades behind?" Smith said nothing for a while, head bowed avoiding her gaze and scratching the earth roof distractedly with a stick. He thought of his brief contact with Lhotse, the man sent by the Americans to kill him. How they had fought and how he had forced Lhotse to stay behind and defend the group's rear. And he had. Had slowed down the Chinese. Taken a bullet for them all, and worse.

The others waited. Finally, Smith swept his long hair behind his ears and looked up.

"Yes they do, Chungla. Soldiers everywhere do. But not often and never lightly. Pemba is right that what you suggest is likely suicidal," and then he thought for a moment before continuing. "But so is heading for Mustang. That is exactly what the Chinese expect us to do. They know more or less where we are and that we have to cross the river. You know they'll be waiting, Pemba."

"Our only chance is to get to one of the crossings before them, or to find a crossing they don't know of. In either case we must move as soon as possible," insisted Pemba, undeterred.

"Wait, Pemba," and turning to Smith, "what are you proposing?" It was Tendruck, the leader of the parachutists and Lhotse's friend, who spoke.

"Well. The only advantage we have is surprise and rescuing Lhotse is one thing the Chinese wont expect us to do."

"That's certainly true," agreed Rinzing ironically, "because it's insane. Look how few of us there are." He waved his hand around the small circle of men to emphasise his point. But the infection of uncertainty was now spreading through the group. Chungla sensed the doubt and pressed on.

"We will fight. Give us your rifles and we women will fight if you men do not wish to."

"There are enough rifles for everyone." Tashi had remained silent until know, but a look of horror spread across his face at this statement from Smith.

"Are you mad? You've had your fun playing soldiers with her here, but don't let her think she can go and fight the Chinese," Tashi raged. "Chungla asked you about your army in the West. Tell her whether women fight in that army."

"No they don't, Tashi, but my country hasn't been invaded like yours and if it had they would. You all know that women have been fighting in Tibet for years and we need all the firepower we can get.

If these women want to fight for their freedom why shouldn't they?" Others in the group nodded in agreement. They all knew from experience of the bravery of Tibetan women in the face of the Chinese onslaught on their country.

Before things became more acrimonious, Pemba took charge of the meeting again.

"I do not like what Peter is proposing, but he is right that our chances of getting back to Mustang now are slim. Perhaps by acting elsewhere we will draw the Chinese away from the river and give ourselves a better chance later. And the more willing fighters we have the better."

Chungla beamed triumphantly. Smith avoided the harsh glare of Tashi's gaze.

"So, here is the map, Peter. Tell us, what is your plan," enquired Pemba.

"I don't have a plan," responded Smith.

Chapter 29

ཝ

US Embassy, New Delhi

Pat Reagan stood looking out of the window of his office in the US Embassy to the manicured garden below. Beyond the trees and the wall of the compound, Saturday afternoon traffic headed towards central New Delhi, unheard behind the blast-proof glass. Regan, dressed casually, but expensively in grey Italian styled slacks and a polo shirt with a Martha's Vineyard Sailing Club logo embroidered on the left breast pocket, sucked pensively on a foul smelling cheroot before turning back to his two guests.

"So, Martin, It seems the news from Tibet isn't good. Your man, err ...what's his name?"

"Lhotse." Larsen supplied the name of his friend.

"Yeah, this Lhotse, it looks like he fucked up big time."

"That's one way of putting it," replied Larsen defensively. He had been dreading this meeting since receiving the news of Lhotse's capture from the signals people at Haus Kaus the location of the CIA's Tibet Project safe house in Delhi. At least they were still in contact with the group. Over the years numerous insertions had never been heard of again, betrayed, and/or lost and quickly mopped up by the PLA. He realised with genuine sadness that this was virtually certain to be the last insertion operation into Tibet and that it had only been authorised due to Regan's eagerness to deal with this man Smith. And it was, as Reagan described it, a fuck up.

"Well, what would you call it, Martin? We spent a lot of time and money training this guy and the first proper job we give him he gets himself caught in five minutes flat. Not many bangs for the buck there."

Larsen shuffled uncomfortably in his seat. He wore dark blue trousers and a white short sleeved shirt open at the collar, but even in the cool of the air conditioned office he could feel a trickle of sweat run uncomfortably down his right side. Taking a drink of his coffee to gain time to think of a measured reply, he was about to speak when the limey Chivers butted in.

"Perhaps you're being a little harsh, Pat," interjected the MI6 operative in a conciliatory tone. Stephen Chivers sat opposite Larsen, the two men separated by a low table on which they had both placed their briefing papers for the meeting. Chivers looked every inch the British civil servant of indeterminate rank in his dark suit, white shirt and regimental tie.

"Harsh?" spluttered Reagan. "That's rich coming from you, Steve. It was you wanted us to waste this guy as far as I recall."

"You are correct in saying that we wanted the situation dealt with, Pat, but all I am saying is that we don't have all the facts and, in any event, what's done is done. We need to decide where we go from here."

Reagan turned from the window and wandered over to join the other two men at the table, wafting the smell of strong tobacco over them unconcernedly as he did so.

"Hey, Steve, you're right. No-one can call me unfair. Well, not and live to tell the tale!" He laughed loudly and un-self-consciously at his own joke. Chivers and Larsen exchanged glances as Reagan continued.

"Seriously, guys. Steve is right. We need to move on, but first just give us a head's up on what your boys have been up to in Tibet, Martin." Larsen picked up the folder in front of him and thumbed through several loose leaf pages before beginning.

"Well, as you both know, a team of five Tibetans, all trained at Hale, were parachuted into Tsang province about a hundred klick's west of the local capital, Shigatse. Ostensibly, the aim of the mission was to liaise with a group of Khampa's working out of Mustang harassing the PLA in the west of the country along the Freedom Highway. These guys claim to have some potentially useful intel which they picked up in a raid on a PLA convoy. The insertion team was to collect it from them, assess it, and if useful, get it out of the country and back here.

"But the main aim of the mission, known only to Lhotse, was to whack Smith, who we, or you," nodding towards Chivers, "decided had become a potential embarrassment." Larsen paused to take another drink from his coffee. Reagan and Chivers waited in silence for him to continue.

"Everything seemed to be going fine when we had the first

broadcast from them and within a couple of days they had met up with Smith and his band. But before Lhotse had a chance to carry out his mission they got into a skirmish with the PLA and in the confusion Lhotse got caught.

"From the report we had since, most of the Tibetans were killed or captured and Lhotse ended up in the hands of the PLA and was taken back to the local HQ in Shigatse where, we have to assume, he sang like a bird." Talking about the fate of his friend immediately brought back to Larsen's mind dark thoughts of what had happened to Lhotse and what might still, as he spoke, be happening to him. He had to summon all his professionalism to suppress such thoughts, at least for the duration of the meeting, and get on with the job in hand.

"And Smith? What happened to him?" It was Chivers speaking now.

"It seems he survived, or I guess we wouldn't be here now."

"Yes, I realise that," replied Chivers obviously irritated, " but where is he and what is he up to now? What have your people told you?"

Larsen's answer was interrupted by a knock on the door. A smartly dressed woman of about fifty, Reagan's Personal Assistant, always referred to as Mrs. Walker by Reagan, entered the room holding a tray laden down with more coffee, hot milk and biscuits.

"Resupplies," she announced brightly before retreating and quietly closing the door behind her. Reagan didn't invite anyone to take more coffee or biscuits and the inquisition recommenced.

"Yes, as I was saying, Martin, what has happened to friend Smith? The man seems to have nine lives," Chivers added.

Larsen continued.

"The remains of the band managed to disengage from the Chinese and got away to some monastery in the mountains where they've been hiding ever since. Our last report said they had had bad weather for several days which gave them some cover from Chinese planes and patrols, but that's clearing now."

"So they're on their way to Mustang," stated Reagan. "If they make it we'll be able to deal with this Smith there. We have the assets to do that there. I suppose we just have to sit on our hands til he turns up there. What are the chances of that?"

Larsen drew a deep breath. This is where the shit hits the fan, he thought before plunging into a response.

"They're not heading for Mustang. At least not yet." He paused, awaiting the onslaught from Reagan, but all he said was, "Go on." Larsen did.

"I don't know whose idea it was, but they've decided to go and rescue Lhotse."

"The fuck they have," snarled Reagan. "You get back on to those sons of bitches and turn them round, Martin."

"I've tried to contact them, but there's no response. They're out of contact."

"Fucking convenient," fumed Reagan.

Chivers said nothing, picking up one of Mrs Walker's biscuits and contemplatively dipping it in his coffee, before extracting it and dropping it into his mouth. He then repeated the procedure and pulled a paper from a folder on the table before looking up at Reagan who was now on his feet again with his cheroot jammed in the corner of his mouth.

"This made interesting reading, Pat," he began. "This report from the State Department."

"Yeah, I love those things," responded Reagan sarcastically. "I can't get enough of the thoughts of those pen pushing bastards."

"It says, Pat, that relations between you chaps and the Chinese are coming on by leaps and bounds and that everything possible should be done to encourage and enhance this."

"No disrespect, Steve. After all I showed you that paper, to keep you in the loop, but you Brits aren't in this particular dick waving contest."

Chivers looked exasperated, but managed to remain the diplomat. He slowly and deliberately dipped and ate another of Mrs. Walker's biscuits for Reagan's benefit before resuming his train of thought.

"We might not be involved in the current discussions, Pat, but it suits HMG very well for you and Peking to be on good terms. We can only benefit from such an improvement in relations."

Reagan was quiet for a moment before declaring, "Hong Kong," the penny now having dropped. "You've got to give it back to the Commies. When is that?"

"1997," replied Chivers without enlarging on the issue, but Reagan took up the line of reasoning.

"So, you have to hand back the colony in twenty five years, but the better relations are with the US of A and the Chinese, the better relations are likely to be between you and the Chinese. So the smoother the handover the better. No more riots in Kowloon like you've been putting up with lately. So you don't have to use those little brown guys of yours, what are they called? Oh yeah, Ghurkas. You don't have to let them loose to beat the shit out of the local troublemakers in Wanchai any more.

"Yeah, this makes complete sense," Reagan continued, "because everywhere you've pulled out of so far has turned to a complete shit storm, from India onwards. It's good to see you guys planning ahead for once"

Larsen could see with some pleasure that Chivers was struggling to keep his temper with the plain speaking American. It seemed that Reagan was goading the Englishman because that was what he did. It went with the territory as Head of Station. Larsen had no objections.

Chivers resorted to coffee again to diffuse the situation, before responding, in his own time.

"One school of thought has it that we left all these places before we were ready because Uncle Sam was breathing down our necks. But you seem to be in enough shit of your own, Pat. How are things in Saigon at the moment?"

"OK, Steve," Reagan's tone was more conciliatory now. "But all this policy stuff is way above your head and mine. Why are we falling out over this?"

"We aren't. In fact we can play our own small part in this defrosting of relations between you and the Chinese at the same time as solving our own little problem."

"You've lost me there, Steve. How can we do that?"

"Well, if we can't manage to kill Smith ourselves, we might still earn a few brownie points with the Chinese by telling the PLA that the man Smith is about to ambush one of their convoys."

Chapter 30

Tibet

The invading force of about three thousand troops, mainly infantry advancing on foot, but supported by artillery and a small mounted contingent for recce, easily drove the Tibetan defenders from the strategic town of Gyantse, the third largest in Tibet after Lhasa and Shigatse. The *dzong* or fort above the town was captured soon after, following a fierce artillery barrage. A headquarters was then established at Changlo, a fortified farmstead just south of the town, from where further operations were to be directed.

News soon came that the retreating Tibetan force of possibly more than a thousand men had taken up a defensive position at Karo La nearly fifty miles to the west, blocking the approach to Lhasa about a hundred miles beyond. The pass stood at about seventeen thousand feet and was overlooked by high crags on either side where the defenders had taken up positions. On 3 May a force was dispatched from Changlo to take the pass.

At first things went well for the Tibetans as they picked off the enemy from their well defended positions or sangars. Although the invaders had superior firepower, it proved useless as the Tibetans were so well hidden. The invaders' only chance was to outflank the defenders by getting above them, although it looked all but impossible as they stared up at the steep icy cliffs they would have to negotiate.

A contingent of pioneers was mustered and they began the hazardous climb. It took about three hours for them to reach a suitable vantage point from where they began to rake the Tibetans with deadly fire. The inexperienced Tibetans panicked and fled their defences, opening the pass and the road to the capital to the invaders.

"They came from the south, Peter. From Sikkim in India and followed the trade route towards Gyantse. There had already been a so called battle at a place called Guru where our forces were tricked into laying down their weapons before being machine-gunned. About seven hundred men were killed there." Tashi pointed to the names on the map as he explained the course of the invasion.

"Did you know about this, Peter?" Tashi looked at him quizzically. They sat by the light of a camp fire, Smith now almost immune to the pungent odour of burning yak's dung. Ten days had passed since they had left Tsechen Damchos Ling Monastery heading east, away from Mustang. The group now consisted of twelve men, the remains of Pemba's fighters and the parachute team, supplemented by five young nuns who had elected, or was it insisted, on joining them in the attempt to rescue Lhotse? The other nuns had decided to return to their homes with the intention of eventually returning to their monastery if that seemed possible at some time in the future.

"Not the details, Tashi, but I've read about it. The Younghusband Expedition. 1908?"

"1904," Tashi corrected him. "Your Colonel Younghusband and his British army invaded our country and killed several thousand of our people. The numbers are not known. Two hundred and two of your soldiers were killed. They counted those very carefully."

"Hey, Tashi. Don't start all that 'my' business again. He wasn't my Colonel Younghusband. This was sixty odd years ago." The two men had talked a great deal over the past days and evenings as they crept through the valleys north of Shigatse to eventually find a secure crossing place on the Tsangpo well to the east of the town, away from where they thought the Chinese troops would be looking for them. Their current camp was in the fertile valley of the Rong Chu where the daylight fields were now green with the early shoots of barley and wheat. Fodder had been so scarce on the journey that the horses were beginning to show signs of hunger. Horses were vital to the group's survival and it was a relief to both men and animals that they could finally replenish on something more substantial than sparse patches of scrub. They were careful not to let the horses damage the cultivated fields as they did not want to alienate any local farmers they may encounter, but there was plenty of fresh wild growth in the field margins and even on the lower hillsides.

In that one hundred and fifty mile journey the two men had largely repaired their friendship as Tashi came to accept that Smith had not deliberately turned Chungla into a partisan fighter and that she was following the road that Tashi himself had gone down and had indeed led Smith. Tashi could once again accept what he had chosen to forget as they had argued, that Smith, unlike the rest of the party, did not need to be here, and that if anything his commitment was more than theirs and for less obvious reward.

"Yes, you're right, Peter," smiled Tashi in the firelight, acknowledging that Smith had no responsibility for an invasion which took place fifty-five years earlier and that he was actually fighting against the current invasion of the Land of the Snows.

"But it is interesting, do you not agree? The road which Younghusband and his men followed from Gyantse to Lhasa is the road the Chinese still use today and have the audacity to call the Friendship Highway."

Smith took the map from his friend and stared silently at it for some time in the dim light of the fire.

Chapter 31

ㅈ

PLA Military Command Headquarters, Lhasa, Tibet

"Comrades, I am sorry to have to inform you that Comrade Zhou Renshan is dead." There was a stunned silence as the members of the newly formed Revolutionary Committee of the Tibetan Autonomous Region took in the news.

"How? What happened?" one of the twenty-seven members of the Committee eventually asked tremulously.

Zeng Yongya looked at the assembled body of men before him for some seconds before responding, trying to detect if his announcement had had the desired effect. He was sure it had.

"Suicide," he announced simply. Members of the Committee looked cautiously at one another. No-one needed to be told what this meant. Zhou Renshan had been denounced as a "capitalist roader" not long before.

But the Army remained the nearest thing to a stable and potentially unifying force in the midst of the mayhem tearing Tibet apart as the Red Guards and various factions of the Army openly struggled for power in the Autonomous Region . Two new Divisions had recently been deployed to Tibet as the PLA finally flexed its muscle to impose order. Zeng Yongya was Commander of the Army and now he was Chairman of the Revolutionary Committee. Zhou Renshan had been a prominent leader of one of the warring factions and now he had committed suicide. The point was not lost on the members of the Committee, ten of whose members were PLA Officers. They were all too well aware that another prominent Communist Party member and faction leader, Wang Qimei, had already been denounced and disappeared. The People's Daily had recently announced that the struggle against him would continue.

Previous meetings of the Committee had been in the grand Hall of the People's Congress in the centre of the capital, but, in case anyone had missed the point that the Army was now in charge, the current meeting was being held in the austere Committee Room Number Three in the PLA's Tibet Military Command Headquarters on the outskirts of Lhasa. Committee Room Number Three was a large, functional room with white walls and no windows. Bright unnatural light blazed down on the Committee members seated behind tables arranged in a horseshoe pattern. They faced a larger table behind which Zeng and two aides sat. The only decoration was a large photograph, hung behind Zeng, of a benevolent Mao staring wistfully into the middle distance beyond the assembled members. It had not gone unnoticed that Committee room Number Three was also used as a venue for what were considered to be the most serious Military Tribunals where a harsh justice was often dispensed.

"Regrettable as this news is, Comrades, we must move forward," continued Zeng. "We now face a dual threat and we must work together to restore order". Zeng, in his mid-fifties, already bald and small even by Han standards, smoked incessantly as he paced the room. His reputation went before him and no-one questioned his new found authority to effectively run Tibet from now on. Like most of the senior Officers on the Committee, he had been posted to Tibet to fight in the Chinese border war against India in 1962 and subsequently leap-frogged PLA commanders who had been in Tibet from the inception of the invasion of Tibet in the 1950s. Most important of all, he was a protégé of Lin Biao, Supreme Military Commander of the PLA, number two in the People's Republic of China only to Mao himself, and recently designated by Mao as his chosen successor.

"Firstly, we have to put behind us past factional difference and petty personal interests so that we can work for the best interests of the Party and the Revolution," continued Zeng.

"And secondly, we must crush all internal dissent to the will of the people.

"The first task I assume to be completed as from today. I know that everyone in this room will agree with me that the factional fighting of the last three years has caused nothing but harm to the Party. Whilst much progress has been made in ousting feudal practices in the Tibetan Autonomous Region, the danger from revisionists and splitists still exists and it is this which we must now unite to defeat once and for all." Zeng paused for his audience to absorb what he was saying, before continuing to speak in the same quiet, measured tone as before.

"The problem has been that the extent and intensity of the

factional fighting in part of the country has been such that we have lost sight of the insurrectionist violence right under our nose. Right here, virtually on our doorstep, less than a hundred kilometres from Lhasa".

"May I speak, Chairman?" Ren Rong had now risen from his seat a few places to the left of where Zeng stood. Ren, the Chief Political Commissar of the Armed Forces in Tibet who had supported the so called Nyamdrel faction in the recent turmoil, a faction previously opposed to the position taken by Zeng, until recently himself a supporter of the Gyenlog faction. Zeng had managed to out-manoeuvre Ren, but the wily Commissar had avoided being purged and in the interests of compromise and the greater good he was now one of the Central Committee's Vice-Chairmen.

Zeng looked at Ren with an air of distaste, for an instant regretting that he had not come down harder on the Commissar who might now be about to use this very public opportunity to cause trouble or express dissent. So let him, thought Zeng.

"Please speak, Comrade".

"Chairman, I assume that you are referring to what the locals are calling the Nyemo Revolt."

"I am", agreed Zeng, pausing for a moment before continuing.

"And I would like to take this opportunity to report to the Committee, Comrade Commissar, that I have recently received news that the ringleaders of the so-called revolt, including the nun Thrinley Choedron, have been arrested by units of the PLA and as we speak they are being brought to Lhasa for trial."

There was an eruption of voices in the room as members of the Committee took in the news. This was indeed a major coup for the Army. The Nyemo Revolt had been simmering for months beneath the turbulent surface of Party factional fighting as disenchanted Tibetans had taken advantage of the chaos to exact revenge and express their frustrations as best they could. It was in the countryside, where the introduction of the commune system was greatly resented, that dissent was at its most vociferous. It took many violent forms. Thinley Choedron and her supporters were alleged to have hacked to death Chinese cadres and their Tibetan supporters. Indeed most of the violence during the revolt took the form of attacks against PLA soldiers, Chinese cadres and Tibetans sympathetic to Chinese aims and methods. For some time it had been mistakenly seen as part the general faction fighting and as such ignored by the PLA who largely stayed in their barracks.

But the Nyemo Revolt was a cultural response to the continuing and worsening onslaught by the Chinese on Tibetan culture. Once it was recognised as such it was finally crushed by the PLA.

"This is indeed good news, Comrade Chairman, but do you have more information for the Committee regarding the Khampa rebels infiltrating the TAR from Mustang?"

Zeng began to wonder just how much Ren already new. Was he about to try to upstage him in front of the Committee? Thoughts rushed through his mind, but his expression remained composed. His voice, when he spoke again, was measured and even.

"I do not know what information you have, Comrade Commissar, but I do have a further piece of intelligence which may interest you all. We have received a communication from the Americans." Zeng paused again for effect and the whispering and head turning amongst members of the Committee grew more intense as they expressed their wonder at what the Americans might have to say to them, here in the TAR.

"Please continue," encouraged Ren, clearly not a party to this after all. He returned to his seat and waited.

"Well, comrades, it is not every day that we, here in the TAR, hear from the Americans, but this information has been provided through a seemingly impeccable source and we must act upon it. They have told us of the location of an ambush planned by rebels from Mustang. I will not go into details, but the other interesting fact is that they allege that there is an Englishman amongst them."

There was uproar as the members of the Committee clamoured for more information, each one trying to attract the Chairman's attention to extract more details. Zeng leaned forward and emphatically stubbed out his cheap cigarette before raising his hands for silence.

"Comrades! Comrades!" Gradually the meeting room fell silent.

"I will not bore such an esteemed gathering with the details of this operation. The group is small and we will soon deal with them. I assumed, correctly it seems, that you would be interested in this information, as it is, in its way, quite historic."

But the members of the Committee could contain themselves no longer.

"Who is this Englishman?" cried out one.

"Why is he here?" called another.

"Who sent him?"

"Why would the Americans warn us about this?"

"Why should we trust them?"

"Gentlemen, please," called the Chairman, raising his voice to regain order.

"The Americans could only have the information they provided us if they had direct contact with the terrorists and it does match up with what we know about them already. Naturally, it could be some kind of a trap, but what could the Americans have to gain from this?

"I am led to understand, from Lin Biao himself, that the Americans are making overtures to Beijing. I tell you this in the strictest confidence, comrades. So we are given this information as a small token of their good intentions."

There was a stunned silence as the members of the Committee took in this information. Talking to the Americans? The hated Yankees. Capitalist roaders. Hadn't the CIA propped up the terrorists in Tibet for the last ten years or more? The world was being turned upside down. What did all this mean?

"What this means, comrades," continued Zeng, trying to answer the questions before they were asked, "is that the world is changing. Since the fighting along the Ussuri River back in March, relations between the Motherland and the Russians could not be worse. Chairman Mao believes that improved relations with the Americans make strategic sense, as we cannot fight the Russians and the Americans. We need to concentrate on the most immediate threat, the Soviets. And it is good for the Americans because our border dispute with the Soviets means that the Soviets have to direct Divisions away from Eastern Europe to defend the border in the east.

"And closer to home, if the Americans stop supporting the rebels we can redirect troops from the TAR to the Soviet border.

"So some of you may be due a posting sooner than you expected," he added with a half-smile.

"But what of the foreigner?" interceded Ren. "You say that he is not American. Not a CIA agent? What do we know of him?"

"Very little. If we believe what the Americans tell us, he is here of his own volition and nothing to do with any Government." Again there was uproar in the room at this. It seemed too preposterous to believe that this foreigner was not an agent of the Americans.

"Comrades," continued Zeng, regaining the floor. "I was dubious at first, but what motive could they have for telling us of the existence of one of their own men. Surely, if he was one of their men and they had a change of policy as they claim, they would simply pull him out? But if he is not their man and we captured him, we would assume that he was and this would naturally cause a political incident at a time when, it seems, neither the Americans nor our masters in Beijing want such a thing. So if they know about him, but can't remove him quietly, the next best option is to tell us before we capture him.

"I agree that they may be lying, but there is no obvious reason for them to do so and they have too much to lose. In any case, on the one hand this is a relatively minor local military matter. I have ordered the local commander in Shigatse to deal with it on the ground and an operation is under way as we speak.

"And on the other hand, the politics of the relationship between the Motherland and the Americans will be played out at a higher level. As we are in a small way affected by the early stage of these developments, I felt it my duty to inform the comrades of the Revolutionary Committee, but I am sure I do not need to emphasise the importance of this not going beyond this room. We will deal efficiently and effectively with the rebels and leave the politics to others.

"Well, comrades, I feel that this is enough excitement for one meeting and so I suggest that we now adjourn."

With that Zeng began to pack his papers into his leather attaché case and light another cigarette. He rose and left the room followed by his two aides, leaving the other members of the Committee heatedly discussing what they had heard.

Chapter 32

অ

London

Abbi picked up the telephone at the third ring.

"Hello."

"Hello. Is that Miss McBride?" An American accent.

"Yes it is," replied Abbi. "Can I help you?."

"I do hope so, Miss McBride."

"Are you trying to sell me something?" She heard a short laugh on the other end of the line.

"Not at all, Miss McBride. I wanted to talk to you. About Mr. Smith."

An icy chill seemed to rush through Abbi at the mention of Smith's name. Her mind spun at the possibilities. Had he been injured, killed? It had been so long and she was desperate for news. But why this call out of the blue from an American? She forced herself to be composed and answered in what she hoped was a disinterested tone.

"Smith? No I don't know anyone called Smith." More angry now. "But what the hell is it do with you? Who the hell are you? Don't bother to answer. I'm hanging up now."

"Then why are you living in his house?" continued the American voice before she could slam down the receiver.

"It's not his house, it's...." Abbi blurted out before realising her mistake. She had moved into Gus's Lexington Mews house after Smith left. Gus was still in Hong Kong with his Regiment.

"And you're riding his motorbike. Not many women can ride a bike like that."

"You've been watching me. Who the fuck are you? I'm going to call the police if you don't fuck off and leave me alone right now" raged Abbi, thoroughly spooked by the thought that some man, some American weirdo, was spying on her.

"Please don't get upset Miss McBride. I just want to talk to you. About Mr Smith. Please."

"I told you, I don't know anyone called Smith. There are lots of Smiths around and they have lots of friends,but I'm not one of them so you've made a mistake. Please, leave me alone," she implored.

"There's no mistake, Miss McBride. I work for the Government, the American Government." Abbi began to feel sick.

"The American Government," she repeated stupidly, half to herself.

"Yes that's right, Miss McBride .Listen, I'll be in the café at the end of your road, the El Greco, I'm sure you know it. I'll be there in ten minutes. I'm sure a talk would be mutually beneficial so I hope you'll join me.

"By the way, my name's Larsen, Martin Larsen.

Abbi sat and did not move for several minutes. She realised that she was shaking. Who the hell was this person claiming to be some kind of agent for the American Government? How did he know so much about her and Smith and why would he be interested? Trying to calm herself, she went through their brief conversation in her mind for some clue as to what this might be about. What might Smith have got himself involved in that she didn't know about? Was she in some kind of danger?

She considered calling the police, but thought better of it. The El Greco was a café she used all the time. People there knew her so perhaps it was better to meet this Larsen first and see what he had to say. If there was a problem she would call the police.

Abbi was wearing Levi jeans and a tight fitting Che tee-shirt. She put on a wool sweater, combed back her dark hair and fastened it in a short pony tail. On her feet a pair of sensible lace-up heelless shoes – in case she had to run for it, she thought! It was a pleasant late spring morning so this would be fine. She slung her bag over her shoulder and left the house, taking extra care to make sure the door to the mews cottage was securely locked behind her. As she crossed the road into the bright sunlight she slipped on a pair of fashionable round lensed sun glasses.

The El Greco was genuinely Greek, or at least Greek Cypriot, having been owned and run by the same family for years. Abbi came in most days on her way home from work. As she approached the café she could see a man sat at one of the tables located under an awning on the pavement outside. Was this him? Her heart jumped and she nearly turned and ran. She had to force herself to keep going. Having seen her, the man rose from his seat, obviously recognising her, and he smiled broadly. He was tall, well over six feet, tanned and smartly dressed in a light weight brown suit. Taking off his expensive looking gold rimmed aviator sun glasses, he held out his hand to Abbi. She ignored it, but he didn't seem to notice the slight.

"Miss McBride," he announced, "I'm so glad you decided to come." He didn't look or sound like a pervert or a maniac, so what the hell was going on here? Well, she supposed, that was why she had come. To find out.

"Please, take seat." She sat where he pointed. He returned to his seat and put his sun glasses back on. He studied her obviously and without embarrassment for a minute before continuing.

"As I said on the phone, I'm Martin Larsen." Talking as if he'd invited her for a job interview rather than announcing that he'd been secretly watching her for God knows how long.

"What would you like?" He waved through the window to the interior of the café and a waiter appeared. Why were Americans so confident?

"Hello, Abbi. How are you today? What would you like?"

"Hello Ari. I'm fine, thanks. Can I have an espresso?"

"Certainly," and he was gone, glancing at Abbi's companion as he went.

Larsen continued to stir the coffee he already had in front of him.

"Who the fuck are you! What do you want with me?" hissed Abbi in low voice, at the same time looking round to make sure no-one could hear their conversation.

"As I said, earlier, I want to talk to you about Mr. Smith."

"You said you worked for the American Government. So prove it."   Larsen reached into his jacket pocket. Abbi flinched instinctively and began to lean back away from Larsen as he pulled out his wallet and put it on the table.

"You've been watching too many films, Abbi. I haven't shot

anyone in a busy street in broad daylight for ages."

Abbi reddened with embarrassment.

"Here, this is my identity card" It certainly looked official and impressive, but who recognises a US Government ID car? Abbi said as much.

"Well, perhaps I can tell you what I know about your Mr. Smith. You know, I think we've got off to a bad start, so I'll be completely up front with you. If you don't believe me you can walk away and I won't contact you again.

"But can I ask you another question first?" No reply from Abbi.

"OK. Do you know where Mr Smith is?" No problem with this one. She had no idea.

"No."

"Which country he's in?" A bit more tricky, this, but she responded with a resounding, or what she hoped was a resounding, "No."

"You surprise me." Larsen was silent for a moment. He seemed to be luxuriating in the warm sun. Abbi was suddenly aware of the din of the traffic passing only feet away heading towards Kensington High Street.

"Would it surprise you if I told you he was in Tibet?"

"Where?"

"Tibet," repeated Larsen.

"Yes it would surprise me," insisted Abbi vehemently.

"Do you know any Tibetan, Abbi?"

"I did a course a while ago. I wasn't very good."

"Do you know what *Rog Nang-Wa* means?" Abbi was no expert, but she could tell that his pronunciation was good. He obviously had some command of the language. Probably a great deal more than her own. She hesitated, so he answered for her.

"It means 'help' or 'to help'. But then you know that don't you, Miss McBride. Because it's also the name of a charity, if that's the correct term for its activities. A charity based in Katmandu ostensibly helping Tibetan refugees in Nepal. A worthy cause, no doubt. But I believe that you work for them here in London, don't you, Miss McBride."

"What if I do?" Abbi responded, half indignant, but half defensively. It seemed that Larsen knew everything about her.

"I'm an aid worker," she continued. "I've always worked for charities. Is that illegal in America?"

"Not at all. I just wanted it to be clear where we stand before I tell you my story. I believe that you started working for *Rog Nang-Wa*" after Mr. Smith disappeared."

"He didn't disappear. He went on holiday to India." The waiter appeared and Abbi fell silent as he placed the coffee in front of her.

"Thanks, Ari," she acknowledged, before picking up the tiny cup and sipping the hot intensely strong liquid with relief. She held the cup before her, waiting for Larsen to continue.

"Yes, he went to India with his friend the lama, Tashi. And then the pair of them went on to Nepal and up country to Mustang. And now he's in Tibet. Up to his neck in shit, to be quite frank, Miss McBride. As I think you know all too well, apart from the last bit, perhaps. But believe me it's true. So let me bring you up to date with Mr. Smith's adventures in case you genuinely don't know."

Larsen recounted briefly how Smith was now fighting with the *Khampas*, as he guessed that she knew. How the CIA had heard of his existence from a Khampa who had escaped from Tibet. How he was himself now trying to escape with the PLA in hot pursuit in possession of potentially valuable intelligence and hampered by the rescued nuns.

As he spoke Abbi tried to reconcile what Larsen told her with what she already knew. Smith had written to her several times from Mustang once he had established himself there. A regular if infrequent courier system had been established by the Tibetans in Mustang to communicate with supporters in Katmandu. From here Rog Nang-Wa forwarded Smith's letters to England. She could almost remember by heart that first rambling letter she had re-read it so many times.

Lo Mantang
Mustang
Nepal
10 Aug 70

Dear Abbi,

I doubt that you will receive this letter, but I had to write to you anyway. You probably already guessed that Tashi and I moved on from Dharamsala. We went to Katmandu and from there to Mustang (see if you can find it on a map). It took us a fortnight to get here, mostly on foot. Pretty hairy – , disguised as a Tibetan, dodging border guards and trying not to fall into the Kali Gandaki – which is this incredible raging river. It's cut a huge gorge north to south across the country and the only route to the capital is along its banks in or up above the gorge. It's as if we travelled further back in time every day until we finally arrived here in the Middle Ages. We don't come into Lo Mantang, where I'm writing from now, very often, as, to be honest, there's bugger all here. It is, however, the "capital" of Mustang.

Basically, Lo Mantang is a small walled town made of mud bricks with towers at each corner and huge gates which are locked every night. The town is a maze of tiny streets and in the middle is the King's palace, no less. No cars, just carts and yaks .Not much evidence that the Twentieth Century ever happened in fact.

The town's surrounded by fields on a flat plain and at the moment it's all very green. This little plain is about the only bit of flat land in the country as everywhere else seems to be mountains. But the weirdest thing is that we're only about ten miles from the Chinese border (or the Tibetan border if you prefer)

Sorry. I'm getting carried away with the scenery, when I wanted to explain to you what is going on. But this is the most incredible place. It is Tibet as far as I'm concerned. I'm in Tibet! There are monasteries perched on cliffs, monks wandering the streets, peasants tilling the fields and bandits riding round on horses.

There I go again! What I wanted to tell you is that I'm OK and I'm probably going to be here for a while. I've got a job. There's no better way to describe it, although the pay isn't great! I'm advising a group of *Khampas* led by a guy called Pemba. It took a while for them to accept me, but my Tibetan has come on in leaps and bounds and they seem to realise that I know what I'm talking about. It's great. I'm outdoors every day, getting plenty of exercise and getting fit again. I've even got my own horse! I haven't ridden for years, but got back into it pretty quickly.

These *Khampas* come from Kham in eastern Tibet and have been fighting the Chinese for years (I'm sure you've read all about this). They're based here now and we're staying in a *Magar* which is basically a military camp near a village called Tsarang south of Lo Mantang (just about everywhere in Mustang is south of Lo Mantang).

If you're reading this I suppose you're wondering why the hell I'm doing this. But if you know me as well as I think then maybe not. I blame Tashi and my uncle George.

Anyway, I'm writing more and more and not really explaining myself very well. The point is that since I left I realise how important you are to me and I don't want to lose that. I won't be here long, but this is something I want to do. I'll probably have to stay here for the winter now as once the bad weather sets in it's virtually impossible to get out til spring. But then I plan to come back to London and I hope we can pick up where we left off. Maybe that's a bit selfish and presumptuous of me, but it's what I want and I hope it's what you want.

You can write to me care of a charity called Rog Nang-Wa, JDA Complex, 4th Floor, GPO Box: 7832. Ward # 11, Bag Durbar, Sundhara Kathmandu, Nepal if you want to, which I hope you do.

I'll write again soon in any case.

Love

S

Smith's letter had finally convinced Abbi that her feelings for him had been right. They had become very close when they were both in London, but when Smith announced that he was going to India and disappeared without trace and not a word for weeks she began to doubt herself. But he was right. She did know him. The kind of man he was. There had only been one thing in his life, soldiering. That's what he knew and that's what he did. It was an alien world to Abbi at first, but as they had talked over the weeks they had been together she began to understand what drove him. His going to Mustang was him doing what he knew, for a purpose he felt was worthwhile. Wasn't she the same? Working for charities all over the world, trying to make a difference in her own small way? It was both selfish and good intentioned.

"Well, Miss McBride. Does this tie up with what you know of Mr Smith and his activities?" Larsen interrupted her train of thought, dragging her back to the present and the little café in

Kensington. She took another sip of her coffee, the strong bitter taste sharp in her mouth.

"So are you telling me you work for the CIA, Mr Larsen?"

"I guess I am."

Abbi thought about this. Everything he had told her made absolute sense. Terrifyingly absolute sense. She had written back to Smith the very same day she received his first letter, pouring out her feelings for him in a flood of emotion which shocked her with its intensity. She couldn't stop herself, the relief at hearing from him was so great, as was the joy in discovering that his feelings were as strong as her own.

It was nearly a month before the next letter came, but then they arrived every few days until the winter snow finally cut off the route out of Lo Mantang for the rest of the winter.

By that time, it became clear that Smith intended to join the *Khampas* on their raids into Tibet in the spring, even though he did not exactly say so.

Abbi did not try to dissuade him and as time passed she became more committed to the cause to which Smith had surrendered himself and began to work for *Rog Nang-Wa* part-time. Once again the line between the self-less and the selfish became blurred. She felt that the work was valuable, raising money for various projects carried out by the charity to help Tibetan exiles, people driven from their homeland by a brutal invading army. She often wondered what it might be like to be forced from the comfortable life she led in London into exile in a foreign country where she did not speak the language, had no possessions but those she had been able to carry. A country which was already mired in poverty and did not need or want a flood of unwelcome foreigners. How would she cope? But she enjoyed the work and being involved in the same cause made her feel closer to Smith.

She soon made friends with some of the Tibetans working in the office and her own increasing knowledge of the language made her popular and useful. Through them she also became more attuned to the clandestine side of the organisation which communicated with the *Khampas* in Mustang and sent them what funds and other support it could.

Neither Smith nor Abbi mentioned it in their letters, but by the spring she knew that he had indeed gone with the *Khampas* into Tibet. The work with *Rog Nang-Wa* helped to keep her mind off the awful and all too likely possibilities that could follow Smith's actions, but she knew that she would never change his mind even if she could speak to him. It also comforted her to think that, however indirectly, she was doing something to support him. But in her all too many sleepless nights she could think only of what might happen to the man she now realised she loved.

So what Larsen was telling her made complete sense, as did the fact that he was this alien creature, a CIA agent. How had thing come to this? Nobody in the real world found themselves in love with a man who was on the run from the largest army in the world in one of the most desolate and isolated places on earth, with a CIA agent telling you what a desperate situation he was in. Suddenly, all the fear and worry came welling to the surface and glistening reflective tears began to well up in Abbi's eyes.

"Hey, Abbi," said Larsen solicitously, standing and pulling a clean handkerchief from his pocket. He put his arm gently around her shoulder and pushed the handkerchief into her hand. She did not resist him and for a few seconds continued to cry into the clean white cotton material.

"Are you alright, Abbi?" it was Ari, the waiter, who had seen that she was upset and come outside to see what was he matter.

"I'm fine, Ari. Thank you," she sniffed, wiping her eyes and beginning to regain her self-control. "Just some family news. It's nothing, but thank you." Ari looked suspiciously at Larsen and began to retreat into the café.

"Hey! Could you get us a couple more coffees?" called Larsen. Ari did not answer, but disappeared inside.

"Well, Abbi, can I call you that?" He continued without waiting for an answer." I think you've answered my question. As I said before, your Mr. Smith is in deep shit. You obviously knew that already, but perhaps not just how deep." Abbi looked up at him, at his handsome, tanned, confident face.

"So if you know all this already, Mr. Larsen, if that's your name, what do you want with me? I don't have anything else to tell you."

"Well, Abbi, what I haven't told you is that your Government knows about his activities and they know about you. That's how I know about you. They told the CIA and persuaded them to come up with a plan to get rid of him." Abbi went cold as Larsen's words crashed over her like icy waves. The colour drained from her face as she stared at Larsen in disbelief.

"Get rid of him?" she repeated. "What do you mean 'get rid of him'?" Larsen didn't answer, but just looked at her with a 'what do you think I mean?' expression on his face..

What had Smith got her involved in? What had she allowed herself to be talked into? It had happened so gradually. Meeting Smith at a night school class, for God's sake. You don't meet men at night school who turn out to be on a CIA hit list. Being charmed by him, his confidence, his competence, his good looks. Then he goes abroad for a few weeks. Then he disappears and turns up having joined a band of guerrillas. Then he's fighting with them in Tibet. Then the British and American Governments get involved. Good God, she thought, how could she have been so naive?

"I know, Abbi," began Larsen after a moment." It sounds frightening. It is frightening But how well do you actually know Smith, really know him? What kind of a man he is and what he's capable of?" She was beginning to realise that the picture she had had in her mind up to that moment probably bore no resemblance to the world Smith was living in or to the dangers he was facing.

"The only good news in all this" continued Larsen cheerfully," is that the guy seems to be a natural. That's why he's still alive. Believe it or not, I tried to stop the plot to eliminate him over there, but he managed to foil it himself anyway."

Inside the café they could hear the roar of the Gaggia machine over the noise of the traffic and Ari arrived with the coffee. Larsen stopped speaking. The waiter looked at him suspiciously and then at Abbi, who smiled back weakly. Not knowing what else to do, Ari put down the two coffees and left without a word. As soon as he was out of earshot Larsen continued on his theme.

"The other thing which I guess has helped them avoid being captured or killed is the general chaos in the country. In China as well. You know about the Cultural Revolution?"

"A bit. I've seen the students on their demos in London waving their Little Red Books."

"Dumb bastards", snorted Larsen contemptuously. "If those spoilt shits could see what's happening in Tibet they might think again before spouting Mao's Thoughts. But probably not", he reconsidered.

"Anyhow, the country's slid into deeper and deeper turmoil since '65. It seems to us at the Agency that Mao's just covering his ass, directing attention away from his own problem. But that really don't matter 'cos the result has still been chaos. Young kids tipped out of school and university and unleashed on anybody Mao claims is anti-revolutionary, namely anybody without a good peasant pedigree." He paused for breath.

"Sorry, I'm starting to give you a lesson in modern politics here. But the reason this is relevant is that faction fighting has broken out amongst the Chinese in Tibet, even in the PLA. Added to this the Red Guards have been stamping up and down the country trying to force collectivisation on the Tibetans. Thousands of folks have been killed. The PLA's been so pre-occupied that they haven't been able to concentrate on the few bands of insurgents like the one Smith is with. At least not until now."

Abbi was not sure she needed the big picture, but she listened to Larsen's words, trying to take in what he was saying.

"Why until now?" she asked, the question he was obviously waiting for her to pose.

"Because it seems the PLA have finally come to their senses and got a grip of the situation. Basically, they've started banging heads together amongst the Chinese factions, rounded up a whole load of Tibetans who'd snuck in under their radar and started killing Party cadres without anyone really noticing, and now they're beginnin' to concentrate on the likes of your Mr Smith and his band. So it's time for them to get out. And fast."

Abbi was silent. Larsen seemed keen, almost eager to continue, so she said nothing.

"Let me tell you a bit more about myself, Abbi, it might make things a bit clearer," began Larsen, sipping his scalding coffee.

So he told Abbi about his years of involvement with the Tibet Project, as he described it. He told her about Camp Hale in Colorado, how he'd worked there as an instructor, learnt Tibetan and got to know the men who trained there over the many months they spent isolated from the world in the high fastness of the Rocky Mountains. He told her about the recruits who were parachuted into Tibet or infiltrated across the Indian border and about the many who were never heard of again, walking into PLA ambushes, being betrayed by hostile locals or disappearing who knew where. But he also told her of the successes and how they were now fewer and fewer as the US Government withdrew its financial support for the Tibetans and closed down Camp Hale.

"So you see, Abbi," he mused, "Me and a couple of other guys are the end of a long and noble line of CIA guys stretching back over maybe fifteen years working on this Project. Unlike some of the things we get involved in, a lot of us had a genuine feeling that we were doing something right here. That the Tibetans had a just cause, if you like. We loved those guys. Still do".

"And now I'm supposed to be helping to wrap the whole thing up. The Agency's efforts are now going into directing the Tibetan fighters into a Special Forces unit of the Indian Army. Not to use in Tibet, you understand, but probably against the Pakistanis, should the need arise. As far as my bosses are concerned the fighting in Tibet is history. There's a new game in town and the old one needs to be shut down asap."

The traffic continued to build up along the road by the El Greco Café. Customers came and went at nearby tables. As the sun rose, shadows crept over the table where Abbi and Larsen sat. But Abbi was oblivious to all this. She was miles away. Thousands of miles away. Trying to imagine again what the life Smith had taken on was really like and how she had become involved in it. How she found herself sitting at a table with a CIA agent telling her about US policy on the other side of the world and how it could have possibly come to have anything to do with her. But it had.

"So why are you telling me all this, Mr. Larsen? Why are you here? Why isn't someone from the British Government here if they know about my supposed involvement in this?"

"Well, Abbi, but please, call me Martin. Well, the British Government aren't that interested in you. You can't get in touch with Smith and neither can they, so they can't use you against him. The easiest thing is to keep it simple and get rid of him and that's what they're focussing on.

"And why am I here? I'm here because I still care about the Tibetan Project, the Tibetan cause if you like. As I told you, I got to know a lot of those guys real well. Sent too many of them off to their deaths as it turned out. But they all went willingly. More than willingly. So since I heard about your Mr Smith I've been giving him a lot of thought. This boyfriend of yours has wandered into a completely alien country with a bunch of rebels on horseback and taken on the PLA. Now he's got the US and British Governments on his case as well. But he's still on his feet and doing fine. I respect that. I admire that. He's doing what he does and he's doing it because he believes in it.

"And I sit behind a desk in New Delhi pulling levers and

pushing buttons and generally doing what I'm told in order to keep my career and my pension on track.

"What kind of a guy does that make me, Abbi?" Abbi looked at Larsen. Really looked into his tanned, confident, successful face for the first time. Into his Scandinavian blue eyes. She couldn't see the stalker, the weirdo, the sinister government agent she had expected to see. Instead she saw a man who was telling the truth. For good or ill, she believed him, believed his story, believed that he knew about her and Smith and where Smith was now, but also believed that in some way he did care about what happened to them, to her and Smith.

"So maybe you are telling me the truth, Mr Larsen."

"Martin."

"OK, Martin, perhaps you are telling me the truth, but I still don't see why you bothered. All you've done is made me even more frightened for Peter than I already was. I didn't know all these details so I was safe in my naivety, thinking there was a good chance he was coming back." Her voice became more hysterical as she continued. "But now you tell me half the known world is out to kill him and it sounds to me as if he has no chance of getting out of there alive."

"Hey, Abbi, that's not quite true. That's why I came to see you. I want Smith to get out of there and I think the two of us can do something to make that happen."

Abbi looked at Larsen again, a flicker of hope in her own eyes now, in spite of everything.

"What? What can we do?" she asked doubtfully. "I'll do anything you say."

"I'm in London on Agency business, but in a couple of days that'll be done and I've got some leave owing. What I'm suggesting is that the two of us take a trip to Katmandu."

Chapter 33

ༀ

The Tsangpo River, Tibet

Colonel Zhou set up his headquarters for the operation to intercept the Tibetan insurgents near the small village of Napshi on the northern side of the Yarlung Tsangpo River. This was the first crossing point over the river west of Shigatse and Zhou was sure that the Tibetans would have to use this or one of the few others on the river if they were to make good their escape to Mustang. The units he had deployed at every bridge and ferry across the river had reported in that they were in position. This had happened within twenty-four hours of Zhou's initial briefing to his commanders at the Garrison Headquarters and he was convinced that the fugitives could not have reached the river on foot or horseback before his men.

Zhou's headquarters consisted of four armoured personnel carriers, one of which was the colonel's command vehicle, three trucks and two jeeps. Hidden behind a large moraine, the vehicles were invisible from the north or west. Poles had been erected between and around the vehicles and camouflage netting draped over them to make detection even less likely. Movement within the camp was kept to an absolute minimum, and bored soldiers passed the time cleaning weapons, preparing food and eating, drinking tea, playing mahjong and smoking.

A couple of shell scrapes had been dug on the top of the moraine and from here men took turns to scan the approaches with binoculars. Other troops had been deployed on the rough road north of Napshi and in the village itself.

Napshi was a couple of kilometres to the north of the headquarters and an unmade road ran from the village southwards to the river, this road being itself crossed by the main road which ran east-west back to Shigatse about eighty kilometres away. A low wooden bridge wide enough to take one vehicle at a time ran out across the wide rocky plain for several hundred meters before it began to span the milky water of the river itself. Soon melt water from the mountains would swell the river and cover the plain, flooding under the whole width of the bridge, but at the moment it was about five hundred meters wide.

The grey rocks and pebbles of the river bed eventually gave way to low sandy banks along which juniper bushes and a few squat willows struggled for survival. The dry dusty plain then extended towards the low foothills on which Napshi was established beyond the danger of flooding. The cultivated fields of the village in which the first green shoots of the season were beginning to appear already stood out in the distance, so marked was the contrast with the surrounding barren earth.

Zhou sat at a table outside his command vehicle, making the most of the sunshine breaking in dappled bursts through the cam net above him. He gazed briefly at the cobalt blue sky, struck once again by the contrast between the drab landscape and the intense colour of the cloudless sky, the likes of which he had seen nowhere else. After a winter trapped in his office and the garrison he was finally starting to come alive again as he settled into the routine of what he considered to be the proper life a soldier, the life he sorely missed in camp, even at his age.

He turned his attention back to the meal of rice and vegetables rapidly cooling in the mess tin in front of him and began to eat with a relish for simple food and the simple way of living of an infantryman which he had almost forgotten.

Before Zhou could finish his meal a signaller came rushing excitedly over from the signals truck.

"Sir, the Commander is on the net," he blurted out. Zhou rose wearily from his canvas chair wondering what the hell this could be about and strolled at a leisurely pace towards the vehicle.

In the back of the gently lit signals truck, with its tiny red and green lights glowing and flashing sporadically, Zhou was given headphones and a handset into which he spoke gruffly.

"Zhou here, over."

"Zhou, at last." Zhou recognised the voice of his overbearing and ambitious Senior Officer immediately, even over the radio's crackling static. The professional soldier found it difficult to disguise his resentment at having to kowtow to a younger man who he felt owed his meteoric rise in the PLA to his father's senior position in the Party back in Beijing.

"It seems," continued the Commander, "that your little band of traitors have had a change of heart about their future plans. I'm sending you a secure signal with the details, but I wanted to speak to you myself to emphasise that you are still to sit tight where you are. Do you understand, Zhou? Under no circumstances are you to move the men you have deployed until you get a direct order from me, over."

Zhou's mind was in turmoil. What had changed? Was he going to be left out of the action? Where had this new information come from? He pressed the button on the handset and began to speak, aware of the agitation in his voice.

"Can you provide us with some more information? How long are we to stay here, over? "

"Do you understand my order, over?"

"Yes, over," acknowledged a deflated Zhou.

"Good. Read the signal. It's on its way, out." Then silence. Zhou dejectedly handed the headset back to the signaller and climbed down the steps leading from the vehicle and back into the bright blue day. Returning to the command vehicle, he sat before his now cold meal and began to prod it with his chopsticks. His mind struggled to assess the information he had been given and work out what might have happened to suddenly marginalise him in an operation he had thought he was running.

But it was not long before the signaller re-appeared, brandishing a piece of paper with the Commander's secure signal on it. The Colonel snatched it from him and began to read:

"Have received reliable intelligence that Tibetan fugitives are NOT currently proceeding to Mustang. Are instead intending to rescue prisoner being transferred to Lhasa. Prisoner left Gyantse under armed escort this morning. So far unable to contact convoy. Have deployed forces from Gyantse and Lhasa garrisons plus air support to assist convoy and capture fugitives. Remain in your position and await further instructions.

Message ends.
Garrison Commander"

Zhou rocked back in his chair as if the signal might spontaneously combust in his hands. His sallow features turned crimson as rage at his own impotence surged through him. A sudden pain in his chest turned his rage to momentary panic as he thought he might be having a heart attack.

"Are you unwell, Colonel?" it was the signaller still standing at his side in case there was a response to the message. From his expression it seemed that this was not the response he had been expecting.

The words brought Zhou back to his senses. He breathed deeply and the moment was passed. What was the matter with him? He wasn't going to keel over and die in this hell hole. He was in control again.

Other Officers might have raged and taken out their anger and frustration on the young conscript, but the old colonel had a genuine affection for these men, dragged away from home and family and dumped down in this God forsaken place on the other side of the Motherland, probably with no real notion of just where they were.

"I'm fine, comrade. I think I swallowed something." He coughed loudly for effect. It was true that he was being forced to swallow something he would prefer not to. But he was a soldier and such things were part of a soldier's lot. And he was an old campaigner not about to be out-manoeuvred by the rebellious Tibetan scum or his effete and dilettante superior Officer.

He needed to think through the possibilities, be patient, and see if, no not if, but how he might still be able to turn the situation back to his own advantage.

"Get me Major Tang."

Chapter 34

ལ

Karo La Pass, Tibet

Following the modern road from Gyantse to Lhasa fifty-five years later, Francis Younghusband would have seen little discernible change to the road of his day. Perhaps it was more hard packed, but it was still un-surfaced and often impassable in bad weather in winter. It also remained the main highway from Shigatse to Lhasa, regularly used by Chinese vehicles.

The two drab green painted trucks now driving at speed along the Friendship Highway had left Shigatse the day before and spent the night in Gyantse at the garrison there. The first vehicle had the traditional canvas cover of military trucks the world over, but the second had a squat rectangular box body on the back, with no windows and one solid looking door, locked with a heavy padlock outside, allowing access at the rear.

They expected to be in Lhasa before nightfall and were making good time as they approached the Karo La pass. Had he been interested, the driver of the first vehicle might have seen in the distance the damaged remains of Ralung Monastery in the hills to the south, recently ravaged by Red Guards. But he could not fail to notice the towering peak of Nojin Kangstang, its brooding snow-capped twenty-two thousand foot bulk dominating the skyline to the north.

As the vehicles climbed, the crags of the surrounding mountains crowded in on them more and more until the road was tightly confined within the pass. The drivers worked noisily through the gears to maintain speed as best they could, but the incline was against them and they slowed inexorably. Not that it mattered. They had plenty of time to complete the journey.

Rounding a sharp bend, they were suddenly confronted by a rock fall. Large boulders had fallen from the northern side of the road and spread right across the carriageway, completely blocking it.

Rock falls were not an uncommon occurrence on this road, especially after the recent rain and the trucks carried the gear and manpower to shift it. They might not make Lhasa by nightfall after all, but they would soon be on their way again. The driver of the front truck was relaxed and almost pleased. Clearing the fall would break the monotony of the drive and give him a bit of a story to tell in the barracks that night. He put the vehicle into neutral and took out a cigarette, lit it and passed one to his passenger. There was no hurry. He wound down the window and sucked in the cold thin air.

As the driver's hand brought the cheap cigarette to his mouth his body suddenly convulsed. An instant before, the windscreen had shattered and his head was now catapulted backwards to impact sickeningly against the rear panel of the cab. But he was already dead, the tumbling 7.62 round from the Dragunov having caused a massive trauma to his brain and killing him instantly.

Not registering yet what had happened, the other soldier looked in horror at the mess which was now his comrade's head. He instinctively leaned across to help him, although it was already too late. As he did so a second round struck him in the back of the head and he slumped forward over the driver.

Tendruk had been watching the vehicle through the telescopic sight of the sniper rifle for several minutes from his sanger in the crags above the road, waiting for the vehicles to come to a halt at the rock fall. By that time they were only about three hundred metres below him. He had done well on the sniper course at Hale, but at this range and with this rifle it was almost too easy.

"Fish in a bucket," he exclaimed delightedly in his American English to Tashi who crouched beside him, peering down the sight of his rifle.

"Barrel," corrected Tashi without looking at Tendruk.

"What?"

"Its barrel, shooting fish in a barrel," insisted Tashi in English, firing a short burst at the trucks below. Tendruk began to look for other targets, other fish.

The front vehicle was immobilised by the loss of its driver, but suddenly the sound of screeching tyres echoed between the crags as the driver of the second truck jammed it into reverse, spitting out plumes of gravel from the rear wheels as it careered backwards down the hill. Immediately, a burst of automatic fire raked the cab, shattering all the windows. The truck swerved violently out of control to come to a jarring halt as its back end crashed loudly into the rock wall at right angles to the road.

Almost at the same time the tailgate of the front vehicle crashed down and PLA soldiers in their green fatigues poured out onto the road, scattering instinctively in every direction. They were met by a hail of gun fire, stumbling and falling as the rounds struck home. But enough of them managed to get to the only obvious cover, beneath the two vehicles, and a couple, more composed than the rest, opted to stay inside the truck. Pressed flat on the floor, they were hidden from sight by the canvas cover and given some protection by the thin metal sides.

The surviving soldiers were now much harder targets for the Tibetans firing at them from the cliffs above and as the Chinese began to realise this they started to return fire in the general direction of their antagonists. Knowing that the operation needed to be over as quickly as possible, Smith stepped out briefly from cover and tossed a grenade downwards at the first vehicle. It landed on the road in front of the truck, rolled a few feet and exploded with a bright flash of flame and a deafening roar, scattering lethal shards of metal in all directions. In the confined space between the rock wall of the pass and the truck the effect was devastating. A second grenade followed, landing near the rear of the first vehicle and adding to the carnage.

"Cut off groups, cover us!" shouted Smith. Rounds began to tear into the stranded trucks again, fired by the two small groups of Tibetans deployed further up and down the road to cut off any of the enemy who managed to escape from the ambush site. Smith and the men from the main ambush party now scampered down the steep rocks towards the road, dodging behind cover when the y could as it was impossible in the noise and chaos to tell whether they were still being fired at.

As they reached the level of the road Smith stretched out his arms on either side and waved them in a downwards motion to indicate that everyone should get down. They dived for what cover they could find, as did Smith himself.

"Stop firing!" he bellowed, now waving one hand above his head to reinforce the order. Gradually the Tibetans ceased fire. There was no returning fire from the Chinese and for a short time, little sound apart from the groaning of the wounded.

Having clipped on a new magazine, Smith now leapt the last few feet from his cover onto the road and immediately flung himself full length onto the hard damp surface. For a second he was aware of the smell of the musty earth, cold and damp beneath his body,

Without aiming he pressed the trigger and swung his rifle in an arc at ground level. Rounds ripped beneath the two vehicles tearing mercilessly into flesh and rubber as the trucks' few undamaged tyres hissed and exploded and the vehicles sank down onto their wheel rims.

Instantly, Pemba and the other men came charging down behind Smith onto the road, sprawling out on their stomachs, chins pressed into the hard earth to present as small a target as possible. They stared anxiously down the length of their weapons, ready to engage a target. But there was only stillness and silence.

It was several minutes before Pemba was satisfied that it was safe and called to Smith.

"You take the front vehicle and we'll take this one." He nodded towards the second vehicle skewed across the road to their right about fifty yards away.

"OK".

Pemba indicated to three men to follow him. They stood and began to walk almost casually down the road, but holding their weapons at the ready. Smith rose to a crouching stance and indicated to the rest of the group to advance towards the first vehicle.

They followed his example, keeping as low as possible to present a small target to any survivors.

Suddenly a burst of automatic fire lit the darkened interior of the canvas covered truck catapulting two of Pembas men forward and downward, crashing to the ground as the rounds tore into their backs. Immediately Smith and the others returned fire into the truck. The firing from within stopped. They darted forward and ducked under the truck, waiting.

Smith looked to the Tibetan nearest the rear of the vehicle, Gyalo, and made a gesture to him of a man throwing a ball underarm. Gyalo produced a grenade from inside his *chuba*, and, reaching round to the tailgate, tossed it gently into the vehicle. Smith and the Tibetans dived to the ground as they heard the grenade roll almost lazily along the metal floor before exploding and ripping the canvas roof to shreds in a plume of flame. For a couple of minutes they were all stunned by the closeness of the explosion. As Smith eventually gathered his wits and looked to the others he could see a trickle of blood running from Gyalo's left ear, his eardrum burst by the pressure of the blast.

"Gyalo!" Smith called at the top of his voice. Gyalo didn't respond and Smith realised that he had not heard his own command as they had all been deafened by the explosion.

Waving to attract their attention Smith indicated that the others beneath the vehicle should check to make sure there were no more enemy survivors. He then dashed, still bent double, towards Pemba and the two men who had fallen to the ground. Pemba was squatting at the side of them.

"Dead," he said as Smith arrived next to him in a few hurried steps. "Both dead."

"Too fucking casual" muttered Smith to himself in English. Then in Tibetan to Pemba.

"OK. We've got to leave them for now and finish the job." Pemba nodded his agreement. Smith looked back to the first truck to see that the other men had now completely checked it. He and Pemba then ran the last few steps to the other vehicle and dived beneath it. Other Tibetans in the rocks above were now covering them as they quickly made their way to the back of the truck and peered up at the stout back door and its hefty padlock. Pemba looked around and then, satisfied that there was no obvious danger he clambered up the back until he was high enough to attack the lock with the butt of his rifle. This had little effect so he turned the weapon around and shouted "Get down," in Tibetan. An instant later he pulled the trigger, giving the lock a short burst.

Smith half expected Pemba to be killed by a ricocheting round, but, amazingly, he was unharmed and the lock, not as solidly made as it looked, fell away. Pemba swung open the door and entered the rear of the vehicle as Smith clambered up behind him. The interior was in darkness and neither man had a torch. At first they could see nothing, but they could smell the acrid stench of sweat and human fear. Then, as the light from the rear filtered inside and their eyes adjusted to the dim light, they could make out three figures in Tibetan dress chained to the sides of the vehicle. Two of the men were squatted on their haunches looking terrified and the other, Lhotse, lay on a rough wooden pallet.

"It's OK," said Pemba in a loud whisper. "We're here to help you." Then looking at Lhotse, "Lhotse! It's Pemba. We've come to get you out of here." Lhotse looked back at his two rescuers with no obvious sign of recognition.

Although no-one had voiced further doubts once they had agreed to try to rescue Lhotse, Smith was undoubtedly not the only one to have wondered how they would cope if they did succeed only to find that Lhotse was still in a bad physical condition. After all it had been a far from unlikely scenario with the intelligence they had. As the adrenalin of combat seeped from his body, Smith's mind raced, confronting the reality of rescuing a possibly badly injured man from a high mountain pass on foot or horseback and hundreds of miles from safety with the PLA in hot pursuit. An added concern for which they could make no definite plans beforehand, but which they now had to face, was who and in what condition any other prisoners in the vehicle might be.

But the first problem was how to release the three men from their chains. Although Pemba had been too impatient to wait for it in order to force the lock of the rear door, they had had the foresight to borrow a heavy hammer and makeshift chisel from the monastery workshop before they left Tsechen Damchos Ling for just such an eventuality. Smith leaned out of the back of the lorry and called for the tools. A couple of minutes later, Chungla, quickly hitching up her robes, was climbing into the back of the vehicle.

Both men looked at the girl as if they were wondering again how they had allowed her to talk them into this mess. It might have been the right thing to do morally, but tactically it was starting to look more and more like a suicide mission.

"Give me the tools," requested Pemba in an even voice, not showing any doubt or concern he was feeling for the way things might turn out. As he began to hammer away at the locks Smith looked up and down the road with his binoculars for signs of Chinese reinforcements then up into the crags to make sure that the others were still looking out for potential dangers.

"OK, check all the soldiers are dead and get any gear worth having," Smith shouted to the Tibetans down on the road. They would use the opportunity to resupply with anything useful the Chinese casualties might be carrying, especially ammunition, but also medical supplies and even rations. Food was always in short supply to fighters who had to live off the land. As more monasteries were ransacked by the Red Guards so there were fewer places the fighters could rely on for food and shelter. Peasants and nomads living in the countryside lived constantly on the edge of starvation and did not see the *Khampas* as their saviours. But if they had any surplus they might want to sell or trade so any personal items of value which could be used to barter for food with locals later as well as cash in yuans would also be taken.

"Get the horses, Tashi," he called to his friend once he was satisfied that they were safe for the moment. The animals had been hidden higher up the road out of sight. In a few minutes they appeared led by Tashi and three of the nuns. Four extra horses, all they could muster, had been brought from the monastery for Lhotse and any other prisoners they could rescue. The two dead Tibetans were laid over their saddles face down and their hanging arms and legs tied tightly together to prevent them falling from the horses once the party was under way.

The sound of metal hammering on metal still echoed in the narrow pass as Pemba continued to work in the back of the prison truck. First one and then another Tibetan eventually came blinking into the daylight, looking suspiciously to right and left as they did so. Then, seeing the horses and armed Tibetans around them they began to smile as they realised that freedom from the Chinese was at hand.

"Here, take a horse each," called Tashi to the two men. "Can you ride?"

"Of course," replied the first as they took the reins of a horse each.

"I'm Tashi," the lama introduced himself. "Who are you?" The two men briefly glanced at one another before responding.

"I am Lobsang and this is Mila," volunteered one of the men. Smith had been watching the scene from the back of the truck. For some reason he could not have explained, these two men gave him a bad feeling. But before he had time to analyse his concerns Pemba was calling for his help from inside the truck

Smith ducked back inside and as his eyes accustomed to the dim light he could see Lhotse sitting on the pallet, his hands now free of the chains. Even in the poor light Smith could also see that Lhotse was in a bad state. A bandage was swathed around his head and covered one eye. His face looked white and damp with sweat, his one good eye not seeming to recognise the people who had come to rescue him.

"Let's get him out of here," said Pemba. The two men helped him to his feet and began to walk the few steps to the back of the truck. Once on his feet, Lhotse did seem to be stronger than he looked and was able to support himself.

"Bring a horse," called Pemba and one of the nuns lead an animal to the back of the truck. It stood about the same height as the top step of the vehicle and so it was not too difficult to get Lhotse to straddle the horse. A horseman all his life, he immediately seemed more comfortable and alert, although he still did not acknowledge those around him.

"Can you ride, Lhotse?" enquired Pemba. Lhotse looked at Pemba apparently uncomprehendingly, but at least he stayed on the horse.

"Do we need to tie him on," asked Smith.

"I think he'll be alright," replied Pemba. "Let's see how he gets on. I will lead his horse to begin with." Then in a louder voice to the whole company. "Alright, mount up. Let's get away from here." Men and women scrambled down the crags to the road and grabbed the reins of their horses. Those who had been collecting equipment from the dead now finished packing what they had found into their bags ready for redistribution when they were in a safer place.

"Just one more thing to do," announced Smith. "Gyalo, come with me. We'll catch you up."

The men and the nuns were soon all on their mounts and the party was heading down the road back towards Gyantse.

Soon Smith was back at the rear of the small party. The plan was to leave the road as soon as they could, heading south.

Chapter 35

ཕ

Karo La Pass, Tibet

In the dim light of the interior of the vehicle men sat stern faced, feet braced against the lurching and sliding of the APC as it rumbled at top speed towards its destination along the rough unmade road. They faced each other in two rows with their backs pressed into their seats, weapons standing upright on their butts and clutched in nervous hands. Each soldier was in full combats with webbing pouches strapped around their waists and helmets fastened. Even Private Cheng, the universally acknowledged Company clown, could find nothing to make a joke about.

It was hot in the close confines of the crew compartment and sweat trickled down the faces of a couple of the soldiers. But it was not only the heat that made them sweat. Neither Cheng nor anyone else in the section had seen a shot fired in anger since being conscripted into the PLA and posted to the farthest reaches of the Motherland. Of the eighteen months or so that most of them had spent in the Tibetan Autonomous Region, the majority of their time had been spent confined to barracks in Lhasa or Gyantse. Some of them had seen action in one desolate Tibetan village or another, where they had been called upon to harass the villagers for misdemeanours against the Party. Property might be smashed and arses kicked, but no-one fought back.

Then there were a couple of occasions when the Platoon had been used to remind those hot heads in the Red Guards who was actually running this country. Hundreds of them running through the streets of Gyantse, waving their Little Red Books, chanting slogans and smashing windows. Permanent revolution might be a nice idea for the Party bosses back in Beijing, but it couldn't be allowed to be more than a good idea out here, near to the border, where rebels were still apparently operating, even after all these years. That's what the Company Commander said. So out they went from the garrison, clubs and shields in hand to crack a few skulls. What an adrenalin rush that had been for Cheng, the peasant boy from Canton. Apparently, one young lad in the Red Guards had died and about ten of them wound up in hospital. But they were running amok and the Army just couldn't let that continue, could they?

"But this is different," said the Platoon Commander when he had briefed the platoon in front of their vehicles on the parade square in Gyantse garrison that morning.

"These splitist rebels are well armed. They have certainly already murdered some of our comrades in cold blood. Cowards that they are, they always attack when we do not expect it and never fight in open battle. Our intelligence says that they are setting up a cowardly ambush for one of our convoys on the road to Lhasa even now as I am speaking to you.

"Our job is to get there to support our comrades as fast as possible. So get to your vehicles. NOW!"

Cowards they might be, but the whole section had heard the rumours of the attack on the convoy on the Friendship Highway only days before. Officially, it never happened, but the word in the barracks was that every man had been killed. Even the wounded had been finished off and they had all been stripped of their kit and the vehicles burnt. This was a different proposition to street fight with a mob of students.

So the APC raced on towards its destination, accompanied by the two other armoured vehicles in the Platoon, thirty men in all. They knew that others had been deployed behind them, but they were the advanced guard.

After what seemed like hours, but had only in fact been about ninety minutes, the soldiers in the rear of the lead vehicle became aware of a loss of speed as they began to ascend the pass. Progress became slower and slower as the road became steeper. But they kept moving.

"Perhaps we'll get right over the pass," volunteered one of the men, breaking the long silence inside the vehicle.

"Perhaps those cowardly bastards never got here, or we got here before them," responded Cheng, smiling one of his cheeky smiles for the first time since they had left Gyantse. Murmurs of agreement spread around the compartment and the tension was broken. They continued to climb.

"Stay alert back there," came the command from the section commander over the intercom from his position next to the driver.

Then silence, except for the increased revving of the engine. The minutes passed and with each minute the optimism of the men in the lead vehicle increased.

They came to a sudden halt. At first there was only silence. A frisson of fear ran through Cheng and he instinctively grasped his rifle more tightly.

Then the rear doors of the APC burst open, flooding the dim interior with harsh light.

"De-bus left and take cover!" came the barking command before any of them had time to think. They had no idea what they were stepping out into, but, as so many times in training, they instantly poured out of the vehicle, to find themselves in the narrow confines of the pass, its massive crags towering thousands of feet above them, dwarfing them. They dived for what cover they could find and flattened themselves against the ground, already breathless with fear and exertion and fumbling to get a firing position.

"Cheng, Lo, Yuang. Get ready to move. The rest of you cover them." It was the Platoon Commander. As Cheng glanced quickly over his shoulder to where the command had emanated he saw the Platoon Commander's vehicle in the middle of the narrow road about fifty metres behind his own APC, which was pulled in close to the wall of the pass. The vehicle mounted heavy machine guns pointed menacingly up the road, their lethal potential giving Cheng much needed confidence in his precarious position. Some distance back he could see the third vehicle. Men were pressed against the sides of the rear vehicles, ready to move forward when called.

Looking to his front now, Cheng registered for the first time two other PLA vehicles about a hundred metres ahead of him, slewed across the road, most of their tyres flat, the pock marks of bullet holes clearly visible in the bodywork of each one.

There was no sign of life and no sound except for the diesels of the Troop's APCs, occasionally revved by their drivers as if ready to pounce into action. To Cheng's discomfort, several bodies in PLA uniforms were clearly visible sprawled on the ground around the vehicles. He realised with a start that he undoubtedly knew these men, or had known them. Men? No more than boys really. Country boys like him.

Trying to clear his mind of the awful possibilities of the situation, Cheng scanned the crags for signs of movement. To his relief, he could see no motion. No rebel adjusting his firing position or dislodging loose rock beneath his felt boots or peering into a telescopic sight. They wouldn't still be here. Why would they? They had done what they came to do and cleared off, sharpish. That's how they operated.

"They're long gone," called out the Platoon Commander, as if reading Cheng's mind.

"But we need to check this out." A pause.

"You three men, move forward carefully and check the first vehicle. AND SPREAD OUT!"

"MOVE!"

But Cheng wasn't ready to move. His limbs were lead as he tried to force them to rise him from the ground. Then finally, after an age, he was on his feet. Trying to hide behind his rifle as he struggled to propel himself forward. He felt utterly naked.

But nothing happened.

He began to move forward. Out of the corner of his eyes he could see Lo and Yuang on either side of him, looking up nervously at the crags above. Finally they found themselves alongside the first vehicle. It was at right angles, the front pointing into the centre of the road. The windscreen was shattered into a million pieces and the driver's door riddled with dozens of bullet holes. Looking up, they could see the bloodied head of the driver pressed against the amazingly unbroken side window of the driver's cab.

The three men looked at each other, visibly shocked at the first sight in their lives of the reality of a dead comrade. Instinctively, Private Lo stepped forward and put a foot on the step of the vehicle.

"Careful!" cried the Platoon Commander, his binoculars trained on the three soldiers. Cheng and Yuang crouched a few metres from the vehicle and again scanned the crags above them as Lo pulled himself onto the step. Grasping the handle he gently opened the door. The weight of the driver slumped against it pushing it wider.

The explosion blew the door completely off, killing Lo instantly.

"Fucking hell," cried the Platoon Commander in shock and disbelief.

Cheng and Yuang were smashed to the ground by the blast. Almost as one, the other men of their section began to dash forward.

"STOP! GET DOWN! GET DOWN!" screamed the Platoon Commander. "STAY WHERE YOU ARE. NO-ONE MOVE!"

"Cheng, Yuang! Can you hear me?" No response. The Platoon Commander called out to his men again. Focussing his binoculars on them, holding his breath, he waited. And then he saw, yes, Cheng was moving.

"Cheng!"

"What?" came the confused and somewhat irritated reply. The Platoon Commander could not help smiling to himself.

"Cheng! Are you alright?" By now he could see that Yuang was moving as well.

"Medics!" Two men with satchels over their shoulders came scuttling forward, bent almost double, as the rest of the platoon covered them.

The medics checked Cheng, but to their and his amazement he seemed to be unharmed, as was Yuang. They carried the two men into cover and both drank greedily from their canteens. Apart from a raging thirst and a ringing in his ears, Cheng was relieved to realise that he was not injured. He sat and watched as the rest of his section now moved cautiously forward and took cover crouching on either side of the road close to the doorless truck.

A stretcher was brought forward and the grisly task of removing Private Lo's remains was quickly conducted. Covered by a blanket, the stretcher was then carried back to the armoured ambulance which had now arrived with the rest of the Company farther down the road. But no other troops came forward. Following the booby trap incident it would be the forward Platoon's task to clear and secure the area. No more risks could be taken, but the road had to be re-opened. Time was ticking away. Time in which the insurgents were getting further away.

"Alright!" shouted the Platoon Commander. "Spread out in a line across the road a couple of metres apart." The men of Cheng's section began to cautiously emerge from their scant cover and form a line facing up the dirt road.

"Move forward. Scan the ground in front of you as you go. Keep away from the vehicles." The line progressed slowly forward, dark eyes scanning the ground in front as they went. Cheng watched as the line drew level with him and then passed him to proceed up the incline. The acrid smell of detonated plastic explosive hung heavily in the air.

Taking a last swig from his water bottle, he began to struggle to his feet.

"I'm fine," he said in answer to the unasked question from the surprised medics. They let him go and he began to walk towards the receding line of troops. He stopped momentarily as the rush of blood to his head made him feel dizzy. But the dizziness soon passed. He was fine.

The Platoon Commander was about to call Cheng back, but he looked alright. He obviously wanted to get back into the fray with his comrades. Probably the best thing.

By now he was part of the short line of men still plodding cautiously up the road.

Like most modern weapons, anti-personnel mines are not designed to kill, but to maim. The one Cheng stood on took his left leg off just below the knee, leaving behind a ragged mess of bone and tissue and blood soaked cloth.

Chapter 36

ༀ

Near Ralung Monastery, Tibet

The *Khampas* left the road only a couple of hours before the Chinese relief column arrived at the ambush site. But it would take three more hours before the Chinese troops were able to deploy men in pursuit, the time it took to clear the booby traps and deal with the casualties. Even then they could not be sure which way the fugitives had fled. They split into two groups, advancing tentatively in both directions, led by soldiers on foot along the road until they picked up signs of the Tibetans.

Although it was a dangerous option, the *Khampas* had taken the risk and initially followed the road in the direction of Gyangtse, from where the relief column would come, knowing that they could soon leave it on a narrow trail leading into the high mountains to the south. The trail led by a circuitous route to Ralung Monastery where they arrived as the light began to fade.

"We'll rest up here for a few hours," announced Pemba to the other riders as they approached the buildings.

"It doesn't look too inviting," said Smith as he drew his horse alongside Tashi's.

"No," replied Tashi. "Not any more. But this was once an important place, Ralung means 'the heart of the lotus' because the monastery is set in this bowl surrounded by eight high peaks capped with snow. It reminded its founders of the lotus heart circled by its petals."

"Very poetic," replied Smith in a flat tone.

"There were so many auspicious symbols in the landscape here that the monastery became the seat of the Drukpa Order, one of the most powerful in Tibetan Buddhism before the invasion. It was one of the most sacred sites in Tibet."

"Not any more, I guess," retorted Smith as they came closer to the cluster of buildings which formed the monastery complex, or what remained of them.

"That." Tashi pointed in the direction of a pile of rubble surrounded on four sides by a badly damaged stone wall.

"That was once a *chorten* which stood five stories high."

Smith could see now that not a single building was undamaged, and most of them were completely destroyed. Low walls, heaps of stone and mud brick now defined what had once been a thriving religious community.

"It was here for seven hundred years. Until the Chinese came with their artillery. The Red Guards burnt the books and everything else was loaded into trucks and taken away. No doubt for some Party boss to sell to line his pocket."

Smith did not need to ask Tashi what had happened to the inhabitants of the monastery. The story was the same as in thousands of monasteries across the Land of the Snows. The monks were driven out, forced to marry and work on the land. Thamzing was the fate of many, enforced re-education in the ways of Communism and the Thoughts of the Chairman. Many were re-educated to death.

Pemba had selected one of the buildings, an old stable, which offered most protection from the wind and where a cooking fire could be lit unseen. The horses were led inside and men and nuns quickly began to unload what they needed for the night from the uncomplaining animals. Without need of further orders a fire was lit, fodder collected and the animals on which they all so depended quickly fed. When possible they were hobbled and allowed to forage for themselves when the party rested, but so close to their Chinese pursuers they could not risk the horses being out in the open.

The fire raised spirits and soon tea was being distributed to everyone, including those unlucky enough to be on guard at a distance from the camp. The rare smell of wood smoke in a treeless land filled the room as splinters of damaged roof beams were heaped on the fire. Smith wondered if he should be feeling guilty for enjoying the fire now consuming a small part of these once sacred buildings, but decided that the gods no doubt realised their predicament and would not be angry.

Lhotse was laid by the fire in an attempt to revive him. He had managed to stay on his horse during their flight from the ambush, but one of the *Khampas* had had to lead his horse the whole way as the injured warrior stared blankly ahead. Still he showed no sign of recognising those around him as he cradled a mug of steaming tea in both hands and the firelight danced on his ghostly white sweat glossed face.

"Let me look at him," said Tashi leaning forward and starting to peel back the bandages on Lhotse's head. Chungla looked on with a mixture of shock and fascination as the suppurating wounds on Lhotse's head, back and chest were gradually revealed.

"What did they do to him?" exclaimed the girl as she and the others now saw the full extent of horrors inflicted on another human being.

"It's a miracle he's still alive," interrupted Smith. "But he's not going to be for long unless we can get him somewhere he can be treated. What are the options Pemba? You know this country."

"Not as well as I do." Everyone in the room turned to see the figure of an aging lama standing in the open doorway of the stable, his dirty maroon robes dimly illuminated by the flickering fire. In a second Smith had his Kalashnikov in his hand levelled in the direction of the intruder. But then out of the darkness appeared one of the guards.

"We found him wandering in the ruins down by the stream," the guard announced. "He says he lives here. Thought I'd better bring him up for a chat." He led the old man into the light and Smith cautiously lowered his weapon.

"Who are you, old man and what are you doing wandering around here in the dark?" asked Pemba, not unkindly.

"My name is Lhamo Tsering. I am a monk of Ralung Monastery and have been for sixty-two years." He hesitated. "Or is it sixty-three? I'm not sure." Pemba smiled. The man was probably mad, but harmless.

"I came to the Monastery when I was about seven years old. My mother was never sure just how old I was. She told the Abbot I was seven, anyway. What did it matter? I've lived here ever since."

"What about the Chinese?" asked Tashi. "Didn't they take you away?"

"Yes, they took us all to Gyantse. Told me I had to get a job. I told them I'm a monk. That's my job. So I came back. I'm old. No-one bothers me here."

By now the old monk had ingratiated himself into the group and a place was found for him by the fire. He squatted on his haunches, hitching his threadbare robes up around his bony knees. There was silence as he greedily devoured the food in the wooden bowl presented to him. More black tea was crumbled from a tea brick into boiling water and a mug was passed round to the old man. He sipped the hot liquid slowly, seeming to savour every drop as his rheumy eyes darted unselfconsciously from one face to the next until he had taken in the whole scene.

"What has happened to your friend?" he asked at last, looking at the injured Lhotse.

"That's the work of the Chinese, old man," said Pemba. "They weren't as kind to him as they were to you."

"Are you a doctor?" the old lama enquired, looking at Tashi as if he intuited the other monk's calling.

"I am. But we have little medicine and he needs drugs and rest or he will die."

"There's a barefoot doctor who has a clinic at Sansa."

"Where is that?" asked Pemba.

"To the south, towards the border with Bhutan. Over the Chanda la."

"How far?"

"Oh," he paused and thought for a moment. "A day, perhaps two days. I haven't been that way for a very long time, but men from the village sometimes come this way to Gyantse. They give me food and news. They say this doctor is a good man. Very young, but a great healer, they say." He fell silent.

For a few minutes the old stable was quiet save the crackling of the fire and the occasional snort of one of the horses. Smith was now aware for the first time of the musty smell of the animals as they chewed their fodder and shuffled around on the packed earth floor at the far end of the building.

"What's a bare-foot doctor?" he asked Tashi at last in English.

"One of Mao's few genuine achievements," replied Tashi. "After the revolution the Communists realised that hundreds of thousands of peasants died in the countryside every year from illnesses that were very easy to treat, because there were virtually no doctors to treat them. So they trained a huge number of people.

Gave them enough medical knowledge to treat these illnesses and sent them out amongst the people. It was a great success. And now we have them here in Tibet. The man Lhamo Tsering is talking about must be one of these."

"So he would be trained by the Chinese?" asked Smith.

"Probably. And trained in China."

"So can we trust him?"

"I have no idea."

"What about you, Tashi? Can you treat Lhotse?"

As they had been talking Tashi had continued to clean Lhotse's wounds using one of the Chinese medical kits taken from the ambush. If he was aware of what was happening, Lhotse showed no sign of it. Chungla watched silently from the other side of the fire as if trying to memorise the procedures for future reference. Her dark eyes met Smith's across the fire and she smiled, an embarrassed girl's smile. Smith wondered, not for the first time, what effect recent experiences were having on her.

"I can make him comfortable," replied Tashi, interrupting his wandering thoughts, "and possibly keep him alive until we get to Sansa, if that is where we're heading, but probably no more."

"Well if we don't keep him alive we've all risked a hell of a lot for nothing."

"Not for nothing. We have gained merit by this act, and if he dies it is amongst friends, not amongst the Chinese who despise him."

"Merit, Tashi?"

"We must accumulate merit in this life if we are to return in a higher form in a future life or gain Enlightenment. Unless one is a *Tulku*."

"Like Chungla?"

"Yes, Peter, like Chungla."

Smith glanced over at the girl again. She still watched Tashi intently, but could not understand the two men's conversation.

"In a past life she achieved Enlightenment, but chose to return to this world time after time in order to assist others in their search for Enlightenment. That is why there is such merit in us rescuing Lhotse. Who was it who guided us to this act?"

"Chungla," replied Smith sceptically. He remembered how vociferous the girl had been in persuading them to try to save Lhotse. But couldn't believe that his own chances of salvation had been seriously improved by killing more Chinese, which had been the result. But this was not the time to get into a metaphysical discussion with his friend.

"Can I help?" asked Chungla in Tibetan across the fire, seemingly no longer able to contain her desire to learn about healing as well as fighting. Tashi nodded and beckoned to the girl who rose and stepped over some of the others gathered around the fire in her eagerness. Smith watched for several minutes as Tashi directed the girl in how to clean and bandage yet another of Lhotse's wounds. Finally, Tashi plied the unresponsive patient with pain killers and laid him down in the hope that he would sleep and survive the night. Chungla covered him with a blanket.

Pemba had also been watching the whole procedure. Apparently satisfied that as much had been done for Lhotse as possible for the time being he now called for everyone in the old stable to gather round the fire. Men and nuns shuffled around so that a rough circle was formed. Lobsang and Mila, the two men rescued with Lhotse, looked doubtfully at one another, but Pemba beckoned them forward into the circle.

"At times like these all ideas are welcome," said Pemba, addressing the pair directly. "Tell us, where are you from. Do you know these parts?"

"We're from Shigatse," responded the one called Lobsang quickly. "We do not know the countryside around here that well."

"What had you done to upset the Chinese?" continued Pemba.

"We're Tibetans. That seems to be enough to upset them." There were mumbles of agreement around the fire at that and Pemba seemed satisfied with this.

"Very well," continued Pemba turning to the rest of the party. "The old man says we should go south to the village of Sansa. Is he right? What do the rest of you think?"

During the brief exchange Smith had been watching the two newcomers. He had felt an antipathy to them as soon as he saw them in the back of the Chinese prison truck. It was just a feeling, an instinct, and he had tried to dismiss it as irrational. But his instincts had saved his life on more than one occasion, so he had continued to watch them on the journey to Ralung Monastery. Watched their furtive glances at one another, watched the whispered conversations, watched the discreet nods and lecherous smiles exchanged as their eyes fell on Chungla riding ahead of them.

He had shared his concerns with Tashi, but the lama had noticed nothing strange about the two men. Tashi saw the best in everyone and dismissed Smith's doubts. But Smith knew he was right. He had been tempted to press them when Pemba failed to question them further about their crimes, but instead he decided to watch and wait.

"I think we should head south," announced Tashi to the group, interrupting Smith's train of though and bringing him back to the business in hand.

"I agree," said Smith. "We have little choice. If Lhotse can travel we need to get him to somewhere where he can rest and be treated if he is to have any chance of recovering. The doctor and his surgery at Sansa sound like Lhotse's best chance. If we can trust him. If it's possible to leave him there we can continue south towards Bhutan. How far is the border from here?"

Pemba was already studying his map, supplied by the Americans, but based on maps produced by British military surveyors in the wake of the Younghusband Expedition sixty years before and surprisingly accurate. Still the best available. But maps, foreign maps, were not Pemba's strong point and he soon conceded defeat and passed the document to Smith.

"About thirty miles," he announced, answering his own question. "Fifty kilometres." He smiled. He had not realised until now just how close they were to the border and possible safety. It wasn't Mustang, but Mustang was probably two hundred and fifty miles away. A long way, an impossible distance on horseback or on foot with the PLA relentlessly searching for them.

"Fifty kilometres," he repeated, only now realising how the danger of their situation had been weighing on him. Suddenly, it seemed as if they might make it. Before the ambush he had not allowed himself to think beyond the mission. But now such thoughts were possible. It was far from over, but the possibility of surviving suddenly seemed very real. For the first time in weeks he allowed himself to think of Abbi and home as his finger gently traced the faint line on the map leading south to Bhutan.

Chapter 37

ཨ

Sansa, Tibet

The village of Sansa was about half way along the line which Smith had traced on the map with his finger. Crossing the Chanda La on a bright moonlit night the party managed to follow the route described by the old monk, Lhamo Tserin. Within thirty six hours of leaving Ralung Monastery, Smith sat alone on the flat roof of the barefoot doctor's house. Out of long habit, the parts of his Kalashnikov were neatly spread on a cloth in front of him as he cleaned and oiled them. The powerful late morning sun burnt through the thin air and he luxuriated in its warmth on his back. Prayer flags hung limply from thin poles in one corner and a pile of precious firewood lay heaped in another.

Beyond the rear of the house a grey plain, dotted with sparse vegetation ran out towards the huge expanse of sapphire blue that was Lake Phurma. A wide shallow stream flowed towards the lake a few yards from the house. Smith was distracted from his task by startled gasps. Looking over the parapet he saw a young girl stepping into the icy water. She wore a pink short-sleeved bodice and a heavy black woollen skirt with a traditionally embroidered hem, which trailed in the fast flowing water. As Smith watched, the girl bent forward and her long black hair cascaded down into the milky melt water. She began unselfconsciously scrubbing it between the palms of her small brown hands numerous times before wringing out the excess water. Finally, she threw back her head with a flourish, producing an arc of water droplets flashing and sparkling in the bright sunlight.

The girl was suddenly aware of Smith on the rooftop and looked in his direction. He hastily looked away, at once fascinated by the scene and embarrassed by his seeming voyeurism. Stepping haughtily from the water and smiling to herself at the foreigner's attention, she headed back towards the house, coiling her wet hair above her head with both hands as she went.

"Tea, Peter," called a disembodied voice from somewhere below. It was Tashi.

"OK, coming," replied Smith as he deftly slotted the parts of the Kalashnikov back into place to the accompanying sound of metal sliding smoothly on metal, followed by a series of satisfying clicks and snaps. He slung the weapon over his shoulder and tied back his own long dark hair before crossing the roof to the ladder leading down to the family's living quarters on the first floor of the squat white mud and stone built house. The ladder itself was no more than a log protruding from below through a hatchway. It leaned against one corner at a steep angle and had a series of steps notched into it. Smith descended deftly into the living room below, leaving the wooden roof hatch open, as it was the main ventilation for the smoky fire burning in an old iron stove in the centre of the room below. As he descended he was met by the sounds and smells of cooking – chattering voices, a metal utensil scraping on the bottom of a pan, the rattling of a boiling kettle on the stove – boiled vegetables and seared meat.

After the intense light of the rooftop, it took Smith's eyes a couple of minutes to adjust to the dim room he now emerged into. Apart from the light streaming in from the hatchway above, the only other illumination came from an open door at the far end of the room and through a few tiny windows set high up in the walls covered, not with glass, but with what looked like grease-proof paper.

"Here you are," said Tashi in English without thinking, handing Smith a tin mug of butter tea.

"Cheers," responded Smith taking the hot drink in both hands.

"Would you like some food?" It was the barefoot doctor's wife, Yangzom.

"Yes, please," replied Smith sitting on the floor next to Tashi. As he waited for the food he took in the room in more detail. It had been dark when they arrived and this was the first time he had been able to study it in anything approaching daylight. Most Tibetan homes consisted of two floors, as did Lhalu, the doctor's, house. The ground floor provided shelter for the animals and storage for fodder and grain. The flat roofs were outdoor living rooms where the light was good enough to prepare food, mend clothes, dry and winnow grain and burn incense to the gods as well as socialising and drinking chang, Tibetan barley beer.

The first floor, where Smith now sat, was the family's dimly lit living room, kitchen and altar room. By Tibetan standards it was quite large, indicating the status which Lhalu had achieved. Having trained in Beijing, but also knowing traditional Tibetan medicine, the people trusted him. He was much in demand and prospered, though never so much as to draw the attention of the Red Guards. His family was also of good peasant stock, a vital credential with the Guards.

Smith noted the good quality carpet on the planked floor, the wooden pillars painted red and the ceiling embellished with strange tantric patterns, barely visible in the dim light. An altar stood at one end of the room and the smouldering scent of incense pricked Smith's nostrils. Above the altar, Chairman Mao gazed down beneficently on the rebels below.

"Please, eat," exclaimed Yangzom, ladling *thenthuk* from a cauldron into dishes and passing them round to the men seated around the room. In addition to Smith and Tashi the diners included Lhalu and his younger brother Dorje. The soup was steaming hot and consisted of nothing more than barley noodles and vegetables, but Smith savoured in silence the subtle tastes of the first meal cooked for him by a woman in a longer time than he could remember.

"How's the patient?" he ventured at last.

"Not good," replied Lhalu, devouring the last of his soup and passing the bowl to his wife for more.

"He needs rest, food and medicine, but I think that he will survive. Tashi probably saved his life. I've given him some antibiotics and some morphine so he is resting more comfortably. We have also put poultices on his wounds." He looked at Tashi, seemingly in recognition of their joint effort.

"But he must not be moved for some time."

"Is it safe for us to leave him here? Safe for you?"

"The Chinese rarely come here. We are quite isolated." If a Tibetan thought he was isolated then he probably was, mused Smith.

"But the Chinese are looking for us. They will come here eventually. And what about the villagers?"

"Nothing is certain," continued Lhalu, taking another bowl of soup from his wife, "but we have to trust our own people here. You will be safe here for a day or two, but then you must leave. We can hide Lhotse, but we cannot hide all of you. The Chinese probably think you have headed west towards Mustang and it will take them a long time to search the mountains."

No village had been spared the turmoil of the Cultural Revolution, but Sansa had fared better than most. The villagers had managed to cling discreetly to many of their traditions and avoid the worst excesses of collectivisation. Lhalu had lived in China and spoke the language and so was trusted by the Chinese as well as by his own people who respected him. At a time when ordinary people sorely missed the tangible presence of the mainstay of their culture, Tibetan Buddhism, with the loss of the monasteries and their lamas, the traditional knowledge of healers like Lhalu was invaluable. This knowledge was not only of herbs and potions, but also of astrology and the ways of the gods. He was as at home telling fortunes as prescribing aspirin.

And so it was that the haughty *Khampas* who towered over the locals, could be billeted, at least for a short time, in a village in western Tibet with a reasonable hope that they would not be betrayed to the PLA. They were spread amongst four families in the village, mainly housed in their barns as the animals were now out grazing after the long winter inside.

Following their meal Smith returned to the flat roof of Lhalu's house, joined now by Tashi and Pemba. They chatted as they sat in the sunshine waiting for Chungla, Lhalu and some of the others to join them to discuss their next move.

"Do you think Lhalu's brothers live in the house as well?" asked Smith of the others. Pemba smiled.

"Of course they do. They are all married to Yangzom." He paused for Smith's reaction.

"OK," commented Smith doubtfully. Pemba continued.

"Lhalu told me that Yangzom was originally married to his elder brother and they had a daughter. The girl you saw this morning, I think." He paused meaningfully.

"But the brother died and so Lhalu married her. As the other brothers came of age they married her as well."

"So she sleeps with them all?" asked Smith, intrigued by how this arrangement could work.

"I didn't ask! But it's usual for a wife to circulate in these circumstances, if you understand what I mean." The old warrior smiled at the younger man, seemly pleased to have shocked the liberal Westerner.

"Listen, Peter, such arrangements are not uncommon and can work well. But Tibetan women in Tibet have more freedom than in many so called Third World countries. The Communists want to teach us about equality, but Tibetan women never had to bind their feet as Chinese women did right up to the Revolution in1949"

"Usually," continued Tashi, "a girl will marry in her late teens and the family chooses the husband. I know you will think this is outrageous, but quite often the girl will not know that she is getting married until a day or two before the wedding and probably won't know who the groom is until the ceremony itself. This is probably what happened to Yangzom.

"And then later, as the brothers come of age she might be asked to marry them."

"Or told?" enquired Smith.

"Or told," agreed Tashi. "But Peter, the Land of the Snows is an unforgiving place. You know this. Until the Chinese came, nearly a quarter of all men entered the monastery. Many families are like Lhalu's, sharing a wife. The result is that the population has been stable for centuries and we have been able to continue to live in this land."

Smith thought about this and could see that it made a kind of harsh sense. None of this was any kind of government planning. It was almost as if over the centuries the Tibetans as a people had subconsciously developed a culture which allowed them to live, albeit frugally, in balance with the harsh demands of life in highest country on earth. Many poor countries were struggling to support burgeoning populations, but Tibet had maintained a kind of delicate equilibrium. Until now, as Peking continued to encourage Han Chinese to emigrate to Tibet and place increasing stress on this fragile place.

"Here they are," announced Tendruk to the dark space below him as his head and shoulders appeared through the hatchway, blinking into the searing sunlight. As he clambered agilely onto the flat roof Rinzing scampered up the rough hewn ladder behind him followed by Chungla.

"Sit", invited Pemba and the new arrivals squatted down to

form a rough circle on the dusty earth floor. Bright as the sun was, it was not hot and for a few moments the small group sat in silence enjoying the warmth, like lizards as they waited for Pemba's lead.

"The radio is now working again," began Pemba eventually. The rest remained silent. It was an open secret that the radio had never not been working. They did not know that it was at Smith's behest that Pemba had decided to stop using the radio once he had been convinced by Smith that the CIA had sent Lhotse to kill him. Not knowing who they could trust, Smith and Pemba had decided to trust no-one.

"And we have been able to contact the Americans." There was a murmur of interest at this from the little group.

"We have told them of our situation and of the intelligence we have captured from the Chinese. They have agreed to help us. There is a small airfield not far over the border into Bhutan. If we can get there in five days time they will send an aircraft to pick us up, or some of us, and transfer us to Katmandu. From there we can make our way safely back to Mustang."

"Some of us?" enquired Tendruk.

"Yes. They can only provide a light aircraft. Those who cannot be taken can wait for another flight to be organised, but I assume that everyone will not want to leave the country. Perhaps some of the nuns?" He looked at Chungla.

"I think that you are correct. We all wish to stay in the Land of the Snows."

"That may be so for the others, Chungla, but it is too dangerous for you to stay. And your destiny is now to take our religion and culture to the West," interjected Tashi.

"My destiny is to stay here and fight," reposted the young nun forcefully. She looked at Smith as if hoping to summon his support. He ignored her gaze, not wishing to get involved in such a debate if he could avoid it. He was the outsider and when it came to such things the Tibetans had to decide themselves.

"Pemba. What do you say?"

"I say, little one, that Tashi is right. You have fought well in the last days and proved you are the equal of any of us. But when it comes to the future of our culture, you are more than our equal. Go with our friend, Peter. He knows the ways of the West and he will help you to succeed there."

Smith shuffled uneasily at the prospect of this new and unexpected role which Pemba was casting him for. The ball was now firmly in his court. His instinctive reaction to object was stifled by the intense look, at once commanding and beseeching, which Pemba directed at the young Englishman. All eyes were now on Smith. Smith the warrior, or Smith the nursemaid?

And anyway, was this the right thing for her? He had never consciously encouraged her to take up arms, but when she had approached him back at Tsechen Damchos Ling Monastery he had seen the anger and hate in her eyes and he knew better than anyone why she felt it. He had seen her being raped. He knew how seeing it had made him feel and he could not begin to imagine what it had done to her.

"It is time for you to leave," said Tashi, apparently sensing the doubt in Smith's mind. "Only yesterday you were saying how you were looking forward to getting home. To seeing Abbi," he added pointedly.

"That was yesterday", replied Smith in English. "It was just the relief at knowing we could get away, but I've been thinking about that, Tashi," he continued in the same language.

Smith was a manager of violence. That's what the British Army had taught him to do and he did it well. It was his answer to the kind of problems he was used to facing. It was natural that Chungla recognised that in him and was drawn to it. Even after Tashi had berated him for training her to use the Kalashnikov he had not doubted that he and Chungla were right. She was tough and resilient. She rode as well as most of the men and had proved she could keep up with them when they travelled. At the ambush he had seen how fully she had played her part. Unlike with Tashi, he had no doubt that she was firing her weapon and making every round count. The look on her young face told him that.

"So you see a different future for you and Chungla. I know you Peter. The hero, the romantic. But you've seen enough here to know we're not going to drive the Chinese out by force, as I have. The dream you have for her probably leads to a public execution in a square in Lhasa or years in Drapchi Prison."

Smith considered this as the others became increasingly impatient with the two men arguing in a foreign language.

"Perhaps they're right, Chungla,"Smith began, turning to the girl, before he even realised the words had formed in his mouth.

"You don't mean that. I know you don't." She seemed to sense the turmoil in Smith's mind.

"I do. Listen to me, Chungla. There is already a Tibetan Buddhist monastery in my country and some of its lamas are not even Tibetan. I can take you there and help you." What was he saying? He'd come to Tibet to fight, to see action, yes, to have an adventure. It sounded puerile when he articulated it, but that is what he lived for, adventure. And now he was promising to give that up. But perhaps the girl would not give in that easily. Smith's hopes were short-lived. He could tell as soon as she began to speak that she was weakening already.

"I cannot imagine your world, Smith." He had long ceased to wince or correct her or the others for the way they mispronounced his name, but he was suddenly tempted to again. Before he could, she continued.

"I don't know what I could do there for my people or how." She paused.

"I can show you," said Smith, doubting whether he could, but then more optimistically adding "Tashi and I could show you. You are coming, Tashi?" The monk nodded his agreement.

"Well, if you and Tashi could show me then maybe I could." Tears of defeat began to well up in her eyes.Tashi and Pemba looked at one another exchanging what Smith guessed to be looks of relief. They had done the job they had obviously set out to do.

"So," said Pemba, seemingly relieved to be able to return to more immediate matters, "I think we should leave in the morning. That will give us enough time to get to the rendezvous. In the meantime we need to decide if anyone else wishes to leave us and return home themselves.

"It might be possible for a small number, such as some of the nuns, to stay here longer until they are fit to travel and make their ways back to their families once they are ready. Lhalu thinks that they could safely absorb a few strangers here without suspicion even if the Chinese do arrive, but it will have to be for those who might want to stay to decide if they want to take that risk. Please talk to them about this, Chungla." He turned to the girl and she nodded.

"Our mission was to join you and support you, Pemba," began Tendruk. " I think that we will be too exposed if the few of us try to operate in this area on our own. We need to go to Mustang and then return to the Land of the Snows with a larger group, or see if the Americans have another plan for us."

"I think yours was the last mission the Americans will send to the Land of the Snows. You have been closer to them than any of us, but from what we now hear the CIA have lost interest in us."

"You might be right, Pemba. It seems that ours was an exceptional mission." Tendruk looked at Smith, but made no further comment about Lhotse's roll in it. The Englishman had known very little of the American involvement in Tibet when he had crossed the border from Mustang earlier that spring. He was still getting used to the idea that he had unwittingly become such a focus of their attentions and wondered with hindsight at his own bravado. Or was it naivety?

"You, know, Tendruk, I only just realised. I never asked if you knew what Lhotse was up to. I just assumed you didn't."

"Are you asking me now?"

"Perhaps this is not the time," interrupted Pemba forcefully. The wrong answer could have an explosive effect on the group and their chances of surviving.

"No, Pemba. He is right."

"And?" enquired Smith forcefully, puzzled now that Tendruk had not immediately denied knowledge of Lhotse's mission.

The little group sat waiting, all eyes now on Tendruk. Kitchen noises rose through the door from the room below to fill the silence. The plaintiff calls of sheep could be heard out on the plain running towards the distant blue lake.

"I knew that Lhotse had been briefed separately by Larsen, but no, I, we," he looked at the remaining members of his team, "we knew nothing about any separate plots and plans. Our task was to rendezvous with you and help extract the intelligence material. That's the mission we're still trying to complete."

"Good," announced Pemba, obviously relieved at Tendruk's answer. "So that's an end to the matter. We need to put this unpleasantness behind us and concentrate on the future. On getting away from here in one piece. We leave at first light so rest now and be ready to move then."

Pemba rose and the others followed his lead. The members of

the little group began to disappear into the dark room below. Only Smith and Tashi remained sitting on the dusty flat roof of the house.

"What has remained unspoken is now spoken, Peter," began Tashi. "It is good that it is out in the open. Tendruk and the others were not involved." Smith was silent.

"Do you still doubt them?"

"Why wouldn't I?" he replied in English now.

"Because Lhotse himself told you about the plot and that this man Larsen had changed his orders. Why would he lie about this?"

"I don't know, Tashi. But I can't trust them. That's why I never asked them before. Because the answer was obviously going to be no, they didn't know anything about it. That doesn't make it true. I decided the best way was to assume they all had the same orders and make sure they never had a chance to carry them out.

"I trust you and Pemba with my life. I don't think you can be a threat to them, so as long as you two were around and I kept my wits about me I figured I was OK."

"So what happens when we get to Bhutan? Can we trust the CIA once we get there?"

"I don't know, Tashi. I suppose it depends who we are dealing with. If this Larsen guy is organising this then perhaps we're alright. Lhotse trusted him one hundred percent, but am I being naive to trust Lhotse, a guy who by his own admission was sent here to kill me?

"I'll go to the airfield expecting and being ready for the worst and see what happens."

Both men looked towards the ladder as they heard the sound of someone clambering up towards the roof.

"Chang", announced the barefoot doctor as he emerged into the sunlight clutching a jug precariously in one hand. He placed it carefully in front of Smith and Tashi before turning and disappearing again, to re-appear in a few seconds with three mugs. He poured generous amounts of the frothy beer into each mug and passed one to each of the two men before crouching down to join them on the hard earth floor, now comfortably warmed by the heightening sun.

"Drink," he urged, although the other two men needed no

encouragement.

For a while, no-one spoke as the three men enjoyed the heat and the taste of alcohol. Smith realised how thirsty he had become as he gratefully drank the barley beer. It would never pass muster in what had become the nearest thing he had ever had a to a local pub, the Admiral Nelson just round the corner from the mews cottage he had shared for such a brief time with Abbi. Abbi, whom he forced himself to think of as little as possible.

Lhotse knowing her name had unnerved him more than the fact that the man had plans to kill him. He had not discussed it even with Tashi, but for a while after the fight with Lhotse he could think of nothing but the fact that she was in danger. That she was in danger because of him. That he was thousands of miles away and could do nothing. Finally, he had managed to squash it all into some compartment he had in the back of his mind where it wouldn't bother him. It was an ability he had and the only way to survive the kind of life he chose to lead.

"So you leave us tomorrow Pemba tells me. Probably for the best. A great pity all the same. I have never talked to a westerner before and would have liked to hear the stories you have to tell about your country. Which country is that? America?"

"No, England."

"England? Is that near America."

"Not really." Smith looked hopefully at Tashi for help, but none was forthcoming. The strong beer and the warm afternoon air were already fuddling his brain. He couldn't face having to try to explain what his homeland was like. The mere thought of it sapped his energy.

"Pemba says you will take the *Tulku* to this place... England?"

"It's possible," replied Smith noncommittally. Tashi looked at Smith.

"That's right, Lhalu," added Tashi emphatically. "She is going to go to England. To a monastery there so that she can teach our religion to westerners. Many of them are very keen to learn." Lhalu nodded approvingly at this. Smith closed his eyes and tried to think of something else.

*

Smith awoke into absolute darkness. So dark that he was not

sure whether his eyes were open or shut. After a second his mind told him where he was. The barn below Lhalu's house was now devoid of animals as they grazed contentedly on the plain beyond the village. So Smith and some of the group had been billeted there, with the horses hobbled outside. Something had woken Smith. He lay still, hardly breathing, listening intently as his eyes slowly adjusted to the weak starlight filtering into the barn. Above the total silence of the Tibetan night came the sound of rustling straw in the barn next door. Then insistent whispering. He relaxed. Probably just someone getting up to piss. A door scraped across the earth floor on its rope hinges as it was pushed carefully open into the night. Someone was being very considerate.

But then the distinctive and all too familiar sound of well oiled metal sliding over metal. Smith tensed in the darkness knowing that someone was carefully cocking a weapon.

Rolling onto his side he reached above his head to the saddle he was using as a pillow. From a pouch he cautiously extracted his pistol and knife. With a weapon in each hand he rose cautiously to his feet and began to move slowly towards the faint light outlining the closed door. By now he could hear the sound of feet moving quickly away from the buildings. Then, before he reached the door, the dull thud of horses' hooves on the hard ground.

Smith dragged open the door of the barn and stepped out into the night, the cold air a shock after the fug of the barn. There was no moon, but in the clear thin air the light of the incredible display of stars was enough to illuminate the silhouette of two horsemen furiously encouraging their mounts into action. Smith dropped to one knee, simultaneously dropping his knife and cocking the Browning nine millimetre pistol. Holding the weapon firmly in both hands he discharged eight rounds into the night.

As Smith turned and ran back towards the building the eerie flicker of butter lamps began to illuminate the tiny windows of the house. There was as yet no light in the barn from which the fugitives had emerged, but this was also where Smith's horse was tethered. He bounded through the open door into the darkness beyond and immediately sprawled headlong over an unseen obstacle. Confused, he lay there for a couple for seconds in the total darkness, aware only of the musty smell of last summer's barley crop in his nostrils. Then, regaining his momentum, he sprang to his feet and turned towards the door just as Tashi's lamp cast an insipid light on the scene before the two men. They both stared in horror at the sight of Pemba's prostrate form stretched out face down between them. By the Khampa leader's head was a thick patch of black oil staining the straw beneath him. As Tashi bent towards Pemba the lamp turned the oil a deep red, almost the colour of Tashi's robe. Smith's heart went cold as he quickly squatted by his friend and rolled him over. As he did so Pemba's headed lolled back sickeningly to drag open the horrific knife wound across his throat like a second grotesque gaping mouth.

"Jesus," was all Smith could say as he slowly rose to his feet. It was obvious that no more could be done for the old warrior in this life. Tashi, seemingly in shock, began to mumble a Tibetan prayer as he fingered his prayer beads.

"Jesus," repeated Smith, this time with clear anger and frustration in his voice. He brushed quickly passed Tashi and out into the night. Before Tashi began to move, Smith re-entered the barn with his saddle cradled in both arms.

"What are you doing?" asked Tashi stupidly.

"What do you think I'm doing?" Smith hoisted the saddle onto his horse's back and ducked beneath the animal to fasten the straps across its belly.

"Those bastards killed Pemba. I had a bad feeling about them from the start. Jesus. Why didn't I do something about it before this?" he ranted, half to Tashi and half to himself.

Only minutes had passed since Smith had awoken, but already it seemed like hours. The whole building was now alive with activity as lights appeared in every room. Several of the *Khampas* had already begun to crowd into the doorway of the barn, staring in shocked disbelief at the mutilated body of their leader.

"It's them," announced Tendruk over the shoulders of men crowded round Pemba's body.

"Who?" asked Tashi, seemingly beginning to regain his composure.

"Mila and Lobsang. I just checked where they were sleeping and all their stuff's gone." Smith was already leading his horse towards the entrance.

"Wait," shouted Tendruk. "We're coming with you. You can't track them on your own."

"I'll give you two minutes," hissed Smith. He swung onto the saddle of his horse and allowed the animal to walk slowly in the direction the two fugitives had fled. Once away from the light of the buildings his eyes soon began to adjust to the darkness. He pulled out his binoculars and methodically scanned the countryside ahead of him. After a minute or so he could distinguish various dark shapes in the distance against the bland grey background, although he couldn't tell what they were. He willed his night vision to improve, straining to see anything he could identify. Long minutes passed.

And then he saw it, or thought he did. Holding the binoculars as still as he could he gently twisted the lens adjuster back and forth to sharpen the image. He could not make out the shapes, but there was no doubt in his mind. Two black forms moving away from him. It was them. It had to be.

Still staring into the night, Smith could now hear the sound of horses behind him. In seconds Tendruk and two other mounted men were alongside him.

"Have you got a lamp?" he demanded without moving the binoculars from his eyes.

"Yes, here."

Still concentrating on his prey, Smith dropped one hand and began frantically searching in one of the pouches on his saddle.

"Here, do you know how to use this?"

"Of course," replied Tendruk, taking the squat metal cylinder of a prismatic compass from Smith, the metal cold and smooth in his hand. He flicked the cover open.

"I can see the bastards. Get a bearing on the direction I'm pointing." Tendruk lined up the small brass instrument, squinting at the luminous dial in the faint light of a butter lamp now held by one of the other men.

"A hundred and ninety-five degrees," he reported.

"OK. Can you cover that lamp and keep it lit?"

"We can try."

The four horsemen lurched forward into the darkness.

Smith had also noted in his mind a prominent peak on the dark horizon more or less on the line the killers were taking. The small group rode as fast as they dare through the night, aware that at any second one of their mounts could stumble on an unseen hazard. After about ten minutes Smith called a halt.

"Are we still on the bearing? I reckon we are." Tendruk retrieved the lamp from somewhere and removed the rag wrapped around the glass. A faint glow illuminated the faces of the four men as they peered at the compass.

"We're still on the same bearing," Tendruk confirmed. Smith jammed his binoculars to his face. He had kept one eye shut when the lamp was revealed so that he did not lose his night vision. Again he scanned the darkness ahead of them and then stopped, staring intently ahead. He could not believe what he was seeing. There they were, clear as daylight in his lens only a few hundred yards ahead of them.

"Is that them?" whispered Tendruk gazing in the same direction as Smith, but without the aid of binoculars.

"Yes. They're hardly moving. A couple more minutes and we'd have ridden right onto them. Or straight past them. One of them looks like he's slumped over the front of his horse."

"You must've hit him."

"Tashi! What're you doing here?

"The same as you."

"Good. So let's finish this. I reckon we can take them from here." He pulled his Kalashnikov from his shoulder and in one deft movement slid back the cocking handle ready to fire.

"Wait," hissed Tashi before Smith had a chance to fire. Feeling back in control of the situation, Smith was now not in such a hurry so he indulged his friend.

"Wait? Wait for what?"

"To find out who these men are and why they attacked Pemba."

"It doesn't matter, Tashi. They're dead men."

"So you've become judge and jury and executioner now?"

"No. Avenging angel."

"But you said yourself they're probably hurt. You can't just kill them in cold blood."

"There are no rules of engagement for these guys. No Geneva Convention. They killed your friend. You saw what they did to him not fifteen minutes ago. You can't have forgotten that."

"I haven't forgotten. But killing them doesn't make you more sorry for Pemba's death than I am."

"OK, Tashi. I can't believe we're having this conversation, but we are. So what are you suggesting? If we don't take them from here before they know we're on them, we're just risking more lives. Is that what you want? I thought you were a fighter. You know the stakes."

"I want to fight the Chinese. I brought you here to fight the Chinese, not to carry out summary executions on my own people."

"What do you say, Tendruk?" The Khampa was a Hale graduate and spoke good English, which the two men had been speaking. He responded in the same language.

"Give me your binoculars." Smith handed them to him and he stared into the darkness for a few seconds.

"They've stopped. Looks like they've dismounted. I'm guessing that one of them at least is pretty badly injured. They're not going much farther."

"So?"

"So we can probably take them alive. You two stay here and cover us, and Rinzing and me," he nodded in the direction of the other Khampa sitting patiently on his horse, "we can swing round in an arc on foot and see if we can get close enough to capture them. Any sign of a problem and you finish them."

"But why?"

"Tashi is right. They are our people."

"And what do we do with them once we've made our citizen's arrest? Hand them over to the Chinese?"

"It is not an easy situation, Peter, and I don't know the answer yet, but I know it is wrong to just shoot them. We're fighting to get our country back from the Chinese. There's no point in that if we don't have higher standards than them."

"OK. I give up. Do what the fuck you want." And looking at Tendruk, "get on with it."

The two Tibetans dropped from their horses and, bent low, scampered away into the darkness to the right of the two horsemen. Smith raised his weapon and stared along its length towards his target. As he let his reins go slack his horse began to walk slowly in the direction of the two fugitives and Tashi followed. Neither man spoke. There was no sign that they had been seen, but Smith guessed that it would not be long before the two could hear the horses. He half willed them to react to their presence. Just give him a reason to shoot.

It wasn't long before Smith saw movement in his peripheral vision. Tendruk and Rinzing were almost on them. Suddenly they were running and shouting as the four dark images blurred into one another. Smith stared anxiously, but dare not fire. What the hell was happening?

He encouraged his horse forward at a walk and Tashi came alongside him. Still the sound of voices, but no firing.

Then very clearly, "we've got them!" Smith and Tashi picked up speed and were on the party in seconds. Tendruk and Rinzing stood pointing their rifles at two men on the ground. One sat with his hands behind his head and the other lay sprawled on the ground.

"This one's dead by the look of it," announced Tendruk, turning the prostrate form with his foot. Tashi swung down from his horse and produced the lamp from his pack, still alight, to Smith's amazement. He examined the body for a couple of minutes before confirming Tendruk's diagnosis.

"So who've we got left?" asked Smith. Tashi held the light towards the seated figure, revealing the terrified eyes of the man calling himself Mila.

"OK, Tashi, now what?"

"We take them back to the village."

"Then what?"

"The dead must be correctly dispatched to the next world." Smith looked puzzled.

"How's that going to happen?"

"A sky burial."

*"Why the juniper sprigs?" Smith enquired as the small party approached Lhalu's house. The first rays of the sun were just beginning to illuminate the mud walls of the building as they rode back into the village, turning them from black to blue-grey. Mila trotted and stumbled behind, his hands bound, and the rope which tethered him to Tendruk's saddle tied round his neck. Lobsang's body was slung unceremoniously over the back of Rinzing's horse, behind the rider himself.

"It's tied to the door to warn strangers not to come near. They may frighten the soul of the dead. The body should stay in the house for three days before the burial. Tomorrow was the day we were going to release the soul of the two *Khampas* killed at the ambush. You have not visited their bodies?" Was it a question or a reprimand, Smith wondered.

"I know, but what about Pemba? We can't wait another three days. The Chinese will be here."

"As we have so little time it's more important that Pemba is helped on his way to the next life by friends than that he be left here with strangers. We will do this tomorrow as well. But we must also release the soul of the bandit Lobsang." Smith looked at his friend.

"Isn't that taking compassion a bit far? We should have just left his body to rot on the plain."

"It wouldn't rot here. You know nothing rots here," Tashi corrected him. "But it doesn't matter. It is not for us to decide what happens to a dead man's soul. We must help it to the afterlife. His next life may not be good because of the way he lived in this life. That's karma. The cycle of suffering will most certainly continue for him."

The horses came to a halt in front of the house and the riders climbed down. Chungla and several of the *Khampas* appeared from inside the building. The horses were led away, Lobsang's body still lolling on the back of one of them.

Mila was dragged forward and instantly several of the men, Pemba's men, surged towards him punching and kicking him to the ground.

"Stop!" cried Tashi, but the beating continued for several minutes until Tendruk and Rinzing could drag them from the unfortunate victim and order the men back inside. Mila made no attempt to get up, laying almost motionless in a foetal ball, his clothes covered in dust, patches of blood already visible in his now dun coloured hair.

"Not as compassionate as you, these guys," observed Smith.

"They fought with Pemba for many years. It is understandable, but that does not make it right." Tashi leant forward to help the injured man to his feet, but he only huddled more tightly into himself and began to whimper.

"Come on. You'll live." It was Smith, his voice unexpectedly gentle, taking hold of Mila and almost lifting him to his feet. The other man winced when he realised who was helping him up, obviously expecting another blow at any second. Instead Smith just guided him to Tashi, turned and headed towards the house. Tashi's eyes followed his friend for several seconds until he disappeared inside, before leading Mila to one of the barns to treat his injuries. Rinzing followed, the rope tethering Mila still in his hand.

*

Smith sat in Lhalu's kitchen, the inevitable cup of butter tea steaming in his hands. Chungla entered the room and sat silently beside him. Pemba's body lay on a table by the house altar at the far end of the room, one of the nuns mumbling incoherently at his feet. Smith found this open acceptance and public display of death strangely comforting.

"She is reading from the Book of the Dead," began Chungla, answering the unasked question. "During the *bardo* the soul needs guidance and the book can provide that for the unenlightened."

"What's the *bardo*?"

"There is no need to whisper."

Smith repeated the question in what he hoped was a normal voice.

"The bardo lasts for forty-nine days," began the girl in a tone which gave away her obvious pleasure at finally being able to inform the man who always had all the answers.

"And in that time the soul of the dead travels to the next life. The Book of the Dead gives guidance for the uninitiated so that they can make the journey safely and successfully. The karma passes through six stages, like a flame from one candle to another and finally from this life to the next." She paused, obviously pleased with the analogy. Smith assumed this was how the young girl had been taught to explain this strange concept to laymen.

"If the soul pays proper attention to the reading of the Book, and it is read correctly, it is possible for enlightenment to be achieved and the cycle of death and rebirth ended." Smith thought for a moment, sipping his tea and watching the melted butter swirl like oil on the surface of the liquid.

"So Pemba could achieve enlightenment?"

"Most certainly," agreed the girl brightly.

"And Lobsang?" He immediately regretted asking the question as the look on Chungla's face changed in an instant to one of consternation.

"Never mind," he quickly added.

"No, you are right to ask," responded the young nun, regaining her composure. "All have the chance of enlightenment."

"I don't care what happens to his soul," snapped Smith. "He got what he deserved in this life. But what happens at this sky burial"? He continued, changing the subject.

"The Sky Burial Master has already been summoned by Lhalu for the dead *Khampas*. He will also conduct the sky burial for Pemba." She paused "And I think also for Lobsang." Smith chose to ignore this.

"When will we meet him, this Sky Burial Master?"Smith was surprised by the look of horror which had appeared on the young nun's face.

"We will not meet him." Smith turned at the sound of his friend Tashi's voice. The lama looked more tired and drawn than Smith had ever seen him.

"In Tibetan society the Burial Master is the lowest of the low, along with butchers and blacksmiths. I am afraid that no-one here will drink or share food with him. His work is seen as unclean."

"I'm confused, Tashi. If this ritual is so important and this guy is an important part of it, why is he not welcomed by people?" Tashi looked wearily at Chungla before replying.

"You will understand tomorrow."

*

Smith walked up the slope away from the village accompanied by Chungla and Tendruk. The others had chosen or were told not to come, instead praying with the nuns in Lhalu's house. After about twenty minutes they crested the rise and the rough dry ground fell away gently before them, grey in the half light of early morning. A couple of hundred metres ahead Smith could make out the seated form of a lama in maroon robes rocking rhythmically from side to side. Beyond Tashi was a small stone hut and further down the slope a number of large stone slabs. To one side a fire of juniper and *tsampa* burned dimly, discharging great plumes of white smoke.

"This is close enough," indicated Chungla, and the small party stopped. As they waited the light gradually improved and Smith could soon make out the forms of four naked bodies laid face down on the slabs of rock. It was impossible to tell from this distance which was which.

Soon three men emerged from the hut, the first holding a large knife similar to a machete and the others brandishing long handled hammers. As Smith and the others watched, the man with the knife took hold of the first body and began to cut large strips of flesh from it.

"That," said Chungla, as if to make her point of the previous day, "is the Sky Burial Master."

As the flesh was passed to them, the other two men began to pound it with their hammers on one of the rocks. Soon bones were also being passed over to meet the same fate. Smith had read enough about Tibet and seen enough carnage in his short life not to be shocked by what he saw, but in spite of himself, he was deeply disturbed by the fate of his friend's body, a body which had been full of a warrior's passion for life and action not thirty-six hours before.

In the short time he had known Pemba they had shared experiences which most men never would and in spite of their very different cultures and ages they had become close. No friend could be unmoved to see that body now remorselessly cut to pieces.

Smith's memories of Pemba were suddenly interrupted by the sound of shouting in the distance.

"Come on! Come on!" The voice repeated. It was the Sky Burial Master bellowing as he scanned the heavens and pitched balls of flesh onto the open ground beyond him. He continued to do this for several minutes before turning to the next body with his long sharp knife and continuing his macabre work. As he began to dispatch the second body Tendruk pointed into the distance.

213

"There," he said. "They are coming. They have seen the smoke." At first Smith could see only a black speck in the now cobalt blue sky, but he knew what it was.

In no time the huge vulture was circling the funeral site maybe a thousand feet above them before descending gracelessly to the place where the balls of flesh had been thrown. Trailing its great ragged brown wings on either side, as if to defend its prize, the bird's long bare neck cautiously extended to take one of the balls in its beak. Smith watched with morbid fascination as the creature devoured first one and then another of the gruesome balls. Looking up he realised that the sky above them was now dark with vultures, twenty or thirty of them, huge wings outstretched, criss-crossing overhead. One by one they descended like a squadron of fighters returning to base, to greedily devour the flesh, organs and crushed bone laid out for them.

The three men began to work more quickly, the giant birds consuming the feast as rapidly as it is served up to them.

"This is good," began Chungla to Smith. "If the creatures eat everything quickly then reincarnation will be swift. This is a very good sign for Pemba and the other men." Smith did not bother to articulate his hope that Lobsang would reincarnate as the rat that he obviously was, but instead asked "What happens if everything is not eaten?"

"Then they would burn it." She nodded towards the three men. "Nothing must be left." Smith was silent and the girl continued. "Tashi told me that in your country you bury your dead, that you hide the body in a box and put it in the ground. Or that you burn the box. Is that true?"

"Yes." Chungla looked surprised at this, as if she had not quite believed Tashi.

"Here the ground is too hard." She looked towards the vast plain below them as if to emphasise the point, as if Smith might not have seen the harsh Tibetan landscape before. "Where it is not, it must be used for crops. As you know there is no wood to burn.

"And besides, traditionally we are a nomad people and to bury someone in the ground would be to leave them behind when the herd moves on. This would be wrong. Instead, the birds take the dead soaring to the heavens. It is also a kindness to the birds." They both fell silent, watching the spectacle before them.

Soon everything was devoured by the voracious birds. Chungla indicated that it was time for them to go. As they rose to return to the village Smith noticed that the vultures were in no hurry to soar to the heavens, satiated as they were by their funereal feast.

Chapter 38

ग

Tsangpo River, Tibet

"Ah, Major Tang. Sit, please," beckoned Colonel Zhou to his Company Commander.

"Bring us some coffee," he called to his orderly before sitting opposite the Major at the table outside his command vehicle. The sun continued to shine intermittently through the camouflage netting above them. The smell of ozone rising from the mighty Tsangpo River reminded Zhou for an instant of a rare visit to the sea in another life. He sat contemplatively for what must have seemed to Tang an age. Interrupted from his reverie by the arrival of two mugs of coffee, the Colonel finally got down to business.

"Read this," he said, tossing the orders he had received contemptuously across the table. There was another silence as Tang quickly scanned the document.

"Well?"

"Well, Colonel, it seems that we're going to be spending time sitting in the sun at the expense of the People," he smiled. Zhou liked and respected Tang whom he considered to be a proper soldier like himself and he knew that Tang was no happier sitting around whilst others charged into the fray than he was.

"We're not sitting here any longer than we have to, and believe me, that won't be very long. As soon as we find out what the hell's actually going on we're going after these bandits."

"The Commander won't like that one little bit."

"He won't like it when I personally shove his orders up his arse. And the only way I'm going to get a chance to do that is if we can find out where these bastards are and catch up to them before he does. I've got the Signallers scanning all our local frequencies for the next few hours to see what they can pick up.

"I want you to get the men ready to move at thirty minutes notice. They can start taking the cam down now and packing everything in the vehicles. Then report back to me. As soon as we have some useful intelligence we can make a plan and get moving. Dismissed, Major."

Tang took a last mouthful of his coffee, rose, saluted and left. The thought of action had raised the Colonel's spirits again. He smiled to himself as he rolled out a large scale map on the table in front of him, using Tang's and his own coffee mugs to help hold the huge document in place. As yet he had no idea what he was looking at, but he would spend the time studying the countryside, re-familiarising himself with every road, every river, every mountain range within striking distance of his camp where he thought the outlaws might be.

Colonel Zhou loved maps, seeing them almost as works of art. He loved the way they cleverly portrayed the nuances of the landscape with their sweeping contour lines, so tightly packed in this vertiginous country. He was intrigued by the symbols of forts, monasteries, villages and towns, telling those who could read them of the history, culture and politics of the land. A map could make it obvious why any of these man- made features were located where they were, at a river confluence, commanding the entrance to a valley, high on a mountain side for defence or isolation.

And all this information was vital for the soldier, especially the infanteer who lived so intimately in and on the land and whose interpretation of a map could mean the difference between living and dying. Zhou, the infantry commander, could tell at a glance whether the terrain displayed on a map would provide the cover his men needed for a frontal assault or whether they should go left or right flanking – where best to deploy machine guns for covering fire – where mortars should be sited. It was in his veins, his second nature.

When Tang returned to Colonel Zhou's impromptu headquarters he found his superior officer still sat at his camp table, still with a mug of coffee in front of him. Zhou looked up and nodded for the Major to take a seat. Also seated at the table was the Signals NCO. Spread out in front of the two men were various print-outs which they had been poring over prior to Tang's appearance. The light was now beginning to fade and the scene was lit by the glow of a kerosene lamp. In the approaching darkness, the sounds of the distant river seemed nearer, competing with those of soldiers occasional movements around the camp.

"Tang, are your men ready to go?"

"Yes, Colonel. Just waiting for you to give the order."

"Good. The Corporal and I have also been busy." He looked over appreciatively to the young man next to him, who in turn concentrated more intently on the documents before him.

"We managed to get an aerial erected on higher ground," began the NCO at Zhou's prompting." The atmosphere is so clear here and there is so little interference that it's possible to pick up signals from much farther away than the normal range. We've picked up comms from Headquarters to units on the ground, which isn't such a surprise, but we managed to get some stuff from the chatter nets of the squadron deployed to intercept the insurgents. They must be a hundred kilometres away, way out of normal range, but it's just bouncing off the ionosphere or something."

"Enough of the technical talk, Corporal, but well done. The upshot, Tang," continued Zhou, turning to the Major, "is that they arrived too late. It seems the bastards ambushed our trucks and released their man who was being taken to Lhasa.

"And even worse, they walked into a couple of booby traps."

"Shit."

"Shit indeed. The Corporal's men transcribed everything they could pick up." He nodded to the documents on the table. "We haven't got the full picture, but it makes grim reading. Two vehicles destroyed, several men dead and one or more badly injured.

"As it was obviously intended to, all this has slowed to a standstill the pursuit of these bandits. They managed to get clean away even with a badly injured man." He paused, dismissing the Signals Corporal before continuing.

"So Tang. There are the facts, or nearly all of them. It seems that our Commander in Shigatse has, in his wisdom, concluded that the bandits are now heading back to Mustang." He paused.

"A reasonable conclusion," agreed Tang. No response. Tang continued, filling the silence. "It's their base. It's where they're safe. Where else would they go?"

"Well Major, consider a couple of things. First and most obvious is that it's a hell of a long way on foot or horseback with at least one injured man."

"So they hijack a vehicle."

"They know we're after them and there are so few roads we'll have them all covered. They're not going to risk that."

"OK, but that doesn't mean they wont try to keep off the roads. They've avoided us for weeks already doing that."

"Agreed. But here's something else. That first ambush they carried out. What if the documents the commander had, very important documents apparently, weren't destroyed? Suppose these terrorists have them and have been able to contact the Americans. They aren't going to want to wait weeks and months before this stuff makes its way half way across the TAR and then over the mountains to Katmandu. By the time they get it, whatever it is, it will in all probability be long out of date. So what do the Americans do?"

"Send some kind of rescue?" suggested Tang incredulously. "Into the TAR?"

"Of course not, but the quality of this intelligence might make a rescue a reasonable proposition for the Americans when otherwise these scum would be left to fend for themselves. Look at the map, Tang." Zhou waved his hand in the general direction of where the band had last been operating. Tang leaned forward to make out the details in the light of the kerosene lamp, hissing and wheezing above them. After a couple of minutes he looked up at his superior officer.

"So you think they're heading south? Going to cross the border into Bhutan and get picked up at an airfield there?"

"Well done, Major. That's exactly what I think."

"But the border is very mountainous. There are peaks there above what?" he consulted the map again. "Above seven thousand metres."

"They're not going over the peaks. One thing these people have is local knowledge and help from deluded locals. If there's a way across they will know about it. And we have nothing like the number of troops on this border that we do further west on the Indian border, since the war. It's going to be easy for them to slip across undetected, an unmarked plane waiting and they're gone, to New Delhi or who knows where."

Tang pulled a packet of cigarettes from a pocket of his tunic and handed one automatically to his boss. Zhou produced a slim battered steel lighter, igniting it with a flick of his nicotine stained thumb and lighting both cigarettes. The two Officers smoked in silence for some time, each seemingly considering the implications of their conclusions. Tang was the first to speak.

"But where does this get us, Colonel? Even if you're right."

"I am right," interjected Zhou harshly.

"Yes," agreed Tang more cautiously. "But we still have our orders."

"Orders, Major? Duty. We have our duty to the People to root out their enemies and destroy them. There can be no higher orders than that. If others are too blind to see the situation clearly we have to deal with it ourselves. We're heading east. There are a few places these terrorists must pass through or near if I am right. They need rest and they need supplies and they need medical treatment. That means they must visit some of the villages on their likely route. Look here." He pointed again to the map.

"Heading south from the Friendship Highway they are certainly already past Kuchung, but these others need a visit from us. Sema, Seralung and this one, Sansa."

Chapter 39

ᛒ

Kathmandu, Nepal

"Hey, Abbi. Over here." Larsen seemed more ebullient and tanned than ever to Abbi as she caught sight of him standing and waving to her across the hotel lounge. He wore beige linen trousers, a white short-sleeved shirt and sported what looked to Abbi like a college tie. A nervous, hesitant smile flashed briefly over her face as she acknowledged the CIA Officer and crossed the room towards him.

"Please, take a seat." He pointed to a comfortable looking brown leather armchair at the opposite side of the low table to which he was standing. She sat and he then resumed his own seat, reaching for a glass on the table and taking a sip of the clear liquid.

"G and T," he commented. "Would you like one? I know it's a bit early, but I got quite a taste for these in London. Or what about a cup of tea? I know how you guys love that stuff. Never really got a taste for it myself."

"Tea would be nice. Darjeeling. When in Rome as they say, or near Rome," she decided that she needed a clear head when dealing with Larsen. Abbi glanced round the room, taking in the very ex-colonial atmosphere of the hotel with its huge fans whirring lazily overhead, large potted plants spilling luxuriant greenery and an obviously well-heeled clientele dressed for the early summer heat of Katmandu. Abbi herself wore an A-line skirt with a floral pattern which she now smoothed over her knees. A simple blouse of light pink contrasted easily with her almost black hair, cut in a bob and swept back by two tortoise shell slides.

"When did you arrive?" asked Larsen once he had ordered tea and cakes for Abbi.

"On Tuesday," answered Abbi, although as Larsen had bought her ticket she assumed he already knew. She always had the feeling that he knew everything about her.

"I'm staying with some people from *Rog Nang-Wa*. I've never met them before, but they're treating me like a long lost sister."

"It's a good organisation so I'm not surprised there are good people working for it."

"Yes." That feeling again. That he, the CIA, knew everything. Whether he did or not the trick worked and kept her constantly on the back foot.

"And how long have you been here?"

"Oh, about a week," he replied enigmatically.

"And are you staying here, in the hotel?"

"As a matter of fact I am. Great place, don't you think?" Abbi's thoughts quickly reeled back to the uniformed doorman with the thick waxed moustache who had greeted her moments earlier, the expansive black and white marble tiled lobby, the bell boy by the lift and had to agree that it was a world away from the grinding poverty which was most of the city and indeed of Nepal, one of the poorest countries on the planet.

"Yes it is. But why are we here, Mr. Larsen?"

"I thought it would be a good place to meet again."

"Don't be obtuse, Mr. Larsen. Why are we here in Katmandu?"

"Please. I told you before. Call me Martin."

"OK, Martin. Why are we here? You never really explained in London. I've trusted you and travelled half way across the world on the basis of that trust, so I hope it's going to have been worth it."

"Ah. Here's the tea." Turning to the waiter, a slim Nepali boy in white trousers and shirt. "Please, put it down there." He indicated to the table in front of Abbi. The boy ritually removed the items on his tray onto the table and poured the rich golden liquid from a silver teapot into the white china cup.

"Milk?" enquired the boy.

"That's fine, thank you." The boy retreated

"That looks great. I almost wish I'd tried it myself. Perhaps I could get into this tea drinking if I did it up here where they grow the stuff."

"Mr. Larsen. Martin." Abbi had a faint note of exasperation in her voice.

"OK, Abbi, you win. I was just enjoying myself so much. This place. Taking morning tea with a lovely young Englishwoman. Drag me back into reality."

"You said we could help Peter by coming out here."

"You know that's not his name, don't you?"

"What? What are you talking about?" Abbi looked flustered and the colour drained from her face as she tried to avoid Larsen's eyes.

"Mr. Smith. You know that's not his real name?" He waited for a response, but none was forthcoming. Abbi looked nervously over her shoulder and then picked up her tea cup, hoping that Larsen would not notice her hands shaking as she sipped from the delicate white vessel.

"You do know, don't you?" he said at last with what sounded like surprise in his voice.

"So this is serious for you. And for him."

"Why did you think it wasn't? Would I have come all this way if I wasn't sure about him?" Abbi almost hissed, looking intently at Larsen now.

"So stop you bloody games now, or I'm leaving." She began to rise, but Larsen reached his long arms across the low table and took hold of her before she could stand.

"Please. Stay. I'm sorry. I play games. It's my job." His tone was contrite and Abbi half believed him. Removing his hand from her arm she retook her seat.

"OK. No more games. Please. Just tell me what you know and what we can do to help Peter."

"Like I said, I've been here about a week. Officially, I'm on leave and that's what the Agency thinks. But I just dropped into the embassy here to catch up with some old buddies. Nothing strange about that. But one of these guys is an old Tibet hand still plugged in to current ops over there, such as they are. Normally, in the job I do, I'd know what was going on anyway, but since the operation I organised involving your Mr Smith didn't work out I got the feeling my boss back in Delhi cut me out of the loop. Nothing was said, but next thing I know I'm due for some leave. So I headed for London to talk to you."

"Forgive me Martin. I don't know anything about these things, about the world you live in, but if your boss has doubts about you, aren't you taking a risk contacting me and coming out here asking questions?"

Larsen lowered his voice conspiratorially. "Perhaps you're getting the hang of this, Abbi. I am taking a risk. A risk for you and this guy Smith, because, like I told you before, for once I believe in the cause. The cause of the people of Tibet who we, the CIA, nobly helped in their fight for freedom. And now we're in danger of selling them down the river for political expediency. I don't want to be a part of that.

"However, just so you're not too worried about me, I'm staying here under an assumed name and the meeting I had with my colleague was well away from the embassy. In any case, what are they going to do? Sack me?" Abbi said nothing, but looked directly into the striking blue eyes of the man opposite her as if to say "or worse".

"Hey, I know that look. You've been reading to many novels. John Le Carre. Great writer, but the real world's not like that. We're just beaurocrats waiting to draw our pensions."

"Well, let's hope you do," replied Abbi, wondering again if she had misjudged this man. She was still unsure whether she could trust him, but what choice did she have?

"Anyhow, this guy at the embassy, let's call him Ted. After all that's his name." Larsen laughed heartily at his own joke. "Ted told me that our boys have got themselves way down south towards the border with Bhutan. You know where Bhutan is?." Abbi nodded. Her knowledge of the geography of the whole region had improved greatly since she started working for Rog Nang-Wa as the charity worked with Tibetan refugees in every country bordering Tibet to the south.

Undeterred, Larsen produced a small map and laid it before her on the table. "Those cakes look great. Do you mind?"

"Please. Help yourself." Larsen picked up a slice of rich fruit cake and took a delicate bite before continuing.

"Here's Shigatse," he pointed. "Tibet's second city and where the local bad guys have their HQ. The PLA are onto your man and in hot pursuit. There's no point in denying that, but so far he's kept one step ahead so let's hope he can keep it up.

"Now, the group were operating west of Shigatse so they could dash back to Mustang and safety when they needed to, but for reasons we won't go into they headed west way beyond Gyantse which is here." He pointed to Tibet's third city on the map. "After a run in with the PLA they decided or were forced to keep heading south. Somewhere here," his finger prodded vaguely at a mountainous area south of the Gyatse-Lhasa road, "they miraculously got their comms working again and started talking to us."

"Why miraculously?" interrupted Abbi.

"Well, we heard nothing from them for weeks when they are supposed to check in regularly and then suddenly here they are, way off the route we expected. They've been up to something we don't really know about, although to be fair Smith's band are not Agency guys. Only some people we sent to join them are.

"So it seems they were only about fifty clicks from the Bhutan border and asking us for a lift. Now I have to be honest. Usually, these people are on their own and there is no way we could or would extract them from Tibet. But it seems they picked up something on their travels which the Agency could be very interested in. So a plan has been hatched. If they can get themselves across the border to a designated airfield, an unmarked plane will pick them up and hey presto, whisk them off to safety."

"And where is safety?"

"Here, Abbi. Kathmandu. Most of these men are going to want to return to the fight and that means going back to Mustang. So they have to come through here. And that's why we're here. Why I talked you into coming here." Abbi thought about what Larsen had told her. It all made a kind of sense, so why was she not convinced? Smith was nearly at the Bhutanese border. Might even be over it by now if Larsen's intelligence was days old as it probably was. She dared to hope that Smith could be in Kathmandu at any time. That they could be together again. At that moment that was the only thing she wanted.

"This all sounds good news," began Abbi, "but why. Why bring me out here. I could have waited in London for him."

"Would you have wanted to do that? It might be ages before he could leave. We might want to debrief him or .." Larsen hesitated.

"Or what?"

"Or he might decide to go back to Mustang."

"Why would he do that and why would you care?"

"I care because, although I've never met this guy, perhaps I know more about what makes him tick than you do. I'm sure you've thought about this, but it's a certain kind of person who takes off into one of the the most remote places on earth in the middle of a war and joins a small band of guys on horseback who are in the business of fighting the biggest army the world has ever seen. And whatever he may have said to you in the past, that kind of guy doesn't suddenly change. Not in my experience and I've known not a few guys like that.

"But sadly there's only going to be one end to this fight and I don't see any point in your man getting himself killed. Perhaps if he sees you here you can make him go back with you. But if you're way off in London I don't think you have a chance.

"Why do I care? Just because one more wasted life isn't going to change anything. But if you want a pragmatic CIA reason to convince you, it would not be good for us for a Brit to be caught fighting the PLA at a time when the US is looking at improving relations with China. We and your Government don't need that kind of political embarrassment just now.

"So it's in both our interests to get your man out of here soonest."

Again Abbi tried to weigh up Larsen's words and again it all made a kind of sense. What else could she do but trust him for the moment?

"So what do we do? What do I do?"

"Just wait, Abbi. Enjoy this incredible town and I'll contact you as soon as I have any news."

"Shall I give you my address? The phone number of the people I'm staying with?" Abbi reached for her bag.

"No need," replied Larsen.

Chapter 40

श्री

Sansa, Tibet

Lhalu the barefoot doctor was awaiting the return of the funeral party.

"Did you see it?" he asked as they entered the house. He paced the room as he spoke and his dark eyes were wild, darting back and forth.

"Did we see what? What's happened?" asked Smith, taking Lhalu by the shoulder to stop the incessant pacing which was already beginning to annoy him.

"A plane. It flew right over the village. About thirty minutes ago. I wanted to ride out and tell you, warn you, but Yangsom said we shouldn't go out in case they came back and thought we were panicking." Smith looked appreciatively over at Lhalu's wife, calmly stirring some concoction on the stove. She looked the Englishman full in the eye for the first time.

"Our only chance is to appear that everything is normal. They are checking everywhere looking for you. As long as they see nothing unusual they won't send the troops here yet. They will come eventually, but hopefully you will be long gone by then," Yangsom pronounced.

"You are right," agreed Smith. "We've put you in enough danger. We must leave as soon as it gets dark. Where are the others?"

"They're keeping inside their billets. I think they are packing up already."

"Good. How is Lhotse?"

"He is much stronger."

"Strong enough to travel?" asked Smith with doubt in his voice.

"No. It will be some time before he can ride, but I am beginning to think he will make a good recovery."

"Will you still keep him here? He is putting you all in terrible danger."

"We said that we would look after him and we will. We can take him to one of the shepherds' huts on the high pasture, well away from the village. He'll soon be able to look after himself and someone will keep an eye on him. Take him supplies. Until he is well enough to travel." Lhalu's composure seemed to have returned, much to Smith's relief.

"And Mila? What will you do with him?"

"I think you will have to leave that to us as well. Once you leave here you must forget about this place. All we ask is that you never tell anyone you were here. We will provide you with a guide to get you to the border." At that moment the door opened.

"Ah! Here is your guide." Smith looked behind him to see who had entered.

"Mola, are you ready to leave?"

"Yes, father," replied the girl Smith had watched washing her hair in the stream on the day of their arrival.

"What?" was all that Smith could manage.

"Mola will make you an excellent guide. She was born on the saddle of a horse. We were herders once. She is strong and has travelled the trade route to Bhutan with me many times. She knows it as well as anyone. She will not let you down."

"And she will be company for Chungla," added Tashi, who had said nothing until now.

Smith smiled at his friend, acknowledging the rebuke, namely that he could hardly refuse the girl when he had encouraged Chungla.

"Who knows," added Yangsom, stifling any possible protest from Smith.

"She may be safer with you than staying here. She will leave you once you reach the first village inside Bhutan. We have friends there. She will return with the next caravan."

As the light began to fade, fighters and nuns began to assemble in front of Lhalu's house. Horses were led from their stables, already saddled and final checks were made to ensure that everything was properly loaded for travel. The horses stamped their hooves loudly on the rocky ground and snorted their displeasure at once again becoming beasts of burden after the lazy days spent grazing in Sansa. They had recovered some of the weight and strength lost in the hard march over the mountains to the ambush and subsequent escape. To Smith's relief they looked fitter than they had since leaving Mustang, what seemed now like years before, but was in fact only a matter of weeks.

"So, it is time to go. We will miss you. Our sleepy village has not had such excitement in years."

"You have been very kind, Lhalu," replied Tashi, speaking for them all. "Let us hope you have no more visitors for a while."

Lhalu and Yangsom and several of the villagers who had billeted the band reached up to shake hands with the riders and exchange final farewells and thanks. Amongst the riders sat Mola, her hair now swept back from her youthful Asiatic face with a single braid protruding from her round fur hat. She wore a dark blue *chuba* edged with a simple narrow multi-coloured pattern. On her feet were stout felt boots and on her face a smile of immense pride. She bent low to kiss her mother.

"Time to go," called Tendruk, assuming the role of leader since Pemba's death. Smith did not aspire to such a position himself, but he did wonder how this would play out amongst the two groups within the party, *Khampas* and CIA men. With these thoughts in his mind he turned his horse away from the Sansa, looking back and waving one last time as the village receded into the night.

Chapter 41

ና

Near Gyantse, Tibet

Colonel Zhou's squadron was already south of Gyantse on the Friendship Highway. They had broken camp before dawn. The only route open to them led back through Shigatse and it was much less likely that the column of vehicles would be challenged by the Garrison as they trundled through the town in darkness. This had proved to be the case. Nor were they challenged as they passed Gyantse, but here the road swung south of the town, making detection less likely.

The column was now hidden from sight on a rough track which dropped steeply below the road before levelling out parallel to the Tambayang Chu River, visible far below. Soldiers sat with their backs to the heavy black tyres of their vehicles trying to get some warmth from the early morning sun as they ate a breakfast of noodles and drank hot tea dispensed from an urn at the rear of the cook vehicle.

Zhou, with a mug of steaming black tea in hand, pulled the headset from his head and handed it back to the radio operator. He strode over to where Major Tang sat in the passenger seat of his command vehicle, his legs trailing out of the open door. Tang lowered his chop sticks from his mouth as the Colonel approached.

"That was Lo on the radio. A man we can trust, I think."

Tang said nothing, waiting to hear what the Recce Flight Commander had reported.

"He's been detailed by the Garrison Commander to cover as much ground as possible looking for the terrorists so he and his men have been flying from dawn till dusk. I persuaded him," Zhou paused and smiled before continuing. "I persuaded him to extend his range south of the area designated by the Garrison Commander. Yesterday afternoon he found himself down by Lake Phurma and buzzed the villages to the west of the Lake, the ones on the likely route to Bhutan, if my hunch is right."

"And what did he see?"

"Nothing."

"Nothing?"

"Well," continued the Colonel, "not quite nothing. The pictures of this village, Sanso, show several horses grazing outside. Possibly more horses than a village that size would have. But who knows? Maybe it is a prosperous place.

"It's not proof, but it points the way I'm thinking, so it's good enough. Give the men another ten minutes, then we move out."

"Sir, vehicles coming." announced Major Tang's radio operator, who had received the message on the chatter net from the rear vehicle of the column, parked some way back up the track. "It looks like they're ours." Tang clambered out of the turret of his vehicle and stood on the roof. He could see a troop of what looked to be three or four armoured personnel carriers heading down the track from the Highway towards their position at some speed.

Tang relayed the message, "Colonel, vehicles approaching from our rear." Zhou stepped away from his vehicle and looked back down the track. Within seconds the first vehicle was alongside him. As it came to a halt the commander's head and shoulders rose through the open turret. He swept the dust from his goggles with the back of a gloved hand before lifting them onto his helmet.

"Good morning, Colonel," said Captain Deng, saluting smartly.

"You almost look like a soldier from down here, Captain. It must be a trick of the light," retorted Zhou. "What brings you here?" continued the Colonel, attempting to disguise his annoyance at being found, especially by Deng. "How did you know where we were?"

"I am the Intelligence Officer, Colonel." As if Zhou needed reminding.

"Alright. Stop pissing around. Why are you here and what do you want?" Deng, at his casually most arrogant, produced a packet of cigarettes before continuing. He offered one to Zhou who declined. Deng lit the cigarette, inhaled deeply and scanned the countryside around them as the blue-grey smoke seeped slowly from his nostrils. Finally his gaze returned to Zhou, almost as if he had momentarily forgotten he was there.

"Well, Colonel, we've been receiving information that the bandits may not be heading in the direction we, that is the Garrison Commander, assumed they would. We're also led to believe that you subscribe to this point of view."

"And who told you that?"

"I am afraid that we have to protect our sources, Sir." That was the second time he had called Zhou "Sir." he tried to detect the old sarcasm, but could not. Perhaps their last encounter had convinced the Intelligence Officer that the old Colonel was not a man to be crossed. The only thing that confused Zhou was that Deng for once seemed to have the whip hand, having probably caught Zhou disobeying orders. So why the apparent deference?

"However," continued Deng, "the consensus now is that the bandits are probably heading south towards the border, possibly with the intention of escaping into Bhutan. So our effort is to be redirected. The troops deployed to the ambush site are now heading this way, but at the moment you are the lead unit.

"I have written orders for you here Colonel, but in essence they require you to take command of the operation on the ground with all troops in the area, including border units, under you command." Deng produced the documents and climbed down from his vehicle to hand them to the Colonel, followed by another sharp salute. Zhou took the orders with a wry smile. Back on top. No longer the furtive fugitive, but the field commander, as it should have been all along. But no time for recriminations, or gloating.

Zhou opened the folder which Deng had handed him. It was a short document with little more detail than Deng had described. He knew what needed to be done and the Garrison Commander knew it as well.

"Let's see your map Deng. Show me what you know, or think you know." Deng produced a map and Major Tang was called to join the two Officers. Having pointed the likely escape route of the bandits on the map, Deng then showed Zhou where the other units now under his command were currently located.

"And what about border crossings?"

"As you know, Colonel, there are no official crossing points and the terrain is pretty wild, even by local standards so our few border troops are currently located here and here." He pointed to two points on the map north of the border. "They are mounted as there are few tracks suitable for vehicles. There are other places where these people could slip across the border undetected, where smugglers and refugees cross." Deng pointed out likely crossing points and marked them with small pencil circles. Never use a cross on a map as it obliterates the detail.

"We turn a blind eye to a certain amount of unofficial coming and going, as you know. Even encourage it to keep our territorial claims alive." Zhou did not need to be reminded that Beijing had unilaterally redrawn this very border on maps it had published back in 1961 and continued to pressurise its tiny southern neighbour about disputed territory.

"So there are only a handful of likely crossing points. That makes our task easier. Much easier with your assistance, Captain." Zhou nodded to Deng in acknowledgement. "Now we need to formulate a plan and brief the other units. What about these villages, Sema, Sansa and the rest? The bandits could have been given refuge in any of them."

"As we think they are already in the mountains south of there I don't think there's any useful intelligence to be gained from them."

"Very well. We can put them on a back burner to visit after the success of our operation and then round up any collaborators"

"With respect, Colonel, you don't need to worry about that. It's already taken care of." Zhou was going to leave it at that as he had enough on his mind, but found himself asking.

"Taken care of? How?"

"The Garrison Commander has requested a tasking."

"A tasking? For what?"

"For a Tupolov."

"What! Why would he do that?"

"These people need to be taught a lesson"

"And what lesson are they going to learn from a strategic bomber flattening their villages?"

"The Americans have a saying about winning over the locals, Colonel. It translates as something like "get them by the short hairs and the hearts and minds will follow". We must be prepared to learn even from our enemies."

"I'll talk to the Garrison Commander. This is unnecessary. And we could learn a lot from questioning the right people"

"It's too late for that, I am afraid, Colonel. The tasking has been accepted by Beijing. The aircraft will take off from Xinziang tomorrow." To Zhou the bombing was wasteful and vindictive. He was here to fight a war, not extract vengeance, but seeing defeat on this issue a foregone conclusion, he forced it from his mind and returned to the business in hand.

With a map spread over the bonnet of one of the vehicles, Zhou briefed Tang, Deng and the troop commanders before his orders were relayed by radio to the other units in the battle group.

"We will spearhead the operation," announced Zhou, "by heading south and then sweeping westwards along the border to form a barrier, along with the existing border units, into which the fugitives will be driven. The units currently to our rear will strike west here," he pointed to a location on the map, "towards Lake Phurma, and from there turn south to drive the quarry into the trap. A simple hammer and anvil tactic." He paused for effect before continuing.

" The only problem is the terrain, which will limit the use of our vehicles in places.

"Deng, contact the border units and get them to round up as many horses as possible. All of you, make sure you know which of your men can ride. Movement on foot is to be a last resort. The enemy could easily get ahead of us.

"And Deng, get that plane in the air again."

"Any questions? No? Good. Then let's get moving."

Along the length of the convoy engines roared into life and one by one the vehicles pulled out onto the track. The air was soon thick with the smell of diesel fumes and dust as the operation got under way.

Chapter 42

ॐ

Kathmandu, Nepal

"Can I speak to Abbi?" The question was posed in good Nepalese, but any native speaker would have recognised that the caller was not.

"There is no-one here of that name," came the reply, also from a foreigner, but in the local language

"Listen, Abbi," in English now. "It's me, Martin. Don't talk. This line's safe, but I need to see you, urgently. Be where we met before in an hour. Wear some sensible clothes."

There was a click and the phone went dead. Abbi held the receiver in her hand, just looking at it for several seconds before replacing the black Bakelite instrument on its cradle. She had not heard from Larsen for three days, since their meeting in the hotel. Then suddenly this. The summons to meet in an hour. The obvious urgency in his voice. And the request that she wear sensible clothes. What the hell did that mean?

Guessing, she changed into denim jeans and a dark blue tee-shirt. On feet she wore tennis shoes. She tied back her hair in a short pony tail and slung a bag with two shoulder straps over her left shoulder. A pair of sunglasses completed the ensemble. From where she was staying she could walk to the hotel in about forty minutes. She slipped out of the door of the shabby concrete apartment, looking cautiously to right and left and headed quickly down the hill towards the old town.

Larsen was waiting for her in the lobby of the hotel. Seeing her, he crossed towards the doorway where the doorman was pointing her in the direction of the reception. She had hardly crossed the threshold when Larsen took her arm and gently but firmly swung her round and back out into the busy street. His face was fixed and determined, his usual casual bonhomie having apparently deserted him. He led her across the wide pavement and waved authoritatively for a taxi.

"Where are we going? What's going on?" stammered Abbi as a battered black vehicle pulled up beside them. Larsen pushed her into the taxi and as she slid across the bench seat he ducked his head and followed her inside.

"To the airport," Larsen instructed the driver in Nepalese. Abbi understood the command, but not why they were going there.

"What have you heard?" insisted Abbi. Larsen looked out of the window for several seconds before replying. The taxi had immediately driven into heavy mid-morning traffic as a mêlée of cars, mopeds, bicycles and rickshaws battled with pedestrians for the limited space available. The cacophony penetrated the car through the open windows. Kathmandu lies in a bowl surrounded by high mountains and Abbi could almost taste the pollution trapped by the high pressure air crushing down on the poverty stricken city.

Finally, Larsen seemed to come to his senses.

"A plane is due into Tribhuvan Airport sometime today. An unmarked Air America plane from Bhutan. Air America's the CIA's cover name for its air ops. It'll park up on the far eastern perimeter, well out of sight of the main terminal."

"Oh my God!" exclaimed Abbi. "They're coming. Today?" She did not attempt to hide her excitement and pleasure. When Larsen had called she assumed things were about to happen, but had forced herself to be circumspect. Now, after all these months, they were coming back, he was coming back. There had been times when she had hardly dared to hope that she would see Smith again.

Then she looked at Larsen. He had no reason to be as excited as Abbi, but his face was stern. Unduly so it seemed to Abbi.

"What's wrong? What aren't you telling me?" There was suddenly an edge of concern, almost panic in her voice.

"It's probably nothing, Abbi. Don't worry." He smiled weakly.

"What's nothing?" her voice louder now. The traffic lurched slowly forward and a moped weaved its way through the traffic behind the taxi.

"I haven't got the full story, but there was some fighting as they crossed the border."

The moped inexorably closed the gap on the taxi.

"Fighting!"

"Don't sound so surprised. What do you think these guys do for a living?" Larsen was sounding more like the Larsen Abbi knew, if indeed she did know him, at all.

"OK, yes of course. It's just suddenly all a bit close to home. I had it in my head that everything was going to be fine now they were so close."

"I can understand that, Abbi, but shit happens. Let's hope not too much shit in this case. I'm just trying to prepare you. Not for the worst, because I don't know much more than you, but I just know that things aren't always that straightforward." Abbi was not quite sure what that was supposed to mean, but it was obviously not a discussion topic they were going to make any meaningful progress on so she decided to concentrate on what she could control, namely her own composure.

The moped rider and his pillion both looked like locals, slim and wiry men with brown skin, wearing battered, grubby shorts and flip-flops on their feet. Both wore full face helmets.

Suddenly the road ahead cleared and the taxi driver sped pointlessly ahead towards the next set of traffic lights.

"So are we going to the airport?"

"There's no hurry. The plane's not expected for a while, but I just thought we would be better early than late. Then we can check out the situation before they arrive."

"Will we be able to get onto the airfield or will we meet them in the terminal?" Larsen looked at her.

"This is an Agency op, Abbi. They won't be going through customs or any of that stuff. They'll be whisked away to the US Embassy, or more likely a safe house in the first place. I'm out of the loop here so I don't know for sure."

"So what's the plan?"

"This is the plan. What I told you. We take the taxi to the other side of the airfield, we wait, and then we make it up from there." This was not Abbi's idea of a CIA agents plan, but she had no better ones and anyway she was convinced that Larsen only ever told her half of what he knew. She was certainly praying that was the case today.

The traffic lights turned to red as the taxi approached and the driver braked hard to avoid careering out into the oncoming traffic. Abbi instinctively braced herself, but both passengers slid forward on their seats. As they regained their positions on the bench seat Abbi became aware for the first time of the whine of a two stroke engine through the open window. She looked across Larsen to see the moped pull up and stop right along-side them.

The pillion rider wore a thin dark blue windproof baseball jacket with a number twenty-three on the right breast. As Abbi watched he tugged the zip half way down and reached inside the jacket. Larsen was suddenly aware of the man and yelled, "Abbi, get...." The dull black of the Glock 9 mm was only visible for an instant. Two shots were fired into the taxi. Larsen slumped back, his face suddenly expressionless, eyes glassy. The moped instantly pulled away and swung wildly to the left through the red light, into the stream of traffic and was gone.

Screaming "Oh God! ... Oh God!", Abbi cradled Larsen's head as the blood seeped onto her T-shirt. The lights changed to green, but the taxi did not move as the driver looked with horror over his shoulder at the scene of carnage on the back seat. All around them horns blasted as cars and motorcycles tried to swing around the marooned taxi.

"He's dead! Jesus Christ, he's dead," sobbed Abbi over and over.

"I get to hospital," announced the driver, finally regaining his senses.

"Too late," muttered Abbi. "It's too late. Can't you see? He's dead!"

"I get to hospital," repeated the driver. "Only five minutes." He crashed the car into gear and launched it in the direction of the Bir Hospital located only a few streets away.

Within minutes the taxi was braking hard outside the hospital. The driver glanced briefly into the back of the vehicle to see Abbi clutching Larsen's prone body in her arms. She stared straight ahead of her as if in a trance. The driver leapt from the car and ran up the stone stairway into the building shouting for help as he went. In no time he returned with a small team of medics who dashed to the taxi and opened the rear nearside door. One of them began checking Larsen's vital signs. The taxi driver peered inside over them looking for the foreign woman. She was gone.

*

Knowing that Larsen was dead, Abbi had suppressed the rising panic as the taxi had approached the hospital. Realising that she could not help Larsen and that if she stayed with his body she would soon be consumed by officialdom, only one thing was now on her mind, finding Smith. If he was indeed arriving in Kathmandu today she had to be there. So as soon as the driver left to get help she stepped out into the traffic and ran across the busy Kantipath Road in the direction of Ratna Park. She immediately began frantically waving down a taxi and one stopped for her within a minute, a young Western woman being a good fare for any Nepali driver. She ducked down low on the back seat as the taxi pulled away, instructing the driver to head for the airport. He did a u-turn, passing the hospital entrance and the commotion of Larsen being pulled from the other taxi with barely a glance before turning right into Bag Bazaar Road.

"Sorry, I dropped my purse on the floor," announced Abbi as she appeared in the driver's rear view mirror for the first time, in case he was interested. He smiled into the mirror in acknowledgement. Within minutes they were crossing the river, just a kilometre or so to the airport. Abbi had decided to stick to Larsen's plan, accepting to herself again that it was not much of a plan, but it was the best she had.

At the airport she paid the driver and went into the terminal. There were not many shops inside, but Abbi had vaguely remembered one from her arrival in the city, what now seemed like weeks before. And there it was, a camera shop. They had what she was looking for, a pair of binoculars. West German as it happened so she assumed that they would be more than up to the job.

Slipping them into her shoulder bag, she returned to the airport entrance and joined the queue for taxis. It was not long before she was in her third Kathmandu taxi within an hour, the slightly puzzled driver taking her north on the Ring Road and not into the city centre where most Westerners headed from the airport. Abbi produced from her bag what was by now a well thumbed map of the city and studied it intently, trying to decide which way was best. She looked up, suddenly aware that the vehicle was slowing. They were now behind a large wagon which was slowly pulling into the middle of the road in front of them to avoid something. As they came closer Abbi could see that the obstacle was one black and one brown calf, each sat in the edge of the road whilst their mother

239

casually chomped on some weeds growing on the edge of the walkway. The taxi driver followed the wagon round them before picking up speed again, making no comment on this apparently normal incident.

They turned off the Ring Road at Mitra Park and soon turned right again to cross the river. Abbi could see a couple of temples marked on her map and they soon passed them, confirming that she was where she hoped she was. The airport was now just to their south, but what she had hoped was an open area between the road and the runway was in fact densely wooded.

"Keep going," she commanded the driver as he looked questioningly in the mirror. Finally, to her relief, the trees were replaced by a small area of scrub and she could make out the wire perimeter fence and taxiing planes beyond.

"Stop! Here!" she yelled at the driver, who jammed on the brakes in response to here frantic commands. He looked around to see what the emergency was and then at Abbi, bewildered.

"Back up," then in a more measured tone, "please back up a few yards." The car rolled gently backwards as Abbi stared out of the rear driver's side window until she was satisfied that the view was as good as possible.

"Yes, here, please," she commanded and the slow-moving vehicle came to a halt again. Taking the newly acquired binoculars from their case she twisted the adjusters until she was happy with the image quality. The criss-cross of the wire fencing was slightly out of focus, but did not impede her clear view of the aircraft beyond.

"Will you wait for me?" enquired Abbi in what she realised was an unnecessarily loud voice. She was not quite sure how much English he understood, but he understood more of the situation than Abbi realised. He answered her question with one of his own.

"You going to look at planes?"

"Yes. I'm a plane spotter," she lied unconvincingly.

"That not a good thing, Miss. Police don't like people watching planes." My God, he was right. How stupid was she. There were probably military planes on the tarmac. She had read stories of tourists who had run into serious problems watching planes abroad. Nepal was probably well down the list of places sympathetic to plane spotting, with its massive warring neighbours and less than democratic government.

"You watch planes from here if you want," added the driver encouragingly, but at the same time tapping his meter to remind her that this was a business transaction.

"Yes of course. Thank you. I can pay you " she re-assured him.

They sat in the taxi for over half an hour as Abbi systematically scanned every plane within sight and the driver read the newspaper he pulled from behind the sun visor, occasionally scribbling on it with a pencil he kept behind his right ear. Planes from BOAC, Pan Am, Indian Airways came and went along with private planes and ones belonging to what she guessed were local airlines she had never heard of. But no unmarked ones. She looked again at her map, trying to decide whether they would get a better view from another position. There were clearly some parts of the airfield she could not see. She decided to move.

"Can we go further on?" Without answering, the driver folded his newspaper, started the engine and moved slowly away. After a few minutes Abbi realised that they had indeed found a place which revealed a section of the airfield they had not been able to see before.

"This will do." The vehicle stopped again and the engine was extinguished. Abbi pushed the binoculars to her face and continued her search. After a few minutes the driver put down his newspaper and looked at his cheap watch.

"This becoming risky. I think we go soon." He had an anxious look on his face and Abbi agreed that they were pushing their luck. She was not concerned about the police arresting her as she was sure she would talk her way out of it fairly quickly, even if it meant getting the local Consul involved. But if the police turned up, that would be the end of her chances of seeing the plane should it come in today. What should she do? What were the choices? Leave and come back later in another taxi or persuade someone to bring her? That had the advantage of extending the possible time she could spend watching, but would leave a time gap now. If she stayed much longer the police may well come. They no doubt patrolled the perimeter as a matter of routine. What had Larsen said? An unmarked plane was due in. Not now, there was no hurry, but later in the day. And how long ago was that? She looked at her watch. It was nearly two hours since Larsen had pushed her into the taxi. Nearly two hours since he had been shot dead, sat next to her, in broad daylight in the middle of a bustling city. What the hell was she doing here? What had she got herself involved in?

It was then that she noticed the next plane landing, taking her mind back to the business in hand. She automatically trained her binoculars on it as it smoothly touched down. A turbo-prop. Four engines. Not the first she had seen since becoming an instant plane spotter. Her hopes had been raised before, but from what Larsen had told her this was the type of plane she imagined she was looking for.

As the aircraft taxied away from the runway it at first headed in their direction and then began to bear to the right and into profile as it moved slowly towards the north-east corner of the airfield, away from the terminal buildings. This had given Abbi the chance to examine the plane from the front and the side, but she could not distinguish any obvious markings on the olive green fuselage or wings.

"Hercules," announced the driver suddenly.

"What?" responded Abbi, continuing to stare through her binoculars.

"That plane. Called Hercules. American." How did he know that? It didn't matter. He was probably right. It did remind her of planes she had seen in England. Perhaps they had belonged to the American airforce or the RAF. But it helped to make it more likely that it was a plane the CIA would use.

"Uh, uh," she finally acknowledged, still scrutinising the aircraft as it came to a halt within her vision. Abbi was becoming increasingly excited that this might be what she was waiting for. Could this really be it? Could he finally be coming back to her? And how would he react on seeing her here, in Kathmandu? A shot of adrenalin like a double espresso surged through her body, making her feel suddenly weak and anxious.

The cargo door at the rear of the aircraft began to lower, a man in a flying suit, presumably a crew member, standing on it, his whole frame gradually coming into view. As the ramp touched the ground so did the loadmaster. He turned and beckoned back into the plane. As Abbi watched other people began to appear. She could not make out their faces, but she recognised what they were wearing – *chubas*.

"It's them," she said aloud. The driver looked up from his paper again in the direction of the plane.

"We go now?"

"In a minute."

"Must go soon. Police," he reminded her. She had put down the binoculars and now saw movement in her wider field of vision, a vehicle heading in the direction of the plane. An ambulance. She picked up the binoculars again and watched with increasing terror as the white van with its blue emergency lights flashing, approached the Hercules. First one and then a second stretcher appeared on the ramp as the ambulance pulled up at its base.

As the stretchers were loaded into the ambulance other people disembarked from the aircraft, more Tibetan men, then what looked like a young nun and a lama, the latter visible for only seconds before he climbed into the ambulance. Abbi's heart leapt. Tashi! She was sure it was him.

Another vehicle, an unmarked minibus, had arrived by now and everyone clambered aboard. No-one else came down the ramp. No Peter. But perhaps one of the "Tibetans" had been him. She knew he had grown his hair and dressed like a Khampa, so perhaps she had not recognised him. No. Impossible! But if he wasn't there, where the hell was he? The driver looked over his shoulder at Abbi.

"Are you alright, Miss? Are you unwell?" He could see that her face was white and clammy.

"N... no, I, I'm fine," she stammered. Looking back across the airfield she saw the small convoy moving quickly away towards the terminal.

"Follow them!" she commanded. "Where will they come out of the airport?"

"There is an entrance by the terminal. Perhaps they will leave there. I don't know for sure."

"Let's try it," she responded, trying to sound in control. As the taxi swung round to retrace its earlier route Abbi thrust her head out of the open window and gulped in the cooling air.

They soon found themselves once again near the main entrance to the airport where Abbi had earlier purchased her binoculars.

"This is the gate." The driver pointed to a large double gate made of wire with a metal frame and barbed wire coiled along the top. It was firmly closed with a large padlock hanging from the centre.

"It's the wrong gate!" Abbi's voice was almost hysterical. "Or they've already gone."

"I do my best, Miss. There is another gate further down." He pointed along the Ring Road heading southwards. "Shall we try?"

"No. We've missed them. I'm sure." There was still an edge of panic in her voice. Oh God. What should she do? Her mind was a blank.

"Ambulances, Miss. Must go to hospital." Obviously. What the hell was the matter with her?

"Which one would they go to if they had an injured man? An emergency?" Suddenly it came to her. Was Smith on one of the stretchers? Why hadn't she thought of it before? Because he's invincible, that's why. But it could be him. Her emotions raged between relief at the thought that he was here after all and terror at what his injuries might be.

"Bir Hospital," answered the driver interrupting her turmoil, then plunging her into more.

"The Bir?" she repeated stupidly. Larsen. That's where Larsen was. Or his body. No she couldn't face that. She couldn't go back there. And maybe the other taxi driver would still be there and recognise her. She'd be dragged into the investigation of his death, perhaps arrested. She'd never find Peter.

But the driver had taken matters into his own hands and was already heading in the direction of the hospital. Abbi's mind was racing and she was about to tell him to pull over and jump out of the taxi when she noticed market stalls along the roadside. She did tell him to pull up, but to wait. He still had not been paid so Abbi was confident he would not leave her. She ran to a nearby stall selling clothes, quickly grabbed several items, paid for them, and without waiting for change dived back into the taxi. Getting into the mood of events the driver sped away in the direction of the hospital.

As the driver glanced wide-eyed into the rear of the vehicle, Abbi removed her tee-shirt, replacing it with a floral blouse in pastel colours which almost fit her, wriggled out of her jeans and pulled on a simple white A-line skirt. She slipped her sunglasses into her bag and reluctantly put on her round gold rimmed glasses which vanity normally prevented her from wearing except when reading. She tugged a wide brimmed straw hat onto her head to cover her thick dark hair. The driver looked puzzled, but impressed by the resulting transformation of his strange passenger. Their eyes met momentarily as Abbi checked how she looked in the mirror. She smiled at him and said a silent thank you.

*

There was no sign of the ambulances or minibus at the front entrance to the hospital.

"Can we drive round the back?" The driver dutifully pulled out into the road again and turned down the side of the building, a two story stone edifice, solid and confident as the British Empire had once been. Rows of ornately decorated arched windows stared out from each floor and the second floor was capped by a balustrade which ran below the tiled roof. Protruding from the side of the building was a covered entranceway similar to those that Abbi had seen on stately homes she had visited with her mother as a girl back in England. She imagined for a second, horse drawn ambulances pulling up under its shelter to disgorge wounded Ghurkhas following some colonial skirmish.

Then, as they approached she saw the red flash of brake lights in the deep shadow of the entrance way. The lights instantly went out and the vehicle pulled away into the sunlight. An ambulance. Not surprising, but Abbi was sure it was one from the airfield.

"It is them," confirmed the driver.

"Stop by the entrance," Abbi directed. She scrabbled in her purse and produced a bundle of notes as the taxi came to a halt.

"You want me to wait?"

"No. Here." She pushed the notes into his hand and opened the door.

"Too much," he said. Abbi leaned in through the open driver's window, kissed him on the cheek and was gone.

She pushed open the swing doors and looked to right and left down a wide tiled corridor with cream painted walls stained brown with generations of smoking patients, nurses and doctors. The ubiquitous smell of hospitals seeped into her nostrils. There was no-one to be seen so she turned left for no good reason and ran down the corridor. At the far end the corridor turned at right angles and as Abbi rounded the corner orderlies were wheeling a gurney only yards ahead of her. She slowed to a brisk walk, closing on them with each step. They wheeled the gurney into a side room with Abbi right behind them. The room was obviously some kind of treatment room with cupboards and cabinets around the walls and a couple of what looked like operating tables in the centre. A man already lay on one of the tables and various people busied themselves around him.

"You can't come in here," said one of the orderlies, becoming aware of Abbi's presence.

"It's alright," said a familiar voice.

"Tashi! Oh, thank God it's you." She threw herself into his waiting arms and closed her eyes, burying her face in his rough woollen robe. After a moment she stepped back from him, wiping the tears from her face as she took in the sight of the monk.

"How are you?" she asked eventually.

"I'm fine, Abbi. How are you?"

"I don't know, Tashi. I don't know"

Tashi put his arm around Abbi and led her back into the corridor.

They sat on tubular steel chairs with brown plywood seats. An orderly brought them cups of tea.

"Is he here, Tashi? Tell me."

"Drink your tea, Abbi," Tashi encouraged. She sipped the hot brown liquid, peering up at the Tibetan lama over her cup, terrified at what he might be about to tell her.

"Is he injured?" she insisted, and then after a pause, "is he dead? Is he here, Tashi?" She put her cup down beside her, becoming increasingly agitated.

"No."

"No what?"

"No, he's not here."

"Was he on the plane?"

"No."

"You left him?" Her voice was incredulous.

"We didn't leave him, Abbi. It wasn't like that."

"What was it like then, Tashi? You left him you bastard!" She suddenly lunged at the lama and began to hammer with her fists on

246

his unresisting chest until he engulfed her, sobbing, in his surprisingly strong arms.

"It wasn't like that," he repeated.

Chapter 43

ॐ

Tibet-Bhutan Border

Even in late spring snow still lay on the high passes. Black rocks protruded though the dirty white blanket, the snow now the consistency of sugar. Cold grey clouds smothered the towering peaks. The horses struggled and slipped as the terrain steepened. Everyone was on foot, even the nuns, dragging at the reins of their mounts, the animals wild eyed with dumb inexpressible fear.

In his delight at seeing how close they were to the border when sat by the fire back at Ralung Monastery, Smith had conveniently failed to take in the densely packed contour lines on his map. Had not wanted to see them, or think about what crossing any part of the Himalayas on foot was actually like. It was now two days since they had left Sansa and it was looking less and less likely that they would make the RV with the American aircraft in time. Would they wait, and if so, how long? The party had no choice except to push on. There were no other options left.

Smith's lungs screamed for more oxygen and his head pounded in the thin air as they struggled towards the col of yet another of the interminable mountain passes. Even after all these months of living at altitude he was still not entirely acclimatised to the morale sapping environment he had to live in. Only his high level of general fitness allowed him to keep up with even the women in the party, adapted over generations to the harshness of the Land of the Snows.

Reaching the col, he threw himself to the ground and rolled onto his back, arms outstretched, not caring about the damp clammy snow beneath his body as he sucked in great lungfulls of air. Tashi and several of the *Khampas* were already there, recovering from the strenuous climb. The lama walked over and sat by Smith, smiling at the prostrate figure wheezing beside him.

"Bloody hell!" exclaimed Smith in an unusually Yorkshire accent for the ex-British Army Officer used to suppressing his dialect, as he recovered his breath and composure. Tashi smiled again, but said nothing. Smith sat up and stared back down the endless valley they had just climbed as the last few members of the party crested the col and slumped down in heaps to recover. There was little talk as the party took advantage of the small amount of time they knew they had before forcing themselves to move again. Some sipped water from yak skin canteens and others, those who still had any appetite, forced themselves to eat a handful of *tsampa*.

As they sat, a distant rumble seemed to march slowly up the valley towards them.

"Thunder," said someone. They all listened as the sound repeated itself. Then silence. No, there it was again, but more muted, perhaps farther way or reaching them from a slightly different direction.

"Thunder? That's unusual at this time of year," announced someone else.

"Maybe it's time to get moving, Tendruk?" suggested Smith, rising to his feet and looking the other man in the eye as he picked up the reins of his horse. "Before this weather catches up with us," he added pointedly, still not sure if Tendruk could differentiate between the sound of thunder and high altitude bombing.

*

Going down should have been easier, but it wasn't. The ground fell away steeply and the horses struggled to find their footing on the loose mud and rock hidden just below the almost melting snow. Still fighters and nuns had to walk, or be dragged, wrestling with the horses to slow them as they slid down the vague track bearing away diagonally to their right, a gash of white where the snow had drifted into it.

"You didn't tell us how bad it was," called Smith as he came alongside Mola. The track, such as it was, had finally levelled out enough for everyone to mount their horses for at least a short time.

"And what would you have done if I had?" the girl reposted. Smith had not expected an explanation, but the girl continued. "We usually only use this route in summer, at least a month later than now. And also the snow has stayed later than usual this year. Could we have waited another month?"

"How long do you think to the border?" asked Smith.

"Tomorrow. By about midday if we are lucky."

"Are there border guards near where we will cross? Do they

know the crossing points?"

"There are no official crossing points along the whole border with Bhutan. It has been closed since the war with India. The Chinese patrol it as best they can, but there are few tracks and virtually no roads near the border so it is difficult for them. Fortunately for us." Fortunate indeed, thought Smith, though he did not say so. They had very little else going for them.

"And most refugees head for India where they get a better reception and the border is easier to cross," she added, "so the Chinese don't put too much effort into guarding this border." Smith looked around at the mountains towering above them and the bleak countryside ahead of them. They had seen no other humans for two days and no sign of them except the track, such as it was, and an occasional cairn to mark the way. A day earlier a flock of nar, Tibetal wild sheep, had been seen on a rocky spur high above them, staring down imperiously. Later a lone vulture had circled on the rising air above them before losing interest and disappearing above the surrounding peaks. Tashi said there were snow leopards in the mountain here, but there were no signs of the elusive creature. Smith could see why patrolling here was normally a low priority for the Chinese, but could not help wondering if that priority had changed in the last few days. The earlier 'thunder' convinced him that it had.

*

Time passed in a blur of mud, loose rocks, melting snow and burning lungs as the party struggled forward over the unforgiving terrain. Most of them moved like zombies, staring blankly ahead, one foot mindlessly following the other. In spite of the physical demands and the, at times intense cold, Smith new that he was luckier than most. As one of the leaders he was able to focus on pushing the others forward and concentrate on possible dangers such as an ambush. Far from adding an extra burden, Smith knew from long experience that the responsibility distracted the mind from the physical discomfort and actually made it easier to keep going. His thoughts occasionally wandered to similar marches in the jungle in a previous life when the responsibilities of leadership had kept him going when soldiers who were fitter than him struggled.

"How far now? To the border?" The question had been gnawing away at him for hours, but like some luxury to be savoured, he had put off indulging himself until he could resist no longer.

"Remember the ridgeline before last?" asked Mola.

"No," replied Smith honestly, as the whole area had long since ceased to have any distinguishable features for him. Mola forced a half smile.

"It was about three hours ago, I guess. Well that was it. That was the border. We're in Bhutan."

"Well into Bhutan!" Smith almost laughed at the thought of it. They had made it. "Why didn't you say? Do the others know?" He looked back at the ragged line of riders strung out for several hundred yards behind him. Some were almost falling from their horses, slumped forward over the trudging beasts' necks, ragged black ghosts against the white snow. "They need some good news."

"Because there is no good news. Not yet. The Chinese have disputed the border for years and their patrols regularly wander for miles south of where we are now. The Bhutanese government can do nothing about it. So if they are on our trail they will not think twice about following us. In fact they will probably want to make a point of it."

"So when can we be sure that we have shaken them off?"

"When we are out of the mountains. Which is still a while yet. Another day at least."

*

It was less than an hour later that the plane came. Flying low from the north down the valley, it was virtually on them before the machine guns began to fire. The pilot must have only seen them at the last minute. Rounds tore into the dirty blackened late spring snow to the left of the ragged column, but intersected it in fractions of a second. They cut into the flanks of one of the horses. The stricken animal collapsed in a pitiful heap, its rider, a young nun, Nyachang, crushed beneath it, but already dead. One of the fighters, Rinzing, was pitched from his horse, several rounds piercing his back, the blood quickly soaking his *chuba*.

In the panic everyone ran for the nearest cover, scattering in all directions.

"Dismount! Get ready to return fire!" bellowed Smith into the chaos. The plane had passed them in an instant. "Get ready! He'll be back." They tried to force themselves into the very rock or earth of their chosen hiding place, dragging their horses down in front of them for extra cover. They waited, hardly daring to breathe, as if they pilot might actually hear them. Only Rinzing's sobs disturbed

251

the silence.

Smith and several of the fighters cocked their weapons and now anxiously scanned the horizon to the south as they counted the seconds, shutting out the sounds of their wounded friend.

The longer they waited the more confident Smith became. They were ready for him. The longer the pilot thought about his run the more likely he was to stay high for fear of being hit in the relatively slow and unprotected aircraft.

"Come on," whispered Smith to himself, adrenalin flowing in his system like hot oil after the monotony of the last few days.

But he didn't come. They waited, but the silence remained. After several minutes, heads began to appear tentatively from their hiding places. Growing more confident as the minutes passed, some stood scanning the sky, weapons raised. Still the plane didn't come.

"Why isn't he coming?" hissed Tendruk to Smith, still crouched nearby. Finally, Smith stood, still staring down the valley..

"There's only one reason I can think of."

"And what's that?"

"That they've got a patrol on the ground near enough to us for them not to need to risk the plane."

Smith quickly detailed half a dozen of the fighters to keep a watch for the return of the aircraft, assigning interlocking arcs of fire so that all points of approach were covered. Running over to where Rinzing lay, he signalled for Tashi, Tendruk and Chungla to join him whilst the rest continued to huddle in what cover they could find. They pulled the dead nun from beneath her horse, satisfied that no more could be done for her. Tendruk dispatched the still writhing animal with a single shot. There was no point now in worrying about giving away their location.

"It looks bad," said Smith to Tashi in English as the lama and young nun knelt over Rinzing, trying to staunch the bleeding. Tashi nodded in agreement. Rinzing lay on his back, at least three exit wounds in his chest and stomach now evident, and terror in his eyes. Chungla cut through the material of his *chuba* to reveal the full horror of the gaping wounds and audibly gasped as she saw them. She looked at Tashi for guidance.

"Strap him up as best you can. We need to get the hell out of here," directed Smith. Standing, he nodded his head to Tendruk, indicating that they should move away from the sickening scene. A few yards away, Smith squatted and instinctively scanned the horizon before looking at the Tibetan. Tendruk squatted beside him. "Any ideas?"

"No good ones," the other responded with an ironic smile. Both men knew that they were being looked to for leadership and that they had better come up with something. Anything. And quickly.

"OK, we need to get out of the open now. This is what we'll do," began Smith. "Six men ride ahead to find somewhere we can defend. We'll regroup there, study the rest of the route with Mola and see if we can come up with an alternative which might take us away from where the Chinese are expecting us to go. That's as good as it gets. Call them in, Tendruk."

Tendruk gave a shrill whistle and everyone looked in towards him and Smith. He indicated to several men who came running, bent as low as they could, AK56's clutched against their bodies. They were quickly briefed and returned to their horses to gather together and head away from the group towards the south with Tendruk at their head.

Soon the rest of the party was gathered together and began to move slowly in the same direction. Nyachang's body was strapped across one of the horses, led by a nun who muttered prayers for the young woman as they went. Four men struggled with the burden of a makeshift stretcher carrying Rinzing, the wounded man still whimpering in agony, but at least no longer losing blood. Smith doubted that he would burden them for long. He reflected, not for the first time, on how in an instant an invincible young warrior like Rinzing could become a helpless victim. These were thoughts no soldier could harbour for long and had to be quickly locked away in that dark place at the back of the mind from where they occasionally escaped.

"There are no options," insisted Mola to Smith. "This is the route to Bhutan. You can see," she waved her right arm at the towering peaks which surrounded them, "that it is impossible for us to go any other way. In any case, it is not far now. We must just keep going and we will be safe. Less than a day's march." Smith could almost believe that he could see a green haze in the far distance down the valley, beyond the snow and rock, where Mola said they had to go. Perhaps that was Bhutan proper. And safety.

But they were not there yet.

They had set up a defensive camp hidden as best they could amongst the rocks a short way up the side of an un-named mountain which reached higher than any in Western Europe. Guards had been deployed and everyone else huddled in what shelter they could find, eking out the rations they had left and trying to melt snow for drinking water with the warmth of their bodies. Fires were not allowed, but in any case there was virtually no yak dung left to burn. Filthy, emaciated brown faces started back at Smith and Tendruk as they made their rounds of the camp to check on everyone and try to keep up morale.

Finally, Smith found Tashi and Chungla.

"How is Rinzing?"

"Dead." Smith tried not to show his relief.

"What should we do with him?"

"We will see to it. We will leave them here, both Rinzing and Nyachang," answered Chungla."For them this is still the Land of the Snows. The birds will come for them and take their souls to the gods. We will perform the ceremonies as best we can." This was better news than Smith could have hoped for. The prospect of the already exhausted party having to try to outrun the Chinese whilst struggling with the burden of two bodies had not filled Smith with hope for their future.

"How long will it take?"

"Why?"

"Because I think that to have any chance of making it we need to travel tonight, in the dark. The Chinese are closing in on us and in daylight they're going to pick us off. But according to Mola we've not far to go, so the more distance we can cover before morning the better."

"We'll be ready," replied Tashi.

*

Smith, Tendruk and Mola squatted on their haunches in a tight circle under cover of a large sloping rock, the map spread out between them.

"I've no idea how accurate this map is, but I've been keeping a track of our progress as best I could and I reckon we're here." He pointed to a location where two sets of closely packed contour lines butted up against each other like two elongated u-shapes. "I think that is the col we're on at the moment. What do you think?"

"I don't have a map so I've not been able to follow the route except when you've showed me where you thought we were. I have to trust you," responded Tendruk.

"And as you know, I do not understand your maps, so I must trust you as well," added Mola.

So," Smith continued unperturbed , "if the Chinese have a patrol on the ground which they expect to hit us wih soon, it's either coming up behind us, waiting for us on the trail ahead, or," he paused, "or they're coming down this side valley which runs into our valley about five kilometres from here." He pointed the way they were currently intending to proceed towards Bhutan.

"If they're behind us we have to outrun them, but I think that's unlikely because they were a couple of days behind us and probably not sure of our route. So I don't think they would have caught up with us, and they would realise that.

"If you look at the valley I mean," he pointed with the tip of his knife, " it heads west and it looks to me as if they could have got vehicles, especially tracked vehicles, a long way up there from the Gyantse road." Smith had years of experience of reading terrain from a map and literally living or dying by whether or not he was right. So far his record was good, he was still alive, and he was confident that, if the map was reasonably accurate, this was the Chinese commander's most likely approach route if he intended to cut them off.

"Assuming you're right, what do we do about it?"

"Fair question, Tendruk. First, we get moving tonight and travel as far as possible in the dark with our patrol scouting ahead. Second, if we get as far as this side valley without a contact we leave a stay behind party to defend our rear and slow the Chinese down to give the rest the best chance possible of escape. If they are already here, I reckon they will have an ambush near where the valley runs into our route so we don't need to worry about them too much until we get closer.

"So I suggest the patrol waits for us here." Again he pointed to a spot on the map. "There's a cairn marked so it's something to aim for if it's there. Hopefully, it will still be dark and we might be able to slip past them if they're waiting for us, but we can decide that there. What do you think?"

"It all makes sense," agreed Tendruk. "I guess we don't have a lot of options."

Mola agreed.

"Good. OK, Tendruk, let's get round everybody and tell them what's happening. Get the patrol away in twenty minutes with you leading them. Here's the map. Keep on the trail and wait when you think you're in the right place. As long as you wait on the trail we'll run into you, even if the cairn doesn't exist. Just don't go beyond where it's supposed to be."

"Mola, can you find the way to the cairn in the dark?"

"I think I can remember it, but from here the trail is easier to follow so we should not be able to miss them."

Every yard of progress they made now was both a relief and an ordeal to Smith. Were they passing the Chinese undetected or walking deeper into a trap? He had no way of knowing, but they must keep pushing on. Get as far as possible under cover of darkness.

They successfully rendezvoused with the patrol group and then, still in darkness, continued down the valley. Everyone led their mount as it was impossible to ride in darkness on the rough, rocky ground. Assuming that any ambush would come from the west, as that was where the side valley joined the main route, they left the trail and moved as far to the east as they could, parallel to the route, to put themselves as far out of range as possible of any attack.

Smith had positioned himself near the middle of the line of weary fugitives, scanning the darkness for any sign of the enemy.

Suddenly there was a muffled cry from someone near the front of the procession. The Tibetans ahead of Smith stopped. Probably someone had stumbled, fallen over a rock or something. Jesus, get moving! Before he could articulate his thoughts, the whole group were exposed by a strange ethereal light, hard black silhouettes against a ghost white background.

The flare hung in the air, suspended on its tiny parachute, illuminating the whole sorry scene. Before anyone could move a shot rang out, and then another and another. Someone behind Smith fell to the ground with an agonised cry.

"Down, get down!" screamed Smith, as did others right along

the line. As they flung themselves to the ground the hillside to their right was suddenly speckled with white flashes as the automatic weapons opened up. The firing continued as another flare replaced the first, and then a third.

Body pressed hard into the ground, mind racing for ideas, it was a couple of minutes before Smith realised the earth was not kicking up round them, in spite of the weight of fire. At first he thought they were just trying to get their range, but then he realised that they were actually out of range, at least of the light weapons.

He cautiously raised his head, feeling he could take the risk, just in time to see an arc of green tracer heading for them as a heavy machine gun with more range replaced the AK56's. At first the rounds went high over their heads, but the firing came in short disciplined bursts, and after each one the range was shortened. Between the bursts, the fire of the original sniper could be heard as he probed for targets. Screams and then whimpers to both his right and left told Smith that the sniper was finding them. It wouldn't be long before the machine gun was tearing into them as well.

They were disorganised, caught out in the open and nearly half their number were nuns. They had no radios to communicate with. They were finished.

And then it occurred to him. They were finished, but he wasn't. He'd done his best for these people, but now they were going to die. Did he need to? What purpose would it serve? Alone he could slip away into the darkness and no-one would be the wiser. The Chinese didn't know who they were looking for or how many were in the group. He had the skill and the cunning to do it. Keep heading south. He could be well away before dawn and once it was light he could travel quickly. He would soon be in that faint green haze he had seen earlier down the valley. Find a village and tell people he was a lost climber or hiker separated from his expedition. He would think of something.

As his mind raced he began automatically to unfasten the saddle and pack from his horse. He had pulled the obedient animal to the ground when the firing started and held him there. But perhaps he could make it as well. He had served Smith loyally over the last year and he deserved his chance. Smith began to take everything from the bags he thought would be useful that he could carry, water, food, as many rounds as he could cram into the small shoulder bag he had, his knife and finally a Dragunov sniper rifle.

Unwrapping the weapon from its covering of rough brown

hessian, he felt the weight and balance of it, comfortable in his hands. He rolled onto his stomach, an almost instinctive reaction, and peered through the sight. Scanning quickly back and forth, almost immediately he saw movement in the darkness. The stupid bastards. He could see them! They were so confident that they were being careless about their cover.

What had he been thinking of? He wasn't going to run and the Tibetans weren't going to die. Or at least not all of them. Releasing the bridle, he threw the reins over the horse's head and gave the animal a slap on the rump. He leapt to his feet, fear in his eyes.

"Go!" yelled Smith, hitting the animal again. He bolted into the darkness, away from the direction of fire. Smith wished him well and hoped he would never see him again

"Let the horses go! Make them run! Tell the others!" shouted Smith to either side of him where he could just make out the shadows of other members of the party in the eerie light of the flares. He kept shouting until he saw someone doing as he said. A horse stood up and ran wildly into the night, a great black shadow. And then another, and another. Within a couple of minutes horses were running in every direction, some away from the Chinese and some towards them.

"Get ready to move! South!" Smith shouted as he saw the first horse crumple to the ground in a blizzard of Chinese small arms fire. The machine gun also swung its aim towards some of the careering beasts. Perhaps, hopefully, its operators thought the Tibetans were making a run for it. Smith scanned back along the cone of tracer through the lens of the Dragunov, twisting the mechanism to get a clear focus. And there they were! The gun crew. Exposed. Too confident. His lungs filled and emptied rhythmically as he tried to control the pattern of his breathing. He began firing, shot after single shot until the magazine was empty, relying more on instinct and luck than the deadly skill of a trained sniper. But the machine gun stopped firing.

"Hold your fire!" he screamed, as the Tibetans had began to fire when he had. They were out of range, but it was at least a distraction from his position. He leapt to his feet, slung his bag and the Dragunov over his should and, clutching his AK56 began to run, head bowed forward as far as possible.

"Lets go!" He waved to those behind and dragged to their feet others as he passed them. Small arms fire rose again from the Chinese ambush site and the horrible screams of wounded horses pierced Smith's ears through the chaos. But what else could he have done? He kept running, not looking now to see who was following. Ahead he could see more Tibetans following his example and running, stumbling over the rocky ground, but moving away from the deadly trap.

Then he caught up with Tashi and Chungla, still huddled behind a small boulder.

"She wouldn't move," said Tashi, almost apologetically. "I couldn't get her to move until she knew you were coming."

"Well I'm here now so let's get the fuck out of here," Smith gasped in English. He dragged them to their feet and began to run again, shouting, encouraging, cajoling as he went. Another flare lit up the sky. Small arms fire continued, but still the machine gun was silent. Smith knew it couldn't last, that even if he had hit the crew they would be replaced pretty soon, but it was a breathing space. Also the replacements were likely to be less well trained on the gun and so with any luck slower and less accurate.

Tendruk and several of the *Khampas* had been at the head of the line of fugitives when the attack began. They had taken cover and returned fire until it became obvious they were out of range. Everything had happened in a matter of minutes when the garbled message to release their horses got to them. They were not sure what to do until they saw other horses running at random away from their riders. Only then had they removed all the kit they could and released their own mounts. But they remained in position until Smith, Tashi and Chungla stumbled onto them, having now caught up with or passed several others along the way.

They threw themselves to the ground by Tendruk. Within seconds others started to arrive. Smith leapt to his feet again. "Come on, we're bunching up. If that machine gun picks us up we're all dead." They all set off again, away from the firing, bent low and running as fast as they could, the fit young men soon leaving the nuns behind.

"I'll wait for them," volunteered Tendruk. Smith did not argue.

"Take a couple of men with you. We'll wait for you where it's safe." Tendruk nodded to a couple of *Khampas*. They stopped running, crouching low with weapons raised, staring into the darkness. Behind them the automatic fire continued. Ghostly wisps of smoke from the extinguished flares wafted across the battlefield, its acrid smell heavy in the air. But even above the sounds of battle could be heard the worst sound of all, the cries of wounded people and animals.

Almost hating himself for it, Smith knew that these were the sounds and smells that brought him alive. Exultant in the fear and the adrenalin, he continued to run. Could have run all night and left the others behind, or turned and joined Tendruk, possibly waiting to be overrun. But he had to concentrate on keeping the others moving as fast as possible and keeping out of range. It was only a matter of time before the machine gun started up again and the Chinese came after them on foot. At least they had no vehicles. But maybe they had horses, wondered Smith. In any case, with the light would come the aircraft. How would they deal with that? One step at a time. They might not be alive long enough for the plane to come and finish them off.

*

They careered on into the night, which grew blacker as they escaped the umbrella of light created by the flares. Gradually their eyes began to adjust to what light the stars provided.

Periodically, they rested for a few short minutes, calling to those behind to keep up, or sending someone back to rally them. It was impossible to tell how many had survived so far. Undoubtedly some had been killed or so badly wounded they had not been able to join the initial exodus. Two wounded *Khampas* were half running, half dragged by their comrades. They were both stoical as they collapsed beside Smith, Tashi and the others for another brief rest. In the darkness the extent of their injuries could not be seen and no-one enquired too closely so long as they could keep moving.

"We leave no-one behind," said Tashi suddenly in English as they caught their breath.

"This isn't the fucking US Marine Corps, Tashi."

"I don't know what you mean by that, but we cannot leave anyone for the Chinese. You know what they'll do to them." Smith did not need to reply. He was not going to argue. It was something he would deal with when he had to, which was hopefully never.

"Well let's make sure it doesn't happen." He stood and gave Chungla his hand. The young girl accepted his help and they trudged forward again. Her fragile frame belied her determination and stamina, fuelled, Smith assumed, by her instinct to survive and to carry her faith to a new land, now that she accepted that was her destiny.

"You've done well, Chungla."

"I've done what I had to, but whatever happens your help will not be forgotten." Smith was silent for a moment, deeply touched by the girl's words.

"You don't need to say anything. It doesn't matter why you came here. You have done what you have done and we all thank you."

"Well it might be a bit soon for that."

"It's not." She strode along beside him in silence now, the sound of her AK56 slapping rhythmically against her back.

*

"This will do," announced Smith, calling a halt to the plodding progress of the small band of survivors. "Get down behind those rocks and get some rest. We're only stopping for a few minutes so make the most of it." They had been running, or trying to run, from the ambush for several hours already and most of them were in a state of almost collapse. Daylight had not, amazingly, resulted in another enemy onslaught so they kept moving, constantly listening and scanning the skies for aircraft. But none came. So they kept moving.

It had been light for over an hour, but as long as they were making progress Smith had put all thoughts of the condition of the wounded out of his mind. Now that they had stopped he had no choice but to see how they were, before making any more decisions. Glancing back up the valley to make sure the coast was clear, he scrambled across to where the two injured men were hidden.

"How are they?" he asked one of the nuns who had been helping them to keep going.

"We're fine," answered one of the *Khampas* before the nun had a chance to reply. He looked into the face of the nun and saw a different story.

"Here, let me have a look." The nun opened the first man's *chuba* to reveal the makeshift bandages she had managed to apply at some stage during their flight. They were soaked in blood, but high up on the man's right shoulder. Beneath the bandage the wound looked jagged and painful, but not life threatening. Smith guessed that he would be alright until infection set in, which it would if he didn't get some proper treatment soon. It didn't look as if he had lost enough blood to seriously weaken him yet. Smith patted him gently on the back.

"You're right. You'll be fine. Let's have a look at you," he continued, turning to the other casualty. The young Tibetan lay on his back staring unseeingly at nothing in particular, his normally bronzed face ashen. Smith forced himself to examine the wound, which revealed itself to be a terrible gouge across his abdomen, through which the livid red of his intestines was clearly visible. Fear gripped Smith's own guts. Fear for the life of a comrade in arms, but also fear for himself and the group. The man wasn't going to survive, but neither were the rest of them if they tried to help him. He nodded to the nun to re-bandage the wound.

"Just hang on in there. You're going to be fine as well," he lied to the man as convincingly as he could. It wasn't the first time he'd had to do it.

He dashed over to where Tashi, Chungla and a couple of others were hidden close together. "OK, Tashi, this is the plan." He quickly drew breath before continuing. "I'm going to stay here with a couple of the guys to wait for Tendruk," he began in English. "And anyone else he's managed to drag down here with him. No, don't interrupt," he held up his hands. "Just listen to me. If the rest of you are going to get away we need to slow the Chinese down. And we need to wait for Tendruk. So we'll wait here. It's a good defensive position. Plenty of cover. Element of surprise. They'll think we'll just keep running.

"Then we'll follow you to the airfield. But if the CIA guys won't wait, you go with them. You've got to get out. You've got the PLA documents and you've got Chungla. They've both got to get to the Americans."

"I'm not going," said Chungla in Tibetan.

"Not going where? What are you talking about? You don't know what I just said to Tashi."

"I don't need to speak your language to know what you think, Smith. You promised to get me to the West and you think you have to send me with Tashi while you stay here and die."

"I've no intentions of dying."

"And I've no intention of leaving til you leave." Smith looked at Tashi, exasperated.

"Listen, Chungla," the lama began. "We discussed this before. You know that the most important thing is for you, a *Tulku*, to take our culture to the West. That is your destiny. And he," he nodded towards Smith, "is doing what needs to be done to make that happen. He is a soldier. He knows what he is doing. They must wait for Tendruk. Once Tendruk gets here they will follow us. In a few hours. Then we'll all be together again."

"Rimpoche," replied the girl, "you know how much I respect you. Please, do not destroy that respect by lying to me. As long as he stays I stay. I can fight. I can kill the Chinese." She dragged the AK56 from her shoulder. "Have you forgotten what they did to me?"

"No I haven't," interjected Smith. "And that's why you need to get away from here. So they don't have a chance to do it again." Smith's mouth felt dry as he uttered the words, but the girl needed to be reminded of the reality of their situation. She was silent for a moment, before replying.

"Do you think I don't know that? But they can't take any more from me than they already have. I am staying." The girl lay on the ground behind her weapon and stared determinedly through the iron sight back up the valley.

So Smith, Chungla, one fit fighter and the badly wounded Khampa remained. They took up defensive positions as directed by Smith and he scanned the countryside to the north looking for signs of Tendruk or of their Chinese pursuers. The band was now so depleted that only Tashi and three *Khampas* set out with the less injured casualty, three nuns and Mola. The young woman led them in the direction of the airfield and what they hoped would be safety.

Chapter 44

ॐ

Bhutan

"This is One Zero. Send sitrep!" bellowed Colonel Zhou into the radio handset. "Get Alpha One Zero now! Over"

"Contact. Wait, out," came the response.

"Don't fucking....," began Zhou, but he could already hear the crackle of static. No-one was listening.

"They're in contact, Colonel, they're fighting," interjected Captain Deng, trying to placate the boss without success.

"I still need to know what's going on, Deng. Have we finally got these bastards?"

"We're not far behind them, Colonel. As soon as it's light we can move. With the horses we'll catch up with them in no time. If Bin hasn't finished them off already."

They sat on the cold hard earth, surrounded by utter darkness as the massive peaks, pressed in close around them, seemed to block out even the sky. A hissing Tilly lamp nearby provided the only visible light, casting a circle of shadows around them. The rest of the company were sheltering as best they could amongst the rocks a short distance away, trying to keep warm and impatiently awaiting orders.

A longer burst of static interrupted the two Officers' conversation. They both looked in the direction of the radio operator.

"It's a sitrep, Sir." He began scribbling notes on his pad as Zhou paced back and forth beside him. After a couple of minutes he tore a sheet from the pad and handed it to the Colonel.

"Good news?" enquired Deng hopefully, but guessing that it probably wasn't.

"They got the ambush set up and the terrorists walked into it, but somehow at least some of them managed to get away. And even better, they managed to take out the gun crew. How the fuck could they do that in the dark?"

"I don't know..."

"Well, I do. They were too casual. Probably wandering around instead of getting into cover. Assuming a bunch of Tibetans couldn't hurt them. But whatever these bastards are, they're not amateurs and we underestimate them to our cost. Have underestimated them to our cost."

"So what are your orders, Sir?"

"It's simple enough Deng. Tell Lieutenant Bin to get his platoon off their arses and down that valley after those rebels. And not to come back til he's finished them off."

"How far should he keep up the pursuit? You know we're already in Bhutan. We're going to need authorisation from above if we're likely to run into Bhutanese troops or officials. Might I suggest that we need to cover our own arses if there's going to be an international incident."

"Stop worrying about you career, Deng. You cross me and I'll sink you without trace. That's all you need to worry about. But if this goes wrong it'll be my career on the line, and that's no longer a great loss. Now get on with my orders."

"Sir!" Deng saluted and turned to the radio.

Having briefed Lieutenant Bin, Deng returned to find Zhou deep in conversation with Major Tang.

"How is Lieutenant Bin?" Zhou greeted him.

"Well, Sir, he's not a happy soldier."

"The People don't pay him to be happy."

"But he should be moving as we speak."

"Good. Then so will we. I've just been arranging with Major Tang to get the Company ready to move. It'll be light in a couple of hours at most, but we could be at Bin's current location by then. We'll lead the horses over the pass and once it gets light we'll be able to ride. Then we'll soon catch up with them. With any luck we'll be in at the kill."

"And the aircraft, Sir?"

"Good point, Deng, but I don't think we need them."

"Sir?"

"As you said yourself, we don't want an international incident. Warplanes flying into another nation's sovereign airspace." He smiled. "No. This is a job for the infantry."

Chapter 45

र

Kathmandu, Nepal

"It took us another day and a night to get there. But the Americans were as good as their word. They had waited for us and they brought us here." Tashi looked round at the drab, surroundings of the hospital corridor. "You see, Peter insisted that he must stay behind to wait for the others. To protect us whilst we made our escape. What did you expect me to do, Abbi. Refuse to go, like Chungla? Fight with him? You know what he is like better than I do. He wanted us to leave and he wanted to stay. Objectively, it was the right decision. If we had all stayed we would have all died."

"So you left him to die instead."

"No, I told you. And in any case he is a very resourceful man. He is not dead. He was waiting for Tendruk. That is all. Once he came they would leave."

"So where are they? Did you wait at the airfield?"

"That was not my decision. None of this was my decision, Abbi. Once the Americans had the intelligence we had promised them they wanted to leave. That's what they came for. They'd already waited three days. And we had casualties who needed treatment."

Abbi sipped her tea and thought about what Tashi said. She wanted to believe that what he said was true. Not that she thought he was lying, but he obviously had no idea what had happened to Smith. Was he already dead as they sat here in safety? Or worse, had he been captured by the Chinese? This possibility had never been far from her mind since she had discovered that he had gone into Tibet all those months before. But now it was more likely than ever that it had happened. She had never been in any doubt as to how he would be treated. A foreign combatant in an undeclared civil war that most people had never heard of, he had no rights and would disappear without trace. She felt weak with fear.

"I might never see him again, Tashi," she almost sobbed. "I might never even find out what happened to him." She slumped

267

into the arms of the lama, her body shaking with grief and fear.

"Listen to me, Abbi. He will turn up. Mola, the girl who led us out of Tibet, stayed behind in Bhutan. She knows people there and they will let us have any news immediately. Soon, once she has rested, she will return to her village by the same route we came out, so she will meet them if they are not already safe."

Abbi was unconvinced, but could take no more reassurances from Tashi. "Who is this Chungla who stayed behind with him?" Tashi began to explain to Abbi about the girl and the events which had befallen them since she had joined them.

Chapter 46

Bhutan

Smith was still alive. He, Chungla and the others huddled behind several large rocks, part of an outcrop stretching half way across the valley. It gave them cover and enough options to be able to move to another position if they came under fire. The cold seeped slowly through Smith's clothing as he lay staring relentlessly up the valley. He fought to keep its insidious fingers at bay as they sought out the weak spots of his body. In the past, in the Army, he had spent hours hidden in OP's and ambushes, watching, waiting. It was part of the job and you got used to it. Found ways of blanking out the time and the cold, or the heat. Now he was drawing on all that experience again.

He guessed that Chungla was at least as good at this as he was. As a nun, especially one destined for great things, her training had been vigorous and her self-discipline cast iron. She had proved that to him many times already in the short time he had known her. He had no doubt that she could cope with the waiting, probably deep in some meditation.

The firing finally began about midday. But the noise came from some distance away, up the valley. It was no threat to them, yet. Smith guessed it was at least a couple of kilometres away. There could be no doubt that the Chinese had caught up with Tendruk. Apart from an occasional puff of smoke, he could see nothing of whatever was taking place. Part of him wanted to be there, in the thick of the action, but they were so few in number it was worse than futile to attempt to move up the valley. They could do nothing except get themselves killed. So they waited and hoped that by some miracle Tendruk could extricate himself from the fire fight with the Chinese.

After about ten minutes the firing became more sporadic. Then it ceased altogether. Chungla looked at Smith with wild frightened eyes, but said nothing. There was nothing to say. They knew that

Tendruk and the others were not coming back. He'd known it all along. They were just buying vital time so the others could get away. Tendruk had now paid with his life. It was a sacrifice Smith knew that the man would make without a second thought, to die fighting for what he believed in, an end to the oppression of his people. Although Smith had not known him as long as he had known the *Khampas* of Pemba's party, in that short time he had recognised the humility and nobility of the man. He hoped that his sacrifice had been worth it.

Before Smith could begin to think about the sacrifice he may be about to make, his thoughts were disturbed by one of the warriors who had stayed with them. He had crawled over to Smith from his own position next to the badly wounded Khampa.

"He's dead," the man said blankly. Thank God, thought Smith. At least if they had to run it would be unencumbered by a badly wounded man or the guilt of having left him behind. He would now never have to find out which he would have done.

"Get his ammunition and bring it over here. We'll divide it between us." After a moment Smith called after Tenzin. "No, wait. I'm coming over." He crawled on his belly, dragging himself over the cold earth and rock, presenting as small a target as possible if anyone was already looking out for them. In a couple of minutes he was laying beside Tenzin, breathing heavily.

"Let's drag him over here" Tenzin looked puzzled. "Perhaps we can still get out of here. If we leave Dawa's body behind that rock, just visible with a weapon in his hand after we're gone it might slow them down thinking they have to take this position and give us a bit of extra time." Tenzin nodded in agreement and the two men began to wrestle with the unwieldy corpse of their comrade as they dragged it towards what looked like a suitable position. With much exertion they got the body into what they hoped looked like a defensive pose and put his weapon in his hand, just protruding from the side of a rock. They quickly rifled through his kit for anything useful . Tenzin also took his prayer beads which Smith guessed he would give to Dawa's family in the unlikely event that he ever met them.

Smith threw himself down beside Chungla and was about to tell her to get ready to move, when the first mortar round landed. The earth beneath them shook and shuddered and the pair were showered with gravel and small rocks. They instinctively tried to bury themselves in the hard, cold ground, arms wrapped around their heads. Another round came in and then another. Still not very close, but making the earth tremble and fraying their nerves.

Smith knew that, whilst a well dug trench would have protected them from just about anything but a direct hit, being out in the open as they were, they were almost certainly finished. But the bombardment was so intense there was nowhere to go and the shock to their bodies was rapidly draining the will to do anything except protect themselves as best they could. Smith struggled to get close to Chungla to shield her with his body, almost laying on top of her as she sobbed and shivered. The terror in her eyes intensified his own feeling of helplessness as he prayed that the noise would stop.

When it did stop Smith was almost beyond realising the fact. His ears rang as if he was trapped inside Big Ben at mid-night. His hands were shaking uncontrollably. Before he could even move, his mind vaguely registered the smoke. He couldn't hear the rounds landing, but he could see to his front the white clouds billowing out to be fanned into a dense mist by the wind.

"Tenzin, attack coming!" he shouted, having no idea whether any sound came from his bone dry mouth. He looked across to where the other man had taken cover, but could see no sign of him. Attempting to raise himself onto one elbow, he struggled for his weapon. He could feel the strange warmth of Chungla's trembling body huddled in a foetal ball next to him. His fear for the fate of the girl forced him to continue the one sided struggle with the AK56. After what seemed like forever he managed to get the recalcitrant weapon pointing in more or less the right direction and drag the cocking handle back towards him. When he let it go, to his immense relief the working parts shot forward. He was ready to engage the enemy again. Just.

Only now did he become aware of the earth being spat up around them. He still couldn't hear a thing, but realised that the heavy machine gun was now being trained on them. When the firing lifted above their heads the poor bloody infantry would make a frontal assault hidden by the smoke. Wiping away the blood dripping from his nose he tried to concentrate on where the rounds were falling as they probed slowly forward towards their pathetic hiding place. The gunners couldn't see their target through the smoke, but they were mighty close.

And then rounds were pinging off the rocks right in front of the pair and Smith had to bury his head in the ground again. Rounds ricocheted in all directions only inches from them as the smell and taste of cordite and acrid smoke crawled into the back of their throats. Smith realised that his senses were returning, as he could now plainly hear Chungla's incessant screaming.

They were pinned down by the machine gun fire for what seemed like several minutes as the Tibetan girl continued to scream. Smith closed his mind to it knowing that the line of infantry was probably already moving towards them. He stared unseeing into the swirling smoke, waiting. At last the machine gunfire lifted well above their heads so the attackers could get in underneath it. Still he waited, shaking hands holding the AK as best they could until, through the mist, he could hear the war cry and small arms fire of charging soldiers. And still he waited.

As if of its own accord, the weapon suddenly came to life in his hand. The feel of it settled his nerves immediately and in an instant the magazine was empty. Still he could see no-one to his front, but they were there alright, their war cry now disrupted by cries of agony. It took only seconds to replace the magazine, with barely a pause in Smith's rate of fire as he sprayed rounds to right and left like a fireman's hose.

He soon had a third magazine clipped into place, squeezing gently on the trigger, intent on inflicting as much damage as possible on the enemy. In the noise and chaos he never even noticed that they had been out-flanked until a Chinese boot exploded in his face.

Smith was thrown backwards by the force of the blow. As he struggled to maintain consciousness he was kicked from every side. He managed to focus for an instant on a figure towering above him, silhouetted by what now seemed to him an intense light. He was staring into the barrel of an automatic rifle. Just as the soldier seemed about to fire, what sounded like a command in Chinese deterred him and he pulled back his weapon.

Several pairs of hands grabbed Smith and dragged him to his feet, holding him so firmly that to struggle was impossible. The iron taste of blood seeped into his mouth and he could feel a warm dribble of liquid on his chin. With his one good eye he could now distinguish another figure who seemed to be giving orders to the men around him. Sweating heaving figures continued to gather around Smith, pesumably those who had taken part in the frontal assault, or those who had survived, arriving on their objective. Smith expected no mercy from men whose comrades he had just killed or wounded.

And then he saw Chungla. She was pinned to the ground by several soldiers a few yards away. Her robes were hitched up above her waist revealing her naked thighs, spread wide apart. Some kind of rag was stuffed into her mouth, but the fear in her eyes spoke louder than any scream.

"So, we finally catch up with the terrorists," began the soldier who had prevented Smith from being shot, speaking in good Tibetan. "You've certainly caused us a lot of trouble and killed too many of our men." He stepped forward and calmly, with no obvious sign of anger, punched Smith full in the face. Smith's head reeled backwards as if his neck would snap as the pain of the blow surged to his brain.

"Now it's our turn. Sadly, we didn't manage to get the other two alive, so we'll have to make sure we get all the information we need from you" continued the man, who Smith guessed to be a Chinese Officer. "But I think we're going to start with your friend here." He nodded his head in the direction of Chungla. " Don't you think it's unhealthy that young girls like this should deny themselves the pleasure of virile young men?" He gestured at the soldiers surrounding Smith. By now his face was so close to Smith's that Smith could almost taste the foul odour of cheap cigarettes from his breath. "It's not natural," he persisted. " She's obviously got some catching up to do, so let's see how many of these fine young comrades it takes to satisfy her." He leered at the young nun struggling wildly on the ground.

With a superhuman effort Smith suddenly lunged forward, taking his captors momentarily by surprise and managing to get one hand free. He grabbed the Officer's face in his fingers and drove his nails into the man's left eye with all the effort he could muster. A high pitched scream burst from his lips as Smith was dragged back and thrown to the ground. In the seconds before the world went black for Smith, as the butt of a rifle smashed into his forehead, he thought he heard shouting not far away, in Chinese. An authoritative voice.

Chapter 47

ཕ

Tibet

"Jesus. Where the fuck am I? I feel like shit." No reply. Smith gingerly put a hand to his pounding head. There was something wrapped around his forehead. Tight. What the fuck is that? Then he heard a voice. Not English. He sort of recognised it, but it made no sense at first. Then like a clearing mist the words began to take form. He turned to where they were coming from, at the same time aware of something warm pressed next to him. A body.

"How are you? Are you alright?" At last he realised that it was Tibetan and that he understood Tibetan. Was that his language. He doubted it, but could not yet be sure.

The speaker was a woman. A young voice. Yes. It was Chungla. He was alive. She was alive!

"I think so," he finally replied, not really sure whether he was or not.

"They bandaged your head," she continued as if to explain his earlier confusion.

"Who did?"

"The Chinese. A soldier." Smith's senses were slowly recovering and with them the pain. Pain in his head, in his right eye. All over his body. As if he had been kicked all over. Vaguely he remembered. He had been kicked all over.

Wherever they were it was dark, with occasional flashes of daylight bursting into the room. Was it a room? It seemed to be rocking from side to side. Chungla was sat half upright with her back leant against what looked like a wall. She held Smith in her thin arms, his head, he now realised, resting against her chest.

"Where are we?" he finally asked.

"I don't know. We've been in this truck for hours, or it seems like hours." A truck. That made sense. The rocking. They were in the back of a moving truck.

"Where are they taking us? Why didn't they kill us?" Then he remembered. The last thing he had seen before the world went black. "Did they......? Are you alright."

"I'm fine. They didn't touch me." Smith's relief was palpable

"They were going to rape me, but another Officer came. An older one. Perhaps their commander. There was much shouting, but they only spoke in Chinese so I don't know what they were saying. The Officer who hit you was sent away. They called a medic who bandaged your head and then we were loaded into the truck. Perhaps they're taking us to Lhasa. For a show trial or something." Followed by a public execution, thought Smith, not articulating his thoughts to the girl.

Smith struggled to raise himself up a little so he could better see his surroundings. As his eyes, or eye, adjusted to the restricted light he began to distinguish more of his surroundings. Not that there was much to see. For an instant in the semi-darkness his mind returned to the hours spent bouncing around in the back of army four tonners going to one exercise after another as a Cadet at Sandhurst. Apart from himself and Chungla this one contained only two Chinese soldiers who stared impassively out of the rear of the vehicle.

"Perhaps we could overpower them and make a jump for it," whispered Smith. He could see her smile in the dim light. The first time he had seen her smile for a long time.

"You can hardly move," she reminded him. "And in any cases, they're not taking any chances." She nodded towards their feet and at the same time raised her right leg a few inches so he could see the manacle holding her to the floor of the truck. He tried to move his own leg, only to realise that he was similarly restrained.

"Get some more rest." She cradled his unwilling head in her arms. "Save your strength for whatever they have planned for us. Where not finished yet," she concluded defiantly. He gradually succumbed. She was probably right. He was so tired. So incredibly tired.

Chapter 48

ཕ

Tibet

He woke to the sound of shouting. "What's happening?"

"I don't know. We've stopped."

Suddenly the tailgate of the truck dropped with a loud clatter and bright light exploded into the rear of the vehicle as one of the guards raised the back canvas and jumped to the ground. He stood facing Smith and Chungla, his head and shoulders silhouetted against the intense light, weapon at the ready. The other guard came towards them swinging his rifle at them in short jerks to indicate that they should move back as far as they could. He produced a key and undid the manacles and immediately stepped back from them, never taking his eyes off them. Once he was far enough away from them he grunted some command and again waved his rifle, this time in the direction of the back of the truck.

Chungla slowly stood, stooping below the low canvas roof, and took hold of Smith. He began to shuffle painfully towards the light. He could now see other soldiers standing behind the vehicle, also with their weapons at the ready, staring intently at their captives, as if they expected them to pounce like snow leopards at any second. If only, thought Smith as he forced his pain racked body tentatively forward. The girl jumped down and turned to help Smith negotiate the four foot drop to the ground. The guards still stood well back.

With his feet on terra firma Smith, with Chungla's support, managed to stand upright and take in his surroundings with his one good eye. They were not in Lhasa, or Shigatse, or a military base of any kind. They stood at the side of a road seemingly in the middle of nowhere. The barren Tibetan countryside, he assumed it was Tibet, stretched way behind them to the ubiquitous snow-capped mountains in the distance. But no buildings. Nothing. No-one, apart from heavily armed PLA soldiers.

So this is how it ends, thought Smith. A bullet in the back of the head and dumped in a ravine five thousand miles from home. One man lit a cheap hand-rolled cigarette. Smith expected him to offer him a final drag before sentence was carried out, like in some corny war film. But before he had a chance to think beyond this sorry fate he and Chungla were being guided at gunpoint around the side of the vehicle. Perhaps that cigarette would have spun out his short life by another precious couple of minutes.

They were now on the road facing in the same direction as the truck and two other vehicles which had apparently accompanied it. The road dropped away steeply downhill and Smith could now make out a few squat buildings about half a mile away. They walked to the front of the truck where they were stopped by an NCO. He walked up to Smith and cautiously forced a grubby manila envelope into his hand. He quickly stepped back and pointed down the road. He began to shout, becoming more agitated as Smith and Chungla stared uncomprehendingly at him.

"I think he wants us to go," said Chungla. "I think we should."

Smith nodded and began to shuffle down the road, the envelope clutched incongruously in his hand. It made no sense and with every step he expected the deadly punch of a high velocity round in the back. But he shuffled on, leaning heavily on the slightly built nun, the sound of his boots scraping against the gravel surface of the road.

After a few minutes he dared to stop and glanced quickly over his shoulder. They had only come about three hundred yards, but the soldiers had not moved. They stood watching their progress, but they were not following and several of them had now slung their rifles on their shoulders. Others encouraged them on with unintelligible shouts.

As the buildings came closer Smith struggled to focus his one good eye. He heard shouting in a language he did not recognise and men began to appear in his vision from one of the buildings.

"Soldiers!" snapped Chungla. "It's a trap. We must turn back."

But what was the point? They were dead if they turned round and anyway Smith had no strength to trudge back up the road into the hands of the PLA.

"No," he mumbled through bruised lips. "keep going."

By now the soldiers were running towards them and Smith could distinguish the weapons in their hands. They continued to shout and gestured for the two to raise their hands. Smith and Chungla stopped walking and did as they were directed. He could now make out the buildings more clearly, a bar painted red and white blocking the road, and the guard hut next to it.

"It's the border! It's the bloodly Nepalese border."

Chapter 49

Nepalese Border

Pressing against Chungla, Smith forced himself to stand as erect as possible as the border guards approached, still shouting and obviously nervous about unexpected visitors on foot from China. They could no doubt see the PLA soldiers loitering on the hill above.

Smith had in the past worked with Gurkhas as the Army regularly used them for jungle ops. He had even learned a few basic words and phrases in Gurkali, but these were now long forgotten, or perhaps he had just forgotten them today, knocked out of his head by a Chinese soldier's boot. What the hell. Someone was bound to speak English.

After more shouting and much jostling, Smith and Chungla found themselves seated in the office of the lieutenant in charge of the border post. The young Officer was accompanied by a corporal who spoke Tibetan. The interrogation lasted for at least half an hour, by which time Smith was beginning to find it difficult to concentrate. In the course of the interview, as it switched back and forth between English, Tibetan and Nepalese with many opportunities for misunderstanding, Smith and Chungla managed to concoct a story in which Smith was the son of a Christian missionary who had been based in Lhasa before the invasion and using his father's knowledge of the country and his contacts had been able to enter the country where he had met Chungla and helped her to get to the border. Unknown to Smith an agreement did exist at the time between China and Nepal to allow so-called religious pilgrims to cross into Nepal without passports or visas, and by good fortune this undoubtedly made it easier for the Officer to not ask too many questions.

He probably did not believe a word of the refugees story, especially as he never asked about the Chinese soldiers and why they had let them go. Smith would have been unable to explain this even if he had been asked. However, it soon became apparent that as the two were no immediate threat the best thing was to get rid of them.

Phone calls were made and before long Smith and Chungla were seated in another army truck, though this time in the front seat.

"Here, you forgot this," said the Officer, pushing the manila envelope into Smith's hand. He looked at it stupidly, hardly able to remember where it had come from, before slipping it automatically into the folds of his *chuba*. The vehicle pulled away from the border post in the direction of Katmandu.

Chapter 50

व

Kathmandu, Nepal

Several hours later the truck entered the city. The driver spoke no English or Tibetan so Smith and Chungla had not been able to find out where they were being taken. Smith had dozed for much of the journey, waking occasionally as the vehicle jolted over some obstacle in the battered road. At first he was disoriented when he woke, but as the hours passed his mind cleared as his body stiffened.

It was now early evening and the city was alive with workers heading home or to the markets, cafés and bars of the city. Everywhere was a blur of light and sound as they approached what Smith assumed to be the city centre. He rested his head against the passenger window, half open against the warmth of the evening, as if still half asleep. The driver took little interest in his charges.

They slowed to a crawl as the traffic became heavier and eventually stopped in the outside of three lanes surrounded by standing vehicles. Car horns blared and drivers struck their steering wheels in frustration as minutes of inaction passed.

Smith casually opened the door and, dragging Chungla behind him, stepped out into the chaos of cars. Leaving the door swinging open behind him, the last thing he heard as they fled into the night was the frustrated shouts of the driver, powerless to pursue them.

They had no idea how many, if any, troops were in the rear of the truck, but assuming they were being chased they dodged through the mass of cars and down an alleyway running at right angles to the main road. It was lined with stalls of every kind and the smells of cooked food invaded Smith's nostrils with an urgency that made him salivate even as he struggled to keep momentum away from possible pursuit. God, when had he last eaten? If he did not eat soon he would surely drop down dead from starvation and exhaustion.

But they kept moving, Chungla taking the lead now, dragging him by the hand through a maze of streets and passageways until, breathless, they pushed themselves into the darkness of a doorway, pressing their bodies into the beckoning shadows. They stood for several minutes, supporting each other from collapsing, ever alert for any likely signs of pursuit. At least they knew they would be soldiers in uniform and so obvious to them.

Eventually, Chungla peered cautiously out into the street in the direction they had come.

"I think we lost them," she reported. "What now?"

"You tell me. We've no money, we're in the middle of a city neither of us have ever been to before, we don't speak the local language and we're both in Tibetan dress. And I'm starving to death." He also had a huge bandage swathed around his head from which his long dark hair fell almost to his shoulders.

"I was hoping for a plan," responded the young girl. "That's what you're good at." Smith wasn't feeling that good at anything at that moment, but the girl's continuing disarming faith in him made him resolve to get to grips with their situation. After all, compared to what they had experienced in the last few weeks they were at last relatively safe.

"Come on!" he said with all the determination he could muster.

"Where?" He did not reply because, at that moment, he didn't know. The narrow street soon led them into a wider one, again crowded with street sellers. Kerosene lamps brightly illuminated their wares, displayed on rough tables beneath stripe awnings. The smells of food alternated with that of an open sewer as they passed along the street, pushing on through the crowd and attracting only the occasional second glance.

"There."

"What?"

"A telephone box."

"Who are you going to call?"

"I don't know yet." He swung open the door and glanced around the tiny kiosk at the cards advertising taxis and girls for rent in English and Nepali.

Then he saw it. One in Tibetan, advertising the services of the Jakalakhela Tibetan Refugee Centre. Knowing that tens of thousands of Tibetans had poured into Nepal since 1959 he guessed that such a place would exist and how it might advertise its services.

And it did!

Chungla also read the words on the small card. "You call them," said Smith. "They need to hear a native speaker so they know we're genuine."

"But..." began the girl.

"But what? Call them."

"How? What do I do?" Then he realised. She had probably never been in a public telephone box. When would she? Never used a public telephone. Perhaps she had never used a telephone at all. He didn't ask. Picking up the receiver, he dialled the number, hoping that no money would be needed as neither of them had a single rupee. He heard the number ringing and waited.

"Just tell them we've arrived from Tibet today and have nowhere to go. We need help." Then he heard a voice in Tibetan and handed the receiver to Chungla.

Chapter 51

Jakalakhela Refugee Camp, Kathmandu, Nepal

"How do you feel, Abbi?"

"Fine," lied Abbi. She was feeling sick and nervous and her legs felt like they were about to buckle beneath her.

"You don't look fine, if you don't mind me saying so," insisted Tashi as they walked towards the yard of the refugee compound. The centre was in the southern suburb of Patan and consisted of a number of two and three storey buildings painted mainly white and in a vaguely Tibetan style. It was afternoon and the place was a hive of activity as Tibetans of all ages bustled here and there, coming and going from the various offices and workshops of the Tibetan craft centre which Abbi knew was the economic mainstay of the community in exile in Kathmandu.

"Are you sure it's him? Have you seen him?"

"I'm sure it's him, but no, I haven't seen him. Like you, I've only just got here. I called you as soon as I heard that they might be here in the city."

"So it might not be him?"

"Who else is it going to be? How many Englishmen have left Tibet lately?"

"God, I know you're right, but I won't believe it til I see him. You said he was injured."

"Abbi, he's fine. Relax. We'll be there in a minute."

They entered one of the buildings, suddenly blind as the bright light of day gave way to deep shade. Her eyes soon adjusted to the ambient light as she followed Tashi down a narrow corridor, watching as he checked the inscription on each door they approached. The smell of stale cooking lingered in the air as they progressed into the depths of the building.

"Here," he said at last. Abbi took a deep breath and followed the lama into the room.

"Jesus, what the hell happened to you? Oh God." She rushed forward as Smith rose from the battered armchair he had been sitting in and threw her arms round him, crying uncontrollably now. "You're alive. I can't believe it. You're alive."

"Just about," retorted Smith with a cock-eyed smile as he returned her embrace. They stood, holding each other tightly for several minutes as Abbi continued to cry from a combination of joy and relief. Finally, she stepped back to take in the image of the man she thought she would never see again, hardly able to believe that it was true. He wore a pair of old jeans and a grubby white tee-shirt with a pair of leather sandals on his feet. His arms were covered in bruises and his head was still bandaged. He had a patch over one eye. She began to cry again.

"What did those bastards do to you?"

"I just got beaten up. It's nothing. I'll be fine in a few days."

"What about your eye? Can you see?"

"Like I said' it'll be fine. How are you?"

"How am I?" Suddenly all the fear and frustration of the past year welled up inside her. "You mean apart from the months I've spent wondering whether you were dead or alive? Oh, and the time a guy was shot dead next to me in a taxi? Well apart from that, I'm fine as well." Seeing the look on Smith's face, she immediately regretted the outburst. She knew that her moral indignation was justified, but she also knew what kind of a man Smith was when she got involved with him. It was never going to be an easy ride. And this was not the time for self-pity. This was the happy ending after the months of fear and worry.

"I'm sorry. I didn't mean that."

"No Abbi, I'm sorry. And what's this about someone being shot in a taxi?"

"It doesn't matter. No, that's stupid. Of course it matters, but not now. We can talk about it later."

"No, tell me now."

She hesitated, not sure whether she wanted to go down this road so soon. Then, with a deep breathe, she briefly recounted the story of Larsen, from his first contacting her in London to his sad demise in Kathmandu only days before. Smith listened intently as she spoke. When she finished there was silence.

"Jesus, Abbi. I'm sorry. I think this Larsen was Lhotse's boss. He was one of the good guys. Do you know who he was in contact with here? We might be able to work out who set him up."

"What the fuck? You're off again aren't you? You only just got out of there alive and you're thinking of wading into another battle."

"That's not what I'm saying."

" Haven't you got enough people after you already, what with the PLA, the CIA, the British Government and probably the Nepalese Army?"

"Not forgetting the Tibetans," added Smith.

"What?"

"I think he means," began Tashi, picking up the story, "that the in- fighting amongst the *Khampas* got a lot worse since we left Mustang last year. The factions fight over what little CIA money is left and it is said that several fighters have already been killed in these squabbles right here in Nepal. No-one is safe."

A knock at the door interrupted Tashi's speech. The door opened.

"One of the *Khampas* gave me this. He said there are some things for you in it."

"Thank you Chungla. Put it down there. This is Chungla," announced Smith. Chungla put down the battered suitcase as Abbi's eyes fell on the girl, her maroon Tibetan nun's habit hanging from her slight figure. Intense black eyes in a round brown face stared confidently, almost defiantly, back at Abbi.

"She doesn't speak English," began Smith, realising from Abbi's reaction that an explanation was needed quickly. "We rescued her from a monastery weeks, or was it months ago? I don't know. Anyway, she joined us and we decided the best thing was to get her to the West. She's a *Tulku*..You know what that means?" Abbi nodded.

"Well, she turned out to be a tenacious little.... nun." He laughed. "In the end there was only her and me left at the border. All the others were dead, except the group who escaped with Tashi. The Chinese finally overran us. I thought we were finished, but for some reason instead of killing us they took us to the border.

Chungla kept me going after they beat me up and she finally dragged me to the Nepalese checkpoint.

"I don't know why they let us go" he added, almost to himself.

As if understanding what he had been saying, Chungla stepped forward and produced a grubby manila envelope. She said something to Smith in Tibetan, too quickly for Abbi to understand, and handed it to him, never taking her eyes from Abbi.

"What is that?"

"God, I had almost forgotten about it. One of the Chinese soldiers gave it to me before they let us go. I left it at the border post and the OC there came after me with it. I stuffed it into my *chuba*, but Chungla remembered I had it and wanted to know what it was. So here it is at last." He worked his finger along the seal to open the envelope and extracted a single page of white paper. On it were a series of Chinese characters written by hand with a blue biro.

"Can you read it, Tashi? It's in Chinese." The monk took the paper from him.

"Seeing you reading that reminds me, Tashi. What happened to the stuff we got from the ambush? Did you get it to the Americans? Did they tell you anything about it?"

"One of Tendruk's men took it when we separated from you. He gave it to the American who met us at the airfield in Bhutan. I haven't seen either of them since we left the airport here. I think it must have been valuable or they would not have taken the trouble to rescue us. But I guess we'll never know for sure. They're probably back in New Delhi or even Washington by now."

"We need to know about that, Tashi. That would make the whole thing worthwhile, wouldn't it?" Tashi didn't answer, but turned his attention back to the paper.

"It says something like 'We warriors should both live to fight another day. Do not think us all dishonourable' and it signed by someone, I think, called Zhou."

"Zhou? Who the hell is that? Do you know Chungla?"

"Perhaps it was the old Chinese Officer who stopped them raping me. He dragged the other Officer away and I didn't see him again."

"They tried to rape her?" asked Abbi, incredulously, having understood most of what the girl said. There was a short silence.

"Yes," began Smith in English. "And they already had raped her in the monastery where we found her."

"Oh God, the poor child."

"She's not a child any longer. We've all grown up a lot in the last few months."

"I hope so." Abbi stepped forward and unselfconsciously embraced Smith again.

The room was silent.

After a couple of minutes Abbi dragged herself from Smith and dropped exhausted onto a chair. Smith looked at Chungla to see her staring intently at him, her eyes glistening with tears.

"Chungla ... " he began, confused, but the girl turned and rushed from the room, the door crashing shut behind her.

"What was that about?" asked Smith to no-one in particular.

"Don't you know?" responded Abbi, smiling sadly. "I think you need to go and talk to her."

"What?"

"Go. I think the poor girl needs you to explain a few things to her."

"Like what?"

"God, Peter. Do I need to draw you a picture?"

"Ok, no I....." mumbled Smith, leaving the room. He headed down the corridor in the direction he guessed the young nun had gone. In seconds he stepped blinking into the intense sunlight of the courtyard where he spotted Chungla entering a doorway on the opposite side.

"Chungla," he called. "Chungla!" She turned at the sound of her name and Smith stepped forward across the courtyard. As he did so, Smith was suddenly submerged in a tidal wave of pressure, dust and debris pitching him forward onto the unforgiving flagstone floor and into an impenetrable blackness beyond.

Chapter 52

ༀ

Kathmandu, Nepal

Item from the English language Kathmandu Post May 2 1971

"A massive explosion rocked the Patan Tibetan Refugee Centre in the suburbs of Katmandu at about 3.30 pm local time yesterday. Eight bodies have so far been recovered from the two storey building which was completely destroyed by the intensity of the blast. There are fears that further victims may be trapped in the wreckage, although it is thought unlikely that anyone could have survived, the damage to the building being so severe.

A spokesman for the Kathmandu Metropolitan Police said that the explosion may have been caused by a faulty cooking gas canister, but a full forensic investigation would be undertaken in due course. He stated that there was no reason to believe at this stage that the explosion was anything other than an unfortunate accident.

Early reports suggested that two Westerners visited the building in which the explosion occurred earlier that day and it is believed that one of the bodies recovered is that of a western woman. The other bodies were so badly damaged as to be so far unidentifiable."

"What does it say?" asked Chungla.

"It says," replied Smith wearily, "that they're dead. All of them"

"Who would do this?"

"There's no shortage of suspects. That's for sure," replied Smith bitterly.

"What will you do? What will we do?"

For a moment Smith said nothing, staring blankly from the bench where they sat, across the sparse grass of the park to the trees beyond through tear-filled eyes.

"We can find who did this," she insisted. "The Khampa who

gave me the suitcase. We can find him."

"Someone will know. They will tell us. Someone in the camp."

Smith ripped the article from the newspaper and screwed it into a tight ball in his hand.

"No Chungla, they won't, because we're not going to ask. Tashi was right." He drew back his arm and threw the ball of paper as far as he could before rising to his feet and taking Chungla's small hand in his.

"Come on. I'm taking you home. To England."